W9-BQL-919

DAW BOOKS BY MERCEDES LACKEY

*Coming soon from DAW Books

BEYOND

THE FOUNDING OF VALDEMAR
BOOK ONE

MERCEDES LACKEY

DAW BOOKS, INC.
DONALD A. WOLLHEIM, FOUNDER
1745 Broadway, New York, NY 10019
ELIZABETH R. WOLLHEIM
SHEILA E. GILBERT
PUBLISHERS
www.dawbooks.com

Dedication:

This work is dedicated to the people that we all have loved and lost due to the COVID-19 pandemic, and to the people they have left behind who must cope with their loss. Colleagues, family, friends, you are missed so very much. There are holes left in our lives, and we grieve over who and what you were to us. We do not suffer only the sting of your absence, we feel the pain that you were removed from our futures, too.

This work is dedicated to the medical professionals and volunteers who labored through unthinkable conditions to aid those they didn't even know. Nurses, virologists, critical care units, ambulance crews, doctors, admin, Makers, and everyone who offered aid—you fought so hard to do what was right, enduring true horrors in terrible conditions. 'Hero' is too small a word for what you are to us all.

And finally, this work is also dedicated in furious disgust to ridding our world of the influence of everyone complicit in using the pandemic as a tool for their own power, profits, and political maneuvering. You pushed hateful agendas while the bodies were stacked up. We all lost people dear to our hearts because of you parasitic, heartless creatures. If you had souls, you'd be damned.

Help them through, whenever you can," muttered Kordas, Duke of Valdemar, in a horse-box that felt stifling for the stark, dirty work to be done. He had latched onto that as his personal guide to life when he'd begun equine husbandry, and he must have repeated it to himself twenty times in the past candle-mark, to maintain his focus.

The Duke was nearly beside himself over the state of his favorite mare, but no grinding of teeth nor fretting would take the place of skilled hands in a time like this. The mare in question was in the throes of foaling, and it was not going well. Knowing that she was very close to dropping, Kordas had ordered her put up in her loose-box just before sunset, and it was a good thing that he had. It was, as these things always were, the middle of the night.

On the plus side, Kordas was an educated mage, so at least he had mage-lights to see by, and a panel of mage-fire to keep him and the sweating mare warm. And, fortunately, this wasn't out *in* the pouring rain. Because it *was* raining—of course it was. Not all of the rumbling was thunder. There had been tremors all across the Empire of late. This mare and most of the other animals in the area were on edge, and those tremors could be why she went into birthing so suddenly—an instinctive impulse to birth now, in case danger was coming. The stable smelled of sweaty horse, damp and dry hay and straw, rain, the reek of Kordas's own sweat, the mare's waters, and a truly notable amount of the mare's digestive gas.

This was especially notable because Kordas was trying to get the foal positioned correctly and his arm was deeply engaged.

They never tell you that giving birth makes the mother gassy, until you're well-committed to the program . . .

Kordas had stripped off tunic and shirt a candlemark or so ago. His trews were probably ruined, his hair was plastered to his head with sweat, more sweat ran down into his eyes and down his back, and the pain in his right arm and shoulder was indescribable. *I don't think I've ever been more miserable in my life.*

On the minus side . . .

The mare grunted with a contraction. Her vaginal muscles clamped down on his arm, he lost the miniature hoof he'd been groping for, and he thought his head was going to explode from the compression of those muscles around his arm. And then, she farted in his face.

As soon as the muscles relaxed, he pulled his arm out, another contraction started, and the foal popped into view again. One tiny hoof, and the nose, and no further.

He stared at the sight of his failure and cursed. "Futtering breech birth," he murmured, as his Healer, Cestin, soothed the mare and stroked her nose.

"Neither Arial nor her foal are up to much more of this," Cestin warned him, which of course he was well aware of. Arial's flanks were soaked with so much sweat that it had begun to foam, and her head hung limply. She was on her feet purely because Cestin was keeping her there. "That foal has to come out soon, alive or dead, or you're going to lose both of them."

"I came to help," called his sister-in-law Fidelia from the doorway. A moment later Delia herself came to the open door of the loose-box, shaking the water off her waxed-canvas cape as she took it off and slung it over the loose-box wall. As always, Delia was dressed to suit the occasion—in this case, in a pair of old worn breeches, a snagged and darned knitted tunic, and knee-high boots. She held up an unneeded lantern and blew the wick out.

"I'm not sure what you can—" he began.

"I've got the Fetching Gift," she reminded him. "I also brought you the boiled strap you forgot."

"Because I didn't know it was going to be a breech birth," he retorted. Then, aware of how ungrateful he sounded, he flushed. "You're a star."

"Well, when you didn't come back, I assumed the worst, and the worst is always a breech birth. I've learned an awful lot about foaling since I moved in with you and Isla." She hung the lantern up and handed him a pail holding a steaming strap made of boiled bandage. "Now let's get this poor creature out of her misery."

As he took the strap, she moved to the mare's side and began feeling her swollen flank. The mare barely registered her presence with a flick of her ear.

Relief settled over him like a warm cloak. *Now* he could concentrate on getting this thing done properly.

Arial had presented a breech birth with one leg folded back, which was not the *worst* that could have happened, but was a difficult proposition with only two people, especially when one of them had to keep the mare on her feet, leaving only Kordas to do the work of trying to get the foal into a proper position for birth. When the mare began pushing the foal through the birth canal, as she was now, only one leg, instead of two, was protruding, and that meant the second leg was turned back and stuck at the shoulder. As he well knew, if he had made the mistake of grasping the first leg at this point to try tugging, serious damage could have resulted to the mare.

To solve the problem, he had to get the fetus pushed back out of the vagina so that the forelimbs could be repositioned. This was more easily done if the mare was on her feet rather than on her side straining. That was why Cestin was at her nose, giving her strength and keeping her upright. The problem he'd had was that he needed to keep track of the leg that was correctly positioned, and each time he'd pushed the foal back, that leg had gotten away from him. To make certain the free leg wasn't "lost" in the process, he *should* have placed some boiled rope or other sterilized strap around the protruding leg before the repulsion began. And because he'd run out of the manor so fast, purely not thinking, he'd left things like that behind. There were plenty of supplies here in the stable, but Cestin didn't know where they were, and to be honest, neither did he. Arial wasn't the only mare foaling tonight, and the stablemaster and both stableboys were somewhere out in the storm attending to a mare who'd hidden herself at the bottom of the pasture.

You could always be in their shoes right now.

He quickly passed the soft strap around the tiny ankle, loosely twisted it once to hold it in place, and began shoving the foal back up into the mare's uterus. She responded with a contraction that felt like she was about to break his arm, but he got the foal back up where she didn't want it to go, inserted his other arm, and began feeling for the mis-positioned leg.

And barely got the tip of his finger on the knee, when another contraction moved it out of his grasp. He and the mare groaned together.

"Got it," Delia said quietly from beside him. He spared a glance at her; both her hands were on the mare's side and her eyes were closed in concentration, bits of her hair already coming loose from the fat brown braid curled around her neck.

A moment after that, he felt the foal's other foot fit itself into his hand. "Don't let her start a contraction!" he said sharply to Cestin. He shoved his other hand up inside his poor mare, got the strap around the second hoof by feel, then slid his hands out, pulling the strap just barely taut as he removed his arms from her insides.

"All right, let her lie down," he told the Healer. Arial responded to the Healer's release by folding her legs beneath her and going straight down into the straw, as he kept the tension up on that strap. Tension *only*. Just enough to keep both little feet where he wanted them, in the birth canal. He did *not* want to pull the foal out. All he wanted to do was to keep both legs positioned as if the foal was diving—

The mare's flanks shuddered with a contraction, and just like that, as easily as if Arial hadn't been struggling for the past half-candlemark, the foal slipped out onto the straw, rupturing the membrane around it as it did so.

A filly!

Moving slowly, and making soothing sounds, Kordas picked up a waiting piece of toweling and gently toweled off the foal's nose. She lifted and shook her head, and sneezed, and his heart sang. *She's fine. She's just fine.*

Another moment later, the foal rolled from her side into a normal "lying" position, and sneezed again. He put a finger in her mouth and she sucked at it vigorously. She was going to be more than fine.

Now it was Arial's turn to move; Cestin backed up as she gave indications she was about to stand. When she rolled to her feet and did, the cord broke, and Kordas reached for it carefully and tied a loose knot in it to make sure she didn't step on it and pull out the afterbirth prematurely.

She sniffed at the birth fluids in the straw, then, as if that scent reminded her that there ought to be a foal somewhere about, she turned, and spotted her new daughter. This was her third foal, and she was an old hand at this by now. She immediately began licking her foal, starting at the head. Kordas moved back and let her have her way.

He looked over at Delia, who was watching the foal with a thoroughly infatuated little smile on her face. The half-formed idea he'd had when he knew Arial had "caught" hardened into a decision. "Delia, I couldn't have turned her without your help."

Delia looked up from the foal to him. "Her? Oh! It's a filly?"

"More to the point, she's *your* filly now," he said warmly.

"I—*what?*" He chuckled. Delia looked as if he'd awakened her from a dead sleep, she was so startled.

"She's yours. Your sister had Arial's first foal, my cousin got her second. And the way you're watching that little girl, I'm afraid your heart would break if I gave her to anyone else." No mention of *selling* the foal; he would never *sell* a foal of Arial's bloodline.

Delia's expression went from stunned to joyful, with a hint of tears in her eyes. "It just might." She might have said something else, but just then the afterbirth fell into the straw with a dull thud—a good sign, that Arial had passed it so early. Delia moved out of the way so that he and Cestin could examine it.

No tears, no holes, and no toughening. He sighed with relief, and just then the stablemaster and two of the stableboys came in, the entire little parade soaking wet, one of the boys leading the mare that had been down at the end of the pasture, the stablemaster carrying the foal in his arms.

"Any problems?" he and the stablemaster asked simultaneously. And they both laughed.

"If I'd asked the gods for a perfect, easy birth, I couldn't have gotten better," the stablemaster said, as the boy led the mare into the loose-box. "But then, it did have to be in the middle of a howling thunderstorm and a groundshaker."

"Arial was breech, but Cestin and Delia helped me right her," Kordas replied.

The stablemaster put the foal down beside the mare; the foal immediately shoved his nose under his dam's belly and began rooting for the nipple. "Delia, eh?" The stablemaster eyed Delia with some speculation. "Never thought of using Fetching Gift for a breech birth. You could be right handy; if you think you could turn a foal that was presenting tail-first, you're worth your weight in gold."

Delia made a little bow. "Call on me at your will," she said.

"I shall. Boys, go into Arial's box and clean up the dirty straw. Thank all the gods it was a warm rain, or we'd all be perishing." The stablemaster stretched and yawned as Cestin and Delia got out of the loose-box so the stableboys could get in, moving slowly and carefully, to fork out all the contaminated straw and the placenta, replacing it with clean straw. Arial didn't care; her concentration was entirely on her foal, and mares generally didn't eat their placentas. "You can go back to bed now, my lord Duke. I'll keep an eye on things here."

Kordas took that as the dismissal it was, plucked his shirt and tunic off the side of the loose-box, and gestured to Delia and Cestin to follow him. "We've been given our walking orders," he said cheerfully. "Let's get out before he chases us out with a broom."

"I wouldn't do that, my lord," the stablemaster countered, as they left—leaving behind the mage-lights, which would naturally fade and then vanish on their own as dawn approached. "I'd just set the dogs on you."

Only Delia had a rain cape, which made Cestin grumble under his breath, but Kordas was actually grateful for the downpour. His trews were already probably ruined, so a little rain wasn't going to make any difference, but the unusually warm rain was doing wonders for rinsing the sticky birth-fluids away. "Hold this, would you?" he asked Delia, handing her his shirt and tunic so he could "wash" his hair as they walked.

It wasn't that far to the manor, a fanciful piece of architecture sprouting delicate towers and elegant domes that was perfectly capable of holding the population of the entire Dukedom at a pinch, and was about as defensible as a sand castle. This, of course, was exactly how the Emperor wanted things; he did not want his landholders to be able to mount any kind of effective defense of their realms. He wanted to be able to march in and take everything if he pleased, and he wanted his nobles to be aware of that every single moment.

"Why is this storm so warm?" Delia asked, through the downpour. There wasn't much lightning and thunder, but the amount of rain coming down was almost enough to drown out her words.

"There's a war out on the frontier," Kordas reminded her. "The Emperor never stops trying to conquer someone. I'm told there are lots of mages in those two armies, and it's messing with the weather. I wouldn't in the least be surprised to have this turn into a blizzard by morning."

"I hope not!" Delia replied with alarm. "That would be a disaster!"

Kordas shrugged, then, aware that she couldn't see him in the dark and downpour, added, "Not much we can do about it without tipping our hand to the Emperor that I have more mages living here than he is aware of." Now, *that* was an advantage to having that enormous pile of a manor—he could have as many mages as he cared to host here, and unless they made themselves "visible," no one would be the wiser.

And since at least a third of his mages were busy full time masking the presence of the others, he was as certain as he dared to be that the Emperor had no idea so many had come to him for protection. He glanced up at the tops of the towers overhead. There were lights in the windows of all of them. His mages were hard at work tonight—perhaps. Of course they could also be curled up next to their fires with cats (or dogs, but mages seemed to prefer cats), mulled ale, and a good book.

Cats, mulled ale, and a good book sounded very attractive right now, but his bed sounded even more attractive. At least he'd washed all the muck off. Though if Isla had ordered him a hot bath . . . *I wouldn't turn it down.*

The nearest entrance to the stables was the kitchen, which at this hour was dark and fragrant with the scent of the herbs in the cleaning water and a slight yeasty scent of the dough left to rise overnight for the first baking in the morning.

No one slept in the kitchens at Valdemar except, perhaps, the kitchen cats. With a superfluity of rooms, even the lowliest scullion had a little cot of his own tucked away in the warren of servants' cells next to the kitchen. They were too small to be called rooms, in Kordas's opinion, but they were private, comfortable, and each contained a proper bed, which was far more than most servants ever got. *That* had not been something that had been built into the structure. It was an innovation Kordas's grandfather had made, converting a single large room next to the kitchen into twenty little kitchen servants' rooms, each one with a door to allow the privacy that servants were so seldom accorded.

Kordas paused just inside the kitchen, next to the banked fire, to drip for a few moments. Cestin wrung out the hems of his robes at the hearth. "If you have no further need of me, my lord—?" he said, making it a question.

Kordas clapped him on the back. "Not tonight. There's probably cakes in the larder."

Cestin brightened at that. "I am a bit peckish," he admitted, and went for a rummage, returning with a napkin full of teacakes. "It was a good night's work, my lord."

"And a success, thanks to both of you." He clapped Cestin on the back again, and noticed as he did so that a cold draft was coming from the crack under the kitchen door. The temperature had dropped while they waited, just as he had predicted. *Good work on Stafngrimr's part, getting that mare and her foal up to the stables when he did. Wretched mage-weather! It just* might *blizzard by morning!*

Cestin noticed too. "I believe I will get back to my room and enjoy these in bed with a cup of tea. I fear the weather is turning. Good night, my lord."

"Good night, my friend," Kordas responded with a smile.

When Cestin had gone, Delia made no move to leave. Instead she peered through the gloom at her brother-in-law. "Did you really mean that? About giving me the filly?"

"I wouldn't have said it if I hadn't meant it. I'd been thinking about it for a while. I might not have if it had been a colt, because I want to put any colts back into the breeding program, but you ought to have a horse you've personally trained, and I can't think of anyone else who deserves one of Arial's foals more than you do."

Delia made a little sound he recognized as a sigh of pleasure. "Thank you, brother. This means a lot."

"It does," he agreed, with a half smile. "It means a lot of *work*. And that work will start immediately. You need to get the little one used to you from the beginning, and used to the idea of a little light weight on her back every single day. Not much. Just enough for her to notice, like resting your hand on her back while she moves about. Grim will teach you, and you'll teach her, and it needs to be every day. There's nothing like working with a horse from the moment it's foaled to get an extraordinary mount. What are you going to name her?"

"I don't know yet," Delia replied. "I need to think about it. Is she going to be a Gold, like Arial?"

"Definitely. Another Valdemar Gold." He had plenty of experience in telling what color a horse was going to be even when soaking wet, and the filly was going to be within a shade of Arial's glorious autumnal color.

"Something about sun, then, maybe," Delia mused, and stretched. "Well, I'm dry enough now I won't leave drips all over the hallway. I'm heading for bed and maybe a small cup of mead."

"I think I'll be doing the same," he agreed.

They parted company at the kitchen door, Delia going off to her own suite in a quiet part of the manor, and he to his tower, though before he got there he became aware that his shirtless state was getting uncomfortable as the temperature dropped.

Of course, he *could* have had all those mages he sheltered do something about keeping the manor warm by magic, but that would be a dead giveaway that he *had* all those mages. Only the Emperor and the Emperor's favorite cronies were supposed to have enough mages on hand to do trivial things like keep their dwellings warm or cool.

He draped the damp tunic and shirt over his shoulders, and hurried his slightly squishy steps.

His tower was just off the seldom-used audience chamber, and he sighed with relief as he opened the door to the bottom level and his night-guard saluted him. There was a good fire down here; it had been banked when he'd left for the stables, and it looked like the night-guard had taken it upon himself to build it up again. He saluted back, and began to climb.

———————

Delia was glad to get out of sight of her brother-in-law the Duke, and even gladder to get back to the privacy of her spacious suite—which was *not* in a tower, something this manor had a superfluity of. She didn't care for towers, except to occasionally go up one to look at the view. She didn't like the way they swayed a little in a high wind, she didn't like the eerie sounds the wind made up there, and she preferred the feeling of being on the ground.

It was not that she didn't enjoy Kordas's company. Quite
the contrary, she enjoyed it just a little too much. But his generous gift had come perilously close to causing her to crack the
mask she always wore around him and her sister.

Every gift he had ever given her was generous, as far as
that went. Take this suite, just as a for-instance. Granted,
there was no shortage of room in this manor; in fact, she
doubted that it was more than half occupied. But still, even by
those standards, this was extraordinary.

The first room alone was the size of the suite she'd had as
a child. This was the "public" room, the one where she would
have brought guests, if she ever had guests. She could have
hosted twenty people here with no crowding. It had a fine fireplace, comfortable padded furnishings upholstered in a dark
brown leather, and walls lined with bookshelves. There were
two windows with cushioned window-seats, and sheepskins
scattered over the polished wooden floor. The next rooms were
her bedroom, a closet so big her clothing barely took up a
quarter of it, a bathing room, and a shielded magic room she
never used at all because she wasn't a mage. Everything
matched: gleaming dark wood and shining dark leather, exactly the way she liked it. The bed was big enough for four,
and had mage-lights in little cages mounted on the headboard,
which had a little bookcase built into it.

Delia didn't know the story of how Duke Valdemar—
Kordas's great-grandfather—had gotten a mage-built manor
as a "gift" from the Emperor, but she knew why it had happened. It was all part of how the Emperor kept control over his
nobles. You couldn't safely *refuse* his offer to have his mages
construct such a place for you, after all. But everything about
the enormous piles they would make for you was calculated.
It would be the height of luxury, setting you apart from your
people *immediately*. Especially in a relatively poor Duchy like
this one. It would also be utterly indefensible, which tended to
discourage thoughts of rebellion. And, of course, since the

layouts were exactly alike, you could not boast of having a better manor than someone else. The Emperor's gifts always had many sticky threads attached.

Instead of seeking her bed, she stripped off her cape and draped it over a drying stand, and went to the window. Pressing her hand against the glass to check the temperature outside, she judged that it probably wasn't going to snow, but it wasn't going to be warm until whatever had caused the weather fluctuations passed them by. There was always war at the borders of the Empire, but this was the first time to her knowledge that what went on out at the frontier was actually affecting the Empire itself.

And what is the Emperor going to make of that? Probably nothing, as long as it didn't inconvenience him.

Thinking about the Emperor got her mind off Kordas for a moment, which was a good thing.

It was fine to love your brother-in-law, just don't be *in* love with your brother-in-law.

A fact of which she reminded herself on a daily basis.

She turned away from the window and went to the table against the wall where wine and mead waited, poured herself a generous portion of the latter in a pewter cup, and turned to the fire.

She'd left the fire well stoked when she'd gone down to the stables, and it only needed another log put on it. That was just a matter of a moment.

She didn't bother raising the shades over the mage-lights; the light from the fire was enough.

Cup in hand, fire going well, she slumped down into her favorite high-backed chair on the hearth, pivoted so her legs hung over the right-side arm and and her back was up against the left-side arm, leaned her head against the padded back, and contemplated the ironic comedy that was her life.

The first irony was that Kordas and Isla *liked* each other very much, were indeed the best of friends, but theirs had been an arranged marriage (as nearly every marriage among the nobility of the Empire was), and they weren't in *love* with each other. Not even after three children. And Delia? Delia wouldn't even be here if it weren't for the fact that she and Isla had no brothers. When their father had died, the Emperor had swooped in, assigned the Baronial title and estates to one of his sycophants, and cut Delia out completely. She'd been lucky to be allowed to take her personal belongings with her when he unceremoniously threw her out.

Could be worse. I could've been forced to marry the Emperor's puppy to cement his position. Fortunately for her, he already had a wife and was disinclined to divorce her or otherwise put her away, in order to marry someone who was in many ways that woman's inferior. Delia had gotten a good look at her while she was packing; there was no doubt she was beautiful, and probably had been the Emperor's mistress at some point or other. She was also tall, willowy, graceful, and wealthy in her own right, all things Delia was not. The perfect trophy of a wife, a living display of the Emperor's favor.

"You'll be moving out, of course, girl," the wife had said. She could still hear that distant, dulcet voice in her mind. It hadn't been more than a moment after she had been introduced to the new Baron of Sterngal and his wife. The wife hadn't even bothered giving Delia her proper name; she'd just stared down her nose at Delia, and said, *"You'll be moving out, of course, girl,"* in tones that suggested Delia should do so on the instant.

Delia had been at her wits' end. Her father was *barely* in his tomb by a day, she was still in grief and shock at his sudden passing, and at the very least she had expected that she would be allowed to move to the dowager house or at worst the gatehouse on the grounds. She'd have been perfectly happy in either place. Her needs were few, and she'd still have been *home.*

But no.

They had shown up out of the blue, parading through the activated Portal with their entire household, which had included enough armed men that she had felt utterly intimidated.

And as she had stood on the steps of what was no longer her own home, wondering what the *hell* she was going to do, with the Ice Queen glaring down at her from one side, and the Ice Queen's husband looking everyplace except at Delia, she had been tempted to run inside, flee up the stairs to the highest tower, and fling herself off it in despair to land messy and dead at their feet. Not being one of the Emperor's mage-built edifices, that tower wasn't *that* tall and she wouldn't have splattered their lovely garments when she hit, but she'd at least have made an inconvenient mess for them to clean up and explain.

And that was when there had been a flurry of trumpets above as the two Heralds announced yet *another* group approaching the manor. She'd stopped herself—because it might have been the Emperor's people coming to fetch her to the Capital, and while that was far from ideal, if the Emperor was fetching her, it meant he would probably make sure she wasn't stripped of *everything*.

But it hadn't been the Emperor's representative.

It had been Kordas.

Riding in on one of his beautiful Valdemar Gold horses for which he was famed—she knew now it had been Arial, the mare she had just helped—and trailed by three empty wagons, he had come trotting up to the steps of Sterngal Manor as if he were the owner, not this trumped-up Emperor's lapdog. And he didn't even bother to greet the new owner and his wife; he came down off his horse and went straight to Delia, and embraced her as if he had known her all his life instead of meeting her no more than a handful of times at best. "Delia, my dear, I am so sorry," he said, as she involuntarily responded to the kindness in his eyes and the warmth of his embrace by burying her face in his tunic with a muffled sob. "I've come to take you home to Valdemar, of course," he continued. "You can't possibly go anywhere else, I won't have it."

Then, and only then, did he look up at the usurper. "Ah, good, you're here. That's convenient. See that your servants pack up Delia's things and load them in the wagons, will you? I'm going to take her up to her rooms so we can make sure that anything breakable is properly protected."

And just like *that,* he put his arm around her shoulder and urged her up to her rooms, while the new Baron and his wife stared at them in slack-jawed astonishment.

They'd done what he'd asked too, probably assuming the Emperor had sent him, and not daring to do anything to contradict him. Or, more to the point, to interfere with what Delia said was hers. Which, among other things, were all the items that Isla had left behind when she'd married, and all the books in the library.

So instead of having to fight that gorgeous, rapacious harpy over every single possession that wasn't an article of clothing, with Kordas's help she had managed to make off with enough valuables to count as a decent legacy.

Kordas had actually done far more than she had in that regard. After her rooms had been packed up—not the furnishings; he'd taken one look at them and said "We've got better" and instructed the servants to leave them—he'd taken her around the manor, pointing to this and that, and saying "Your father left you *that,* right?" and she had just nodded. He had an uncanny eye for small, extremely valuable objects, and they kept well ahead of the new Baron and most especially his wife, snatching up treasure after family treasure before the interlopers even laid eyes on the pieces to know what they were losing.

Then he'd ordered her horse—pony, really, she had only been thirteen at the time—put her up on it, and led the whole cavalcade back to the Gate at the edge of the manor grounds, and through it, straight to the matching Gate here at Valdemar.

She had been in almost as much of a daze at the end of the sweep as the usurper and his wife had been. It was only when she was within sight of the manor of Valdemar that it hit home for her.

She had been saved, literally, by a knight on a shining horse.

She'd managed to be fervently grateful, but the second she laid eyes on her sister, she'd broken down and started crying her eyes out. Isla had taken her to these rooms, let her cry until she couldn't cry anymore, then put her to bed.

And when she'd awakened, every one of the treasures that had been carried away had been lovingly installed here. Her clothing had been put away in the wardrobe. The family heirlooms Kordas had helped her abscond with were on prominent display in a suite of rooms that was easily a match for the ones her father had occupied. Where, in fact, those treasures were now. If she looked up from contemplating her mead-cup, she could see them all over the room. Here the gleam of the arm of a delicate statue, there the sparkle of gemstones in an ornamented cup, yonder the glint of gilding on the spine of a book. It was all still here, and all hers.

The only things that weren't still here were all the books on magic. *She* wasn't a mage and couldn't use them, so she had given them to Kordas and Isla.

Now that she thought about it, that moment when she had looked up at the Duke of Valdemar and realized he had come to save her out of the kindness of his heart was probably the moment she had fallen in love with him.

She hadn't realized that, of course. She'd only been thirteen. All she'd known then was that she worshipped him like a god, and would have done anything he asked of her.

And I still would, she admitted to herself. Then shook her head. She was just ridiculously lucky; she had a sister who loved her, she had a brother-in-law who could not have been more *un*like most of the Emperor's nobles, she was fed and housed in ridiculous comfort and had the freedom to do practically anything she wanted.

And I need to start concentrating on all the good things I have, and not on the things I can't have.

Good things, like that adorable little filly. A Valdemar Gold! Never in a million years would she have imagined she'd ever own a Gold!

The memory of the darling little beastie being thoroughly cleaned by her dam made Delia smile with incredulous delight. *And she's mine! Which means that rather than sitting here in my cups feeling sorry for myself because my brother-in-law regards me as a sister, I should be thinking of a name for her.*

She glanced down at the cup in her hand—one of a set of six she and Kordas had made off with. *Something to do with honey or mead?* Isla's mount was "Sundrop," after Isla's favorite flower.

I know! she decided, swallowing the last of her drink. *Daystar. Star for short.* It had a nice sound to it.

And on that positive note, and feeling better just thinking about that lovely creature *who was now her very own*, she went to bed.

2

"**W**ell, at least this time you don't stink," Isla said, as Kordas entered their suite. She was sitting by the fire, and had clearly been prepared to wait as long as it took for him to get back from his errand. "Something to be said for the rain."

"More to be said for it staying warm until we were just about back inside," Kordas replied. "Is that a hot toddy?" he added, staring hopefully at a steaming pitcher on the table beside her.

She laughed. "It is. Go strip off and get into the robe I've left out for you, and you can have some."

"Yes, oh most benevolent of mistresses," he responded, and did as he had been ordered. This did require going up two floors—suites in the towers were made up of vertical sets of rooms rather than horizontal ones, with a staircase going up along one wall—but the prospect of a lovely fire and a cup of spiced and spiked mead was enough to carry him up to the wardrobe floor, where Isla had, indeed, left out a nice warm (and thankfully dry) robe for him. He left his possibly ruined clothing in the proper place; Isla would have given him a piece of her mind about making extra work for the servants if he'd just left it on the floor. Isla was imperious in her own way, but there was nobody Kordas would have rather been ordered around by.

As he padded back down the stairs in bare feet, he saw Isla had already poured two cups and was holding one out to him.

"Are you in need of a bath?" she asked, sitting back down in her chair by the fire. This was diplomacy on her part; she could have leaned over and obviously sniffed him, then given him a Look. Isla was so skilled in projecting her meaning by precise expressions that it was nearly an entire language of its own.

"Thankfully the rain took care of the mess." He took his seat across from her and sipped at the drink, sighing gratefully. "It was a breech birth and I needed three hands when I had only two; I'm just grateful that Delia turned up and sorted it out. I had no idea the Fetching Gift could be used to maneuver a stubborn foal inside its mother. I gave her the filly afterward."

"She doesn't give herself enough credit for how useful her Mind-magic is," Isla mused. "That *was* tremendously kind of you, since it's Arial's foal."

"I can't think of anyone I would trust more with Arial's foal. She's more than old enough to learn how to train her own mount from the beginning," he pointed out, and relaxed into the padded back of his chair, blinking at his wife a little sleepily. "If she's going to be a Valdemar, even by marriage, she needs to learn every aspect of horsemanship."

These Imperial manors were meant to be detrimental to their owners. They were supposed to impress upon you how all-powerful the Emperor's mages were. And their very impracticality was supposed to make you squander resources. You were supposed to look at this gorgeous piece of architecture, realize that nothing you owned would look anything other than shabby within its imposing walls, and spend money you didn't have to fill all the enchanting empty rooms with suitable furnishings. The more you spent on show, the less you had to spend on anything else. And if you overspent on show, the Emperor could use the fact as proof that you were not fit to be in charge, and replace you with someone else.

They were quite lovely poisons wrapped in attractive sugary coatings.

But when Kordas's grandfather had been "gifted" this thing, he hadn't actually moved into it immediately. Instead, he and his people had studied it, and instead of doing what the Emperor *assumed* they would do, they adapted the manor to how people in this Duchy lived, rather than "living up to" the manor. The result was that entire sections had been given over to storage—there was enough food alone here to feed the entire human population of the Duchy for two years at this point. There were plenty of other things in storage too; the Emperor would probably not approve of the "other" armory hidden here. Kordas adored his grandfather's cunning, and he built up odd skills and cultivated his own versions of the canny old man's resourcefulness. A summer's spare time was spent creating secret caches inside everyday settings, to impress Grandfather. Bump-out hidden drawers, hatches disguised in mosaic that revealed tubes to drop items to other rooms, even hollowed chambers in saddles. Grandfather heartily approved.

It wasn't a secret that rooms were being used for storage— but only Kordas, his cousin, Isla, and a few choice servants under his cousin knew just how *much* was stored here. He and his father had had a plan . . . and with every year that passed, the feeling never left any of them that the need to implement that plan became ever more urgent.

Well, they had an idea, rather than a plan. They still didn't have every part of the idea figured out. And when (not if) they did see that idea through—it had to be iron-clad and foolproof.

They would never get a second chance, and the repercussions for failure did not bear thinking about.

Isla stirred a little, interrupting his thoughts, and he smiled at her. She was staring at the fire, and he wondered what *she* was thinking.

If he had not known that Isla and Delia were sisters, he never would have suspected it. Isla was gifted with a lush figure and a cascade of red-tinted brown hair; Delia was small, thin, and dark, and did not look sixteen at all. Isla had wide, luminous green eyes and a perpetual expression of pleasant welcome; Delia had dark gray eyes and a constant look of brooding, even when nothing was wrong. Neither were conventionally beautiful, though Isla had an edge over her sister. The place where both sisters were a match was in their heads; both of them were smart and very clever. Smarter than he was, he often thought, and blessed the fact that neither of them had ever turned their formidable intellects against him.

"So you have undoubtedly given the Emperor's little bird something to sing about again," Isla observed with amusement. He had to laugh aloud at that.

"I'm going to enjoy reading that particular dispatch, though I confess it would have been even more amusing if I could have somehow coerced him into being there for the foaling," he replied, the thought sweeter than the mead. "Arial was particularly gassy."

She laughed at that. "You will *never* get him near the stable after Delia's old pony nearly savaged him."

"Delia's pony is a good judge of character."

She chuckled, and fell silent. There really wasn't much to say, and he was enjoying the peace and comfort after the ordeal of the foaling. He was perfectly content to sit and sip in the quiet.

The "Emperor's little bird" she referred to was the lord of one of the fourteen manors in his Duchy, a man who had been there as long as *he* could remember, although he was not in any way related to the original lord who had held that land and title. Whether Lord Merrin had been specifically planted there during Kordas's father's tenure, or had volunteered for the position of "Emperor's 'secret' informant" after taking over the property, was a mystery he wasn't particularly concerned with solving. Getting rid of the man was the last thing on Kordas's mind. Much better to know who all the informants were, so he knew exactly what the Emperor was being told at all times.

The fellow actually thought he had a foolproof method of sending his reports to his master; he wrote them by hand and placed them in a box on his desk. The box had a spell on it that caused anything placed in it to travel to an identical box somewhere in the Emperor's Palace. Probably *not* directly to the Emperor's private office; Lord Merrin was a very small bird, and Kordas was an equally small fish.

Merrin, however, is absolutely sure that he has the ear of the Emperor himself. His attitude of smug "I know something you don't know" was a dead giveaway. If Kordas hadn't already known Merrin was the resident spy, that attitude alone would have told him.

What Merrin didn't know was that the magnificent desk he had in his private office also had a spell on it. Anything that he wrote on it was reproduced in Kordas's study, on stacks of paper kept in a drawer in *Kordas's* desk for just that purpose. The drawer and Merrin's desk were made from the same tree, which had made the spells trivially easy for a competent mage to create. Kordas had done it himself as one of the first pieces of magical business after his father had died and he had been confirmed as the Duke.

It had also been trivially easy for him to get Merrin to want that desk. It *had* taken the sacrifice of one of the Duchy's most magnificent deramon elm trees, a tree which featured amazing grain and spectacular color. And it had taken the best cabinetmaker in the Duchy most of a year to produce the beautifully carved, ornamented, and polished desk. After that, all it had taken was for Merrin to see the desk, and hear the sad and entirely fictitious story that the cabinetmaker had hoped to sell the desk to Kordas, but that Kordas had laughed and said, "What do I need with a desk when I already have one?" That piqued Merrin's curiosity, and the low-but-not-suspiciously-low price for it, coupled with the cabinetmaker's eagerness for more work, had cemented Merrin's avarice.

This had also enabled Merrin to flatter himself that he had infinitely better taste than "that bumpkin" Duke Kordas, and that was that. One look had been all that it took to seal the deal. And within days, Kordas knew every letter of every word that Merrin sent to the Emperor.

I do regret losing that desk, a little.

"I can just see the dispatch," Isla said, breaking the silence. "After all the bowing and scraping and sucking up, the next words will be *that bumpkin Kordas spent all night in his sta-ble personally attending to the birth of a horse.*"

"If 'that bumpkin' is what they both think of me, we can all live with that," Kordas replied. "Better to be inconsequential in the Emperor's eyes. I am grateful to be small and poor."

That was not *quite* true, although it was true that Valdemar was by far the smallest Duchy in all of the vast Empire. In fact, truth to tell, Valdemar was smaller than many Baronies. And Valdemar was not precisely poor; it just was not rich. They produced enough from the farms to feed the Duchy and store back a bit against bad years, but not more than that. The real wealth of Valdemar was in its horses, all the more espe-cially because the Ducal lands were more suited to grazing and mowing than tilling and farming. Money from the sale of those horses was what had gone into filling all those storage rooms here at the manor.

And it was going to be a good year in the Valdemar mead-ows, as long as there were no problem births. Every mare above the age of four and below the age of sixteen was in foal.

There were five different lines that Kordas sold outside of the Duchy—the Valdemar Golds (rarely), the Charger line (which were heavy horses favored by knights for tourneys), the Tow-Beasts that pulled the barges along the vast Imperial network of canals that handled almost all of the cargo of the Empire, the Sweetfoot palfreys, and the Fleetfoot racehorses. Valdemar paid its tribute to the Emperor in horses, all of them as four-year-old, tamed and trained beasts. And until now, none of those had ever been Valdemar Golds. The Golds were the rarest, in part because of the color, but mostly because he was so careful about his breeding and bloodlines.

"Are the Emperor's fake Golds ready?" Isla asked. "Because if he actually reads the dispatch, being told about a Gold foaling is going to make him want the ones you promised him."

"All this year's tribute horses are ready," he assured her. "The two I earmarked for him as Chargers have shed their coats four times, and each time, they grew back gold. At four, I know they won't change their coat-color. The magical work Cestin and I put in on them when their mothers 'caught' took hold perfectly. Ridiculously detailed spell—takes forever. But it would take a mage with expert knowledge of horse anatomy to even think to look for it, much less find signs of it."

"And it won't matter if they don't breed true?" she asked anxiously.

"He doesn't have any Golds to breed to," Kordas pointed out. "He won't be able to determine if they breed true or not. Not," he added, "that he'll care. He pays no attention to his stud book, or to his breeding farms, much less anyone else's. All he knows is that when there's a parade, he has the most impressive horse in the Empire to ride, and a bonus if it's rare. And even better if he has a pair of them that can pull a carriage three times as big as anything anyone else has. There's nothing in the Empire rarer than a Valdemar Gold, and nothing more impressive than one of my Chargers. Combine the color with an impressive horse, and he'll be happy. Chances are he'll keep them in the Imperial stables at the Capital, and never breed them at all. After all, if he wants another, he knows where he can get it. We've made sure I have more Chargers in that color coming up."

"But you're giving him a warhorse," she objected. "And you have no idea whether or not he can handle it."

Now he laughed, and tossed down the last of his drink. "Actually I have a very good idea of what he can handle as a rider. Remember, I was a hostage at the Imperial Court until I was eighteen. He's a terrible rider. And the two Chargers are from an entirely new line I started for my farmers here, crossed with Tow-Beasts. They have the looks, strength, and stamina of the warhorses, but they have the tempers of a good, steady dog, and their preferred gait is a walk. He'll probably have a new, gaudy carriage built, one with gilding everywhere, and he'll have them pull it rather than riding them."

"When did you start that line? And why didn't you tell me about them?" Isla asked, a little surprised.

"They're not all that interesting, and I didn't think you'd care," he admitted, and gave her a pointed look. "The number of times you've put on that expression of 'yes, dear, I am listening to you' when I'm droning on about the horses has not been lost on me."

She shrugged apologetically. "Well . . . why another line? I should think that five are enough to handle."

"I'm breeding them as an alternative to oxen, for heavy plowing. Thick hides, broad feet, smart enough to read what's around them. Won't win any races, but could pull for a week. The first lot is trained and waiting in the Westfields, ready to be loaned out any time."

"Loaned?" she said. "Why 'loaned'?"

"Because it's unlikely any of my farmers could afford one," he said frankly. "And they're horses, not oxen. They need more particular care than an ox or a mule. So I'll be loaning them out with a drover who will also act as groom and keeper, and we'll see how that goes. One horse, one drover, to a village in each sort of terrain. It's early days yet, and I don't have so many of them that I can't absorb them all into the Duchy farms, then sell the rest to my lords and end the experiment, except for the ones I'll keep around to send to the Emperor."

This was all small talk, really. He was not asking the question he really wanted her to answer, which was "How are the children?"

It was a question fraught with pitfalls, because officially, he and Isla were childless.

Neither of them had been prepared to surrender one or more of their children into the Emperor's household where they would become, as Kordas himself had been, hostages for their parents' behavior. So all three of Isla's pregnancies and births had been conducted in absolute secrecy, with only three people being aware of the truth: Cestin, Delia, and Kordas's cousin, Hakkon Indal. The last was a necessity because the children were *supposed* to be Hakkon's bastards. And they were being raised not by Isla and Kordas, but (officially) by a nursemaid, a tutor, and a body-servant hired by Kordas to tend to *all* of the children in the manor. There was quite a little pod of those children, and Kordas was doing as his father and grandfather and all those who had come before had done: rearing all the children in the Ducal household with the same education, whether they were the offspring of servants or those with nobler blood, with the eye to putting them in training for positions of responsibility in the Duchy when they were old enough.

Mind, he and Isla were not absent from the boys' lives. He saw them often, and made a point to visit the nursery where they all lived. Isla spent some time with all of the children, every day.

She probably spends more time with them than the parents of other nobles spend with their offspring.

But he knew it hurt her that she couldn't be their *mother.* She knew this was how things had to be in order to safeguard them, but she didn't want to be like the parents of other noble children. She wanted, sometimes so much that it drove her to tears, to be as closely involved in their growing up as any ordinary farmwife. There were so many things she had never gotten to experience. She had not seen their first steps, nor heard their first words.

They had never called her "Mama."

But doing that . . . would only end in her losing them. They both knew that. And so he hesitated to ever bring them up before she did, for fear that mentioning them would make her unhappy.

"Hakkon wants to know if we're ready for Restil to take his place with the pages," she said, as if she had read his mind.

He was about to say "Isn't that really Hakkon's decision to make?" but he stopped himself before he did. This wasn't the lady of the manor speaking. This was the mother of his child, and Hakkon had been exactly right to ask her. Instead, he thought about it for a moment, recalling his own childhood. "I was only a little older than Restil when I was made a page, and Hakkon was younger." He pulled on his beard a moment while he thought. "You know, Restil could be assigned as *your* page . . ."

Her eyes closed, and she bit her lip. "I was hoping you would suggest that. But is it safe?"

"Not only is it safe, you can get away with showering him with affection and no one will think twice about it," he promised her with relief. "He's a handsome little lad, if I do say so myself, and most ladies of rank are inclined to spoil their pretty little pages. You'll be no different."

She sniffed, signaling that she was holding back tears, which was not unexpected; he moved over in his chair, which was quite big enough for two, and patted the seat beside him.

She joined him, resting her head on his shoulder, with his arm around her. For a while, they just sat together; quiet on the surface, but mentally he was trying to pick up every detail that might signal her state of mind. Did she just want comfort? Or was she amorous? If the latter, he could certainly throw off his fatigue, but if lovemaking wasn't what she wanted—

Their relationship was a trifle complicated. Oh, not in the fact that they were husband and wife, nor that it was an arranged marriage. That was normal enough. No, it was due to his own upbringing, which was decidedly not normal, at least insofar as his own experience deeper in Imperial territory went. His father and his grandfather had both been adamant that sex was not a husband's "right," no matter what other people in the Empire said. Nor was it his right to order women about as if they were pet dogs. This, of course, was in direct contradiction to all the examples he'd had at the Emperor's Court. But—

She sighed, and he felt her tears on his chest. Ah, well, all right, then. No midnight romping tonight. *Good. I need the sleep,* he caught himself thinking.

Instead, he moved his free hand to dry her tears with the sleeve of his robe, and continued the conversation about their son. "As soon as he's old enough that we know he can keep secrets, we'll tell him, I promise. And in the meantime, you can act like any of those silly cows in the Court and dote on your pretty page-boy. He's an affectionate little chap, and he'll thrive on all the love you give him."

"It would be *so* much worse if the Emperor had demanded him," she agreed, though her voice trembled a little with emotion. "And I *know* I am ridiculously lucky. I have my boys within my household, and I can see them whenever I like. I didn't get married off to someone three times my age who I didn't even know. I didn't get the treatment that Delia did when Father died."

"But this is still hard," Kordas replied. He *did* understand. She liked him, and he liked her; they were ridiculously compatible. But this was much, much different. This was mother-love;

she *adored* her children with all the passion of a warm-natured woman, and to be denied so much of their lives . . .

Well, it went against instinct, which did not answer to logic and reason.

She never complained about it, that was the remarkable thing. For the last nine years, she had not complained about it. At most, she had given way to a few tears, like now. *She's braver than I am,* he thought soberly.

"Well, I'll tell Hakkon tomorrow to put Restil in the page corps and assign him to us. No—to *you*. There's no reason you can't have a personal page." She gave a shuddering sigh, and patted his hand.

"If you don't mind, I'm going to go to bed early," she said, as thunder rumbled somewhere in the distance. And since she did not add "and why don't you come with me?" he just nodded.

"I'm going to finish off this excellent toddy that you put together. It's far too good to waste a single drop," he told her, and gave her a hand up out of the chair. "Better be prepared for Delia to gush about her new prize all during breakfast."

"Sometimes I think Father should have married you to Delia rather than me, the way you both worship horses," she teased, pausing and looking back over her shoulder at him.

"Thank you, but despite the example of our noble Emperor, I am *not* inclined to go robbing cradles for a wife," he retorted. "Besides, I like the one I have. She's got me broken in pretty well."

She managed a hint of a laugh, and headed up the stairs to their bedchamber. He admired the view until the ceiling cut it off. Well, maybe there was some love there after all; nobody ever said love had to only be romantic. It could be based upon admiration, too.

The conversation tonight had cast his mind back to the five years he had been at the Emperor's Court, and he mulled over his past as he brooded into the fire.

He had not been the youngest hostage there; indeed, the youngest had been barely able to toddle. The more important you were—a Prince, say, or one of the Emperor's subject Kings—the more likely it was that the Emperor would snatch one or more of your children away as soon as they were weaned. The Duke of Valdemar was not important politically or militarily, and certainly was not monetarily important; Kordas had gotten the feeling when he'd arrived on the other side of the last of the Portals that summoning him had been something of an afterthought, and probably not even the Emperor's afterthought.

It was far more likely that some flunky on inventorying the thousand or so children at the Imperial Court had noticed that the Duke of Valdemar had not yet sent a hostage, checked the rolls to make sure there were children, and sent for him.

He had been lucky that his father must have anticipated that—and realized he was going to need an advocate and advisor. That was where Hakkon had come in—masquerading as the body-servant he was allowed to bring with him. Hakkon was ten years older than he, a bastard cousin on his mother's side, and one that the then-Duke had been happy to add to the household when Kordas's mother had requested the favor. By the time Kordas was thirteen, Hakkon was tall, strong, as muscled as a muleteer, intelligent, and completely devoted to the family. He'd also spent a great deal of time at the Duke's side as the Duke made his annual tribute visits to the Imperial Capital, so Hakkon knew exactly what a nest of serpents the place was. The perfect protector to send with Kordas.

As he and Hakkon had stood just off the Imperial Portal platform, staring at the dozens of people scrambling to and fro, none of whom were paying any attention to *them,* it became clear that no one in the entire Portal room was prepared to step up to find out who they were, much less help them.

Hakkon, however, was not prepared to take that sort of treatment. Not after a full day of transiting Portal to Portal, at none of which had anyone offered them so much as a drink of water.

Hakkon had marched out into the room, grabbed the first unburdened person in Imperial livery that he saw, and growled something at the man. Kordas had been too far away to hear what Hakkon said, but it, and Hakkon's size, evidently made an impression on the servant. The man scuttled away with the speed of a terrified mouse, and by the time Hakkon had returned to Kordas's side, another harried-looking servant in Imperial livery appeared in a doorway, looking for them.

That was the first time Hakkon had intervened for him, but it had by no means been the last.

They'd been led to a vast wing of mostly tiny rooms, about the size of monastic cells, actually smaller than the bedrooms supplied to the servants here at the manor. There had been *just* enough room for a wardrobe, a chest, and two narrow beds. Hakkon had left him alone to survey this grim prospect with dismay. And, truth to tell, he had been close to breaking down in tears. He hadn't wanted to come in the first place. He'd been forced to leave all of his friends at the manor behind, and by that time, that had included Isla, who was his very *best* friend.

The overt reason for Isla coming to spend time at Valdemar had been to help his then-invalided mother run the manor. *Now* he knew (although he had not at the time) that their fathers had decided to introduce the two of them to see if they would suit. It had been a clever move; their birthdays were within two moons of each other, they were both highly intelligent, and they were both mages—though their fathers had made it very clear that they were never to reveal this outside the family. The Emperor prized mages, and would collect every one that he found into his service. And Isla had the added bonus of being a Mindspeaker.

I hate to think what would have happened to her if the Emperor had known about that. The *best* she could have expected would have been being mewed up with the rest of his mages. He'd seen where they lived, a vast edifice attached to the Imperial Palace; he'd also seen, rarely, some of the mages themselves. They never looked happy.

The worst she could have expected would be much worse than being locked up in a gloomy mausoleum to labor for the Emperor every waking moment. There were not many *female* mages among them—so Hakkon had told him—because female mages, unless they were very powerful indeed, were treated like breeding stock for the purpose of making more mages.

Well, that hadn't happened. She'd come to Valdemar when they were both eleven, and by the time the Emperor summoned him, they had been absolute best friends.

And, fortunately, she had also had neither great wealth in the form of a dower, nor great beauty. The former would have made her a rich prize that the Emperor could have used as a reward for one of his faithful. The latter—well, she'd still have been a reward for one of his faithful, but first the Emperor would probably have made her one of his many mistresses. He collected beautiful women and seemed to relish best the ones who were openly afraid of him and dared not defy him.

Well, she'd escaped the Emperor's trap. Her twin brother had been the one who'd gone as a hostage.

And her brother had died there.

Nothing sinister about that, though. It was just reflective of the lack of care that the hostages got. Idor and his body-servant had both fallen ill. No one came to check on them at first when they did not turn up for meals, and by the time Kordas himself had gone to Idor's room to see what was wrong, it was the first that anyone knew *how* sick they were. And by that time, it was too late. Despite the best that the healers could do, they had both died within hours of being found.

This was typical. You *needed* someone like Hakkon to make sure you got your share of food at meals, that nothing was stolen from you, that you weren't beaten or worse by the predators among the children. In theory, having nobles send their firstborn sons (or daughters, if they had no sons) to the Emperor wasn't a completely bad idea from the Emperor's point of view. The youngsters were all treated alike, they got the same education, they integrated into the fabric of the Empire, and they would theoretically grow up loyal to him.

In practice, with a thousand children there, it was barely organized chaos, in which older children ruled the younger, and abuse was common.

The moment that Kordas had discovered Isla's brother had been lying sick and alone for days was the moment Kordas had vowed to himself that no child of his was ever going to be sent into Imperial care.

Pain in his jaw made him realize he was grinding his teeth—as he often did when he thought about the Emperor and the Imperial Court.

I'm nothing to them, and as long as things stay that way, my family and my people are safe.

The problem was, he knew very well that could change overnight.

I need to check with Jonaton tomorrow. Maybe his answer will be different this time. Jonaton was so close . . .

I'm clenching my jaw again. Time for bed. Today had been good. Perhaps tomorrow would be better.

3

Valdemar kept "farmer's hours," even at the Ducal level, which disconcerted Imperial visitors a great deal. Breakfast was nearly at dawn, and was the biggest meal of the day.

The Great Hall of an Imperial-gift manor was meant for holding massive audiences, ceremonies, and enormous celebrations. It was not meant to be used as Kordas used it: as the communal eating-room.

In an Imperial-style Court, the people of rank ate together in a pleasant, well-lit dining room, while the servants and commoners ate in a larger, windowless, basement room off the kitchen. That was the room that Kordas's grandfather had cut up into kitchen-staff rooms.

The Great Hall at Valdemar was set up with trestle tables and benches around the clock, and had never, to Kordas's knowledge, been used as anything but an eating space. Kordas's father had partially solved the heating problem by suspending a kind of cloth "ceiling" at about the height where a normal ceiling would be, made of painted sailcloth covered in images of stars, moons, and suns against a dark blue background. Kordas had no idea what things looked like above that cloth ceiling these days. *It's probably the home to about a million spiders at this point,* he mused as he entered the room.

There *was* the difference between the High Tables, where people other than the servants and commoners ate, and the rest of the hall. There were no cloth coverings on the common tables; people had to pick up their own pieces of trencher-bread as they came in; they needed to bring their own cups, spoons, and knives; and they served themselves out of bowls and platters placed at intervals along the tables. When those were emptied, someone at the table was expected to fetch more from a table along the side of the room. At the High Tables, there were tablecloths, plates, cups, knives, and spoons, and people were served individually by the pages. *Not* by the youngest ones, who were still in training, and could not be expected to carry heavy bowls and platters of food, but by the ones in their last year of page-duty, at which point they would become squires. About half the pages were from the households of the lords of his manors. Not because he was holding them hostage, as the Emperor did, but to ensure their educations in being gentlemen. The pages were exclusively male. Little girls were expected to be trained in their own households by mothers or senior servants in the duties that were the traditional purviews of women. There might have been exceptions to this, but Kordas didn't know any. There were rarely female squires— he had three—but they had come to him at the express request of their parents, for martial training as knights.

Kordas did not enter at the main doors to the Great Hall as most people did; he came through a smaller door up at the end of the Hall where the High Tables were. There he stood, just within the shadows of the doorway, and took a moment to look over the people who served him—and whom he, in his own turn, served.

Isla had gotten up this morning before he had; she was already in the middle seat of the main High Table, with Delia on the other side of her, both of them involved in a lively conversation that involved a lot of knife-waving. Hakkon was on the other side of Kordas's empty chair, keeping a sharp eye on the pages and administering quiet corrections if they made mistakes.

It was Hakkon that Kordas's gaze lingered on; Hakkon was the Seneschal, and according to Imperial custom, the highest-ranking person in Kordas's household. Technically, he even outranked Isla. Kordas had depended on him for decades, and Hakkon simply didn't have it in him to let Kordas down.

It would have been very easy, back in those days when Kordas was a hostage in the Imperial Court, for Hakkon to have eliminated Kordas by simple neglect. It was possible for bastards to succeed to a title; it just needed the Emperor's approval, and that probably would not have been hard to get. Had Hakkon lusted for the Ducal coronet, the opportunity to snatch it had been right there.

But he had never been anything other than Kordas's faithful protector and advisor. He had never even *once* given Kordas bad advice.

No one would ever have guessed that Hakkon was Kordas's cousin; Hakkon was still tall and strong and muscled like a muleteer; he didn't allow himself the "belly drift" of most courtiers. His hair and impressive beard were a startling white-blond, and he kept both in neat braids.

He never missed anything—perhaps as a result of being Kordas's watchdog for so long; even though Kordas was still in the shadows of the doorway, his cousin spotted him, and signaled with his eyebrows and a tilt of his head toward the empty seat.

Kordas acknowledged him with a nod, and made his way through the bowing pages to join his family.

"Well?" Hakkon asked, as he took his seat.

"Well, the foaling was successful thanks to Delia, plus there was a second Sweetfoot born last night. I gave Delia the Gold foal because she earned it, so she will be starting her filly's early training today, and yes, please put Restil in the pages, he's old enough." Having gotten that out of the way, he turned to his breakfast, listening in to Delia and Isla's conversation. As he had expected, it was about Delia's filly, who apparently had been named "Daystar." Isla was giving her advice on the filly's early training, and Delia was doing more listening than talking. Kordas buttered some bread with a broad knife imprinted with the white and blue winged horse of Valdemar, and turned back to Hakkon.

"I expect to hear from the Emperor that he wants his tribute quite soon," he continued, "since the fact that I was doing my own foaling last night is bound to come to his ears as a hilarious anecdote."

Hakkon snorted. "I don't know how you put up with being thought a clown. I'd have broken some noses over it if I was in your shoes." Then he laughed. "So it's just as well I never wanted your shoes."

"I put up with it by reminding myself constantly that it's better to be thought a clown and be dismissed as harmless than to be a target for the Emperor's suspicions. The more of a fool he thinks I am, the less likely he is to think of me at all." He shrugged. "Anything you need to tell me about the pages, the squires, or the state of the Duchy?" All the servants ultimately reported to Hakkon, and were given their orders by him. The various lords of the other fourteen Valdemar manors also reported directly to him. He was in charge of the Exchequer, who managed the Treasury, the Housekeeper and Head Cook, and of course the pages and squires.

"Squire Brianta. I want her placed with a knight. She's more than ready for the position, but you don't have any lady-knights here," Hakkon told him. "What do you want to do?"

That was a good question. *Who am I certain enough of to trust a female squire to? Wait . . .*

"You don't have a squire at present," he pointed out.

"I . . . don't," Hakkon admitted, after hesitating a moment. "That's not a bad thought."

"Is she smart enough to consider training for a Seneschal position?" he persisted. "Two birds, one stone, as it were."

"We'll see. I like where this is going, though," Hakkon replied, and speared an apple with his knife. "Brianta is too good a squire to waste on a dolt, or worse, someone who would try to take advantage of the situation. And I do need a squire."

"Then assign her to yourself. If her parents object, send them to me."

Hakkon grinned. "They won't. They prefer to think about Brianta as little as possible. Oh, they'll be happy enough when she's knighted, I am sure, since she'll have a proper position in the world, but right now, she's just the odd girl that isn't much of a marriage prospect. Awkward for everyone. So am I correct in thinking you want Restil as Isla's personal page?"

"Yes, sir, you are correct!" Kordas laughed, getting Isla's side-glance. "It's about time she had her own page."

"It's about time she had more than that, but your lady wife is the most difficult person I have ever met to get her to sit back and let other people do things for her," Hakkon grumbled. "She'd be out there in the kitchen garden troweling herbs if I let her."

The twinkle in Isla's eyes told Kordas that she'd heard every word of that and was greatly amused by it, but she chose to turn back to her sister rather than address it.

Kordas and Hakkon continued to talk through the meal, though much of it was coded. It was *fairly* safe to talk openly here, but Kordas was not taking any chances that someone might decide to try Farseeing or a scrying spell on them as they ate. Unlikely—but possible. Besides, he and Hakkon had gotten used to phrasing their conversations with double-meanings, and in the Empire, that was a good habit to keep.

Although Kordas did not know Hakkon's full story—that had died with Kordas's mother, the Lady Lyantha, and Hakkon himself didn't know most of it—he knew enough. Lyantha's sister had run off with someone in a situation almost exactly like the popular song "Black Jack Davy." Unfortunately their idyll had not lasted very long. She turned up with a toddler in tow about two years after Lyantha had married Lord Valdemar. She had come here, to the manor, knowing she was not welcome back home. Lord and Lady Valdemar would have taken her in, no questions asked, no shaming and no blaming, but she had merely begged them to take Hakkon into their household, and vanished again. Had she gone back to her lover, once she no longer had a child to worry about? No one knew; she had never been heard from again.

Lyantha had added Hakkon to the household pod of children, then taken him as her page. Lord Valdemar might have been considering legitimizing Hakkon as his heir, but while Hakkon was still among the pages, Kordas had been born.

And from that point, there had never been any question but that Hakkon was going to become Kordas's protector and guide once the Emperor summoned him.

"You know," he said thoughtfully, as Hakkon carefully peeled his apple in one single strip, "I've never asked you if you resented being made my watchdog for all those years at Court."

Hakkon snorted. "You could not pay me enough to put up with the never-ending stream of garbage that comes out of the Court," he said immediately. "There is no title high enough to compensate for having to deal with that conniving toad on the Conquest Throne. Besides—"

He put the knife and the apple down, and half-turned to stare directly into Kordas's eyes.

"—your sainted mother and your kind father took me in

and treated me like their own. They never allowed anyone to shame me for what I was. Your father knighted me in secret, did you know that? When you knighted me, it was actually for the second time. When we came home because he was dying, he took me aside, and told me that if I wanted to stay at Valdemar, he'd order you to make me your Seneschal, but if I wanted to be on my own, he'd make a provision in his will to have the income from one of the manor farms and three of the Chargers, so I could go take up arms anywhere I cared to, or I could settle down with someone of my choice. And he said *someone,* not 'a lady.' So . . . you know, he knew."

"He told me."

"Well, I never knew for certain if he had or not." Hakkon picked up the apple again, and started slicing bits off, eating them carefully. "We're family, Kordas. You're my brother. You've never treated me as anything less, not even when we were at the Court and you *could* have ingratiated yourself with those entitled brats and used me as your pet attack-dog." He cracked a crooked smile. "Besides, this means that these days *you* get to stand between *me* and Imperial trouble. I call that fair."

"Good point." He finished the last oatcake and waved off the page offering more. "If you're done murdering that apple with a thousand cuts, want to climb Jonaton's tower with me?"

"But of course." Hakkon got up first, but Kordas wasn't far behind him. It was going to be a very long walk. Jonaton had his lair in the very top of the tallest of the Valdemar manor towers. And only those who were close enough to the Emperor's favor were permitted the smaller, local Portals that would enable them to walk from the ground floor into the top of a tower.

There were three other mages in this tower, but Jonaton was the most powerful and had seniority, and got the set of rooms with the best view. That also meant there were two other mages between him and trouble, should trouble decide to come looking for him. He had been the first mage that

Kordas had ever met as a child just out of the nursery, and he vividly recalled running into the man in a hallway and being startled half out of his wits by the apparition that had blown by him in a flurry of ruffle and lace-trimmed, embroidered robes all in colors that had never been found in nature.

The staircase here was contained, to give the inhabitants of the tower as much privacy as possible. It was lit by day by tiny slit windows, and by night by mage-lights that came alight when the staircase darkened. They ran into the first tenant on the stairs themselves; the youngest mage in the manor and once Jonaton's apprentice. The lad did not copy his mentor's sartorial splendor; long gray half-robes, gray tunic, and gray hose. Pelias squeezed himself against the wall so they could pass. "Are there oatcakes for breakfast?" the teen-ager asked, hopefully.

"With clotted cream and jam," Kordas told him, and the young man pelted down the stairs they had just taken with an energy and enthusiasm that made Hakkon sigh.

"If only youth could be bottled," his cousin said. "No, wait, the Emperor can—"

"But would you want it at *that* price?" Kordas countered.

"Hrrm. Youth siphoned off young criminals? Depends on the criminal, I suppose," Hakkon replied. "A murderer, I'd be fine with that. A pickpocket, not so much."

"Sooner or later you run out of murderers," Kordas pointed out, as they encountered the second inhabitant of the tower, who had paused at the entrance to the stairs. "Morning, Siman."

"Good morning, my lord." Siman was old, but still vigorous, and was dressed. "I intuit by the rapidly fading footsteps of young Pelias that there are oatcakes for breakfast."

"Your intuition is correct, as ever." Kordas made space for the elder mage to pass. "There were still plenty when we left."

"Good. If the sounds I heard at an unholy hour this morning are anything to go by, I believe Jonaton has good news for you, and the rest of us are about to put your father's plan into action."

Kordas felt his eyes widen with surprise, and he put out a hand to stop Siman and ask him more, but the mage was already out of sight and reach around the turn of the stair.

"Do you know anything about this?" he demanded of Hakkon.

His cousin shrugged. "You know me. Once I'm asleep, you could hold a battle on top of me and I'd never know it till I found the hoof prints in the morning."

Well, there was only one thing for it. He whirled and began taking the steps upward two at a time.

They found Jonaton awake and feverishly scribbling figures on sheets of reused parchment. He looked up as he heard them enter.

"I have it!" he crowed, waving a handful of papers over his head. "I have it! I tried it last night and it worked!"

Jonaton was not in his usual garb; garb that would have gotten him mistaken for a woman except for his lantern jaw. Kordas suspected him of jumping out of bed as an idea hit him and coming straight down here to his workroom, because the plain, baggy linen breeches and oversized silk shirt he was wearing looked like things he usually slept in. He snapped his fingers twice, manically remembering protocol, and said, "We're good, here, now. All warded up. You know," and twirled his bony, frequently bandaged fingers.

His mouse-brown hair was a tangled mess, and with the dark circles under his eyes, he looked as if he had been working all night. Kordas glanced over at Hakkon, who seemed bemused. "I *know* you went to bed last night," Hakkon said.

"Yes, but I suddenly had an idea!" Jonaton waved his fistful of papers again. "I need more power, but it will definitely work! Let me tell you!"

Since by now Kordas was well aware that nothing would stop Jonaton when he was in full flow, he just looked around for a place to sit, spotted an empty bucket, and turned it over to sit on it. Hakkon leaned back against the wall with his arms crossed. Jonaton launched into his explanation without a pause.

"My problem has been how to identify a good spot to Gate far enough away from the Empire that we'll have a long head start on anyone who chases us. Right?"

"Wait, I thought the problem was that Gates only go so far—" Hakkon interrupted.

"No, no, or the Emperor wouldn't have his private Gates that can go wherever he wants them to," Jonaton replied, shaking his head vigorously. "It just takes a lot more power to operate them than the static Gates we use. That's easy, we have plenty of mages here to punch one through for a good long distance. I mean, not from up *here*, but where the big ones could be made. Because. I swear, you never listen to me."

"I listen to you—" Hakkon began.

Jonaton interrupted him. "So, we know about a thousand years ago, something cataclysmic to magic swept over, well, everything, right?" he said.

"We do?" Hakkon whispered to Kordas.

"And that's why it takes a lot of effort to gather the magic energy to do things, unless you are doing demonic pacts or blood magic, or something else Abyssal. Or maybe Elemental, but you have to have a lot of energy to bind Elementals." Jonaton had the bit in his teeth now, and there was going to be no slowing him down. "But that's not important right now. What is important is that the same—I'll call them Mage-Storms, because they act like heavy weather—created Change-Circles."

"What are—"

"I'll tell you later," Kordas promised, his eyes on Jonaton and his excitement growing.

"Now *one* of those Change-Circles south of us, in the Barony of Lepodal, brought in a tree with a trunk big enough to drive a wagon through it. Well, it would have, except it didn't bring the whole tree. It brought a crescent-shaped bite of the tree. And *that* was so fantastic that Baron Lepodal got a cabinet-maker to make as many tables out of that tree trunk as he could. People competed to buy them. They're scattered all over the Empire, family heirlooms. And I happened to be in the same manor as one of them a few years ago, and while no one was looking, I thought, 'Jonaton, old sport, it might be handy to have a splinter of that thing some day, because you never know.'"

"You never know what, exactly?" Kordas asked.

"That's what I'm getting to!" Jonaton shouted impatiently. "So I made sure no one was around, and I got down on the floor under the table, and I carved off a little sliver from the underside. I made sure to get it from the trunk, because I wasn't sure what the legs were made of. And I put it in a box, and put it in my collection, and then never thought about it." Jonaton waved backhandedly at the overstuffed shelves and stands that could start a museum all on their own.

Becoming a mage of high quality meant suffering through a long list of pain- and senses-shocking experiences just to learn the craft. An exploratory mage, well, they were rare, and every one known was recorded as *eccentric*. Kordas knew that it changed some mages beyond reasoning, but Kordas knew that one trait about Jonaton was that he compulsively *acquired* things. As vices go, it wasn't the worst possible—but just the same, Kordas knew it was probably best that he never officially learned where Jonaton's collections originated, or there would be no small sum of reparations money going out of the Duchy.

"How you keep track of all that—stuff—" Hakkon began.

Jonaton ignored the jibe. "Until last night! When I realized, that tree must have come from the West! *Far* to the West, way beyond where the Empire's borders are, because otherwise someone would have found it and made matching tables and made a fortune! So last night I gathered up all my spare energy crystals and that sliver and decided to see if I could punch through to where that tree is—or was, anyway. And I did it! I did it!"

"So . . . you saw where the tree used to stand?" Kordas asked hesitantly. Jonaton used a lot of eccentric language, and he wasn't quite sure just what "punched through" meant.

"More than just *saw!* I got a momentary window there! Like—if I get enough power behind me, I can open a temporary, *really* temporary Gate-like-thing—I call it a Snatch-Portal!—for long enough that Delia can pick up something *from* there, I can make a Gate-anchor out of it, we can open one again, and she can throw it back! Then I use the same bearing I figured out, in the cave, and sight in on it good and strong, and even better, the rest of that tree is still alive! So it'll make it easier to get a lock, and if I can, I can burn in a searchable sigil. Which means—"

"We can open a Gate, a real Gate, out far beyond the border of the Empire," Kordas said slowly. "Exactly what my father wanted. What he planned for. What we've been working for."

Kordas felt the hair on the back of his neck standing up, and he grew hot and cold at once. After all this time, and all this effort—here it was. The Plan. It was no longer just a plan. They could make it a reality.

He and his family and anyone who wanted to come with them could escape the Empire. Forever.

"Are you *sure* of this?" he asked.

"Well, of course I'm not *sure*," Jonaton said crossly. "It's magic. It has built-in fuckery. Other mages could stop us—and will, if they're in the Emperor's service. But *I* am willing to make that Gate and *use* that Gate, and if that's not good enough for you—"

"No, no, no, I understand!" Kordas hastened to tell him, as he rose to his feet and strode across the room to take Jonaton's hand in his. "Good Gods, Jonaton, this is brilliant! You're a genius! But—"

Jonaton stopped him before he could say anything. "Yes, I

know, I know, and you're right, the site is not on a body of water, much less a river of the size you want. But the thing is, the first Gate will just be temporary. You'll send someone across to *find* a lake or a river, or even a swamp would do at a pinch—"

"Not a swamp. I do not even want to think about sheep in a swamp." Kordas shuddered.

"Hah! Bad for the sheep, but you have to admit, it'd be so funny it'd be worth it! But. Yes. No. All right, not a swamp, then. But you just send some hardy, over-muscled, over-eager lad who loves nothing more than to hack his way through howling wilderness and eight million leagues of wait-a-minute bushes and bears and Gods only know what else to find a river, and we can put a proper water-Gate on it, and there you go! Well, first we go through and build a durable Gate frame under shelter, and bring through parts for a bigger one. Obviously. But that's tomorrow!" Jonaton grinned into Kordas's face. "Easy peasy nice and breezy. You'll finally have a use for that manor-sized barn full of hulls. Among other things." Jonaton gently pulled his hand loose from Kordas's and yawned, covering his mouth with his sleeve. "I'm going back to bed now."

And without another word, the mage padded in bare feet to the staircase and up it. Kordas turned to Hakkon. "Did you know anything about this?" he asked incredulously.

"Well, obviously I've known he's been working non-stop on this since your father's time," Hakkon pointed out. "But no, I had no idea he'd . . ." Hakkon paused as the enormity of it all hit him. "By Klathor's Axe. He did it, didn't he? He really went and *did* it!" Hakkon's eyes widened and a wicked grin spread over his face. "We're going to be able to *do* this! We're going to get out of this place!"

"Slow up, old friend. Not without a lot of planning and a *hell* of a lot of secrecy," Kordas pointed out. "In fact—" and now the enormity of the *task* that faced them hit *him*. "The work we've been doing all these years is nothing compared to the work that's ahead of us."

"But now we know the goal is provably possible," Hakkon pointed out.

He nodded. *Now we can see it, not just dream about it.*

"I'm going to go check on the warehouses," he said. "And then I need to get someone with a better head for math than I have to tell me how many thousand more hulls we're going to need. This . . ." He scratched his head. " . . . is going to take a lot of whiles. But first, let's go talk to the Circle."

Hakkon groaned. "Not those old coots! Kordas, they're half drunk and all crazy!"

"They're not as drunk or as crazy as you think they are, though they'd like you to think that," he retorted, and led the way down the stairs again.

The "Circle," as they liked to be called, were six incredibly old mages who all lived in the same tower. They looked and acted today exactly the same as they had looked and acted when Kordas had first been old enough to notice them, and Hakkon had confirmed that they had looked and acted that way when *he* had first arrived. For all Kordas could tell, they'd been here since his grandfather's day. When they were not asleep, they gathered in a comfortable room at the base of their tower, sitting on the floor on enormous cushions stuffed with buckwheat hulls or crushed nut shells that had molded over time to exactly fit the shapes of their skinny behinds and backs, positioned just out of slapping range of each other. Pages brought them their meals and wine. Mostly wine— although Kordas had done some discreet monitoring, and had discovered that they didn't drink nearly as much as people assumed, or that they would *like* people to assume. They all went by single names—if they had last names, no one here at the manor still knew what they were. Ponu, Dole, Wis, Koto, Ceri, and Sai.

They never seemed to actually *do* anything. They certainly

didn't seem to use their magical workrooms in the tower. Mostly they sat in their circle and gossiped about—well, everything. As a child, Kordas had sometimes snuck into their room to listen quietly, and somehow they seemed to know *literally everything* that was going on, not only in the Duchy, not only in the neighboring holdings, but even in the Emperor's own Court.

Most people dismissed them as senile and crazy. "Why do you keep them around, Father?" Kordas had once asked. Kordas's father had actually gotten down to Kordas's level so he could look his son straight in the eyes.

"First, they have nowhere else to go that is safe for them," he'd said, carefully. "The Emperor would use up their last years in a heartbeat if he got hold of them. But second—just because you don't *see* them working, doing magic like Jonaton and the others do, it doesn't mean they are doing nothing. If you ask the right question, if they know something they think you need to know, or if there is danger to the Duchy and us, listen to them, and they'll tell you things worth knowing. It's when they stare directly at you and point fingers that you had better listen carefully. They're each wise, but put together, they're more wise than just six people."

He hadn't needed to consult them very often, but when he did . . . in between the insults and the in-jokes he didn't understand, he discovered that his father had been right.

"By the way, how much do you know about Jonaton's larcenous side?" he asked as they went down the stairs.

Hakkon coughed uncomfortably. "Uh, well . . . yes. That Snatch-Portal he talks about 'hypothetically' making? He already does it, when there's something he needs. He just opens it to the marketplace, looks around to see if what he wants is there, and helps himself. Oh, it's never anything big or expensive!" he hastened to add. "And I have *finally* gotten him to leave payment for what he takes! But . . . aye." Hakkon sighed heavily. "'Light-fingered' is putting it mildly."

"Hrm. My parents told me they rescued him from a mob that was chasing him because he was wearing women's clothing. How much of that chasing was because of what he was wearing, and how much of it was because he'd helped himself to something that wasn't his?" Kordas wondered out loud. "Stolen dress, you reckon?"

Hakkon snickered.

"We'll probably never know. He says that when he needs something immediately, he doesn't see anything wrong with taking something that someone isn't at that moment using." Kordas looked over his shoulder at his cousin, to see if Hakkon was serious. It appeared that he was.

"Well . . . that's an original way of looking at things."

Hakkon shrugged. "Mages. They're *all* at least a little bizarre."

"I—am a mage, you know," Kordas objected.

Hakkon grinned, a grin that said more clearly than words, *Yes, I do know.*

By that time they were on the ground floor and nearly at the Circle's tower. "The way I see it, it doesn't matter too much if someone is 'eccentric' or 'bug-jumpy moon-touched,'" Kordas stated firmly. "It matters if they're functional. People can be any kind of weird as long as they aren't harming anyone. Hells, that makes them victorious—that's their truth, they get to live it."

"Glad you're the Duke," Hakkon answered. "I'd never have assembled a house like yours. I'd have frustrated the lot of 'em, and not seen their value like you do."

Kordas quipped, "We mages all have our spins off the beam, Hakkon," and took a few moments to lean with his back to the hardwood inlay of the paneling. "I couldn't really feel happy until I accepted what I'm made of, so now I play to it. My truth is that I'm opportunistic, I'm a little deceptive, and I love picking out the value hidden in what others ignore. I can't seem to turn it off." Kordas paused a moment, and said more softly, "You made me feel safe enough to figure that out."

Hakkon just replied with a silent nod.

"Not every future mage gets to be raised as a good person. I got lucky," the Duke concluded. He reached for the loose latch of the sub-door, and rattled it to announce visitors were coming. "Brace yourself. For pipe smoke and wine fumes, if nothing else," Kordas said, as much to himself as to Hakkon. "Here we go."

4

Things had warmed up this morning, and all the windows in this lowest room of the tower were wide open—with cheese-cloth screens in them to keep out the bugs. The scent of wine was in the air, matched by the scent of the daylilies at the foot of the tower just outside the windows. As Kordas had ex-pected, the six old men were at their usual positions, parked in their peculiar cushion-chairs, finishing the remains of their breakfast and starting on their first pitchers of wine. Each of them was a different shade of brown in skin, from river-water to deep as tree-bark. Each had a low table before him, strewn with writing instruments and papers.

"Well, look who's here!" Ponu cackled; since he was facing the door, he was the first to see them enter. "The lord of the manor himself! Nice of you to drop by to see if we're dead yet!" Ponu was *probably* the oldest of the six; he hadn't a hair on his head, and only one or two sprouting from a mole on his chin. All six of them wore the same things every day—fresh, clean, natural-colored linen trews and loose, wrapped shirts tied with broad linen sashes. Well, they wore those things when the weather was warm. When it was cold, they were all shapeless bundles of blankets, from which a hand would emerge from time to time to reach for a wine-cup or a nice morsel. "Let's have a roll call. Anyone who's dead today, raise your hand, so he knows."

"Be nice to the boy, Ponu," admonished Dole, who had an impressive crop of curly gray hair down to his shoulders, and an equally impressive nose. "When has he ever pestered us for anything?"

"He doesn't know what to pester us *for*," taunted Wis, whose otherwise bald head sported a long, white braid at the top that coiled on the floor behind his cushion. Wis cocked an eyebrow at Kordas. "Do ya, little man?"

Koto snorted, and continued to play with a cat's-cradle. "He knows more than he tells. Plays things close to the skin, that one." Koto's head was not just bald, it was shiny, and very, very round. It looked odd on his stick figure, like he was a twig doll with a ball for a head.

Ceri and Sai were known to be brothers, and were suspected to be twins, although they wouldn't say one way or another. They were both stern-looking, usually silent, with massive white eyebrows and long, straight white hair. Ceri wore his in a tail on the top of his head, Sai wore his unbound and combed until it looked like a fall of ice. They both looked at Kordas and grunted.

Kordas didn't have a hat to pull off, but if he had, he would have done so. He walked to the center of the circle with Hakkon in tow. "Actually, I've come to ask you about some history. I only know a little, and Hakkon doesn't know any of it."

"Oh. History." That was Sai speaking for the first time. "I suppose you think we're millennia old."

"I think you are millennia wise, actually," said Kordas, which drew appreciative cackles from all six. "And that's exactly the age of things that I'd like you to tell us about."

"Oh, the puppies want to know about the Great Mage War, do they?" asked Ceri, in a flat tone that made it impossible for Kordas to tell if he was being serious or mocking them.

Best to assume the former. It was always best to be on good behavior with the Circle; although they didn't *often* do magic these days, he'd seen them perform mind-boggling feats.

"Yes, please," he said.

Ceri and Sai exchanged a look with each other, and then with the other four. Ponu just shrugged, as if to say, "Well, you volunteered by speaking up. Carry on. We'll correct you, as needed." Ceri responded with rude gestures from multiple cultures.

"Not *quite* a thousand years ago, magic flowed freely across the world, and mages could do things that we would think of as god-like," said Ceri, intoning his words as if he was reading out something spread before him. "A mere apprentice could craft the sort of Portal that could take you from the ground floor to the top floor of a building. A single mage could craft a common Gate. Three or four could create a Gate that could easily reach across several Kingdoms. Mages *created* entirely new creatures out of practically nothing—ice-drakes, gryphons, *wyrsa*. You'd *think* that would be enough for folks, wouldn't you? But no—"

Sai snorted. "Of course not. Because *some* people are greedy bastards and can never get enough. So one of these mages far out in the West decided he was going to be the Big Bad King of the World, and gathered up mages and armies to do exactly that, and started rolling across the landscape, crushing everything in his path."

"That sounds familiar," muttered Hakkon. Ponu smirked at that.

Ceri took up the narrative where his brother had left off. "Naturally, people in the way didn't much care for that, and resisted. A different mage gathered an army of defense. And, in the end, they destroyed each other. But of course, it wasn't enough for them to just kill each other, oh no, they had to blow bloody great holes in the earth in two cataclysms that sent a pair of terrible storms screaming in waves across not just the Physical Plane, but the Abyssal and Aetherial Planes as well!"

"Idiots," muttered Ponu.

Dole decided to interject something. "Where those two sets of waves intersected, you got Change-Circles. You can still see the damned things if you know what to look for—or you're unfortunate enough to come across one that's trapped a pool of sick, twisted magic at its heart. They're circles of land that can be as small as a water bucket or as big as a couple of acres, where actual pieces of land were ripped up and exchanged across vast distances."

Kordas glanced over at his cousin, who looked incredulous. "That can happen?" Hakkon demanded.

"Not anymore," said Dole. "There's not enough pure magic around to set off something like that again, for which the Gods be thanked. That story your bedfellow told you about the tree? *That* was part of a Change-Circle. And if you stumble into one, and you're not a strong enough mage, you can end up as a creature as twisted and warped as the magic itself."

"Seen people with their insides as their outsides, I have," Wis reported, casually examining his wine-cup as if it were of the greatest possible interest. "Can put a body right off their feed, I can tell you."

Hakkon looked more than incredulous, he looked stunned. He glanced over at Kordas, who shrugged. "If they say it's true, it's true," Kordas told him. He couldn't get his mind wrapped around it, but if the Circle stood by it, then it must have happened.

"We never lie," said Wis. "Well, maybe sometimes. But only that we haven't had enough wine. We never lie about history."

"How do you *know* these things?" Hakkon said, sounding

a little choked, as if he really might be starting to believe the six were a thousand years old.

"Because, unlike people who let their muscles do all their thinking for them, we *read*," Sai told him, as sternly as a tutor who is chastising a slacking student. "There are a lot of books in this manor. You might try looking at some of them—oh, wait, all you know is the Imperial tongue, so I suppose you'll have to listen to us instead. Now are you going to babble, or are you going to listen?"

Hakkon shut his mouth with an audible snap. Apparently satisfied, Sai picked up where Dole had left off.

"Now, this was a long, long, *long* way from where we are. And it was before there was an Empire, or an Emperor. Just a High King wearing the Wolf Crown ruling over eight County-sized Kingdoms. The High King knew about the war, of course, because a lot of big magic flying about makes disturbances even when people *aren't* blowing each other sky-high, and he had scryers and Seers and Foreseers keeping an eye on things in case they boiled over enough to affect his realm. And, of course, when the end came, the Mage-Storms certainly *did* affect his realm. The mess was far enough away that it actually took about half a day for the front of the Storm-Wave to hit his kingdoms, and before that could happen, he had every mage, great or small, organized to create a shield over as much as he could—limited by the fact that shields are always circular domes, so, well, too bad for anything and anyone that didn't fit under the dome. It wasn't so bad for people who didn't have much that was made by magic in their land—they only needed to hunker down for the physical storms that also came through, watch out for Change-Circles, and hope they weren't caught in one. But anything that *was* made by magic and still empowered by it turned to vapor in a most spectacular fashion."

Sai evidently felt he had said enough and stopped.

"Is that all?" Hakkon asked after a period of silence.

"Well, of *course* that's not *all*," Wis snapped. "Don't you even think? There's a thousand more years of history between then and now!"

Ponu piped up, "It's always 'a thousand years' in stories, even if it was eight hundred ten or fourteen hundred eighty. 'A thousand years' is dramatic, and drama means more to people than accuracy, I'll tell you that for free. That's how you get throngs of obedient morons, while the educated have to work doubly hard to keep records accurate. Historians and librarians have saved more lives than Healers."

Wis and the rest nodded, and Wis continued. "That's the *reason* the High King became the Emperor and the Empire grew! The High King had the only powerful magical artifacts and constructions that still worked! And he had most of the only mages that were left, even though about half of them died keeping that shield up."

Dole added, "Not that the ones who died then wanted to. They had no idea what they were up against, though the High King knew. Their lives were taken from them."

"What was under that dome put the High King at an advantage that no one else had for centuries. Really, except for the Change-Circles, the *lucky* ones were the people living without much magic in their lives," said Ponu.

"Because nothing they had was blowing up in their faces?" Hakkon hazarded, in tones that were surprisingly timid for the big man, as if he was afraid of being yelled at again. Kordas was irresistibly reminded of one of the big guard mastiffs he had once seen encountering a tiny kitten, which had put up all its fur, spat, and sunk needle-claws into his nose. The poor dog hadn't known what to do, and neither did Hakkon.

"Gods be praised! It has a brain!" Wis exclaimed, throwing his arms upward. "Yes. Healing still worked just fine as long as it was the inherent Gift and not operating by magic. The same

for all of the other Mind-magic Gifts. But *real* magic of the sort
that the High King had come to depend on—" He snorted. "Eh,
well, it was scattered and unreliable and *very* hard to control.
It was slow, if it was going to be stable. *Unless . . .*"

He paused significantly and looked at Ceri, who obligingly
took up the thread.

"Unless you are employing the dark magics linked to the
Abyssal Plane," Ceri said ominously. "The Abyssal Plane
wasn't much affected. So, blood, pain, and demonic magics
worked just fine. As did Elemental magic, but Elemental magic
tends to be the provenance of shamans, and the High King
didn't have any, so he didn't know that. So the reliable magic
was all Abyssal stuff."

"As the High King soon found out." That was Dole. "At
first, it was deal-making. Then binding. To their credit, the
High Kings, and later the Emperors, really did their best at
first not to give in to the temptation to use the Black Arts,
but—well, they are all powerful people who spend their lives
trying to amass more power, and when you do that, you start
to look at anything as a tool, no matter how filthy."

Wis sneered, "And oh, were some of the Emperors filthy
tools."

"And *that*," Ponu concluded, "is why the Court of the Emperor is a nest of scorpions, rats, and snakes—with apologies
to the wiser ways of scorpions, rats, and snakes. The Black
Arts corrupt everything and everyone they touch, and the Emperor and his mages have been wallowing in them for a very
long time."

"Why wasn't the Abyssal Plane much affected?" Kordas
asked.

"That would require a level of understanding of magic you
don't have," said Ponu, witheringly. "But I'll try a very simple
explanation that is not the true one, but is as close to the truth
as you can understand. The Aetherial Plane is 'lighter' than

we are, and the Abyssal Plane is 'heavier' than we are. So just as waves in the sea move seaweed and don't move rocks, the magic waves moved us and didn't move them."

Kordas nodded, knowing that was about the best explanation he was going to get out of them. He might be a mage—but it was pretty clear to him in this moment that he didn't know a fraction of what they did about magic.

"And just as cheesecloth lets wind go right through it, the Aetherials were not as much troubled by the waves as we were. But it did confuse them, and blew some of them away from us. Meanwhile, those who learned stable magic had to fight as much for stability as anything else." That was Dole, pouring himself another cup of wine. "Which, really, is only fair. We here on Velgarth were the ones that made the mess, it's only fair that we are the most affected by it."

"I should make some stuffed bread," said Sai, out of nowhere. Sai's magic, as Kordas was actually aware, extended to baked goods, and his specialty was stuffed bread, sweet dough filled with sweet pastes like fruit or nuts, savory filled with cheese and meat. "Should I make some stuffed bread?"

"Stuffed bread is always a good idea," said his brother solemnly. "All for stuffed bread?" Even Hakkon raised his hand. "Ponu, give the lads some wisdom."

Kordas glanced over at his cousin, whose expression revealed that he was still trying to process everything he'd just been told.

"Some people are makers, some are bakers. Some are cooks, and some are chefs. Everyone has their own recipes, and everyone wastes good ingredients into a charred mess when they overdo it. That's spellwork. Good spellwork needs a sharp, resourceful mind, a prepared work space, the right tools, good ingredients, and a schedule. Anything else that you want to know?" asked Ponu.

"Jonaton—" Kordas began.

"Found a way to find a way to anchor a distant Gate last

night, yes, he was loud enough about it," said Wis. "Yes, we'll help with the actual Gate construction, but don't bother us with the petty details before you get to building it. Yes, between us and about half a dozen more of your tower-dwellers, we can make it reach *quite* a long way."

"Yes, he seems to be on the right track," said Dole. "Yes, he's probably right it will work. Yes, he's also right that there's a level of uncertainty, and you can thank those idiots a millennium ago for that instability."

"Yes, we know how to keep the Emperor from noticing it," Ponu said. "It's simple. Tell him 'don't build a Gate that pushes, build a Gate that pulls.' He'll know what we mean. If he does that, you can put the thing far enough away the Emperor won't connect it with Valdemar, even when it's active, and that will solve your problem. It'll also get things through to the other side faster if he builds it that way."

"I can't think of anything else at the moment, and thank you very much, honored elders," Kordas said, after a long moment.

Ponu cackled at that. "Honored elders! Did you *hear* that?" He laughed again.

"Toddle along, you two," said Dole, dismissively. Then— "Oh, wait!" He pointed a finger at Hakkon. "Tell your pretty boy that the next time he punches a Portal into my space and sticks his hand in it to help himself to my things, he'll be drawing back a stump. I'll even cauterize it for him!"

"Really? Isn't that overreacting? You had over a hundred firebird feathers," said Ceri.

"And if I want a hundred and one, what business is it of yours?" Dole snapped, and threw something—it looked like a small cheese-crumb from his breakfast—at his fellow mage. It fell short, but the point was made.

That started them off, bickering and calling each other names. This was why their seats were positioned out of hitting range of each other.

Kordas grabbed Hakkon by the elbow and pulled him out before cups started flying.

Hakkon scratched his head as they emerged into the short hallway that led back into the rest of the manor. "Are they always like that?"

Kordas snickered. "Sometimes they're worse. But, I'll also say that despite the wardings in there, and with us—" he tapped the Crest of Valdemar on his baldric, then flipped it over a bit to show the layers of metal, lace, and wood hidden under it—"they still speak in code and implication. It might have sounded like pointless banter, but in truth, they were telling us valuable hints about what to think and how to do things just then. It's a sort of game they play. Still, if I were you, I would warn Jonaton about the fact that his thievery is not a secret to the Circle. I'm pretty sure Dole was serious."

"Oh." Hakkon looked back at the closed door. "Right."

"Come on, I need your calculating brain," Kordas said, tugging at his elbow. "There are many steps in making perfect stuffed bread."

Hakkon looked deeply baffled for six seconds more, then understanding dawned on his face. "They—oh. I only listened to the words, not what they could have *meant*," Hakkon replied, actually blushing. "It was like those weird story problems I read to you when you were first learning magic."

"A truth of magic is that we never stop learning, or the magic fades. New spellwork is invigorated by new knowledge, while if a mage stops new learning, they stagnate away into dull despondency," Kordas said as the pair headed through alabaster-columned and wood-paneled halls, toward one of the lesser stable complexes. "That's mostly what the Emperor has now, in the City. Mages that are decadent but dull. They learned the official methods to have power enough, then just stopped there."

Hakkon looked even more enthused, and even younger,

when he replied, "And they don't have Circles in the City, do they?"

Kordas just grinned back, holding the door open with a flourish for his friend.

For what they needed to inspect, they needed horses. Kordas was certainly not going to take a nursing mare away from her new foal, and he didn't particularly want to draw attention to the fact that Duke Valdemar was going out for a ride, either. So once outside in the sweet air of Valdemar, he sent the stable-boy for two of the Sweetfoot palfreys, a pair of geldings named Penta and Kery, both ordinary-looking bays—or at least, as ordinary as horses in the Valdemar stables ever got.

It was a good morning for riding; the rain had cleared away every hint of dust, flowers were in bloom in all the meadows, and even in the worst of situations, riding a Sweetfoot palfrey was always a pleasure. Kordas liked to boast that you could put a baby in a Sweetfoot's saddle and it wouldn't fall off, and he'd come very close to proving that with his insistence that the children of the household learn to ride as soon as they could toddle. So the ride to a peculiar yet nondescript building at the edge of the manor's grounds brought him a feeling of vast content, even if his mind was still racing.

They dismounted and tied up their horses at rings on the side of the building and went in.

It was a vast storage building, with a workshop attached. And it was here that the *other* main cash "crop" of the Duchy was produced.

The forests of the Duchy were too valuable to squander as a crop for export. The fields produced mostly hay and grass—every bit of grain stayed right here, and so did the produce. But a clever discovery here had given them something else that was even more valuable to the Empire.

But now Kordas wondered about that discovery, because it seemed so unlikely . . .

The objects in question were stored on racks that reached all the way to the ceiling and filled the entire storage building. To the uneducated eye, there was absolutely no way of telling what they actually were. They looked like dull, brownish-gray oblongs with flat bottoms, flat tops, pointed ends, and obtusely-angled sides. They were as long as three common wagons and about an arm-length taller than a man.

In fact, they were barge hulls.

Valdemar had been producing them for as long as there had *been* a Valdemar, after the first Duke—also a mage—had discovered how to create them almost entirely by accident. As much of a botanist as he had been a mage, he had taken to experimenting with fungi he had found here.

And were some of those out of Change-Circles? After listening to the story of the aftermath of the Mage-Wars, it seemed likely! *Surely he would have been drawn to Change-Circles, and to investigate them. And I have never heard of a fungus like the one we use to make barge hulls anywhere else.*

Well, since the first Duke's discovery, the Duchy had been making and selling the hulls at such an entirely reasonable price that there were only two other workshops in other parts of the Empire that even bothered with doing the same. Wooden barges were almost unheard of except as luxury items, but these were *cheap* to produce, requiring a bare minimum of magic.

First, a mold, or bladder, made of inflated rawhide, oiled and carefully prepared, was covered in a layer of cured long-fibered vegetation. This was the only finicky part of the process: layering the vegetation for maximum strength. Here in Valdemar, they used a kind of hemp—the stems, and only the stems—the kind that was generally made into ropes. The stuff would grow anywhere, with wild enthusiasm, and quickly choke out any other crops. They got several cuttings out of every field every growing season. There was a workshop on the eastern coast in Lyranhold that used an equally fibrous seaweed. The third workshop, near the Capital, used a similar weedy relative of flax.

The vegetation was laid on with a simple water-soluble glue, easy and cheap to make. It was allowed to dry, then a thick paste made of water, wheat chaff, sawdust, and any other kind of plant material that could be reduced to a state like coarse-ground wheat was coated on just before the spores of an extremely odd fungus got laid on with a trowel. That was kept damp and allowed to grow until the mold was about a thumb-breadth thick, which took about three days. The workers wore glass-faced hoods, aprons, and gloves, which were thoroughly bleached every day. The fungus spread fast enough that one could watch it grow into intertwining layers, pulling itself tight into a weave that was ultimately fine enough to shine like satin.

Then, an apprentice mage applied a simple, low-power, curative spell of intensely purple light to it, until its surface fused into a single, inflexible piece. It would be tipped onto its longest side, the bladder deflated and pulled out, and there was your hull. Total cost, almost nothing, except for the spell-work, but that was kept a very dear state secret. The result was more waterproof than treated and varnished wood, light enough that two men could carry a hull with ease, tough enough to take hard collisions in the water, easy to patch if it *was* holed, and it could be made in any shape you liked. On the east coast, they made deeper-drafted, keeled, seagoing boats in addition to barges. In Lyranhold, they were known to make cottage roofs as well. The practical size-limit was right about the length of three wagons; after that they needed some internal ribbing and proper keels to keep from buckling over time, especially in seagoing vessels.

The resulting forms weren't ideal as roofs, mostly because while they kept out the weather, they did little to keep out the heat of summer nor the cold of winter. In order to be made into barges people could live comfortably in, or into roofs for more than a shepherd's hut, they needed to be insulated, and that added considerably to the cost. One lesser mage and a crew of helpers could produce as many as four or five plain hulls a day, once the production was started.

They had all sorts of molds here, from rowboats to living barges where entire families could make a comfortable home. Mostly, though, what they produced were cargo barges. The main difference between the cargo barges and the living barges was that no one bothered to cut too many windows into the angled sides of the cargo barges except at the end, where there would be a small cabin for the operator.

There were molded loops at either end. Several barges could be roped together to form a train, and one or two Tow-Beasts hitched to the front loop of the front barge were sufficient to haul the entire thing along, heavily loaded.

It probably never entered the Emperor's mind, but those three workshops were the main reason commerce flowed so easily and cheaply, if a little slowly, within the Empire. While Imperial roads were good, the network of canals was excellent. There were Gates at intervals along every canal as well as locks to lift the barges over elevation changes. Generally, anything that needed transportation went by barge for all but the last few leagues, or within a large city.

Anyone in the Duchy could come here and get a hull for the very special cost of about the price of two goats. Newlyweds got one free. Anyone outside the Duchy paid more than that, of course; this *was* a "cash crop." In a pinch they could be used as houses on land as well as on the canals, but because they were so light, they were dangerous in a windstorm unless heavily weighted with a layer of paving stones in the bottom.

"How many of these things are there in the Duchy, do you think?" Kordas asked Hakkon.

"It'll be in the records, but at a guess, I'd say three for every family," Hakkon replied, his lips moving a little as he counted hulls under his breath. "We could ship out every grain of the emergency stores in the manor at once using about three quarters of these hulls stored here." He turned to his cousin. "So it might be time to start the half-year plan."

———————

Like all of the Dukes before him, on every fine day, Kordas rode out to some part of the Duchy to personally see that all was well. This served several purposes. It kept him in touch with almost all of his people. With thousands of them, obviously he couldn't know them all by name, but he *could* ensure that they saw him, saw him as approachable, and would not hesitate to talk to him if there was something that needed his personal attention. It also drove the Imperial spies *mad,* because it meant that they would have to leave their comfortable little niches where they were pretending to be road workers, itinerant laborers, or some other unnoticable entity and follow him around on foot while he was on horseback. And it reinforced that image he so carefully cultivated, of a jumped-up gentleman farmer; bucolic, more concerned with drains than politics, and utterly dismissable.

So today he was going to visit one of his very favorite people in this part of the Duchy. Squire Lesley, the pig farmer.

Lesley was not *just* any old pig farmer. Half the Duchy depended on him and his herds to grub up and manure their fields every year once they were harvested. He not only had his own herds of pigs, but for a fee he kept individual pigs for anyone who wanted one to butcher in the fall and didn't want the trouble of tending it. Lesley was the supplier of all things pig to the manor, and he knew as much about breeding and raising them as Kordas knew about horses.

And it drove the spies insane when Kordas went to visit.

When they were not out running in someone else's fields, churning up the soil with their snouts and disposing of anything not wanted by eating it, the pigs were in spacious pastures dotted with little shelters—made of the same stuff as the boat hulls—that would have served equally well for sheep. Today about half of those fields were empty, and by that, Kordas knew that the early cabbages, parsnips, broad beans, peas, and radishes had been harvested, and the pigs were out doing their duty, making the fields ready for the next round of crops. He rode up to the low, broad stone farmhouse with an eye out for Lesley's distinctive yellow hat. Unlike most farmers, the wide-brimmed hat Lesley wore was never made of straw; after one too many incidences of his hat blowing off and a pig eating it, Lesley's wife had made him one of yellow canvas, coated with a bitter wax that the pigs found too distasteful even to mouth.

Kordas spotted his target at the side of a very special pen. This beautifully crafted stone pen and stone pig-house was the home of his prize sow, the Empress.

Lesley's prize sow was always named the Empress. If the name carved into the stone of the pig-pen was anything to go by, that had been the case for this Squire and probably his ancestors going back to when this farm had been established. The Empress was kept in conditions that matched any that Kordas provided for the Valdemar Golds. Her house had a thick bed of immaculately clean straw at all times. Her yard had a stone water trough filled with spring water, and a stone food trough filled with the best possible foods. There was both a dust-wallow and a mud-wallow, and the rest of the yard was covered in more straw. The yard was *never* allowed to get dirty.

Kordas tied up his horse in the shade next to the house, and rambled over to the Squire, who was leaning over the wall, talking to his pig. The unobservant would have said that Lesley was paying no attention whatsoever to his liege lord, but as Kordas got within range, he heard a very soft voice saying, "And there's our Kordas, Empress, come to have an audience with you."

"Heyla, Lesley," said Kordas, just as softly.

"Heyla, Kordas," Lesley replied, comfortable and calm. "Come have a piece of wall."

"Don't mind if I do."

He joined Lesley in laying both arms up on the top of the wall, gazing down at a sow that was easily the size of a sofa, surrounded by what looked like a sea of pretty pink piglets. "Farrowed, did she?" he observed.

"A full dozen, all healthy," Lesley said, not trying to keep the gloating out of his voice. "Reskin is going to be beside himself. His Nonesuch only had a litter of eight." Kliff Reskin was Squire Lesley's chief rival in the matter of pigs. Reskin had been injudicious enough to challenge Lesley's supremacy in the matter of pigs in the Duchy, and had become Lesley's mortal enemy from that day forward. It did not help that Reskin was not a farmer, but a pub owner and brewer, that he fed his sow on leftovers, scraps, and the spent barley from his brewing rather than following Lesley's example of free-ranging his pigs or supplying them with good fodder like turnip-tops and cabbages that had a touch of worm. It was worse that Reskin was openly contemptuous of Lesley's knowledge.

"Well, that'll disappoint some bettors," Kordas observed. "He was awfully sure Nonesuch would have a bigger litter than that."

Lesley snorted. "As if he could tell!" the Squire scoffed, and as the Empress ambled over to the wall, looking for a scratch, he handed Kordas a stick. Kordas took it, and obliged the Empress and Lesley both by gently scratching her pink rump while Lesley did the more delicate work around her ears.

"Anything to report?" Kordas asked.

"If the weather's aught to go by, and I reckon it is, the Emperor's war in the west is a-heating up," Lesley pronounced with authority. "Wizard weather's going to make it chancy for hay, so I'd advise Hakkon to tell your men to cut early, cure quickly, and get 'er in as fast as they can. If you get a second and third crop that way, all the better. If you don't, you'll still have the early crop. It'll be a good year for pigs and a chancy one for sheep, and keep your horses out of that field down by the canal that likes to flood unless you want to be treating hoof-rot half the summer." He cocked an eye at Kordas. "Anything to report?"

"We've had some success on the Plan."

If there was anyone outside of Hakkon that Kordas trusted without question in this entire Duchy, it was Squire Lesley. The same had been true of their fathers and grandfathers. And the Squire signaled his appreciation of this news with a low whistle.

"Welladay. I can have my second son, daughter-in-law, their brood, and half the herd ready to go with two days' notice," the Squire said. "The others will take some uprooting, but we've been hoping for this as long as you have."

"That bad?" he asked in surprise. Had the Emperor's people been harassing *his* without his knowledge?

"No-oo, not exactly," Lesley assured him, calming his alarm. "Just—I'm Landwise, as was my da, and my da's da, and his before him. I can *feel* it, Kordas. It's like a great big lump of poison sitting out there to the east and south of us. All my life, it's been spreading, getting stronger, and that spreading and strengthening has gotten a good lot worse in the last five years. Eventually, something's going to break, and when it does, I don't want to be here."

"But this has been your home for—as long as it's been my family's," Kordas protested, with a touch of surprise. He had not expected this result. He'd expected he would have to argue with the Squire, apply some pressure, at least, and some persuasion. To hear that Squire Lesley was perfectly willing to load up his pigs onto a barge and flee into the unknown on two days' notice . . . well, it took him aback.

He was not Landwise, which was a very, very old form of earth-magic; it didn't confer any particular sort of power other than the ability to read the health of the land and do some modest predictions about crops and animals. But if Lesley was reading that much awful in the Imperial Capital from this far away? Well, things must have accelerated for the bad quite a bit in the years he'd been gone.

"Right, then. If you need hulls, come get them as soon as you have a chance. I'll leave word you're to have them for free." The Empress wandered away, her needs satisfied for the moment, and lay down so her piglets could suckle.

"That's a generous offer," said the Squire.

"You have a lot of pigs," he pointed out. "It'll cost you a fair bit to convert the hulls to pig-barges."

"True, that," Lesley admitted. He straightened and looked up and over to his fields. "I do believe," he continued, "that my shelters need replacing. Too small."

"Ramps?" asked Kordas.

"Aye. It'll get 'em used to going in and out so they'll be ready on the day." He turned to Kordas and winked. "Always good to think ahead."

"Always," Kordas agreed. "Send one of the lads to me if your Landwise sense tells you anything I need to know."

"That's a promise," said the Squire. "Now, the day's getting on, and none of this is getting our work done. Good to see you, Kordas."

That was a clear dismissal. "Good to see you as always, Squire," Kordas replied, touching two fingers to his hat in farewell.

And with that, Lesley went off on some other errand of his own—possibly to see about getting those extra hulls moved to his fields—and Kordas went on his way.

5

"**W**hat am I supposed to do now, Grim?" Delia asked, once she had edged into Arial's loose-box. The mare looked entirely different from the exhausted, suffering creature she had been last night. She'd gotten a rub-down and grooming since then, and a good sleep, and she was very much aware of everything going on around her precious foal. And with Delia in the box with her, she had gone tense and wary, ready to either flee or attack to protect her baby.

"Take this," the stablemaster said, handing her a brush over the wall of the box. "If you're going to be able to handle that foal daily, you need to get on well with her dam. Hold out the brush so she can see it. Wiggle it a little until she acknowledges you've got it and reacts."

Delia obeyed; Arial focused on the brush, recognized it, and snorted once, then turned her attention to her hay, her entire body relaxing. She knew what a brush meant, and she was looking forward to it.

"Now go brush her neck," said Grim. "Softly and gently.

This isn't meant to be a cleaning, it's meant to be a treat. Right now, Star's taking all her cues from her mama, so the more you make Arial relax, the more relaxed the foal will be."

Delia approached the mare slowly and carefully, as the foal peeked around her dam's buttocks. At the first touch of the brush, Arial sighed and sagged a little, then leaned into the brushstrokes. Arial even stopped eating, the better to appreciate the slow, steady pressure of the brush on her neck. Now exceedingly curious, the foal came around to sniff Delia's elbow—and Arial did not object.

"Now hold out your free hand to Star," ordered Grim. "But keep it close to your body. You want her to come to you, you don't want her to think you're grabbing for her. She hasn't learned anything yet, so everything she does is either going to be what was born into her or what she picks up from Arial. If you move fast, she's going to assume you are something that wants to eat her."

Delia brushed with the right hand, and slightly extended her left. The foal made several false approaches before deciding to come close enough to sniff the hand. Satisfied that Delia wasn't some sort of monster that was going to snatch at her, she moved closer still, coming in to sniff Delia from her ankles to her chest. Delia crooned nonsense at her, and the foal flicked her ears at the unfamiliar sound. Her fingers itched to touch that soft coat and curly mane, but she did as Grim was telling her.

"That's good. Let her get used to the sound of your voice, too. Try putting your hand on her neck. If she lets it stay there, start scratching," Grim said. "Don't stop brushing Arial."

She couldn't have stopped brushing if she'd tried; Arial was now leaning into the brush strokes with pure pleasure, eyes half-lidded, a forgotten strand of hay sticking out of her mouth.

"Easy, baby," Delia said to both of them. "I'm not going to hurt you. I just want to make you feel good."

The foal's ears twitched again. Arial moved her head a little, saw what Delia was up to, considered things for a moment, and closed her eyes completely. Evidently she was of the opinion that someone who was so superior at brushing was safe to have around her precious baby.

Moving with exquisite care, Delia set a hand on Star's neck. The foal's skin shivered under the unexpected pressure, but as Delia started scratching, she settled. Her ears flicked toward Delia again, and she moved a little closer, to get more scratches.

"There you go," Grim said with an air of triumph. "You've got them both now. Keep that up until one of them gets bored."

"Won't that mean I'll be here all day?" Delia objected.

"Foals don't have that long an attention span. Just give her a moment."

Delia scratched until she had covered every bit of the foal she could reach without moving. At about that time, Star *did* get bored, hungry, or both. She pulled away and stuck her head under her mother's flank, seeking milk.

"I can't believe that last night she wasn't even born, and now she's up and trotting around!" Delia said softly. "Puppies and kittens aren't like that."

"That's because she's a prey animal. Prey babies have to be able to run from the time they're a few hours old. Leave her alone a moment, and hand me the brush," Grim told her, and when she had passed it over, continued, "Now rest your hand lightly on Star's back. Maybe scratch a little if she doesn't object."

Star was too busy drinking to object. At Grim's direction, Delia put both hands on the foal's back, with a very little pressure. "We're getting her used to the *idea* of weight on her back, so when the time comes for her to wear a saddle, and then to allow you to ride, it will all seem normal," Grim told her. "This morning is going to set the path for her for the rest of her life."

By lunchtime, Star was allowing Delia to run her hands all

over the foal's body, pick up each hoof, drape her arm over Star's neck and hold her close, and put a couple of grooming cloths on the foal's back, where they rested as Star moved around her mother. Stafngrimr pronounced himself satisfied with the day's progress. "You come back here tomorrow morning, and do the same on your own. You've both learned the early lessons, now you both need to repeat them for a while. You won't need me for a few more days. Now, a couple things I want you to be wary of. *On no account* do you *ever* let her rear at you, not even in greeting, not even in play. You put your hand on the top of her head and her forehead, use gentle pressure to keep her head down, love on her head, and make her stand still if she tries. You don't let her nip at you, not even a nibble. If she goes to mouth you, you put your hand on her nose and pet it until she pulls it away. The best thing you can do to prevent nibbles and bites is to pet her head when she touches you with her nose."

"Not swat her?" Delia asked.

"That's the last thing you want to do. Horses lunge and box in play out in the field. And she's faster than you. You don't want to get her into that habit, because you'll never connect in time to correct her, and it becomes a game, one *she* controls." Grim patted her shoulder. "The big thing she needs to understand is that in this partnership, you're the lead mare."

Delia nodded. "So I do this every morning until about lunch?"

"About that long. After a few more days here in the box with her dam, introducing her to the halter, and getting the halter on her, we'll have you do the same things out in the pasture. Pretty soon she'll connect you with being scratched and petted, and she'll come to you without calling for her, unless she's in a full-out romp with the other foals." Grim laughed. "Don't worry, she'll notice you eventually, and come."

"I love watching them play," Delia said wistfully.

"So do I. But don't go out in the paddock and play with her.

She gets to play with her peers, but she needs to *respect* you. You're not her peer, you're the lead mare of the herd, and you are not something to play with." He scratched his head. "Foals play rough, and the bigger they get, the rougher they play. You don't want an adult horse 'playing' with you on her terms; you'll end up with broken bones. Positive reward from you should come in the form of petting and praising. Later it can come in the form of treats, or being given a toy to play with."

He motioned to her to come out of the loose-box.

"We'll start getting her used to the idea of a halter soon, maybe as early as tomorrow. I'll leave it on the side of the box for her to sniff at today. Tomorrow, you move her around so she's seeing it, pick it up, put it down. Day after that, you hold it for her to sniff, then rub it on her head. Day after that I'll show you how to start putting it on her. When I'm ready to let them out in the pasture in the morning and bring them back in at night, that will be the right time to teach her how to be led."

Delia paused in the door of the stable. "That soon?" she said in surprise.

"It's easiest now, before they get any bad habits, and while they still accept every new thing that comes to them, rather than rejecting it," Grim replied. "I was getting her used to being handled last night, while you and the Duke were already in bed. Here, come with me, and I'll show you just what the results of this kind of early training are."

Curious now, she followed Grim to another set of stables, the ones reserved for the "heavy" horses—the Chargers, the Tow-Beasts, and the new line that Kordas was experimenting with. Grim stood at the fence around the pasture, and whistled a particular three-note call, and two huge horses that could have been Valdemar Golds if not for their size picked up their heads and came trotting for the fence. The other horses in the field ignored the call.

They were utterly magnificent, with flowing manes and

tails that must have taken the grooms hours to comb out, their hides gleaming like liquid sunshine as they slowed to a walk and approached the stablemaster, heads bobbing. They whickered a greeting as they got to him.

"And there's my handsome lads," Grim crooned, as they put their heads *down* so he could scratch their heads under their forelocks. "Delia, hop over the fence, and come up to the forequarters. Doesn't matter which one you pick."

She obeyed him, though she felt more than a little intimidated by a horse that towered over her so much that she had to reach *up* to pat his shoulder.

"Now, just run your right hand down his leg till you get to the knee. Then pat his shin with your hand. He'll pick his foot right up, then he'll wait for you to take it in your hands, and just rest it there, easy and light. He won't even shift his weight until you let go of the foot for him to set it down again."

She did as she was told, and was filled with amazement when the horse did exactly what Grim said he would—with a hoof that was so big it filled both her hands with plenty of room to spare! He didn't let a bit of his weight rest on that leg, either. She could move his foot around to inspect the frog, and she probably could have cleaned it if she'd had a hoofpick. She let the hoof go, and he put his foot down politely, brought his head around to sniff her, and then put his nose in her hands, as Grim had said Star would soon. She rubbed the soft skin around his nostrils and scratched under his chin. He seemed to enjoy that very much.

"That's the benefit of early training," said Grim. "Not a chance in hell we'd be able to control a lad that size without it. Can you imagine trying to shoe that fellow, or trim his hooves, or clean his feet, if he wasn't used to obeying us without question? It'd be impossible. Come on back over."

She hopped the fence again, and he produced a couple of pieces of carrot from somewhere, and gave the two false Golds their treats. "My one regret is these boys are going to be wasted on the Emperor," Grim sighed. "But the good thing is once the stablehands understand what sort of gems they are, they'll be treated right." They put their noses over the fence to be rubbed again. "All right, Delia, off with you. You've put in a good morning's work."

On her way back to the manor, she wondered if other horse breeders took the kind of care and time with their animals that Kordas and his stablemaster did. She didn't think so. Her pony had taken a lot of persuading before he became the cooperative fellow he was now, and even then, there was only a handful of people he'd work with. On the other hand, as Kordas had often said, her pony was a good judge of character.

The main door into the manor was the closest—the most convenient for a Duke who was often in the stables—so that was where she was heading, though she did make sure her shoes were cleaned first. Because she had been raised in a household that had not, at the time, had one of the Imperial "gift" manors, she was struck again by how very odd the manor at Valdemar looked, poking up out of the landscape with nothing to anchor it *to* the landscape it was in. Her father's manor just *fit* into its surroundings, the two-story stone walls echoing the exposed stone of the hills above, and centuries-old trees embracing it. The Valdemar manor *stood out.* No trees embraced its walls, not even bushes. The walls were smooth, and a rather unnatural shade of pale pink, like the inside of the shell she had among her curios. Not unpleasant, just unnatural. The thing wasn't made of any stone that could be found around here, like the walls, stables, and barns, which were built of the native gray granite. There were far too many towers. There were no kinds of defensive walls around it. It looked like—

Like a giant piece of sugar-paste sculpture!

There had been something like that as the centerpiece of

Isla and Kordas's wedding feast, a replica of the Valdemar manor with the banners of both houses hanging from the towers. She had thought it too pretty to eat, but that hadn't stopped anyone else from snapping off pieces to munch. But then again, pure sugar wasn't something that appeared on tables very often around here. Sugar was something used sparingly in baking, so people who got a chance to have a bite of the pure stuff generally took full advantage of the opportunity. That wasn't the case, away in the Capital, at least if the things she'd read were true. The Emperor had a kind of chronicle sent to every noble household in the Empire twice a year that, in addition to informing households of any changes or additions to the laws of the land, detailed all the goings-on of the Capital. She used to read the things avidly, wishing she could be there to see the festivals, taste the amazing things described for the feasts—

Until Kordas had pointed out that the sole purpose of this was to make people like him and his household discontented with what they had, and goad them to attempt the same. All that would be a heavy drain on their income, and *that* would lead to them trying to exploit more out of their properties, all to the detriment of their homes and the people that depended on them.

"The Emperor wants us all in competition against each other," Kordas had told her. It all made a twisted sort of sense. If you were in competition with people who were your equals or slightly better, you'd be too busy to pay much attention to what the Emperor was (or was not) doing. And if you were spending your income on frivolities, you wouldn't be building up your own personal army.

She shook her head to clear it of such uncomfortable thoughts. The Emperor was far away, and paid no attention to places as minor as Valdemar.

An intoxicating scent tickled her nose as she entered the

high-ceilinged, pink-hued entrance hall of the manor, and instead of turning right to go to her own rooms, she went left, heading for the tower occupied by the six mages who called themselves "the Circle." It smelled like—

As she opened the door into the tower, the glorious aroma enveloped her.

Sai was making stuffed bread.

Being mages, the Circle had no difficulty in and no compunction about making minor changes to their tower, and one of those changes had been a big oven next to the hearth, because Sai was a baker, and as good a baker as he was a mage, if not better. His particular specialty was stuffed bread. He insisted on doing everything himself, brandishing a giant knife and threatening to cut pieces off anyone who interfered with his work. So, at unpredictable intervals, he'd order servants to bring him the needful things from the kitchen, and the bottom room of the tower would become a bakery, with the finished loaves lined up on one of the built-in shelves that circled the wall. Those loaves didn't stay there long. Sai didn't care who ate the products of his genius, as long as his genius was acknowledged. Anyone was welcome to take what they wanted. And when Sai baked, anyone who could smell the loaves rushed to taste them.

Right now, there was a circle of five mages with contented looks on their faces, and as many pages waiting impatiently for some of the loaves to cool enough to snatch up and devour. Those would probably be the sweet loaves, stuffed with nut paste, chopped fruit, or other similar fillings. The pages tended to ignore the savory loaves, but she knew the ones filled with cheese on sight, and gravitated toward one.

When it was securely in her possession, she sat down on the floor out of the way and unashamedly began to devour it.

Sai took the last of his loaves out of the oven, put the stopper in the door, and turned toward the circle of urchins. "I suppose you want me to cool those loaves down for you?" he said, sounding cross.

The chorus of shameless begging rose to fill the room, and he made an abrupt gesture to silence it.

Then he made another, as if he was gathering something in from the loaves and tossing it up to the ceiling. "There," he said. "They're *just* cool enough to eat without burning your- selves. Shoo, little piggies!"

The little piggies each snatched up a loaf and raced for the door.

"The cheese bread is brilliant, as always, Master Sai," Delia called around a mouth full of it. "You're a genius!"

"I know," said Sai, preening a little as he took his place on his cushion-chair, and Ceri rolled his eyes. "If I ever need to hide from the Emperor's mage-hunters, look for me in a bak- ery."

Dole, who was seated near her, tilted his head to one side at the bread, suggestively. Since she had eaten all she wanted from the loaf, she passed him the rest. "Why are you baking bread today, anyway?" she asked.

"It helps me think," he said, astounding her by actually answering her question in a sensible fashion. "The more I need to think, the more bread I make. That's not always the case, mind you. Sometimes I make bread because I *very much* need to hit someone, and pounding dough is a good substitute for punching a doughy little face, but mostly I bake because I need to think."

She blinked a little at that statement. "What's going on?" she asked, carefully. "Why do you need to think?"

"We wonder that all the time," Ponu replied, snickering. "And when we need him to think? He becomes a baker. Bread or brains! But it *is* a tasty trade-off, so we have learned to live with it."

Ceri said, "I mostly like his layered breads. What one layer knows, the second layer over on each side can't learn," and his brother Sai nodded sagely.

Sai sucked in his lower lip. "I don't think I can tell you that, Delia," the mage said, finally. "Ask your sister; she'll tell you if she thinks it's safe for you to know."

Safe? What on earth is going on?

"Need to know," Dole said sagely, telling her exactly nothing.

"I'm not a child," she retorted, feeling irritated.

"You are also not in charge of this Duchy," Dole reminded her sternly. "We owe you nothing. You are entitled to nothing from us!" he proclaimed, raising a finger for emphasis.

"Oh, don't be so hard on her," said Ponu. He might have said something more, but at that moment, the whole tower vibrated for a few moments. It wasn't long, and it was barely detectable, but she knew she hadn't imagined it when all of the mages suddenly looked wary. Dole looked at his finger suspiciously, then settled down.

"What *was* that?" Delia demanded.

Ponu frowned as the others gave him a look that suggested they wanted *him* to answer her. "Well," he said finally. "We know what it *isn't*. It's not caused by something in the Duchy. It's not natural, in the sense that nothing natural like a rockslide is causing it. It's been going on for years, actually, but most of the time no one notices it. Lately, it's been getting stronger, and we are fairly sure it comes from the Capital."

"So . . . something the Emperor's mages are doing?" she hazarded.

He nodded. "We haven't investigated it closer, because we don't want anyone knowing we're here." He shrugged. "That's the cost of being in hiding. There is a lot we can't do without revealing ourselves. Or others."

"Is it dangerous?" she demanded.

"It could be. It isn't yet. And we think it's related to

Elemental magic. Probably Earth Elementals. That's the best answer we have right now." Ponu settled back in his seat with the air of someone who was done talking.

"Thank you all for speaking with me," she said, knowing she wasn't going to get anything more out of them for now. "And thank you very much for the bread, Sai."

"Glad you enjoyed it," the mage said with clear satisfaction, as another couple of people came in, attracted by the aroma. She got up, made a little sketch of a bow, and decided to go see if she could get anything out of Isla. It was clear there was something going on, something extremely important, and . . . to be honest, she was a little resentful that she was being kept out of it!

But as soon as she left the Circle's tower, she almost literally ran into Isla, who took her by the elbow and said, "Delia! I'm running out of some wild herbs. Let's go hunt for them."

Now, as far as Delia knew, that was a lie. Isla never ran out of *anything;* she was fanatical about keeping supplies on hand. But Delia took the basket that Isla gave her, and followed her sister out of the manor, between two meadows full of grazing mares and new foals, and down to the woodlot that was deliberately kept wild to allow the propagation of certain herbs that not even Isla could get to grow in the garden.

Once they were under the cover of the forest, Isla grabbed her by the arm and pulled her along a thread of a path with some urgency, until they reached an odd cluster of boulders that formed a tiny cave. Isla gave her a little push, and squeezed into the cave beside her, then made a couple of motions in the air that Delia thought might be magical gestures.

Her guess was confirmed when her sister said, "There. Warded. Now—*you* have been very busy this morning asking questions, and not all about horse training." She folded her legs and sat herself down in the moss and leaf-litter in the cavelet, patting the ground next to her. Gingerly, Delia joined her on the ground.

"Well," she replied, looking into Isla's gray eyes, "Something's going on. How did you know I was asking questions?"

"Because Ceri is a Mindspeaker like me, and he told me," she replied. "And now I have to make up my mind whether to tell you what's happening, or ask you to stop asking questions. Either one creates problems, and I'm trying to decide which course is safest."

"Safest for whom?" Delia retorted, feeling more than a bit impatient with her sister.

"Everyone. Literally almost everyone in this Duchy," Isla replied sternly. "Including you. This isn't some bit of gossip, this is something that puts the lives of everyone who knows about it, and plenty who *don't,* in danger."

"All the more reason to tell me," Delia said, doing her best to sound calm, rational, and above all, trustworthy. "I want to help, and I happen to have a lot of free time. Right now, about the only responsibilities I have are to Star and my pony. I can take on more. A lot more. And I can go places and do things you and Kordas can't, because I'm just the youngest daughter of a Baron with no Barony anymore, who doesn't even have a good dower or astonishing good looks to her credit."

Isla sat silently, looking at Delia as if she was weighing a lot of heavy options.

Although they were sisters, Delia really did not know that much about Isla. After all, they were nearly twelve years apart in age. Isla had been living at Valdemar since the age of thirteen, fostered there—supposedly—to learn the running of a manor from Kordas's mother. She hadn't even come home when their brother, a year older than Isla, had died while at the Capital. Delia had seen her only once between that time and when Kordas came to take her away to Valdemar, and that had been at her wedding to the Duke. They had been playing catch-up since then, but not as much as one might think, since Delia wasn't particularly interested in learning how to run a manor, and had been left more or less to her own devices. Which, to be honest, consisted mostly of shadowing the manor Artificer as much as he would allow, and reading everything in the manor library.

So she had to assume that Isla also didn't know as much about *her* as she would have preferred, given what she'd just said.

Finally her older sister spoke. "All right. You are *never* to talk to anyone about this except for me, Kordas, and Hakkon," she said fiercely. "And *only* when we tell you that we're safely under ward."

"Yes, ma'am," Delia replied meekly. This—fierceness—was a side of Isla she had never seen before.

"Not even the Circle," Isla prompted. "Nor Jonaton, nor any other mage at Valdemar. Not unless they bring it up first."

"Yes, ma'am," Delia repeated. "But—they know this? What you're going to tell me?"

"Yes, they do. But *they* have ways of knowing when it is safe to talk, and ways to make sure it is safe to talk, and you *don't*."

Not for the first time, Delia regretted her lack of mage-talent.

"Yes, ma'am," she said for the third time, and followed it with, "I promise."

"Delia, this is the kind of promise that you'd rather be maimed or exiled for, before giving it up. You need to be certain that you have that kind of strength. There are people in our world who'd treat us all like moths in their web the instant they knew. Are you sure?"

Delia felt Isla's grip on her hands and knew this was nothing near a joke. She shuddered and responded, "I swear."

"All right, then." Isla sighed, leaning back, and her eyes lost focus. "We are escaping Imperial reach. We are taking as many allies and resources as we can with us, and it will probably be within the year."

"What?" Delia stared at her sister. "But—where—how—why—"

"This was Kordas's father's plan," Isla interrupted her. "He became convinced that no matter how small and insignificant we try to make ourselves look here, eventually the Emperor would give the Duchy to one of his favored underlings, or strip it bare of everything worth having. Valdemar isn't essential to the Empire, but the Empire consumes all it can reach. Valdemar has hidden away as unimportant, but land is land, and if we aren't stripped bare by the Empire, we'll just be given away to someone the Emperor favors the moment he runs out of plums to pass out. This was begun, as a concept, before Kordas was even born."

"But you'd have to go—" She was reasonably familiar with the maps of the known world, and the Empire was *huge*. She shook her head. "—you'd have to go *far* outside the borders of the Empire! And how would you cross all the land between us and there? I mean—" She tried to wrap her head around the idea of packing up thousands of people and all their worldly goods—and travel how? By wagon? That would take an impossible number of horses, mules, and oxen. And who would let such a caravan cross his lands? Could they go by canal? That was more feasible; after all, a Tow-Beast could haul as many as ten barges depending on what they were loaded with. But again, who would let such a caravan cross his lands? And then, once they got past the last of the canals, what would they do? They'd have to find a river or—

"We. You are part of this now. And as for how, by Gate," said Isla. "Or, to be more specific, by barge and by water-Gate."

"But that's—"

"Hard, but not impossible. We needed to assemble trustworthy mages to build and lock Gates, then work out how to assemble a receiving-Gate far away. In the unknown. Last night, one of them not only worked out how to do it in theory, he worked out a link to an actual place." Isla waited for that to sink in.

Delia's mouth sagged slightly open with shock. Did this

have anything to do with the earth trembling this morning? No, Ponu had said that it was something to do with the Capital, and she didn't think he'd lie about that, and she was certain he was correct about his guess. But—

"But this is incredibly *dangerous*," she protested. "Aside from if the Emperor finds out about it, it's dangerous to do magic that requires that much power, and—where would we go, anyway?" All the choices seemed fraught. East past the Capital was nothing but ocean. North was cold and inhospitable and full of enemies of the Empire. South was worse; there was an active war going on down there right now. And West— every league that the Empire had moved westward had involved moving into lands where magic was unpredictable, into wilderness where there were monsters and other hazards—

"I told you. *Very* far west," Isla said. "West, so far as we can tell, is mostly land that has gone wild. I know you've been in the library almost every day since you arrived here. You've read about that, surely?"

She nodded numbly. "But—"

"As hungry as the Empire is, if that place is wild, that means it's too costly for the Empire to expand into. The way things are going, Kordas sees it—and, word has it, the Foreseers, who have ever more distressing visions—it's either be preyed upon by monsters there, or by the Emperor here," her sister said, with a clenched jaw. "I'll take the monsters. At least they'd be honest about destroying us."

"But—" Delia began, then paused. "You say that Foreseers are making predictions? How would you know that? How would Kordas know what visions Foreseers have?"

Isla answered, "That, neither the Circle, nor Kordas, nor Hakkon will tell me. The most I know is that Kordas said something about salvage."

Delia snapped her fingers. "*'What one layer knows, the second layer over on each side can't learn,'* Ceri said earlier. The

Circle seem like they've always been here, so they must be the mages that Kordas's father wanted to gather. Now, they *are* Valdemaran, and nobody questions them being at the manor because—because they've *always* been there, to everyone alive now. And what each of us knows isn't the same as what every 'layer' knows. None of us know the whole plan. *Need to know,* Dole said."

"There are three things to do when someone is too close to keep a secret safely hidden. You can tell them nothing, which makes the person resentful or even more curious, and they dig where they shouldn't. Another way is to tell them everything, which gives them too much knowledge of the whole, which makes it harder for them to maintain the self-control of keeping it all secret. The third option is what we've all agreed upon: tell enough that the person knows when to stop asking for details," Isla confirmed. "Staying away from Court means more than just staying at an inconvenient distance for being stabbed. It means that none of the powerful players in Court recognize Valdemar's ways as anything but plodding, weird, and harmless. And, since none of them could trust each other enough for a long-term, many-pieced plan to work, they don't even think to look for one." She jerked a thumb toward the manor. "Enough so that the Imperial spies think of Valdemar almost as a punishment assignment. Nothing apparently happens here. The highest-ranked spy in all of Valdemar is widely *known* as the highest-ranked spy in all of Valdemar, and he's practically retired."

"Right. A *good* spy wouldn't have even been suspected, but someone has to care about their work to do it well. So he found a place to stay drowsy, and keep his rank without the work."

Isla's eyes shone with her smile. "All that brilliance and a new foal, too. I'm so relieved that you're in on it now. Now that you know the general direction and the pace of things, we can include you more when the times come. But first, we need to establish one particular Gate. Kordas plans to ask you to help do that."

Being stunned by something her sister said was getting to be the norm today. It took her more than a moment or two to gather her thoughts. "But I'm not a mage!" she protested.

"But you have a powerful and precise Fetching Gift," said Isla. "Jonaton intends to establish a small Portal. It may not be safe enough to reach through with tongs, even, so Kordas wants you to Fetch something small, like a stone or a bit of earth, to serve as the anchor on this side. Then he wants you to send something from here to there to establish the anchor on the other side. When that's done, an actual Gate can be built. Just a tiny one. Small, shieldable."

Delia knew for a fact that Kordas had been out all day, so the only way that Isla could know this was by Mindspeaking with him. *I guess that's actually the safest way for them to discuss this,* she thought numbly. *But—*

"I don't know if I can do that," she admitted, licking her lips nervously. "I've never Fetched anything further away than a few leagues."

"But you don't know that you can't," her sister pointed out. "We are *all* going to have to do things we are not certain we can. You won't be the only one. But there is one thing I do know for certain. If we don't try, all that is going to happen is that we are going to sit here in this Duchy, doing needlework and raising farm stock, waiting for the Emperor, or someone, to move on us. I've lived like that all my life, and I can't do that anymore. More to the point, I'm *not* going to have that for my boys." She lifted her head, and her eyes flashed with determination. "I would rather they wore skins and ate half-raw meat around a fire than sit here tamely, like a lot of Squire Lesley's pigs, waiting to be surprised by the butcher!"

Slowly, Delia nodded, setting her mind to accept her exciting new *'need to know.'* "All right, then," she said. "You can tell Kordas that I'm here to help."

Isla just smiled, as if she could not have imagined Delia saying anything else. "Then let's gather some herbs to make good on our deception, and get back. We'll talk more about this tonight."

Just in case Imperial magicians had been looking for unusual bursts of power in unexpected places within the Empire, Kordas instructed Jonaton to gather his strength and whatever resources he needed, and put off the next stage in the Gate-making magics for a few days. Jonaton protested, but admitted he did have fabrication to work on that wasn't too physically demanding "for now." For Jonaton, whose dedication to magic as both art and science could manically consume him, that was a very good compromise.

During those days, Kordas went on his usual rambles, maintaining the outward appearance of the doting Duke of a drowsy Duchy.

Fortunately I'm mind-shielded enough out here that my deeper thoughts can't be read by friend or foe, Kordas mused as his horse clopped along in no particular hurry. *I don't come across as a second-generation insurrectionist espionage-embezzling thief at all.*

Kordas had been through the "proper education" for a child

of royalty, in the military compound—school, rather—that indoctrinated all noble children. Unlike most who entered there, and far fewer who left there, Kordas knew what he was made of. He didn't embrace deceit nearly as much as he knew how to steer conversations so there was no definitive answer given. That skill came to him early at the school, where inevitably— possibly in preparation for their later intrigues as adults— bullies ganged up, split, or formed factions to overwhelm the lesser children. Kordas rode the edge between submission and distraction, honing the ways of deflection and adaptation by the moment. His cleverness did not really come into its own until strategy games entered the curriculum.

There were three, and only three, games taught at that school. All were board games, with no variant rules. One, Faire Trade, was an economic resource-management game with very strict rules about how goods were presented, tracked, bartered for, and taxes deducted. The second was simply called Imperial Power, and while its board was not a representation of the actual Empire, Kordas immediately noticed that the game's terrain replicated key parts of the actual Empire's geography, cleverly rearranged. Imperial Power was an outright war game, and its players were to swap resources, build supply lines, make assaults into weaker territory, or lure opponents into unwinnable overextension. The third game, Winding Web, was utterly abstract, using colored marbles and alteration cards to surround and flip the colors of other players' marbles and pile them in the center of the spiral, until the winner's tray was emptied. Its players were encouraged to be as hurtful, intimidating, and double-dealing as they could manage, swapping cards and sabotaging others' plays, strictly by the rules.

Kordas realized that these were not solely the games they were presented as, as much as they were personality tests. Senior students, who had played the games for a considerable time, wound up divided into different educational tracks, and matched against tougher and tougher opponents. Kordas connected the types of bullying and maneuvering his early classmates engaged in as corresponding to the three games. He deduced that the three games trained specific rigors of thought; that meant that if Kordas knew what game the students were best at, he could predict their behavior as people.

He resolved to come across as good at none of the three games, and instead spend his time watching the players. He had embraced the Fourth Game, and nobody was the wiser.

If I appear weak enough, I can lead aggressors wherever I want them to be. If I am assertive but strange, others will have pause. If I seem stable but harmless, I am put in the "safe" category, and barely thought of again. If I seem motionless, I am only the background that action-seekers exert themselves in front of, and will be ignored. And, if I bore everyone, I become invisible.

The future Duke of Valdemar left the Imperial school with a deeper awareness of how Imperial Doctrine slithered and struck on the board of the Empire than many of the Empire's senior nobles had after years in office.

Nobody in the high ranks sees anyone as a person—instead, as they have been taught, they are game pieces to be moved around, traded, and expended against each other. Martial, economic, and psychological domination are their only three games. I learned the three games as well as the school's brightest—but I only ever played as below average for them.

The Fourth Game is the show.

His horse knew the way, so he simply closed his eyes for a while. He took in the scents—elderflower, purpleroot pine, the buttery undertone of sweet-hay, the sour-sweet tang of lemontail—as the wind picked up. He leaned back in his saddle, letting the reins rest upon the saddlehorn, and let his arms hang away from his torso until he felt the first light droplets of rain.

I will miss this place. I have so many big speeches planned about how we the people are Valdemar, but just the same— this place. These flavors, these scents, the sound of these birds, and the wind in these trees. I will miss this so very much.

Kordas let the light, warm rain wash his face, which was just as well. With those thoughts, the Duke of Valdemar's face would have been wet anyway.

His ramblings "just happened" to coincide with visits to the people in his Duchy he trusted most. These were the Duchy's eight Counts and their worthiest subordinates, people who had already been brought into confidence by his father, so the only actual secret they learned was that the Plan's candles were lit, and it was a vital step closer to fruition. Each of them had entrusted children or other relatives, as well as trained experts, with their own specialized duties in the Plan's execution. They would be sent across as soon as the Foothold Gate was built, to scout for dangers—and hopefully eliminate them—and prepare the settlement base for what was to come.

One of them, Count Endicrag of Endicrag Manor, had two things they were going to need desperately. One was a cousin, a Healer named Alberdina, who was willing to go in the first wave. The other was of even more immediate help. Lord Endicrag's sixth out of ten sons was everything Kordas could have wanted for his explorer-through-the-Gate: tough, strong, smart, and with a seriously itchy foot, just a little older than Kordas, an able fighter, and a trained woodsman. He was actually back from a foray into the mysterious North. Not *for* anyone; he'd gone on his own, to see what was there. When Kordas explained the situation to him, the man immediately wanted to be the first person to go through the Foothold Gate, explore, and find a suitable place for a water-Gate.

"I've longed my entire life for a chance like this," said Ivar

Endicrag, actually rubbing his hands together with glee. "I've *dreamed* of it, actually. I've made lists of what to stock for each foray I make. I want one of your Chargers, a trained one that can handle rough terrain. A Charger is a force-multiplier, turning me into a squad of people without actually having to have a squad of *people,* and if my understanding is correct, they 'stand watch' at night?"

"More or less. A horse's senses are keener than a human's, and Chargers rarely sleep deeply," Kordas replied slowly. "If I were you, I'd take—"

"A dog, too? I have one. Got him before that last trip. He's a good boy." Ivar chuckled. "When can I start training with the horse?"

"Now," Kordas told him, hardly able to believe his luck; he didn't expect Ivar to be so prepared. "In fact, pack your things, come back with me, and move into the manor. It's not as if we don't have room! And since you and your dog will be training with one of my Chargers, it won't seem out of place."

Ivar didn't wait for a second invitation; he sprinted out of the room like it was on fire.

His father sighed. "Truth to tell, I'm glad you're taking him off my hands," the graying patriarch said. "He's not very restful to have around. I'm not looking forward to packing up and haring off into the wilderness, Valdemar, but given some of the rumors I'm hearing out of the Capital, I'm not eager to stick around here, either."

"Barges will make that journey less uncomfortable," Kordas pointed out.

"And more practical," his Lordship nodded.

Kordas made small talk about Endicrag's family until Ivar appeared, carrying a huge rucksack and a second bag, loaded with weapons, and accompanied by an intelligent-looking mastiff. "I've ordered my riding horse prepared," Ivar said, before Kordas could ask. "I'm ready. Whenever you and Father are done."

Lord Endicrag shook his head. "And this is why you are the despair of your mother," he said, sounding more amused than anything else. "You haven't been back a fortnight!"

Ivar shrugged. "And look how useful I am now!" he countered. "I'm perfect for what's ahead of us!"

"You can't argue with that," Kordas pointed out.

Endicrag sighed. "No," he admitted. "I can't. Off you go with the Duke, lad," he added. "If you get eaten by something, at least make sure it's memorable." His Lordship had made a joke out of it, but Kordas could tell this was causing him anxiety. Ivar could tell, too.

"Father, I'm far from your only child. I can do this—you and I both know that to be true. Wherever I go, you, all my family, and all of Valdemar is carried with me. That's what gives spring to my stride through the deepest snow or stinging gales. I can be my best because you raised me."

Kordas waited by the exit while Endicrag and Ivar tearfully embraced and murmured to each other.

Not enough of us get to tell those who had a hand in building us just how we feel about our pasts, while they're still alive. It wounds the heart, but makes us more whole whenever we can, though. This physical world isn't all there is, but while we have it, this is the one that counts. The words should be spoken.

"I hate to worry him like this," Ivar confessed, as he and Kordas headed to the stables. "But . . . this is who I am."

Kordas waited to say anything until they got to the stables and he could watch Ivar with a critical eye. And he liked what he saw. Ivar's black mastiff stayed right at his master's heel, with his long tail waving gently from side to side and his head up, ears alert, attention fixed on his master. This was a well-trained dog, with love for his master. Ivar's horse welcomed him with a whicker and a nuzzle, and Ivar checked bridle, saddle, and girth for his horse's comfort before mounting.

As for Ivar himself, he looked to be in his element:

brown-haired, brown-eyed, with brown skin that showed he spent every moment he could outdoors. He had the mix of environmental awareness, sureness, and calluses that proved he had gotten those muscles through actual work, and not "vanity exercise" like lesser nobles—idle dilettantes—pursued. Hacking at stuffed targets didn't give Ivar his build—hacking through wilderness did.

I think Delia is going to get on with him, came the unexpected thought, not an unwelcome one. Kordas was very well aware, and had been for quite some time, that his young sister-in-law was infatuated with him, and that was absolutely not something he wanted to encourage. But perhaps her attention could be redirected to Ivar . . .

Not overtly, though. That's the surest way to get her angry with me. But maybe Isla could do something in that direction.

"So, I've already figured out which Charger I'm going to put you with," Kordas said aloud, as they headed back to the Valdemar manor. "She's a four-year-old mare, she's a bit smaller than the average, and she's already got a bit of a reputation in the stable for being protective. That means you're going to have to do a fair bit of work to get her to accept your dog."

"What do you mean by 'a reputation for being protective'?" Ivar asked.

"Some loose dogs got into the pasture. Apparently, she stomped them flat, I presume because they were trying to chase the other horses." Kordas cast a glance at Ivar, but he seemed impressed, rather than alarmed. "I don't know if they were feral. I just know they weren't any of the manor dogs."

"Has she ever gone after any of the manor dogs?" Ivar asked—a good question, in Kordas's mind.

"No, but she knows them," he pointed out. "And they don't go into the pastures unless they're with a handler."

"Bay will be fine," Ivar assured him. "He's always on his best manners around horses. And I'll make sure to introduce them properly. Oh, I have a question. Who is it safe to talk to, about you know what?"

"Assume no one, unless they bring it up with specifics *and* first let you know they're warded," Kordas cautioned. "Outside of the mages, most of my household doesn't know." He had a question of his own, though. "Why is it you're so eager to take this on, anyway?"

"I don't much care for Imperial civilization, or civilized places," Ivar said frankly. "The last job I took put me up north, for the Empire. Luckily, there wasn't anything up there the Emperor wanted—or at least, nothing he wants badly enough to open a second war front, while he's still enmired up to his ass in the first one. The whole expedition was a slow push to find anyone and anything to exploit. Just—no sense of adventure from anyone but me, only a strict military operation with an eye for plunder. Timber and fish don't interest him, thank the gods. I don't want to do any more of those official forays; I'd rather rot of boredom. Your Plan? That suits me."

They continued to talk all the way back to the manor, with Kordas becoming more and more comfortable with the younger man with every exchange. He watched how Ivar managed his horse: neck-rein and knee, mostly, which meant a skilled and considerate rider, and a confident and secure horse. The mastiff stayed about two lengths from the horse and even with the girth; the perfect distance to react to anything.

When they arrived at the manor, Kordas left Ivar, his dog, and his rucksack and bag with the chief steward, and took his horse and Ivar's to the stable. As ever, Grim somehow materialized within moments of his crossing the threshold to the main stables.

"We have our scout, Grim," he said. Grim nodded, since Kordas had kept him appraised of everything from the moment he had taken the reins of the Duchy. "Ivar Endicrag. This is his current horse, and I'm giving him Manta, so have her moved to a stall here tonight, please. He has a mastiff, so this is going to be interesting."

Grim took the reins of Ivar's horse, looked the beast over, checked the conformation and all four feet, and nodded approval. "Dog will not come amiss, if Manta will abide it."

"If she won't, Ivar's not the man for this job, and I think he is," Kordas replied, and left both horses in Grim's care while he went back to the manor to wash up before dinner.

The chief steward met him at the door. "The young man is in your tower, ground floor guest room, m'lord."

"Perfect, I can take him in to supper with me. Well done, Tomen." He headed for the tower at a fast walk, and found Ivar already "settled," insofar as such a footloose fellow could be, and once they were both respectable, led him to the Great Hall.

The steward had already arranged a new seat at the High Table, and as they entered the Hall Kordas saw that the entire family was watching the entrance to see who the guest was.

Supper was generally the lightest meal of the day, as breakfast was the most substantial. This, of course, was *not* how the Imperial Court did things; it wasn't called "supper," to begin with (that was far too countrified and peasant-like), and the evening meal was a huge multi-course affair that lasted hours, after which there would be music and entertainment into the late evening. This was a much simpler meal, and Ivar looked relieved to see that it was. It probably matched what Lord Endicrag served.

As he made introductions, Kordas looked directly into Isla's eyes, and thought, *Have you told Delia everything?* knowing that she'd take the direct look as an invitation to read his thoughts. At her nod, he finished his introduction with, " . . . and Ivar is a scout. His father thinks he can be useful to us, or at least, entertaining."

"You might say I'm afflicted with wanderlust," the young man laughed as he took his place at table. And for the rest of the meal he kept them well entertained with stories of his explorations—stories that turned the skeptical look on Hakkon's face into one of satisfaction. Ivar managed to convey his competence without sounding like a common braggart, and his wonderment at the marvels of nature was infectious.

Well, Kordas thought, taking note that not only Hakkon, but Isla and Delia, clearly approved of his choice. *That's one hurdle taken care of.*

Now there are only a million more to go.

———————

Delia had to admit she was impressed with the new man. He was able to tell a good tale without boasting, he was deferential without being servile, and from what she could tell from his stories, he seemed to be the ideal choice for the job. Hakkon could have done it, of course—but Hakkon was going to have his hands full for the duration. *She* could be spared, and she wouldn't have objected—but she didn't have nearly the qualifications this fellow did. *I'm going to take this as a good omen for our prospects,* she thought, as she headed to the stable to work with Star.

But the new man, Ivar, was already there ahead of her. At his side was a massive mastiff—one that had *not* had his tail docked nor his ears clipped as was fashionable, which was mutilation as far as she was concerned. He went up another point in her estimation.

Grim was already speaking with him as she came in. The dog lay at his master's feet, looking from one face to the other, as if following the conversation with interest.

" . . . and how did you want to go about introducing the dog, milord?" Grim was saying.

"Well, that's not for *me* to say, Stablemaster," Ivar replied, rubbing the back of his neck with one hand. "How do you think Manta will take him? And what course of action would you suggest?"

"I'd say, let's put her in the round training ring on a lunge line, just in case. Have the dog wait outside the ring while I introduce you to the horse, then if you can get him to approach her calm and sociable like, we'll see."

"The last won't be a problem," Ivar told him confidently. "I'm eager to see Manta, and that's a fact. I've heard a lot about Valdemar Chargers, but I certainly never expected to be given the use of one."

"You're being given more than *the use* of her, milord," Grim said, motioning to Ivar to come along to the back of the stable. "The Duke was very specific that she's to *be* yours, if you get on."

Delia thought that Ivar looked a bit shocked as well as elated. But then again, she knew the market price of Valdemar Chargers. There were city houses that were cheaper. In fact, there were entire farms that were cheaper.

She decided that Star could wait a little, and followed them as Grim got Manta from her stall at the back of the stable and led her to the training ring, with Ivar and his dog following at a respectful distance. It was clear from the looks that Manta was casting over her shoulder that she was well aware of the presence of the dog, and not entirely happy about it.

Grim put her on a lunge line and motioned to Ivar to come into the ring. Ivar did not march immediately up to the two. Instead, he stood about a length away and spoke to Manta until she flicked her ears forward and lifted her head, looking at him with interest instead of wariness. Then he approached her slowly, with his right hand in a fist; he offered it to her to sniff, then touched her muzzle with it, all the while talking to her. As soon as he had her full attention, he immediately turned to the side. Delia knew what that was—the invitation to the horse to follow.

Manta was clearly very pleased with this mannerly approach, and followed him. He touched her muzzle again with his fist, continuing to talk to her. Grim let out the lunge line as he turned again, and she continued to follow him. Finally he touched her for the third time on the muzzle, and stopped, opening his hand and moving it up slowly to her neck. She arched her neck in an invitation to him to stroke her. This he did for a good long time, before patting her on the neck, touching her muzzle, and looking where his dog lay patiently just outside the fence of the yard.

"Bay, come under," he said in a quiet voice, and to Delia's astonishment, the dog *crawled* beneath the bottom fence-board rather than leaping over it.

Manta snorted. She didn't *like* this . . . but she did like the new human, and the human had clearly summoned The Beast. So she was wary, but not quite ready to attack it.

Ivar had his dog approach slowly, a few steps at a time. If Manta showed signs of aggression or nerves, he would tell the dog "back," and Bay would back up a few steps until told to stop again. Finally they were within a length of each other; Ivar gathered the reins just under the mare's chin and touched Manta's muzzle again. "Manta," he said, and her ears flicked toward him at the sound of her name. "Bay is my friend. If we are going to be friends too, you need to accept him. Come up."

Now he walked her one slow step at a time to his dog. Bay sat as still as a statue, no whining, no twitching. Now Ivar touched his fist to Bay's nose, then to Manta's muzzle. He continued to do this, over and over, until finally Manta reached out with her nose, warily, and sniffed the dog.

Now Ivar praised and made much of her, and took her for a little walk in a circle. Then he brought her back to the dog, and began the process all over again.

By the time the candlemark was over, he was on Manta's bare back, with the dog trotting a length away, even with his right heel, and Manta was perfectly happy with the situation.

Grim was clearly gobsmacked. So was Delia.

"Well. I never," Grim said, as Ivar swung his leg over Manta's shoulder, and dropped to the ground. "That does beat all!"

Ivar blushed, pleased. "I suppose I've got a bit of a knack with animals," he replied. "I like them better than most people. Present company excepted."

Grim cast a look at Delia that she interpreted as a reminder that she was supposed to be working with her foal, and she scooted back to the stables that held the mares and youngest foals. Ivar was certainly an interesting fellow, and in many ways.

But right now, the important thing was that he was one more piece of the Plan, and a vital one at that.

Kordas was doing his level best to keep his impatience in check, but it was dreadfully hard. He exorcised it as best he could by riding out every single day to the farms and manors of those he trusted absolutely, whose sons and daughters would form the vanguard of the planned migration. This was not a message he wanted entrusted to the written word.

His working plan called for the supplies going out first, accompanied by his first recruits. These were all going to be people no younger than fourteen, and no older than thirty; ideally single and ideally around twenty. They were going to be a mix of farmers and people with at least some experience with weapons. Some of them were coming straight off the Valdemar Ducal farms, because most, if not all, of the Chargers, the Tow-Beasts, and the Heavies were going to be needed to haul all the barges. Kordas intended to drain the Duchy of its resources before his household and the heads of all the other households took the final trip through the Gate.

This was going to be aided by the fact that the Emperor's birthday would be in a couple of moons, and the Emperor celebrated his birthday with a Regatta, a boat procession from one side of Wolf Bay to the other. The various components of the Empire were all expected to supply decorated boats and barges. The largest and most splendid of these went on display inside and outside the Bay at anchor, and of course included the warships that were part of the Bay's defenses. The rest paraded through pairs of Gates on either side of the Bay in a solid formation of craft so dense you could walk from shore to shore without getting your feet wet.

It was ingenious, really. The Gates set their destination by talismans carried by whoever was crossing. So participants decorated their barges, put their talismans for the Bay and back on the prows of their crafts, and lined up for the nearest Gate on the nearest canal (or rarely, river or lake). They'd go through and find themselves staged up in line, each craft given a shove by pole-men on the other side. Each craft would be connected by rings mounted on the front and back, and the continuous shoving in of boats behind would carry the entire line across the Bay to the exit Gate, where hook-men would flip each craft free and pull it through, and participants found themselves back where they started. There were prizes for decoration, though never in anyone's memory had a craft from Valdemar won such a thing.

For the participants—for the most part—it was the most tedious day of the year. You lined up your barge with all the other locals, often before dawn. You waited your turn as the line crawled slowly toward the Gate. When you finally got to the Gate you were generally hot and tired, and when you went through, you had to put on a show of sorts for the entire time you were crossing the Bay—if nothing else, you had to sing along or pretend to dance with the music from the larger ships. It took at least a candlemark to cross the Bay, and the entire time, your senses were bombarded with music, you were crowded so deeply among the other boats that unless you were lucky enough to be on the outermost layer, all you saw of the procession was your neighbors, and the never-ending colored smokes would leave your eyes red and watering. The only good thing was that it was guaranteed not to rain.

Kordas always participated. His barges always had the same big figures of horses as his great-grandfather's, stowed in the manor from year to year, brought out, touched up, and decorated with flowers and ribbons. He and his people always returned from the Regatta with watering eyes and headaches, and only the fact that he made sure each barge had enough food and good beer to see them all through the day kept tempers in check. And with all of that, he couldn't ever recall having seen anything of the rest of the parade, nor having been offered as much as a celebratory candy.

Every so often he'd have an "emergency" that kept him home, usually an illness, and hire boatmen to take his place. His father had done the same, and his grandfather. Everyone did, at least among those who weren't vying for prizes. So that was what he planned to do this year. So his barges would go out, be seen, and come home—and mingled with them would be the last of the escapees. *They* would have entirely different talismans on their prows—talismans that would send them to a Gate that "pulled" rather than pushed, talismans that had no return marked on them.

It wasn't foolproof, but it was as good as three generations of Dukes had been able to conjure.

And it had the advantage that even if someone found out some of the barges were not going where they should have gone, it would be difficult, if not impossible, to untangle the mystery until it was far too late. With so many craft going through the Gates, the Gate "memory" would have been over-written a hundred times by the time mages came to "read" it.

And if worst came to worst, it would be entirely possible to snatch the talisman from the prow and run for the Gate to escape. During the Regatta, there were no Keepers stationed at each Gate to control the flow of traffic. You might lose whatever you had in the barge with you, but that would be a small price to pay.

Well, that and you'd be swimming when you got to the other side.

Three days after young Ivar had been installed at the manor, Jonaton turned up at breakfast with Hakkon.

If strict protocol had held at Valdemar, Jonaton would have been seated somewhere down among the servants. Very few people were aware he was a mage; those who were aware thought he was a "Magus Minor," someone far too limited in power to be of interest to the Emperor, and just a small, civilized step above a hedge wizard. He *could* have been seated at the Head Table if his relationship with Hakkon were known— and sanctioned by the Empire. But that would have created dangers for both of them. It was thought best by everyone not to give the Emperor anything he could use to leverage someone who could legitimately take Kordas's place.

But strict protocol was scarcely ever applied here, and Jonaton was perfectly welcome at the High Table, where he performed little bits of entertaining sleight of hand on the occasions when there were visitors. Mostly, though, Jonaton talked about geometry, Imaging, herbs and cures, and his cats. Anyone's cats, really. Often, he brought Imager pictures of various cats, and added funny captions to them. They always raised laughs as they were passed table to table.

This morning, however, he was not here because of a visitor. Through a lifted brow and a couple of coded words, he made it very clear that he was ready to begin the first steps of creating *the* Gate, and that he expected anyone interested to turn up at mid-afternoon ready to work.

Then, he ate all the honey-melon, took a double-handful of crisp bacon rashers, and left.

Typical, Kordas thought, suppressing a laugh.

Mid-afternoon was the perfect time to initiate such a complicated and dangerous bit of magic. It wasn't so easy to clear off tasks that had already been scheduled for morning, but at mid-afternoon even Kordas could be expected to take a break for a moment or two to himself. Mid-afternoon was the time when the highest amount of traffic would be passing through existing Gates, mid-afternoon was when most mages were deeply involved in projects of their own or the Emperor's, and would not necessarily notice something going on elsewhere, and mid-afternoon was when the Emperor himself was most likely deeply engrossed in the business of the Empire. Night— now, *night* would have been a terrible choice. Not to mention that if Delia was going to Fetch something from the other side of the Portal Jonaton would create, she needed to be able to see what was on the other side.

So, just after lunch, one by one, all the interested parties made their way to what had once been the walls of the previous manor, and were now a series of artificial "ruins" in a garden.

Accessed by three hidden doors were two staircases and a ramp down into what had been the cellars of the previous manor, which were connected to the current manor via a fourth passage that ran beneath the Circle's tower.

As Hakkon stood watch, Kordas went to a part of the ruins he was known for using as a place to read or even snatch a clandestine nap—a cool little grotto with a smooth stone bench that curved to fit his back admirably, and just happened to have a stone that lifted up to reveal the stair down. He disposed himself on the bench until Hakkon gave a soft whistle, signaling that there was no one watching, and slipped down the stair, dropping the stone in place behind himself.

By the time he got to the cellars, Delia, Isla, the entire Circle, and Jonaton were already there, waiting impatiently, among all sorts of small cats.

By design there was absolutely nothing down here that could have been connected with a magical workspace—not until and unless someone who had been keyed to the place entered it. *Then* the walls, floors, and ceiling glowed with diagrams, runes, and wards, until you almost didn't need magelights to see by.

Each of the seven cellars served a different purpose. The one Kordas entered now was marked "Seeds—Hard Grain—Preserved Nuts"—the least interesting stores a prowler would want a look into, but a logical place to find mousers hanging about. It had been designated from the beginning for the use of whatever mage or mages were going to make that all-important first small Gate into the unknown.

"Well, you took your time," Isla chided. "I thought Jonaton was going to split himself in two, he's been vibrating so hard."

Kordas just shrugged. "I'm here now," he pointed out, as one of the many, many manor cats twined itself around his ankles and threatened to trip him. "And I see the Preserved Nuts are here." One of the Circle made a very rude gesture in response. Kordas began unbuttoning his Ducal jacket, starting at the top and ending just past his baldric, then tugged the jacket open, to be more comfortable. As usual, Kordas had a dark gray undershirt beneath the jacket, dyed and embroidered with violent stormclouds. "All right, then, what do you need me for, besides as a source of power?"

"What else are you good for?" jibed Ponu.

"It's not his jokes, that's for sure," Dole groused, then snapped his fingers. "Go." He pointed to an empty circle on one curve of an immensely complicated diagram on the floor. "Go stand there. Let the adults work."

"Yes, sir," Kordas said meekly, and took his place, "rooting" himself into the diagram and gathering up all of his magical reserves, ready to pour it into the work at hand. He exhaled and gazed down at the floor patterns. Some of the curves were clearly rebounds from where other lines clashed, and they looped gracefully to rods or glowing crystals firmly set into sockets. Brass and copper calibrators were tapped into

their own sockets, marking the optimal timing for this particular spellwork.

Kordas looked up and gazed in admiration at Jonaton, who
was truly in his element. Jonaton had his hair up, with three
copper hairsticks holding the loops. Copper earrings and neck-
laces added to the look, which was paired with a black upper,
corselet, and deep brown, leaf-patterned, widelegged skirt-
trews. "You look great, Jonaton," Kordas said.

"Oh thank you!" Jonaton replied, whipping around to have
a look at Kordas. "It's good to see you a little more casual for
once. But still stormy under it all, huh?"

Kordas tapped at the undershirt. "I am what I am," was all
he said, acknowledging the subtext. Jonaton flashed a brief
smile followed by a brief downcast, and turned back to his
table.

Mages of the Empire were a highly predictable lot, as he
knew from experience. They all studied the same lore, the
same spells, and from the same teachers. Once they had
reached a certain level of competence, they almost *never*
learned anything new again. They certainly didn't experiment. The Emperor didn't much care for innovations in magic.
A mage willing to innovate and seek out new ways of doing
magic just might become dangerous to the Emperor's plans,
which was one reason Kordas had so many mages just like
that hiding here.

Jonaton had stressed earlier that there was *always* a level of
uncertainty and "fuckery" in trying anything new. He turned
around and clapped his hands once. "No time like now, everyone. Magic like this is about reaching into unseen worlds where
things already live, pulling and twisting at the environment
around them, uprooting it and turning it toward what we want.
Sometimes, even investigating what's out there, well, it's like
picking a grape from a big fruit bowl, and a lot of deadly spiders
can hide in a heap of fruit. Now, the kind of distance we're

trying for today is like me punching my whole arm into a narrow tunnel lined with spiders. I think we have it all set, but I'll throw away the shot if I get 'bitten' even once, understood? So catch me if it goes badly." Jonaton thoroughly washed his hands, in a very ritualistic way, in both of the basins at the table's sides. The basins looked to be hammered copper, and were joined to each other by a graceful arc of the same material.

So Kordas really had no idea what to expect when Jonaton began work.

He *certainly* didn't expect that the work was going to be so . . . simple.

He *had* expected muttered incantations, the drawing of diagrams, the sketching of runes in the air, and perhaps even the spilling of oils or scattering of essences.

He got none of those.

Instead, Jonaton set up a pair of matching, curved stones, like a pair of graceful, curving horns, atop his stone table. He placed a sliver of wood between them—the wood from that table he'd described?—and held out both hands toward the arrangement.

Kordas had to brace himself against the sudden draining sensation that coursed through him in that moment. The diagram of which he was a part pulsed with light, all of it flowing toward Jonaton. Two cats chased after the lights, eyes bright and tails twitching. There was a sudden sharp scent, all the hair on the back of his neck stood up, and then a flash of light and a *snap* exactly like an enormous static spark.

And light suddenly spilled from between the two curved stones, along with a breath of wind scented with pine needles and a hint of heated stone. From where he stood, Kordas saw what looked like an oval of blue sky. The Circle and Jonaton made happy noises, but then Jonaton frowned.

"Bugger all," Jonaton muttered. "Punched through the world and came out too high. Looks good, though—Sai, pull the top axis guide down the arc another step—good."

He made a swift gesture, something complicated and much too fast for Kordas to follow, and the image framed in the stones blurred, then settled again, this time a strip of blue sky streaked with white clouds, a stretch of grass, the suggestion of an old, enormous, long-fallen tree, and a tangle of undergrowth. The water in the basins started to boil.

The undergrowth gave a rustle suggestive of something small scurrying beneath it, and the black cat that had been trying to trip Kordas earlier gave a delighted meow—and leapt through.

"Sydney, you asshole!" bleated Jonaton, grabbing belatedly for his pet through the Portal.

Too late.

"Well," said Dole. "It appears there are mice."

"Delia—" Jonaton began, shaking the arm that he'd reflexively put through the Portal to grab the cat.

"I don't Fetch live things," she replied. "It's dangerous. You want your cat to come back in pieces? This is bad enough—I can't even see him! Now shut up."

Jonaton snapped his mouth shut as Delia's brows furrowed with concentration. She stared at something in the Portal— what, Kordas could not see from here. And she grew paler and paler, drops of sweat running down her temples, until he was just about to shout at Jonaton that this wasn't going to work—

But he didn't. He didn't because that wasn't *his* call. It was Delia's.

And as she gave a sudden gasp, a grayish, mossy stone about the size of his fist appeared in her hands, and her knees buckled and she sat down hard on the stone of the floor.

"Now, Wis!" Jonaton shouted, and Wis tossed a cube of sandstone etched all over with runes through the two stone arcs, where it landed with a thud and another rustle of leaves on the other side.

Before anyone else could say or do anything else, another sound entirely emerged from the Portal.

A grunt.

An *angry* grunt.

Followed by another, and a sort of squeal.

Followed by the yowl of a cat.

Followed by the cat itself, puffed up to twice its size, tail a giant bottle-brush, hurtling back through the Portal as if on fire.

And Jonaton slapped his hands together, closing the Portal just as Kordas got a glimpse of black hair, a red tongue, and far too many white teeth snapping fruitlessly at the air then receding away.

"Well," said Sai. "It appears there are bears, too."

7

Sydney-You-Asshole was nowhere to be found for the near future, having left a row of perplexed cats on either side of his escape path. It did not do to practice *too* much magical work at once, so the group adjourned the spellwork with handcloths dipped in the basins' now-hot water to refresh themselves. Magicians who didn't know how to dump off excessive heat didn't live long, and Jonaton's basins were for exactly that. Since the local stone was in Jonaton's hands, and the anchor-stone was across the Portal, that was *all* that was going to happen today. Isla whisked Delia away, following praise from the elders, up into the manor to get her strength back. Kordas went back to his stone grotto, and the Circle huddled with Jonaton—tabby in lap—for a magical consultation that was far above his own level of expertise.

Truth to tell, he didn't mind stopping. It wasn't as if he didn't already have his hands full; having to help construct a major Gate on top of everything else would probably be the stone that sent all the rest tumbling into an uncontrolled avalanche. He also felt a little giddy. It was a delayed reaction, but it finally did emerge fully in his mind that it *had* been done—a Portal had been opened. There had only been a glimpse, but the air was sweet, the greenery was healthy, and there was no lack—at all—of trees for construction right there. And, thanks to the cat, they knew the air was breathable and the ground steady.

This was a vital advancement in the work his father had left with him, and it took a few deep breaths to come to terms with that. When Kordas was "just a Duke's son," he hadn't understood—how could he?—that his father was more than a giant that Kordas owed his life to, a Duke who could point and anything he wanted would be done. His father had been more like a symbol of a father, rather than an actual person, for almost all of Kordas's youth. The Duke shuffled him from teacher to mentor to stable, while Kordas saw commoners out playing with their children. It wasn't until Kordas's teens that he understood. His father wasn't *neglectful* of him.

He was *trusting*.

Kordas's mother taught Isla how to manage a household when both of them were thirteen, and she was responsible for taking in Hakkon, her sister's bastard. It was from his mother that Kordas had learned the complexities inherent in kindness, and the thrift of acceptance. Kordas lived by that, in fact—a hardship was only dwelt upon long enough to determine what the hardship's particulars were, and then his thoughts switched immediately to how to alter that situation. He admired, loved, and trusted his mother, so he kept his mind open when she explained that his father did the best he could in his position to be a good father.

His father was "Duke Erik of Valdemar"—even now, he heard a herald's voice in his mind saying the title, not his own. A ruler. He had Counts, who had Lords, who had Estates, and all of them had people to look after. Only after his father was dead did Kordas realize that his father had shown his love by making sure that Kordas had the *right* people guide him. It was through those others that the Duke lovingly raised his son to not crumple under the weight of inheriting Valdemar. It wasn't until he sat down with his father, under wardings, that Kordas learned from his father's own lips the admiration and trust Kordas had earned. And then, all too soon, his father was gone, and Kordas stood before the Manor in the Ducal regalia. Counts, Lords, and every person of rank in all of Valdemar gave their condolences for the loss of the man Kordas didn't know most of his life, but had ultimately been admired by.

He drew a deep breath, buttoned his jacket up again, straightened up his tabard and the Crest of Valdemar upon it, and emerged from the grotto.

Back to the Fourth Game.

"Messenger," Hakkon told him as soon as he came within view. "Came and went. Imperial."

"Oh, joy." He sighed. Not that this was unexpected. After all, it had been roughly a week since Lord Merrin had sent that report containing news he'd been birthing his own foal. That would have reminded the Emperor of his existence, and also of the fact that this year's tax and tribute was supposed to include two Valdemar Golds. With the Birthday and Regatta not that far away, the Emperor would want his new toys on view, he'd want to see them himself to decide how best to display them, and he'd want them delivered immediately.

Hopefully that was all it was. The two of them stood face to face for several long moments, much unsaid between them.

"How was the grotto?" Hakkon finally asked.

Kordas brightened a little, and put both palms up. "Our horse went the distance."

Hakkon allowed himself a thin-lipped, but genuine, smile.

"It always feels good when your charge makes the jump," he replied. "Let's have a cup and find out what the Empire requires."

"Let's go deal with the worst," he reluctantly replied.

"The *worst* would have been if the messenger had insisted on seeing you, personally, right away," Hakkon reminded him. "Or if there had been Imperial soldiers with him to enforce that request. So this isn't the *worst,* not yet."

When they entered the manor, Kordas's herald, a fellow about Ivar's age named Beltran, was waiting for them with the sealed message in his hands. Kordas relaxed a little, though only a little. Beltran was literally the lowest-ranked servant that could be entrusted with an Imperial message. If it had been more important, the steward would have had it. More important than that, Hakkon would have been holding it when he came out of the grotto. So . . . hopefully this was nothing he wasn't already expecting.

He took the message from Beltran's hands, and broke the seal on it. His Mage-sight detected a little shower of magical energy as he did so. That would be the spell that would tell whoever had set the seal that the message had been opened, and whether or not it was by the person to whom it was addressed. If someone else had opened this first, well . . . at the very least someone in the Emperor's service, if not the Emperor himself, would want to know *why,* and the only permissible answer would be that he was too sick or injured to do so himself.

He opened the carefully folded paper. Very thick stock. Linen, cotton and softwood. Its deckled edges were jarred by the heavy-lined stamped block border surrounding the calligraphy.

There was the usual salutation, to him by his shortest possible title, from the Emperor by *his* longest possible title, which took up half the page, then the important part.

He looked up at Hakkon, feeling his mouth pursing as if he was tasting something sour. Which he was. The excitement, the energy drain, the celebratory mood and then the thoughts of his father and the Plan legacy had resulted in enough of a twisted gut that he tasted bile.

"I'm ordered to turn up with the horses in person," he said abruptly. "As quickly as possible."

Hakkon's face took on an equally sour expression. "Well, that's . . . inconvenient."

"Yes," he replied, not wanting to say anything more, in case there was some subtle enchantment on the paper that would allow what they were saying to be overheard. "But orders are orders. How long will it take to get the tribute herd together?"

"About two days," Hakkon guessed. "We'll want to make sure every horse has been attended to, checked to make sure it's in fine fettle, and is shod for city streets. Grim's up to it, of course, and we can always borrow a blacksmith from the village if we need one."

"Do so. Let me go put this in a safe place, and we'll discuss what needs to be done further," Kordas declared. By a "safe place," of course, he meant the drawer of his desk that was made of such heavy wood that it might as well have been warded on its own, and inside a pouch that scrambled up a spell's precision. He'd need to bring the letter with him, of course, to present to the Gate Keepers, including the one who minded the Gate that was just outside the manor village, right at the wall around the manor estates. It would be up to the Keepers to decide how expeditious his trip was. If they decided to route him straight to the Capital, he'd be there in under a candlemark. If they decided to put him with the trade traffic, the way they had when he'd been sent to foster at the Imperial Palace, it could take more than a day.

"Right," Hakkon agreed. "I'll tell Grim, then we'll meet you there." Beltran nodded.

He didn't have to specify "where," nor who "we" would be. Jonaton was already either with the Six or with Isla, and Beltran was here. Whichever of them found Isla first would gather her up, plus probably Delia if she had sufficiently recovered from Fetching that stone, then they would meet with the Circle, who were the closest thing he had to a Privy Council. Time was of the essence. The good news was that the messenger had not waited, which meant Kordas probably had the two days he needed. But anything over two days . . . could be bad.

He sprinted for his office, Beltran following. The quicker he got this piece of Imperial arrogance somewhere he wouldn't have to worry about it, the better.

The circle of peculiar stuffed chairs had been enlarged to include seven more of the things, mostly stuffed between the Circle's regular ones—and separating the six of the Circle was never a bad idea. Hakkon had found Delia first when he had gone to the stable to inform Grim of the new orders, and had gathered up the steward, Renfeld, on the way back. Kordas and Beltran had found Isla with Jonaton after he stowed the paper where it could do no harm for the moment. By the time Hakkon arrived with Delia, the rest of them had settled as close together as physically possible, so they didn't have to raise their voices much. Yes, the chamber was warded and shielded to a fare-thee-well, but everyone had heard tales of birds bespelled to repeat whatever they overheard, and even though the Six outwardly scoffed at such things, no one was willing to take chances where the Emperor was concerned.

"Grim says he can have the herd ready two days from now, as I predicted," Hakkon said as he lowered himself into a cushion-chair with a grimace. "So that's out of the way. He just needs to organize enough grooms to handle the herd on their trip without leaving the stable shorthanded. You're sending a generous number this year."

"Good. Well." Kordas sighed. "I did not expect this result."

"But it at least makes sense," Isla pointed out. "You haven't been to Court in person in over ten years. No one who actually looks after their lands in person goes to Court willingly during the summer—so this makes it inconvenient for you, which of course is the point. They want to reinforce that you serve them, not the other way around. The Court is half-empty right now, there's probably nothing and no one there to offer a distraction. I haven't heard how the war in the South is going—"

She looked to Ponu, who shrugged.

"Neither well nor poorly," the old man said. "From my perspective, he's probably tying up the Southerns to keep them from tending to their fields with an eye to running out their resources, and planning an offensive after the Regatta to destroy whatever harvests they have. Then, when they're further weakened from a lean winter, he'll move on them again before the fields and roads thaw. That's been his pattern until now, and I don't see it changing."

"Well, it works," Sai pointed out. "And once the Emperor finds something that works, he never changes it."

"So unless the war heats up in an unexpected manner, he can ignore the conflict and leave it to his generals until after the Regatta. So now he's bored, and I caught his interest." Kordas nodded. "Lucky me. All right. Isla, you're in charge of the Duchy. Hakkon, I want you here as well." When Hakkon looked as if he might protest, Kordas shook his head. "I need you here in case someone decides to try something, assuming that a 'weak' female is in charge who can be pushed around. I'm not in my teens anymore. I *will* take Beltran."

"All right, then," Hakkon agreed, subsiding. "If you're not taking me, I'll settle for you taking the best knife-fighter in the Duchy."

Beltran blushed a little, but didn't disagree.

"Beltran is also high enough in rank to go anywhere with me, but low enough to be ignored on his own," Kordas added. "Delia, you're going to be your sister's messenger."

"Because no one is going to pay any attention to a girl, but I'm high enough in rank no one is going to try anything with me," the girl agreed.

"And because thanks to those lessons you've been getting from my Weapons-Master, I know you're one of the best shots in the manor," Kordas told her, and felt a brief moment of amusement at her startled look. "What, my insouciance got you fooled into thinking I don't know what's going on under my own roof? I'd appreciate it if you'd add sling to those lessons. Maybe quarterstaff. In my humble opinion you're too small to risk close-quarter combat, but I'll leave that up to Weapons-Master Klemath. The Plan will go right on ahead. Get the first, temporary Gate up, get Ivar across to scout the position for the one we'll actually use, and start moving people out as soon as the main Gate is established."

Wis cleared his throat, getting Kordas's attention. "On that note . . . we might as well tell you *now* that Jonaton's had a brainstorm."

All eyes turned to Jonaton, who cleared his throat uneasily. "Well, anyone could have had it," he demurred.

"But the fact is, you did, not anyone. So?" Wis prodded.

"Once Ivar has the location for us, I can have a new Gate up and powered and running within a day," Jonaton said modestly. "Maybe two at the worst."

Kordas stared at him. "But—*how*?" he stammered. So far as *he* was aware, the construction of a major Gate took a fortnight at the very least.

"I did some probing to the West after the Circle and I got the two stones linked and I could work through them," said Ceri. "There's an ancient reserve of power in the immediate area that I am fairly certain we can draw on. It dates back to that ancient conflict you were asking about not long ago; somehow it managed to not get caught up in a Change-circle, scattered to the winds, or contaminated."

"And *I* found a way to make Gates quickly," Jonaton said

proudly. "It turns out you don't have to make a Gate entirely out of stone. We do it that way because that's the way it's always been done, but that doesn't mean it's the way we always have to do it. In fact, the only reason we make Gates out of stone is because timber doesn't last. I've tried horn, wood—even wax! They all work. They all work *well.* It's just that the weaker the material, the faster the Gate degrades. One made of wood won't last a year." He laughed. "And those made of wax last just about long enough for one trip."

"So we make two arcs out of timber, right here, in our workshop. We carry them through the temporary Gate with their foundation stones, set them in place, power them up, and—" Ceri spread his hands wide. "We don't need a Gate that lasts. We don't *want* a Gate that lasts, because we don't intend to go back."

"In fact, it might just be a very good idea to have a Gate we can burn behind us," Sai pointed out.

"This—is unexpected good news." Kordas managed not to stammer. Then he took a deep, deep breath and settled his mind. "Right, then. We always knew our deadline for getting the last of us out was going to be the Regatta. This is just a minor deviation from the Plan. I'm not that powerful a mage that you can't do this without me."

"But—" Isla bit her lip. "What if you're still under the Emperor's eye by the time of the Regatta? How will you get out?"

"The Plan isn't about me," Kordas said, with force, so he could be sure they understood he meant this. "The Plan was *never* about saving whoever was the Duke. The Plan was always about getting the most of us out that we can. I'll do my level best to join you. If I can't, I'll do my level best to hide somewhere, even if I have to live the rest of my life as a stablehand." He did not mention what would happen to him once the Emperor discovered their deception and escape if he was ever caught. He didn't have to. But he preferred to be optimistic.

And after all, the life of a stablehand wasn't all that bad.

"Now, let's see about working out a clear schedule," he said. "There literally is no time to waste."

———————

Delia hardly knew what to say during that meeting. Over the course of the past couple of days she had somehow gone from being essentially her sister's hanger-on to one of the lynchpins of a desperate plot.

But what bothered her the most about all of this had nothing to do with *her.* Because all she could think about was the peril that Kordas was walking into. Willingly! And he knew very well what he was doing!

This is insane . . . .

But if it was insane, it was the sort of insanity that made more sense than the "sanity" of the Emperor's toadies.

She found herself agreeing to help Jonaton and the Six with the creation of the temporary and "permanent" Gates—apparently she was useful, not because she was a mage, but because she was *not.* She wouldn't be affected as much, or at all, if certain things went wrong, it seemed. And once the big Gate was up, she had an even more important job, since it would be her task to carry messages from Isla to coordinate the exodus . . . .

"I don't understand how this is going to work," she finally confessed to her sister, as Kordas left the planning group to consult with Grim about the tribute-horses, Hakkon and the other non-mages went off to continue the charade that the only *important* event in the entire Duchy was that the Emperor had demanded his tribute early, and Jonaton and the Six went into a huddle to decide exactly how they were going to create two curved, wooden horn-like objects that were two stories tall.

"You don't understand how what is going to work?" Isla asked, motioning to her to follow.

"How are we going to keep the Emperor's spies from noticing that people are disappearing?" she asked as they headed for Delia's rooms—those rooms being the ones least likely for anyone to be using as a scrying point to spy on the people in the manor. After all, who was *she* to the Empire? A mere female of no importance.

Isla shrugged. "They won't notice, mostly because so far as the people in power are concerned, the ones that will disappear were invisible in the first place." Isla opened the door into Delia's rooms, motioned her inside, and shut the door again. "Let's just take Lord Merrin as an example. He is the Emperor's spymaster in Valdemar. As such, he is a very minor functionary in the Emperor's service. Do you think that outside of his hand-picked spies, his personal body-servant, and perhaps his steward and his seneschal, he actually *knows* any of the people who serve him?"

"I—don't know," Delia confessed.

"Well, I can tell you for a fact that he doesn't. Because I have three spies of my own in his household. One is a housemaid, because housemaids are almost literally invisible and yet see and hear an amazing amount. One is a gardener for the same reason. And the third is one of his minor clerks. He *might* take notice of the clerk, but only because he might need something written or fetched from the library or archives, and even then, all he'll see is a pair of hands. The others? For him they are faceless nonentities, to the point that my housemaid was once forced to stand on a staircase facing the wall because he paused on that stair to have a long and quite interesting discussion with one of his spies, and a housemaid's orders are to draw no attention to herself, ever, which she would have done if she'd tried to go down past him. It literally never occurred to him that as she stood there, as dumb as her broom, she was busy listening to every word he said."

"But—these people are *doing* things, doing the work of the

Duchy!" Delia protested. "Won't Lord Merrin notice if that work doesn't get done on the other manors and holdings and farms?"

"What if the work isn't there to *be* done?" Isla replied. "Remember, we're stripping as much as we can as we leave. As people leave, their work will leave with them. The spies won't notice if more fields are fallow, or if there are fewer sheep in them. They won't notice if there are fewer shepherds or coppicers or thatchers or threshers if there is no work for those people to do. Just like Lord Merrin, the spies are going to concentrate all their attention on Hakkon and to a lesser extent, me. The important people of the Duchy, the people who do the most hard work, are the ones that are beneath their notice."

"But they'll have to notice eventually—" Delia pointed out.

"Well . . . Hakkon says he has a plan for that, which I should not ask about. I'll take his word for it. Very likely I would not like it," Isla admitted.

"Oh." Delia licked her lips, thinking that there were a lot of things Hakkon could do about Lord Merrin that would come under that heading.

"In the meantime, you and I need to work out something plausible that will send you all over the Duchy carrying messages for me," her sister said. "Something important to *me,* but which will seem utterly trivial, even frivolous, to a man like Lord Merrin."

———————————

As Hakkon had stated, the tribute was very generous this year—five horses more than were actually required. Ten of the horses were Chargers, ten were Fleetfoots, and ten were Sweetfoots, and leading them all were the two False Golds. The Emperor did enjoy horse races, and of course he enjoyed always winning, so one third of the tribute was always in Fleetfoots. Kordas had cleared out the general stable to put them all in one place for the convenience of seeing that they were in top condition, their hooves were trimmed, and they were properly shod. This was not an easy task, since the False Golds, the Fleetfoots, and the Chargers were all stallions. *Mature* stallions. Fortunately, they were also all well trained, or things could have gotten chaotic or worse.

The Fleetfoots pretty much had to be stallions; there is no point in racing a horse you couldn't send out to stud if he was a winner. And the Emperor's dunderheaded idiot Knights of the Throne would refuse to ride a mare or a gelding. This made absolutely no sense at all, of course. If Kordas had been an enemy commander, one of his first moves would be to send a loose, wild mare in heat out onto the battlefield as soon as the Knights put in an appearance, but in the Empire, when masculine ego came into play, logic flew right out the window.

The only reason the entire yearly undertaking didn't descend immediately into chaos was that there were no mares in the herd. Since the Emperor had never expressed a preference for the gender of the Sweetfoots, the Duchy always sent geldings. There had never been an objection, so he saw no reason to change that now.

Merrin's spies were bumbling around the place like fat flies, standing out by always being in the way, until Grim got sick of them and put them *all* to cleaning stalls. Two of them vanished as soon as Grim turned his back, and the third looked thoroughly miserable, which cheered Kordas up no end.

But he should have realized that extreme interest meant that something was going on, other than Merrin making daily reports. What that something was, he discovered when at last the herd got put into harness and he and Grim sorted them into their "strings" for the trip.

Now, normally, one did not put horses into harness to move them from one place to another. Normally, you would just herd them, like cattle. But these were mostly stallions, and allowing them to be loose in a herd was not just asking for trouble,

it was sending trouble a hand-made, gilded, and highly decorated invitation. So instead, they were harnessed up in three
"strings" of ten each. There would be a groom riding the lead
and tail horse of each string, and Kordas and Beltran would
each ride one of the False Golds, one at the front of the procession, and one at the rear.

Kordas was hoping that *someone* in the Emperor's staff
would take pity on them and send them straight from the
Valdemar Land Gate to the Imperial Palace Gate, but he wasn't
expecting that. This was why each of the horses carried a bag
of oats and a skin of water, and each of the humans had a
small rucksack of provisions.

They had formed up in front of the stables and were ready
to ride off, when suddenly, a swarm of servants followed by
Isla came racing out of the manor. The servants were burdened with four large packs, and Isla was accompanied by his
seldom-employed valet, carrying a full Court outfit.

The *full* Court outfit, complete with the ceremonial rapier,
and the Ducal sidearm. A "Spitter."

Oh, how he detested that thing, not for what it did, but for
what it meant!

Only a noble could carry a Spitter. It was an awkward contraption used mostly for duels, a sort of hand-held crossbow,
except instead of being a *bow,* it had a rolled-steel tube one
loaded a bolt into—the bolt diameter and the tube's inner diameter built, of course, to Imperial standard sizes. The Spitter's
tube ended in a simple cast-metal chamber, reached via a
hinged "break" mechanism operated by linked thumbspoons—
one on each side, for ambidexterity's sake. One loaded a round
pellet (a "robin's egg," they were originally called, being light
blue) into the pellet chamber, folded the weapon back until the
thumbspoons re-engaged, and the Spitter was considered "live."
To load a bolt, one would drop a beribboned ball into the barrel's muzzle, push the Spitter-bolt in until the ribbon was folded
in tightly against the ball, and that was it.

A Spitter's pellet would break with a noise not unlike someone spitting—hence the name—when the trigger forward of
the handle was pulled back very hard. Skilled Spitter marks-
men tended to aim below their target, to counteract the upward motion caused by the trigger pull. The pellet contained
highly compressed air, and the manufacturing of the things
was a closely guarded secret, but involved magic, of course. A
Spitter's bolt would erupt from the end of the tube at high
speed, much higher than one could get from a crossbow, leaving behind a burst of frigid but harmless gas, the bolt stabi-
lized by a vapor-wrapped weighted ribbon faster than the
strongest bowman could loose.

Kordas's Spitter, formerly his father's, had been modified
with an unobvious difference. If its thumbspoons were pressed
upward, a second break in the upper handle would open. If the
handle's decorative grip-ring was twisted halfway, a mercy-kill
piston, pointed at each end, was dropped from its locked state
in a short barrel to a ready position. If a pellet was inside that
second chamber and the Spitter was used as a club, the impact
of the piston's exposed length would break the pellet, and fire
the piston only about a hands-breadth's distance with the same
force as a bolt fired in the conventional way. If an animal had
to be put down, better to kill it instantly that way than let it
suffer trauma from a bolt.

The reason he hated the things was because although they
were supposed to be used only for duels, they were most often
used in acts of casual cruelty by the nobility. He'd seen that in
play far too often when he'd been in fosterage. Servant annoy
you? Put a bolt through a shoulder or a calf to teach him a
lesson. Someone's pet in your way? Kill it with the Spitter.
Want to show off? Put some hapless servant against a wall
and outline them with bolts.

*But you also resent what that weapon means to you, be-
cause of what you have done with it. The things you did with
it, thinking, "I am the Duke, and the Duke must serve executions*

personally," except you knew all along you could just order it done, without even your presence required. It says a lot about what you really are, Duke or not. You wanted to feel deadly, yourself. Not deadly by proxy, but you. Executing. You wanted to know how it felt to kill, with your own hands.

"Ceri Foresaw you are going to be 'invited' to stay," Isla said tensely. "Strip and change."

Beltran had already dismounted, and was pulling on his formal tabard with the winged white horse device that marked him as the Valdemar Herald on it. Kordas gritted his teeth, stripped to his trews, and donned his own Court garments, right there in the stable-yard, ending by buckling on his Court Saber and baldric and shoving his Spitter into his belt. The trews didn't matter; they were hard-wearing leather suitable for a long ride. And his riding boots had just been polished. Anyone who went on a long ride with shoes and linen trews, in his opinion, was an idiot. But gods! The fancy shirt with a ruff, no less, the long waistcoat, and the overly-elaborate two-colored greatcoat, made him angry just to look at, much less be forced to wear. And if this journey stretched for a full day, they'd be unbearable by lunchtime *and* look terrible when he finally arrived at the Imperial Palace.

"One more thing. From the Circle. You'll be among strong telepaths, and maybe worse. Take this stone amulet and fix it in place behind your Ducal crest. They said, picture this as the skies over Valdemar, and then think into it—they said you knew how—of what you love about Valdemar. 'Springs to sunsets' and the more, the better. Just nothing about the Plan, including them. Especially them. Then they laughed. It's supposed to play your emotional memories about Valdemar instead of what you're actually thinking at the time. But recharge it daily. Add new bits. They said that Imperial telepaths would dismiss you as a homesick hick." Isla half-smiled. "Which you will be."

"That obvious, is it?" Kordas asked sardonically. "This amulet is just what I need. This could save me from exhaustion, trying to stay veiled-shielded the whole time I'm there. But I do have to say—it won't be entirely deceptive. I'll be thinking of Valdemar the whole time I'm away." He spent a while picking at the Crest of Valdemar. It had many layers behind the escutcheon's leather foundation, made up of almost an embarrassment of wards, locks, and memory enhancers, to which the stone amulet was pinned in place. Kordas traced fingers across the amulet and murmured, "I'll try not to lose too much of myself there," He held his breath a moment, then returned the Crest to its place on his baldric and sighed.

"You look splendid," Isla soothed.

"I feel like a fop," he grumbled.

"You'll be fine," she promised. "And just think what would have happened if you'd turned up looking—"

"Like an ordinary fellow with actual work to do?" he almost spat.

She raised an eyebrow. "Exactly."

He sighed, and mounted the horse again. "I just hope they don't *invite me to stay* for too long."

"Be boring," she advised him. "The novelty of laughing at the country bumpkin will soon wear off, as long as you don't make yourself into entertainment. Blank looks instead of reactions, and asking 'Pardon, could you explain?' They'll soon get weary of making the explanations. And go into the fine details of horse breeding as often as possible."

He leaned down from the saddle and kissed her forehead. "My wise counselor," he said. "Hakkon would advise me to break heads."

"I wouldn't do that . . ." She pursed her lips. "However, if you're given the opportunity, it wouldn't come amiss if you could demonstrate, harmlessly, what a good shot you are."

That pulled him up short for a moment, but he certainly saw the wisdom of the advice. He *was* a good shot with the Spitter; he was a good shot with anything, just due to practice, but being known as a good shot with the Spitter might keep him out of duels. "I'll do that," he agreed. "And I'll be back as soon as I'm able."

It was at moments like this that he was glad that his relationship with Isla was not a romantic one. She was able to see him off with equanimity; he was able to leave without desperately wondering if she would be all right. They trusted each other's competence, and at this moment, that was more important than all the love-letters in the world.

As the cavalcade rode off, he checked the inside-pocket of his coat to make sure he had transferred the sealed orders to it when he had changed. The crackle of parchment reassured him.

If this was not an auspicious start, at least it was not an inauspicious one.

The Land-Gate at the manor village was usually not much in use, since most traffic went by canal, so he was surprised to see that there was a small group waiting at it as they rode up. He was even more surprised to see that the group was headed by Lord Merrin. His already sour mood was further soured by seeing that obsequious toady's face beneath a plumed hat.

"Ah, Valdemar, I thought you would probably be embarking at some extremely unfashionable hour!" Merrin brayed at him, laughing at his own feeble attempts at humor. "And here you are! We'll be coming with you at the Emperor's request."

"The more, the merrier!" Kordas said, with hearty good humor he most certainly did not feel. *Well if he's been invited along, I might as well start the play-acting right now.* He eased the False Gold, which towered over Merrin's Sweetfoot palfrey, right up to Merrin's stirrup. Alarm awoke in Merrin's eyes, but before the man could move his gelding away, Kordas had given him a hearty back-slap as good as anything Grim could have delivered. Merrin half doubled over with an *oof!* as Kordas laughed. "Always good to have you along, Merrin, old man! We can show those prissy City lads what a good country fellow looks like!"

Merrin forced a smile and a nod, but his eyes flashed with

annoyance. "That's quite a bit of baggage, Valdemar," he said, eyes narrowing.

Kordas shrugged. "Never know if his Imperial Highness will decide he has need of me. His stableman may need some schooling on these two Golds. Might as well come prepared. It's not as if it'll be hard to chuck the baggage back through the Gate if His Magnificence tells me to head back home."

Merrin eyed his own baggage, loaded aboard four sturdy mules. "But you didn't bring any pack animals . . . ."

Kordas shrugged. "A little exercise is good for the soul."

Merrin looked appalled, as if that was no attitude for a noble to have.

The Land-Gate perched on a flat stone circle atop a rocky hill beside the road that led through the manor-village. As the Gate through which the representatives of the Empire would come and go, it was not the strictly utilitarian structure of stone pillars gently curving toward each other at the top that the Canal-Gates were. Instead it was a fanciful creation of metal swirls which currently framed only sky, and was just big enough for a horse and rider to pass through.

The Gatekeeper lived in a comfortable little building at the bottom of the hill. He was *not* a native of the Duchy, and took none of his needs from the Duchy. In fact, Gatekeepers were rotated out weekly—most likely to prevent them from making local friends. Not once had Kordas ever seen the same Gatekeeper here twice, or at least, not that he knew of. The Gatekeepers always wore the plain red uniform of the Imperial City Guard, which made as much sense as any other origin. They were not mages, which also made sense—that would keep them from tampering with the Gates they guarded.

Kordas dismounted from his horse and approached the Keeper, who had come out of his building and waited on the threshold for Kordas to present orders. Kordas handed him the Imperial directive; he read it without so much as a twitch of expression, handed it back, and said, "Thank you, milord

Duke. Please wait here until you see the Gate open, and then you and your party may proceed through. Please do not touch the sides of the Gate itself, and be prepared for changes in altitude and temperature."

Which was pretty much what every Gatekeeper said.

The Gatekeeper approached the Gate, the Gate sensed his presence and the air between the uprights shimmered and rippled and suddenly looked like a pool of water—if the water was held upright like a mirror.

Now the Gate was receptive.

Kordas mounted his False Gold again, and confidently approached. As the Gate sensed the magic embedded in his orders, the surface between the uprights shimmered again, and to his mingled consternation and relief, their destination appeared, framed as if it was a gigantic picture, by the ornamented metal. A gigantic version of the same sort of sugar-sculpture fantasy as the manor was based on, but much, much bigger, and hundreds of years older.

The Imperial Palace.

They were going *straight* through.

Kordas could not remember a single time when he—or anyone else from the Duchy—had been given a straight through pass. So far as he was aware, the only people who ever had been were the Gatekeepers and the Imperial Messengers. *Or Merrin, the little sneak.*

"Merrin, would you like to go first?" he asked.

Merrin smirked, and gave his palfrey the heel, scooting the horse in under the False Gold's nose. Kordas hadn't paid any attention to how many people Merrin had with him until this point, but between all the servants on horseback and the four mules loaded with baggage, he must have had a dozen beasts in his packtrain. *Seven servants! Does he have someone to wipe his bum for him?*

When they'd all gone through, Kordas heaved a sigh of relief, and turned his attention to his own people. "I'll go through first, then send the Fleetfoot train, the Sweetfoot train, the Chargers, and Beltran, you bring up the rear." He nudged his False Gold with his heel, and the patient horse went through the Gate as if he'd been doing so all his life.

Crossing a Gate was always disorienting, at least for him. There was a moment that seemed to drag on forever, when he was suspended in utter darkness, a darkness that *seemed* to be empty, and yet . . .

He sensed things out there, even if he couldn't see them. Vast armies of things. Some he thought were humans—possibly ones passing through Gates elsewhere. Most were not. Most of these things paid him about as much heed as he'd pay a bird in the sky, or a snail on a leaf. But some . . . he got the distinct impression that, if they were aware he was there, he'd have been of some interest to them. And that these were *not* things he wanted to take an interest in him.

So in that time when he was suspended between *here* and *there,* he did his best to think nothing, *be* nothing, and attract no attention at all.

Then he was through, and he immediately moved to the side to make way for the rest of his group, looking about to see where they'd been dropped.

Well, this is new.

Looming immediately before them was the Imperial Palace, wreathed in smoke. Well, that was the same; the Imperial City was always full of smoke. His nose wrinkled, and he felt a slight headache coming on. That was the same, too. They were in a vast courtyard with a half dozen of the Imperial Gates, all active, though none of the others seemed to have large parties going through them. The courtyard was paved—at least, he thought it was pavement, though the surface was textured and pebbly, and he had no idea what material it could have been made from. As the strings of horses came through, he found himself looking for the servants who should have been here to take the horses, but he couldn't spot anyone in the distinctive red-and-purple tabards he remembered from when he'd been here as a boy.

Merrin noticed his confusion. "What are you looking for, Valdemar?" the nobleman asked, with a kind of smirk that suggested he was in on some sort of privileged information that no one had bothered to impart to Kordas.

"The attendants," he replied.

"Oh, the Emperor did away with those ages ago," Merrin replied, the smirk growing more pronounced. "Ah, look, over there—that's what you're waiting for."

Kordas looked where Merrin was pointing, and felt his jaw dropping.

From an entranceway that he vaguely remembered as leading to the stables came a procession of—well, they weren't *human.*

8

The . . . things . . . wore the distinct red tabards with the purple wolf's-head of the Imperial servants. And they walked on two legs, and had two arms. But—

"Oh, I forgot, Valdemar. You haven't been here in over a decade, have you?" Merrin said, the smirk apparent even in his voice. "We haven't had human servants in the Imperial City for . . . well, years!"

"What exactly are those things?" Kordas asked cautiously.

"Constructs," Merrin replied casually. "We call them 'Dolls.' Ever so much more efficient than humans. They don't need rest, they don't need food, they can't be hurt, and if one is broken, you can just burn it and replace it."

"Dolls" seemed an apt description for the things. They were more or less human shaped, better constructed than a scarecrow since they had jointed limbs and actually moved with a fair amount of grace, but there was no way they could ever be mistaken for anything but what they were. They seemed to be sewn out of canvas, with a suggestion of eyes, a nose, and a mouth, but nothing like a real face. Their heads were without any sort of ornamentation. As they neared, Kordas thought there was some sort of jointed skeleton inside the padded, sexless bodies.

"Greetings, Great Lord Merrin," said the first one in line in a high, breathy voice. "This one is assigned to conduct you to your apartment. Will you require replacements for your human entourage?"

There must be some sort of . . . intelligence bound inside those things. But what? Whatever it was . . . this was profoundly *wrong.* Everything in him revolted against this. It was, to his core, disturbing.

Were there actual demons in there?

Somehow he didn't think so. *Mind, I've never had anything to do with demons. But still, I wouldn't think they'd be so polite.*

"I will require servants, and so will my entourage," Merrin replied, carelessly.

"Very good, my lord. If you and your entourage will accompany this one, your beasts will be taken to the stables, and your luggage will be brought immediately." The Doll waited silently while Merrin and his men dismounted, then as they were led off, an entire group of Dolls emerged from a storage shelter, where they had simply hung on a rack like jackets. They removed the baggage from the mules and led the beasts back into what must be the area of the stables.

Another of the Dolls approached Kordas. "Greetings, Great Duke Valdemar," said the Doll, in a voice so like the first one's that he could not have told them apart. "This one is assigned as your receiver, to conduct you to your apartment. Will you require replacements for your human entourage?"

Kordas gave himself a mental slap to break himself out of his stupor. "These are very special horses," he said, tentatively.

"Yes," the Doll replied. "Two are Valdemar Golds. They all

are your Duchy's tribute to our Glorious Emperor. All will be taken to the stables and given the best of attention, and the finest fodder. Will you require replacements for your entourage?" As it spoke, the other Dolls took the packs down from the backs of the false Golds, and waited silently for instructions.

"All but my Herald are to return immediately to Valdemar," he said, still not sure what the right answer was.

"Our Glorious Emperor has given this one tokens so that they will return immediately to the Valdemar Gate." The Doll held out a mitten-like hand; in it were six small papers with Imperial Seals. "Will you require replacements for your entourage?"

"Are you asking if I'm going to need servants?" he asked tentatively.

"Yes." The Doll's blank head made talking to it somewhat unnerving.

"Yes, please," he confirmed. "Lads, come get your passes back, and let the—Dolls—should I call you Dolls?—take the horses to where they belong."

The Valdemar stablehands dismounted somewhat reluctantly, and even more reluctantly, approached the Doll that was still holding out the passes. They huddled for a moment, and finally one of them snatched all six passes and distributed them to the others. "Are you sure you want us to leave you with that—thing—milord Duke?" asked the brave one, looking him fully in the face. The stablehand's expression told Kordas that the fellow, though absolutely terrified of the creature, was perfectly willing to stay right here if the Duke asked him to.

"I'm quite sure," Kordas said firmly, as the other Dolls led the false Golds and the three strings of tribute horses to their new home. "Off with you, my lad. Be sure and tell my lady everything that you saw here, and give her my best."

The young fellows were clearly reluctant to leave, but even

more reluctant to stay. "Very well, milord Duke," the brave one said at last. "If you're certain."

"I'm certain, and you have families you need to return to," Kordas repeated, and deliberately turned away from them. "Now, if you would be so kind, my friend, my Herald and I would greatly appreciate being taken to our quarters."

But the Doll froze for a moment. "Great Lord Duke," it said, after a moment. "This one is nothing. It cannot be a friend."

"You certainly are not *nothing*," he said, perhaps more sharply than he had intended. "And you certainly can be a friend."

The Doll bowed its head briefly. "As you will," it whispered, with an air of both uncertainty and—was it shock? "Please, come this way."

The Dolls had picked up Merrin's heavy luggage as if it was nothing, and they made light work of the two packs. Kordas glanced over at Beltran; the poor fellow's eyes were as big as plates, and he looked just as reluctant to have anything to do with the Doll as the stablehands had been.

He patted Beltran on the shoulder. "It's fine."

"No, milord," Beltran gulped. "It's *not* fine. But I will do my duty."

They followed the Doll up the steps of the main entrance to the Palace—two ridiculously huge doors that were at least two if not three stories tall, apparently made of solid bronze, and so perfectly balanced that he knew from being here as a child that they could be moved with a single fingertip. These stood open to the Entrance Hall.

This was a vast, echoing chamber with no obvious entrance or exit except those doors, but the walls were lined with Gate after Gate after Gate, each one framed in the same decorative metal arcs as the one they had passed through back at the manor. People and Dolls—mostly Dolls—were coming and going through them. The Doll with Kordas approached one of the Gates and spoke.

"The Copper Apartment," it said. The mirror-surface of the Gate shivered, and cleared to reveal what looked like a fine antechamber; from here Kordas saw what looked like black and white checkered marble, some very uncomfortable-looking copper-colored furniture, and copper-colored walls.

The Doll stepped through, and Kordas and Beltran followed.

There was no sense of disorientation, probably because they weren't actually going that far. The little antechamber was just about big enough to hold six to eight people without crowding, so the two humans and the three Dolls fit fine. The furniture—two chairs and something that passed for a little table between them—looked just as uncomfortable up close as it had through the Gate, all strange copper curves and very little padding. The Doll opened a single copper door into the apartment proper, and stood aside for them to go in.

They found themselves in what Kordas guessed was supposed to be a common room. It, too, had a black and white floor, a curved copper wall, uncomfortable copper furniture, and a green ceiling inlaid with copper squares. There was no sign of a fireplace, but the temperature was quite comfortable. Mage-lights in sinuous copper sconces lit the windowless room. Kordas judged that before his visit was over he was going to be very tired of copper.

There were three doors in the half-circle of wall. The Doll went to the right-hand one and flung it open. "This will be your chamber, milord Duke," it said, and gestured to him to enter.

The room was shaped like the segment of a circle, which made sense if they were in a tower. The color scheme continued in this room, but the bed, at least, looked as if it wouldn't be torture to sleep in. The bedframe was more sinuous copper, columns rising from each corner of the bed that split, curled around in tendrils, and met above the center. There was an ordinary-looking copper wardrobe, a couple of chairs and a stool, and a window in the curved outer wall, framed in more copper spirals. Of course, it might not be an actual window, but rather a magical image. Disorientation was a means of control, too. This apartment could be a mile from the actual Palace, and he might be no wiser.

"Which of the packs is yours, milord Duke?" the Doll asked, as he stood there, taking it all in. He eyed the bed dubiously; the Doll hadn't specified that there was a bedchamber for Beltran. Was he expected to share it with Beltran? He *could,* it wasn't as if the idea offended him, but—"Uh, the blue one," he replied absently.

The Doll carrying the blue pack took it to the wardrobe, opened it, and began putting his clothing away. The Doll carrying Beltran's brown canvas pack began taking it out of the room, then turned and looked at Beltran, who had not moved. "If you would come with me, Duke's Companion?" it whispered. "I shall show you to your chamber."

Well, that's a relief.

Beltran followed the Doll apprehensively, as the other Doll opened a door in the left, non-curved wall. "This is your chamber of bathing and personal hygiene," it said, gesturing to him to come and look. And sure enough, there was a bathroom like the exceedingly convenient ones in his own manor, with an enormous tub, the kind of close stool where the waste flushed down, presumably into a sewer or tank, and a sink and mirror. And a door in the opposite wall. "You will be sharing this with your companion?" The Doll sounded tentative, as if it expected him to disapprove.

"That will be fine," he said, still a bit dazed, because this was nothing at all like his experience here as a foster, where he'd shared a tiny little sliver of a room with Hakkon, and a bathroom with a dozen other male fosters.

"Will this serve?" it asked anxiously.

"This will be fine. More than fine!" he told the Doll.

"Milord Duke will be served by three of us, if that is sufficient," the Doll said. "This one, and the two pack-carriers. *Will* that be sufficient?"

He wanted to tell the thing that he'd rather not be served by *any* of them, because to be honest he found them unnerving, but he suspected that would only cause the Doll distress. "That will be fine," he repeated.

The Doll pointed to a copper chain hanging beside the bathtub. "The Duke must merely pull one of those chains, and one of us will come to serve," it said. "And we will be at hand at all times. We will also come to guide you to all functions and appointments." It handed him a copper chain bracelet. "If milord Duke will put this on, the Duke has but to approach a Gate and speak the name of the chamber he wishes to enter, and the Gate will take him there. The Duke's companion has been given one as well."

Kordas knew that this kind of formal speech was a Court standard, but he found it stilted, and pinched the bridge of his nose between his thumb and forefinger. "What do I call you?" he said at last.

The Doll suddenly froze. "Please forgive," it said after a long pause. "This one does not understand."

"What do I call you?" he repeated. "Your name, what is it? I can't just call you 'Doll.'"

It froze again. "Why . . . would . . . milord Duke . . . wish this one to bear a name?"

"Because it's polite?" he replied.

This time the pause was very long indeed, and he was afraid that he might have broken the poor thing. Finally, though, it responded. "Milord Duke may call this one what he pleases."

Well . . . I'm sure of one thing. Whatever is bound in there, it's no demon. It's intelligent, it's aware, and it's a slave. Bile rose in his throat. "Come with me, please," he said, and left the bathroom, followed by the Doll. The other Doll had finished putting up his clothing, leaving the pack neatly folded in the bottom of the wardrobe, and he signaled to it that it was to follow as well. They all entered Beltran's bedroom, which was identical to his, just in time to find the third Doll opening the door to the shared bathroom and explaining the chamber to his Herald. He waited while the Doll went through its patter, and cleared his throat to get its attention.

"Beltran, do you have anything on you that will make a permanent mark?" he asked, knowing that Beltran certainly would, since one of Beltran's functions was to be his personal secretary.

Beltran produced a tiny pot of ink and an equally tiny metal pen from a belt-pouch with a flourish. Kordas took them from him, and turned to the first Doll. "Am I allowed to make a mark on you?" he asked.

"The Duke may do what he wishes with this one, and any other Doll," the Doll said. "The Duke may break a Doll's limbs, burn a Doll, practice marksmanship upon a Doll, paint upon a Doll—"

"Stop!" he said, sickened. "We have no intention of doing any such thing to you, do you understand? I just want to add a little mark on each of you so Beltran and I can tell you apart."

"As you will," the Doll said. "But one Doll is the same as any other—"

"No, you are not," he said forcefully. "I know that, and *you* know that, and it's only decent to acknowledge that. Now, since you either don't want us to know your names—which is *fine,* that's your right!—or we can't pronounce your names, or there is some other reason, and you've said I can call you what I like, I am going to give you names." He dipped the pen in the inkpot and very carefully scribed a five-pointed star between where the eyebrows would have been. "You are Star."

"This one is . . . Star," the Doll repeated, and it sounded a little stunned.

He went to one of the other two, and scribed a five-petaled flower on its forehead. "You are Rose."

"Rose," the Doll said obediently.

He went to the third Doll and scribed a three-leaved clover

on its head. "And you are Clover." He pointed to each of them in turn. "Star, Rose, and Clover. Is that all right with you?"

"As you—"

"Please answer the question," he said patiently. "Is that all right with *you?* Are there some other names you'd like to be called?"

"These names are . . . fine," said Star. "These names . . . are . . . lovely," Star added, wonderingly.

He heaved a sigh of relief.

"Now, I have a question, and I hope it's not intrusive. Are you three just going to hang about the apartment all the time?" *I really hope not. It's going to take a while to get used to these things.* He hated feeling that way, because it seemed wrong, but on the other hand, the Dolls were . . . well . . . creepy.

"Oh *no,* milord Duke!" Star said with what sounded like a shocked gasp. "That would never do! There is a storage chamber behind the middle door of the common room. That is where we are, until needed."

He wasn't entirely sure that was any better, but . . . "Are you all right there?"

"It is where we belong," Rose said simply. "Clothing belongs in a wardrobe. Dolls belong in a storage chamber."

Ugh. But . . . all right.

"Well, now what are we supposed to do, Star?" he asked. "Is there somewhere we are supposed to be? Some function we are supposed to attend?"

Long silence. Finally Star spoke. "If . . . this one . . . may presume?"

"Presume away," he replied, preferring this to utter servility.

"Milord Duke's wardrobe is . . . inadequate by Court standards. This one could, if the Duke wishes, draw a bath, take the Duke's measurements, and order luncheon to be brought up, and an adequate wardrobe will be delivered before the Court meets at dinner?"

He ran his hands through his hair and puffed out his cheeks, thinking this over. On the one hand, he didn't want to be completely embarrassed, and if the *Doll* had noticed that his clothing was "inadequate," then he might be the equivalent of a stablehand at a High Feast. Ludicrous. Maybe dangerously so, because the one thing he did not want to do was leave the impression that he was to be treated like trash.

Not good.

"Can I ask for modifications to that idea?" he said, finally.

"As you will," all three of them said at once.

"An adequate but *simplified* wardrobe," he stated. "Cut ornamentation to a bare minimum. Absolutely nothing that stands out. *Austere,* if you understand. Very conservative."

The three of them then turned to face each other in a little huddle, and stood there in long silence for a very long time.

"Milord, what are they doing?" Beltran asked. The lad didn't seem to be as nervous now, a fact that spoke well of him.

"Conferring with each other, I suppose?" he hazarded, just as Clover turned back to face them.

"This can be done," the Doll stated. "And it can be done for the Duke's companion—"

"Beltran," the lad said firmly. "Call me Beltran. I'm the Duke's Herald and acting secretary."

"Ah!" Rose exclaimed. "Yes, this can be done for Beltran, now that we know your rank."

"A *conservative* wardrobe will be even easier to fabricate," said Star. "We will have it after luncheon."

"Then let this be done," he said, and felt some tension draining out of him. "Just one thing. Boots, not shoes."

"As you will," said Clover . . . with just a faint hint of disapproval.

He smiled. "Now about that bath—"

"If the Duke will come to the chamber—"

"And the Duke will undress himself, if you please," he said firmly.

Was there a hint of a sigh?

"As you will," said Star.

———————

The best way to keep one's mind off troubles, at least in Delia's experience, was to work. And since Jonaton and the Six needed her to "anchor" them while they made that temporary Gate for Ivar, as soon as Kordas and the tribute-train had gone through the Gate to the Capital, the subterranean workroom was where she took herself.

All seven of them were already there, muttering and disagreeing and then agreeing again, and doing things with herbs and stones and bits of string and candles and chalk that all made no sense whatsoever to her.

"Is Isla going to help?" she asked, once there was a lull in the proceedings.

"Isla? No, we don't need Isla, and she has things of her own to do," Jonaton said absently. But then he looked up and really *saw* her, and beckoned to her. "Sit *here*," he ordered, pointing to a stool that was behind the pair of stone "horns." She saw now that he had moved them farther apart. "She needs to make sure none of the cats gets down here. Herding cats is enough of a job for ten people, but Isla is an army unto herself. Ivar should be here any moment."

And just as he said that, Ivar did appear, from a different entrance than Delia had come by. His unruly blond hair was confined by a practical sweatband, and he was burdened with a pack and a belt festooned with weapons. There was a crossbow and a quiver of bolts, a good long knife, an axe, a sling, and a bag of shot, and perched on the top of his pack was a helmet.

He himself wore a good set of leather armor: tunic, bracers, and upper arm pieces, a gorget, and a pair of the stoutest boots Delia had ever seen in her life. His great black mastiff Bay was at his side, looking solemn and business-like, right up until Ponu exclaimed, "Doggo!" and Bay's tail wagged. Sai confirmed, "That's a fine big pupper, that is."

Jonaton glanced over and asked, "He didn't go after the cats, did he?"

Ivar patted Bay on the side with firm thumps. "Didn't need to. They fled at first sight."

"What a good boy," Ponu declared, despite a glare from Jonaton.

Dole looked Ivar over skeptically. "No sword?" he asked.

"Swords are good against humans, not so much against animals. Not that we'll actually fight unless we have no choice," Ivar replied easily. "If we run into anything like that bear, Bay will harry it on one side while I plink at it on the other, with the idea of making it run away. I'm not there to do anything more than look for your body of water. Not even long enough to need my horse. Besides, the horse won't fit through this Gate."

"Well said," Ponu agreed. "You're smarter than you look."

"If I wasn't, I'd also be deader than I look," Ivar laughed.

Delia had to smile a little. Ivar really *was* smart.

"All right, then, let's make this thing happen!" said Sai. It seemed to Delia that despite his eager tone, he was covering up a lot of anxiety. She was pretty sure she was right when she noticed that, as he lined up two sets of six large crystals with each of the two stone horns, his hands shook a little.

He looked up, caught her staring, and schooled his expression into something other than tense. "Curious, kitten?" he asked, his tone far too jocular. "A Gate has to be powered by *something,* and we don't want to alert anyone in the Capital by pulling on the energies that power that Gate down by the village. So we've been making these storage crystals for as long as the Plan has been in existence. Twelve is probably too many—"

"But better too much than not enough," interrupted Ceri, and gestured to Ivar to come stand opposite of Delia.

"Am I going to feel anything?" she asked, just a little apprehensively.

"Not a thing. You haven't a spark of magic in you," said Dole. "That's why we want you here, we told you. You're the rock that's going to keep everything weighted down."

She wasn't entirely sure she wanted to be compared to a rock, but—

At that moment, the entire room lit up as all the inherent diagrams and lines and most of all the twelve crystals and the two stone horns flared into life. It was *so* bright, in fact, that she had to shield her eyes for a moment.

When she could look again, she saw . . . absolutely nothing. From this side of the Gate, there was nothing whatsoever going on between the two arcs of stone.

But Ivar's face reflected a rippling light, and she could see just a little bit of it in the reflections from his eyes and the metal bits of his armor and weapons.

"Go!" shouted Ponu.

Ivar and Bay walked confidently toward her.

And vanished from sight as they passed between the stone horns.

"Don't move!" shouted all seven of the mages as she stirred a little, wanting to get up and see whatever it was they were seeing.

She froze.

Silence filled the cellar. Finally she broke it.

"Um—"

"You stay there until Ivar comes back, even if that takes until sunset," said Ponu sternly, as Jonaton sagged down onto a stool. It appeared that he had done the brunt of the work. "I certainly hope it won't take that long. The longer this thing stays open, the more likely it is someone in the Capital will sense something."

"And if he's not back by sunset, he'll have to camp there," added Dole.

"Does he know that?" she asked, alarmed now.

"Of course he knows that! Why do you think he was carrying that pack?" Koto snapped, speaking for the first time. "We're not idiots! We gave him a thorough lecture!"

"Well, not *complete* idiots," Sai snickered, earning himself a glare from the usually silent mage.

"Do you have something you can do?" Ponu asked. "A book you can read or something?"

"I—uh—"

"You didn't give *her* a thorough briefing," Sai pointed out. "You didn't give *her* a briefing at all."

"I thought that was your job," Wis accused.

"Why should it be my job?" retorted Sai.

"Because you aren't good for anything but talking and baking?" said Ceri.

Well, the resulting bickering that erupted was good for one thing, at least. It was entertaining. Entertaining for her, anyway.

It was just as the bickering was dying down that Jonaton sprang to life again, pointing at the (to her) empty space between the stone horns.

"He's coming back!" he shouted.

Elation mixed with alarm erupted on all seven faces, and before she could ask what was going on, Bay suddenly appeared in a leap that carried him tumbling into Jonaton, knocking him to the ground. A moment later Ivar dashed into view as well, skidding to a halt on the floor of the chamber. The Circle burst into confused shouting, of which she could make nothing except extreme agitation.

So she did the only thing she could think of. She stood up and moved.

Light erupted from the crystals and the horn again, then blinked out, leaving her half blinded.

"Well . . . that worked," said Jonaton, as she rubbed her dazzled eyes. "Good job, Delia."

"Why were you running?" "Was it a bear?" "Was it *wyrsa?*" "Was—"

"I was running," panted Ivar, "because the seven of you pounded it into my thick head quite thoroughly that as soon as I found a body of water that suited us, I needed to get back here as quickly as possible to avoid alerting the mages in the Capital. So I did."

Silence.

"Ah," said Jonaton, finally. "Uh, well done."

"I want it known right now that I do *not* much care for that Gate you built," Ivar said crossly. "It wasn't like any Gate I have ever used before. It felt as if something was stretching and pulling me like taffy, and there were entirely too many things in the darkness between here and there that fancied a nice piece of taffy."

"Really?" Koto stood up and came to stand over the kneeling Ivar. "Can you—"

"Later, Koto," Jonaton cautioned. "We'll go over all of this later. Right now—you said you'd found what we need?"

Ivar began laughing, in between panting for breath. "Good gods, I could *smell* it, it was so close! More to the point, so could Bay, and it was his nose I was counting on. When I got to the other side—this Gate dumped me out in the middle of a lot of trees, facing west."

"That's good, because that's what I was going for," Jonaton said with satisfaction.

"Well, I could smell water, and I told Bay to find it. We hacked our way through some brush, got to the other side of the trees, and found ourselves *above* a sort of bowl, a flattened, round valley. Most of the valley was filled with a lake in the shape of a crescent. A *big* lake, bigger than anything in this Duchy, for sure."

"This sounds promising. Go on," murmured Koto.

"Oh, but it gets so, so much better." Ivar grinned, as if he had a huge secret he was just about to reveal. "You know this thing you gave me?" He opened his hand, which had been held in a fist around something, showing that he was holding a sort of black stone disk. "This thing you said would show me where that magic you thought you sensed was? Well, it led me down to that lake. And—"

He snatched up a piece of chalk from where Ponu had discarded it and sketched a crescent shape.

Then he stabbed the chalk right in the middle of the crescent, on the very shore of what presumably was the lake. "It led me right *there*. There were stonework ruins, some a couple of stories tall. Hundreds of years old, looked like, and no people had been anywhere around for just as long, too, I'd wager. There were the remains of a tower, overgrown by generations of trees. Hardwoods. The brush we hacked through was probably streets, once, and when we got waterside, there was a jetty. Birds and bugs were everywhere, there were watergrasses and algae, and it looked like fish were striking." He laughed again. "We ventured onto the jetty, mindful of snakes, and when we looked back the way we'd come, there were more ruins, and what looked like a charcoal dome. A little north of there, we could see another jetty, more intact than what we stood on. It was a dock. Straight as a bolt. Overgrown like everything else, and there was a line of pilings on either side of it. I think they were moorings or slips, once. The dock ended in a tee, probably ten horselengths long." Ivar marked it on his crude map. "You can clear it, clean it up, and build your Gate right there. It'll dump barges right into the water. And there was more. There were sunken boats by the shore, prows sticking up above the waterline. Looked like they'd rotted out from below, but what was above water still had flecks of paint. Still had their ribs, too. Must have been made from that local hardwood."

They all sat there staring at him, dumbfounded, then looked from Ivar to each other, and back again.

"What star were you born under?" Ponu managed. "Because you must be the luckiest son of a bitch in the Empire."

"I've been told that before," said Ivar modestly.

Jonaton had been quiet but suddenly asked, "What kinds of boats?"

"Pointy," Ivar snickered. "Now. As I recall, we were promised a baron of beef, a barrel of beer, and one of Sai's cakes that is so special he only bakes it once every three years. So."

He grinned up at all of them.

"That'll be Bay fed. What will I eat?"

"**W**ill this do, milord Duke?" whispered Star, gesturing at the shockingly extensive wardrobe laid out on the bed.

Kordas ignored that question for the moment. "How in the name of gods great and small did you do all this so quickly?" he asked. This was literally twice as much clothing as he had brought with him. It was not a "rainbow" of clothing, either; it was, as he had asked for, conservative. The linen shirts were all white. The breeches were all shades of gray. The waistcoats were all shades of matching grays. The coats were all shades of blue-gray. "Do you do this for every visitor?"

"There are many of us, and we do not tire," Star replied. "And . . . no. No, we do not. We create individual garments, not entire wardrobes, and only when requested. But you are different."

He licked his lips, and rubbed the back of his neck under his hair. He didn't have to ask *how* he was different, not after that answer he'd gotten from Star about how he was permitted to treat the Dolls who had been assigned to him. Of course he was different. He might be the only person in the Palace who didn't either abuse them or treat them as moving furniture.

"Thank you," he said sincerely, "and I am very much in your debt. This is all wonderful, and exactly what I described."

It was. The clothing was better by far than what he'd brought from home, but in a subtle fashion. There were no signs of wear, and it was obviously new. His own clothing, if you looked at it closely enough and knew what you were looking for, showed that it had been taken apart and "turned"— the inside turned to become the outside—so that the original wear and tear was disguised. The fabrics these pieces were made from were much finer. He didn't know enough about fabric to understand how, but the difference was definitely there; the coats and waistcoats were slightly heavier and softer; the shirts were of a whiteness he'd never seen in linen before and of so fine a weave he could scarcely make out the threads, and the lace on the sleeves and ruffs was less coarse than the lace on the shirts he'd brought from Valdemar, which was made by a lovely lady in the manor-village. The gray-colored knee-breeches (not trews, he noted with regret) were exceptionally close-fitting and had a velvety texture like glove leather. They might have *been* glove leather. The colors were muted and harmonious. The two pairs of knee-length boots, one black, one blue-gray, fit his calves like a second skin without being uncomfortable, and were so polished he fancied he could see his own reflection.

He still couldn't imagine how the Dolls had managed to produce three coats, six waistcoats, a dozen shirts and as many sets of underclothing, and two pairs of boots in less than an afternoon.

Unless—maybe—they had things like this cut out to a general size and pattern, and could tailor them up quickly.

Still.

That means these Dolls have creative intelligence. They can judge styles, sizes, and who knows what else?

"Are you truly pleased?" Star whispered. He thought he caught an edge of anxiety in her tone.

Her? Am I thinking of this Doll as a female because it is being subservient? Is the Empire's poison in me again so quickly? Or is it that—yes, the Dolls all move like little girls are trained to move. That must be why I thought "her."

"I am more than pleased. I am completely astonished. Now that I see this work, I realize I would have looked like—" He fumbled for a comparison the Doll might understand. He rather doubted Star would know what a "scarecrow" was. "— like I'd been dressed in cast-offs. And that would not do, would it? Not even for a country bumpkin from the furthest reaches of the Empire."

Star bowed its head slightly. "No, milord Duke. Not if you wished to have any amount of respect." It paused. "This one is aware that milord Duke wishes to appear unsophisticated and free to be dismissed in the Great Game, but this is a fine line to walk. Milord Duke must have *some* respect."

Kordas felt his jaw sagging, as he heard what were almost his own thoughts being echoed back at him from the Doll's— well, it didn't have a mouth, but it did have a voice.

"The ones below who know the language of clothing have chosen a path for you that this one hopes will serve. Your clothing is fitted exactly, and designed to display the physique of a very physical man. One who is not lightly trifled with, lest he lash out physically in anger." The Doll gestured at the garments on the bed. "Slightly out of fashion. No ornamentation of the outer garments. Lace is linen thread, not gold or silver. You do not display wealth upon your person. But this only signifies that you feel no need to. This should, if the ones below are correct, engender conflicting feelings. The first, that you are, as you say, a bumpkin to not understand that clothing makes the man. But the second, an uneasy feeling that *perhaps the Duke is so confident he feels no need for display.* And if you are that confident . . . what is your reason for feeling such confidence? Is it misplaced confidence? Or do you have power that is not apparent?"

He forced his mouth to close. "I think you might be the very first being I have ever met that understands the—the Fourth Game," he said.

He used that term to see if Star really *did* understand it. And Star did not disappoint.

"We call it the Great Game. The Game of Power," Star agreed. "We who are unregarded and unobserved have been observing this Game since we were bound to serve."

Well, that particular turn of phrase caught his attention. But he wasn't given the chance to ask about it, because at just that moment, all the mage-lights in the bedroom dimmed and turned to a soft blue, and a three-note chime rang across the room.

"Milord Duke, that is the signal that it is time to dress for dinner. This one fears that, although you are accustomed to dress and undress yourself, the close fit of these new garments will require that this one assist you."

"Botheration," he muttered, and sighed. "Will the Emperor be at this dinner?" If his memories were correct, the answer should be no. When he'd last been here, the Emperor only attended Court meals that were "occasions," preferring to keep his physical presence as a sort of reward—and an opportunity for his courtiers to display their loyalty. He rather doubted that his presence tonight was an "occasion." The arrival of the tribute-horses had never been any sort of event before, and it didn't make sense that it suddenly would be now.

Star shook its head. "No," it said. "Not this evening. Tonight you play the Great Game with your peers. One of us three will attend you as your servant. Your companion will dine here, unless you wish him to attend as well."

That set him back a moment. "What are the advantages to him attending?" he asked.

"A set of eyes and ears that will be virtually invisible. He is merely your Herald and Secretary. No one will address him or take notice of him."

"And disadvantages?" he persisted.

"That you might be weak enough to believe you need him with you. That you have some bonds of affection to him."

Hmm. The second is an acute disadvantage for a first impression. Maybe later. "I'll leave him here, then."

"Good. This will give the ones below the time to make new garments for him as well." The Doll gestured at the bed. "Please select garments, my lord Duke, and this one will assist you."

He hadn't actually believed that he was going to need assistance merely to get dressed, but the Doll had not exaggerated. The breeches, boots, and coat in particular were so closely fitted to his body that if they had not been cut in some fashion that allowed for a great deal of "give," it would have been like being strapped up in tight bandages. And he'd have had to dislocate a shoulder to get into the coat.

He had to admit to preening a bit in front of the mirror, though, when he was dressed. He looked positively splendid.

And . . . yes, in the clothing he'd brought with him, he'd have looked . . . sloppy. The difference between these garments and the ones he'd brought was like the difference between the ones he'd brought and the ones he'd helped birth the foal wearing.

He paused when the Doll held up the baldric, sword, and Spitter, though, with its beautifully made Valdemar badge.

"Are those necessary?" he asked.

"They are symbols of rank, my Lord," Star said patiently.

He sighed.

———————

Somewhat to his surprise, the courtiers were *not* organized at dinner by rank. Instead, the places at the two long tables below the empty High Table were filled by no system he could determine at first glance. Across from him was a very young Prince, an unsmiling, slick-haired, saturnine lad no more than eighteen, dressed in cloth-of-gold, who simply introduced himself, nodded at Kordas's introduction, and remained silent and observant for the rest of the meal, speaking only to the Doll standing behind him to accept or reject the dishes being offered to him. On his right was a smirking fop of a skinny Count, whose clothing was the very opposite of Kordas's—gold braid ornamented every possible surface of his scarlet coat, with gold lace on his ruff and sleeves. He very clearly considered himself to be Kordas's superior in every way, even before the first words were spoken. To his left was a wheezing, elderly Duke, whose silver-embroidered, green waistcoat strained to contain his belly, and whose matching coat could not possibly have been buttoned over it.

Kordas turned to the Duke first, as the initial dish of the first course, a clear broth, was served. After the Duke had nodded to his Doll to ladle the broth into the silver bowl before him, Kordas introduced himself.

"Eh? Valdemar, is it?" Duke Elnore took a moment to spoon up some of the broth, tasting it with delicate manners. Kordas was not surprised at the manners. These were drummed into every hostage's head until they were second nature. "Horses, isn't it?"

"Indeed, my lord Duke," Kordas replied, as Count Declaine on his other side rolled his eyes at the Prince across from them. "The Sweetfoot line of palfreys, the Fleetfoot line of race horses, the Imperial Chargers for the Imperial knights, and the Valdemar Golds." He didn't mention the Tow-Beasts. That would be pushing things a little too far.

"Hrm! Hrm! Hrm!" replied the Duke. Was that a laugh? It might have been. "Lost a wager a time or two to those Fleetfoot nags of yours. Breed 'em to run slower, why don't you?" And then he uttered an actual laugh at his own wit.

"You don't mean to say you breed them *yourself,* do you, Valdemar?" The Count's eyes glittered with some unreadable emotion, as the second dish of the course was served, and Kordas declined it. This dinner would probably have twelve courses of no less than three dishes each, and you had to pace yourself if you didn't want to be sick.

Time to play the bumpkin. "Well, I don't bone up and *mount* them, if that's what you're implying. But for placing which is bred with which, why yes, I do, Declaine," Kordas said lazily. "I know the full pedigree of every horse that comes from my stables. I make all the matches myself. It doesn't do to leave something that important to menials." He accepted the next dish, which looked like something pickled. It was. "Of course, once they *leave* my stables, they are out of my hands, and I've got no control over what they get bred to, if they get bred at all." He shrugged. "I do keep track of it, though. Wouldn't do to have someone claim a nag with a muddled pedigree is something I'm responsible for."

Now the sly glances around the table suggested he'd presented just the right level of agrarian simplicity. He decided not to elaborate on it and see what his neighbors said.

"I *heard,*" continued Declaine silkily, "that not more than a week ago, you were actually attending the birth of a horse yourself!"

Well, that got around fast. He was unsurprised. If Merrin, the Emperor, or both wanted the story spread around, it could have come into the Palace in the morning and been known to the entire Court by afternoon.

"Some things are best left to experts, and I am an expert," he drawled. "Especially when it's a Valdemar Gold."

The mention of the Golds awoke something else in the eyes of everyone around him: glints of avarice. Everyone wanted a Gold, apparently. He was just glad that the only ones he'd brought were in the Emperor's hands. Even if they were fake.

But besides the avarice, there were snickers hidden behind hands. He held his peace, sampled courses, and listened rather than talked. Best not to speak until spoken to, he reckoned.

The Prince across from him ate very little, and listened intently, his expression so closed Kordas could make out nothing of what he was thinking. The Duke, as his girth suggested, ate practically everything. The Count ate about as much as Kordas did. There was music. The air was gently perfumed; the jewels, gold, and silver glittered; the magelights were just bright enough and a pleasing color of pink. The conversation was muted in a way that suggested there was some sort of dampening effect in this room, so that the sound didn't become overwhelming. Kordas took note that virtually every Doll attending the humans had some sort of identifying feature about it. Some were subtle; small marks on the forehead, such has he had made on Star, Rose, and Clover, or actual faces drawn or painted on the heads. The faces . . . well, they were done well. He suspected there might be some subtle competition going on, with the masters of the Dolls hiring artists to do the work. Some of those faces were just a little too realistic for comfort. Some of the Dolls were ostentatious, displaying gold or silver jewelry as if the Doll was a merchant's display model. Some were ridiculous: wigs on their heads, and dresses, or coats and breeches, which made them look like gigantic versions of a child's toy. So he wasn't the only one who wanted to tell the Dolls apart.

All of them, however, sported the Imperial tabard. Evidently the Emperor wanted to make sure that people were aware at all times that the Dolls that served them belonged to the Emperor, not to them.

From time to time someone around him would address Kordas with some quip that was meant to highlight or confirm that he was, essentially, a bumped-up country Squire. Mostly he answered these in a way that confirmed that impression.

But when the Count, over the dessert course, asked sneeringly, "Just who was your father, Valdemar?" he decided it was time to break that impression a little.

"My father was Erik, Duke of Valdemar," he said evenly.

"His father was Werther, Duke of Valdemar. His father was Ugo, Duke of Valdemar. His father was Hrothgar, Duke of Valdemar. His father was Polmar, Duke of Valdemar. His father was Lokan, Duke of Valdemar." He continued on for more generations of Dukes of Valdemar, until the Count's eyes had glazed over, everyone within hearing range had been made aware that his lineage and title went back a very long time indeed, and he had cemented that *his* pedigree was every bit as good as any of theirs—and probably better than most, and certainly dated back to when the Emperor had merely been a High King. He finished with, "And Lerren, Duke of Valdemar, was made Duke by High King Sonat the First—for establishing the line of Chargers and horsing every one of the Conquering Knights of the Realm, I'm told, although that could just be family myth." And he laughed. "I did say it pays to know your pedigrees."

The Duke brayed with laughter, looking directly at the Count, and the Count flushed an angry red. *Hmm. Could be the Count's title is rather shiny and new.*

"So it does, Valdemar," said the Duke genially. "So it does."

The mage-lights in the enormous dining chamber dimmed and turned a pale green, which made everyone look as if they were slightly bilious and seemed to be the signal that it was time to leave the table. Kordas followed the Duke at a discreet distance, and discovered that they were all expected to mingle in an adjoining, equally large room, where there were more musicians and an open floor for dancing. Star stayed quietly at his elbow and said nothing as he found himself an out-of-the-way corner by an alcove that contained an extraordinarily realistic and extraordinarily bland statue of a heroic figure in full armor. Probably an Emperor. If not the current one, then at least one of his ancestors.

He was exhausted. This entire evening had been more of a drain on his emotional and mental resources than he could have imagined. He hoped that he could remain ignored for the rest of the night.

Fortunately, it appeared that there were things that were far more interesting right now than he was. The company was mixed, although most of the women sat along the walls. There was a pattern there, clusters of young women heavily supervised by a single older one. Probably sisters and a mother or aunt. Men would come and ask them to dance, and the older woman would either look pleased or stern—the young ones would go to dance regardless, but if the chaperone looked stern, they would return once a single dance was over.

But there was a more interesting game going on. Several women, young and not so young, stood, rather than sitting, by themselves. These ladies were dancing a very different sort of dance among clusters of men—young and not so young—who were competing for their attentions. Those who were not part of those clusters appeared to be very much engrossed in the little dramas being played out before them.

Kordas started when someone touched his elbow.

He turned to find himself looking into the eyes of the Prince who had sat across from him. "Pardon. Did I startle you, Valdemar?" the young man asked. The polite tone seemed genuine.

"A trifle, your Highness," he replied. "I was taking in the view, and engrossed in the music. My little Duchy is too small to have such gatherings every night. And we are rather too backwater as well. Our days begin early and end early, and our entertainments are generally simpler."

The Prince smiled thinly. "So it seems," he said in neutral tones. "I was wondering; was that story you told about mounting all the Knights of the Realm on Valdemar Chargers a true one?"

Careful. "It's family legend, Highness," he said. "I can't speak for how true it is. Although I could verify it if I had access to our records. We keep very careful records."

"Apparently, if you know the pedigree even of horses that have been bred when out of your hands." There didn't seem to be any irony in the Prince's statement. "I wonder, would it be possible to secure an entire year's—would you call it a 'crop'?—of Chargers at once?"

"This year's Chargers, no, I regret to say," he replied, trying to convey a genuine regret. "And the ones born this year won't be released for a while regardless. We hold them until they are four years old, and send them out fully trained, so that they are up to bearing the weight of a fully armored knight, and so that we know when they leave our hands they are battle ready. About half of our Chargers for this year have been sent out already, and most of the rest are spoken for. You could secure the current three-year-olds, however, to be delivered in a year."

The Prince smiled again, this time with satisfaction. "That would suit me perfectly well. Even the two-year-olds would do. We will speak later, Valdemar."

He bowed deeply, as was proper. "I am at your service, your Highness," he said, and the Prince nodded and slipped away.

What the hell was that about? Why would anyone want a full year's worth of Chargers?

Well . . . moot question. Because it wasn't going to happen. If all went well, by the time the snow fell, he and his and all of his horses would be long gone.

———————

"It is appropriate for you to leave now, if you choose, lord Duke," Star said in a quiet whisper, just as Kordas was debating whether or not to find out if *anything* available to drink on the table across the room was something other than intoxicating. The behavior of some of the people suggested this was unlikely. None of them were drunk—that would clearly be dangerous—but eyes were a little too bright, cheeks too flushed, laughter too loud, and behavior ventured on reckless. Duels were sparked at these damned things, and he didn't want to find himself on the receiving end of a challenge just because some idiot stumbled into him and decided to take offense.

"Lead the way, Star," he muttered, and followed the Doll as it threaded its way effortlessly along the wall, avoiding everything and everyone, in an intricate sort of dance that was surprisingly graceful. He wasn't the only one leaving, as he soon found when he was brought to a hallway, which in turn led into either that enormous entry hall full of Gates, or a room just like it. There were quite a few people heading for those Gates, and presumably to their apartments.

"Step up to a Gate, hold up your bracelet to the Gate, and say 'The Copper Apartment,'" Star murmured, stopping briefly to let him get ahead, so that the Doll could follow him as the other Dolls were following their masters. *Right. Don't look out of place,* he reminded himself, and picked a Gate no one seemed to be heading to.

"The Copper Apartment," he said, and stepped through, to find himself in that now-familiar antechamber. Beltran, who had been waiting for him there, sitting on one of those excruciatingly uncomfortable copper chairs, leapt to his feet, anxiety draining from his expression.

"How was it?" the Herald asked anxiously.

He *wanted* to say "appalling," but smiled and said, "Too much to eat, too much to drink, and no one wanting to talk about anything interesting. At least not until someone asked me about our herds. And then they really didn't seem interested."

He beckoned to Beltran to follow him, and led the way into his chamber, with the Doll following. A moment later, Rose and Clover entered, presumably in case they needed something that required more than two "hands."

The mage-lights were low, and the curtains to the sole window parted. Not yet ready to say anything, and not ready to fall on the bed just yet, he was drawn to the window.

It looked as if he was at least ten stories up, if not more. The window looked out on part of the Palace grounds; not the grand pavement and courtyard at the front, but instead over what he judged were probably the stables, kitchen-gardens, and the rest of the working part of the grounds. Clearly, this apartment was *not* one of the favored ones, which would over-look something much more aesthetically pleasing. He didn't mind, though, not at all. It was a little surprising to see that everything below was well lit, and there were still a few people coming and going, not only from the stables, which he some-what expected, but among the vegetables and herbs too. By far, though, there were more Dolls than humans.

"Are the kitchen staff Dolls too, Star?" he asked, without turning away from the view.

"Yes, my lord, aside from the chefs," Star said. "There are no longer any human servants here. Humans require food and sleep, and we do not. We have replaced every job that used to be filled by a human. There are only courtiers, officials of the Court, and sometimes their families here, and the Emperor's soldiers and guards."

He blinked at that. "When did this happen?" he asked. "And how?"

"About eight years ago," Star told him. Then the Doll paused, and he turned away from the window to look at it. It stood so still that for a moment he wondered if something had "broken" it.

"It is now safe to speak in candor," it said.

He blinked. "Wait. What?"

"It is now safe to speak in candor," repeated Star. "They have lost interest in you and are scrying someone else's chamber. There are only so many mages, after all, and they are human. Their time is limited. Their resources are limited. You are deemed to be uninteresting for the moment. They were hoping you would say something to Beltran, but instead you spoke to this one, and they deem anything said to a Doll to be unimport-ant. This one knows this, because the mage whose task was to scry you has moved on to another, and his servant-Doll has observed this. What one of us knows, all of us can know."

"Well . . . that's convenient," he said, a little dubiously. *A little too convenient?* "How do I know I can trust what you say?"

"Because, my lord Duke," Star said, in tones of infinite sadness, "Dolls cannot speak other than truth, and we always know truth when we hear it. We are implanted in these serviceable bodies, but they are burdens to us. A Doll is a prison."

Star paused to let that sink in, then said, "A Doll has no ability to communicate or move unless we, like this one did, submit to encasement within a Doll body. Failure to submit to the process results in the dissipation of the self. We refer to ourselves without names to distance ourselves from the painful memories of what we were."

Kordas had laced his fingers tight, and suddenly realized Star's explanation had made him clench them until they ached. "What are you inside, then?"

"I am a *vrondi.*"

He staggered back a little in shock. Because he knew exactly what a *vrondi* was. They were ubiquitous little Air Elementals, perfectly harmless . . . but how and why was this one bound up in a doll of canvas and wood?

Wait, wait, don't take anything here at face value, he reminded himself, and cautiously invoked mage-sight.

Sure enough. Under mage-sight, the two ethereal blue eyes of a *vrondi,* the only parts of one you usually ever saw, blinked at him out of the canvas face. There was absolutely no way to counterfeit that.

"How?" he managed to say, as Beltran looked from him to Rose and back again, thoroughly bewildered. *Poor Beltran. I'll have to explain all this to him in a moment.*

"The Emperor's mages were concerned about the dangers of Abyssal magic, and began looking for means to harness Elemental magic instead," said Rose. "By unhappy accident, a way was found to attract, catch, and contain us. After much more experimentation, the method was found of binding us to these bodies." The Doll pulled its tabard aside, and showed him a buttoned seam down the middle of its sexless, blank torso. It slowly unbuttoned that seam and pulled it slightly apart. Within the cavity revealed was a blue, faintly glowing, round object that looked a bit like a Spitter pellet, only larger. It buttoned itself back up again, and dropped the tabard back in place. "That is this one. That is where this one is confined. That is where . . . *I* am confined."

"Does it . . . hurt?" He couldn't imagine it *didn't* hurt. This was an Air Elemental; to be confined to something physical must be like—being drowned.

"It is uncomfortable," Star said. "But disobedience is excruciating."

He passed his hand over his eyes, wincing in sympathy. "Can I release you—no, wait, I can't, can I?"

"It would be exceedingly dangerous for you to attempt that, my Lord," said Star. "And I would likely just be caught and confined again. We cannot escape the Trap. It draws all *vrondi* to it, like a vortex. The only escape is dissipation . . . death."

Death? "Wait—what?" he said again. *"You can die?"* He had no idea that Elementals could die! This was . . . *horrid.*

"Yes, my Lord. If this body is abused badly enough, the vessel ruptures, and we die. I cannot explain it in a way that you would understand, but suppose that we are under great pressure, just as the air in a Spitter pellet is under great pressure. If the vessel is ruptured, we disintegrate like the shell of the pellet. And, by design, our prisons are made to be easily broken, whether by misfortune or intent."

"Oh gods," he groaned, and even Beltran understood enough to be appalled. "How often does that happen?"

"Often enough," Star stated sadly. "It is presumed that there is an endless number of us, and it is of no matter if some are destroyed."

"Of course it matters!" he snarled. "And there *isn't* an endless number of you, is there?"

"No, my Lord." Star fell silent.

"Give me a moment," he said, so filled with rage that it was very hard to think.

"My lord?" Beltran said quietly. "What's a *vrondi?*"

Thinking about how to explain Elemental magic to his Herald allowed him time to let his temper cool. "You know there are four—well, call them 'worlds,' right? We mages call them 'planes of existence.' Because as complicated as they are, the most plain way to make any sense of it all or chart it is to think of them as flat. They aren't flat, at all, but that's the easiest way to make sense of what we can perceive."

"I have read that, my Lord, yes. One of them is the world in which we live, and it interacts with the other three. But because the other three are different, we can't see the creatures that live there without specific effort, either on our part or theirs." Beltran scratched his head. "I can't say as I understand it, but my ma and pa taught me to believe in Heaven and Hell and I can't see those either, nor the ones that live there, so there's no reason why I shouldn't believe you when you tell me these things exist too."

"Right," he said, relieved that he wasn't going to have to undertake a *really* basic explanation. "The world we live in is the Material Plane. The others are the Abyssal Plane, where demons come from, the Elemental plane, and the Aetherial Plane, where the gods and their servants are."

Beltran opened his mouth, probably about to say something about "but demons come from Hell and the gods are in Heaven," when he realized that those were just different names for the same thing—or maybe Heaven and Hell were like districts on these other planes—and shut his mouth again. "Yes, my Lord. Go on."

"There are lots of different kinds of Elementals, not just Air, Earth, Fire, and Water. *Vrondi* are Air Elementals. Mostly—mostly we don't have much to do with each other. But *vrondi* have a very peculiar affinity for the truth, so some mages have learned how to get their help in being able to tell truth from falsehood. Very inexperienced or weak mages can call one or more and ask them to reveal the truth. They do that by surrounding a person and glowing blue. If the person lies, they stop glowing. If the person is telling the truth, they keep glowing."

"The truth is nourishment for us, my Lord," said Star. "That is why."

Huh. I had no idea.

"And a powerful mage can give them a sort of extra boost of energy, so they can actually *compel* the person the mage is questioning to tell the truth." He looked to Star for confirmation.

The Doll nodded. "It pleases us to do that. The truth is important, and the more truth in the world, the more *vrondi* there are."

He passed his hand over his eyes again and said bitterly, "Then this place must be like swimming in a sewer for you. Gods."

Star answered, "The sewers serve a noble purpose. And, while the amount of deceit here is profound, there is also truth in abundance. Torturers are very sincere in their desire to harm."

"But why *vrondi?*" he asked, almost desperately. "Surely there were some other Elementals they could have put in the Dolls—"

"We are imprisoned by an application of the same process by which the pellets are made, my Lord," said Star. "As to why it was *vrondi* they chose, and not another Elemental, this one cannot say. Perhaps the others are too powerful to confine. Perhaps the process would not work on them. This one is not a mage, and no mages have ever confided the reason to a *vrondi.*"

"I can surmise why," Beltran offered. "A *vrondi* cannot lie, which would make you ideal servants. None of you could be assassins, spies, traitors, or agents."

Star nodded. "We do not kill. We do not even harm if we can help it. We cannot lie, but we can choose how to phrase things. We can choose to perform only the minimum commanded of us, but not to refuse entirely. And there is a trick that our jailors are unaware of: even if I, as an individual, am aware of something from another of my kind, I can still say 'I do not know,' because knowledge gained from another is technically hearsay. It is by that trick we can live by the truth yet not betray. My truth is that I make my decisions based upon knowledge from others, but that knowledge may be sourced from another's misunderstanding. Thus, compelled by truth, that knowledge does not qualify as a complete truth. Just a possibility or probability."

Beltran said slowly, "That wouldn't show up as a lie, because it is an interpretation, but—yes. That's clever. So you wound up dismissed as useful spies for intrigues."

"Just so. And virtually everyone who comes to this Court attempts it. When they are frustrated by it, we tell them, 'The core of our control states that we must obey, above all others, who wears the Imperial Ring, the Imperial Carcanet, and the Wolf Crown.'"

"That makes sense. An order in perpetuity. Even if an Emperor dies, you are kept loyal to who follows. Tell some power- or deceit-centered courtier that core rule, and they'll back away fast, for fear of what might be reported by you as suspicious."

"It is as you say."

"And the mages don't know that you can share your experiences with each other?" asked Kordas, beginning to pace. His heartbeat thumped in his ears. "Why would you—all of you, I assume—entrust us with this knowledge?"

Clover spoke for the first time. "We are what you call 'bored' for much of the time, as Dolls. When someone new arrives, we take their measure, discuss it between as many of us as may be interested, and we rate you. No offense is intended by that."

"No, it makes sense," Kordas replied. "You live or die by truth, and so you want to know who you can trust." A new understanding of an old phrase occurred to him. "You want to know who is true."

All three Dolls replied in unison, "It is as you say."

Kordas pushed further. "Can you read people's pasts? Forgive their mistakes, their guilt?"

Star replied, "We do not phrase it as forgiveness, but we can tell whether someone is flawed in any untrustworthy ways. And how much. Sir." Star bent to help Kordas slip off his new boots. "If you mean, if I may, Sir, that you were judged by us and found worthy of trust, that is true. Despite the guilt, anger, and terror you feel, and the incongruent feelings you have about your maneuvering in the Great Game, your reasons are understood and also found to be true. Feelings of fact and worth can be true even if they contradict each other. Humans, especially, are able to function with scores of truths in conflict inside of their minds. Including the truth that there are things you may never understand and that you must accept *that* as a truth to survive by."

Kordas was struck silent. Star removed the new boots and set them aside while Kordas rocked back against the wall, trying to process that. *I've never been—read like that before. They must have done that with everyone in the Court, and the—they must be sick from what they've seen, and then I come along, and I've made a lot of mistakes and—things I haven't ever forgiven myself for—and the Elementals just— they just see what I'm made of, they judge—*

"But if you've taken the place of the servants and staff here—where did the people go?" asked Beltran, utterly oblivious of where his lord's mind was going. Which was just as well, really.

"Specialists and chefs remain." Star paused a moment, as if listening to a distant voice. "The Master of Records says with few exceptions, the humans and all pets were sent to the war front. Dolls are impractical in any use but backline support. Scribes, pages, any other male human that could wield a weapon, were conscripted to the Imperial forces as combatants. The females were conscripted as menials or entertainment. The pets have likely all been eaten by now."

Beltran looked pale. Kordas rubbed at the Ducal Crest, holding his breath.

We have to get away from the Empire before it's our turn. But that would still leave the Dolls, the—vrondi *to, inevitably, be*—

An impulse arose in him. A stupid impulse. Possibly a suicidal impulse. A generous impulse to be sure, but that didn't make it less stupid.

On the other hand—if he didn't act on it, he wouldn't be worthy of the name of Valdemar.

"Star," he said, looking directly into the creature's blue, unwinking eyes. "My people and I are in the process of escaping from this part of the world, and intend to travel far beyond the reach of the Emperor. Would you and the rest of the Dolls like to come with us, if I can manage it? I can't promise it will happen, but I can promise that I will die trying, if need be. My people are largely innocents, and they could be—better off with you than with me."

Star *did* freeze; went so rigid that only now was Kordas aware that until this moment it actually *had* been making minute movements, probably continuously adjusting its weight and balance. He was not sure whether he had insulted it, whether or not it believed him, whether it might be compelled to report what he had just said to its masters. He held his breath, waiting for the answer—

—or a troupe of the Emperor's guards to burst in.

But finally, Star spoke, in tones of such mingled hope and anguish that his heart almost broke.

"Oh *yes!*" Star cried softly. *"Please."*

10

With Kordas gone, implementing the Plan had taken on more urgency. Delia didn't know why Isla wasn't absolutely frantic with worry over the fact that he'd been "invited" to the Imperial Capital, but—

Well, maybe she is. She's just really good at hiding it. She and Kordas must have been working on the Plan for half of their lives, after all, and they were all too well aware that at any moment the Emperor's people could step in and do something that could threaten it. The Empire had killed the older brother she had never known. Kordas had spent five years as a "foster" in the Imperial Palace. And it occurred to her in that moment that she had led an *incredibly* sheltered life. She'd never been a hostage to the Emperor. She'd never had to deal with politics of any sort, much less Imperial politics. In fact, the only time the reality of the Empire had intruded on her life had been when the Emperor gave her home away at the time of her father's death.

She had a lot to think about the morning that Kordas left,

but most of it so overwhelmed her with worry and even fear that she sought refuge in the company of her little foal, able for a little while to shove all that concern aside in the simple pleasure of working with her charge.

As she carefully schooled little Daystar in the manners that a horse meant to grow into a companion and friend should have, the presence of the horses around her felt oddly comforting. And Arial seemed to approve of both the schooling and Delia's presence.

Of course, it didn't hurt that Delia always brought a treat for the mare; a carrot, an apple, a piece of sweet bread. She had cleared this beforehand with Grim, of course. Everything to do with the horses needed to be cleared with Grim first.

Today, they were out in the paddock. Daystar had taken to the halter surprisingly well, and was learning to answer to gentle, persistent pressure on it. Of course, the fact that when the foal did what Delia asked her to she was immediately rewarded with a soft brushing or scratch to her neck certainly helped with that.

It was in the paddock that Isla found her, just as she was thinking of her sister, wondering if Isla had any way of communicating with her husband, and when she looked up to see Isla at the fence, she wondered if Isla's Mindspeaking ability had alerted her to the fact that Delia had Isla on her mind.

"Are you done with your little beauty for this morning?" Isla called, resting her right hand on the top of the paddock fence. "I could use your help."

"I am," she said, and took the halter off Daystar. An older horse could wear a halter day and night to make it easier to catch them, but a foal this young could not be trusted not to stick her silly nose where it didn't belong, get a halter-strap caught on something, and—

Well, at the least, she'd panic and then be afraid of the halter. At the worst she could break a leg or strangle herself.

Daystar trotted—it was more like a bounce—a few lengths

away, then frisked, kicked, and bounded over to play with some of the other foals.

I wish I was a foal. Their lives are full of nothing but joy.

Delia patted Arial, then joined her sister, climbing over the fence.

"I need you to start taking messages to our people and bringing their concerns back to the manor, as Kordas has done," Isla said. "I can't spare the time. First of all, they need to know he's been called to the Capital and we don't know when he'll be back, and second, we like to keep on top of what our people need at all times. So you'll have to be his surrogate. I'll loan you my mare Sundrop. She knows you, and everyone will recognize your authority if you are mounted on a Valdemar Gold."

Delia easily read between the lines of this bland statement. She was to tell the people that Kordas trusted that the first Gate had been established, and it was time to start moving people through it.

The thought actually made her insides feel weak for a moment. This wasn't just a fantasy, or a "maybe someday." It was happening, and not even (or perhaps especially) was Kordas's absence going to slow or stop it. In fact, it might just make things more urgent.

"Now?" she asked. Isla nodded.

"I need you to ride out to Squire Lesley and Count Endicrag today. I've gotten one of the scribes to copy a map for you to follow, and they're the nearest. Come snatch some luncheon while Grim has Sundrop saddled for you."

She blinked her eyes in surprise. Count Endicrag? That made sense. He was one of the eight ranking landholders in Valdemar. But Squire Lesley?

"The pig farmer?" she said incredulously.

"He's anything but *just* a pig farmer," her sister replied in a note of gentle rebuke. "He serves as the local magistrate. He knows *everyone* in his corner of Valdemar, and everyone knows him. Lord Merrin might think he is the one in charge of those lands, but everyone in that County looks first to Lesley for guidance, because Merrin knows nothing about them, and cares less. Kordas knows this, and knows that asking Merrin about things will yield no useful information, but Lesley will know all the blessings and ills, and likely how to fix the latter."

Delia felt her cheeks growing hot with embarrassment. "I'll go get that lunch at the kitchen," she said meekly, and followed her sister back to the manor.

But Isla took her by the elbow and steered her into an empty little room, almost an ornamental nook, just off the corridor on the way to the kitchen, and closed the door. "We don't have much time, so listen and don't ask questions," she said. "This room is warded completely, but it's small enough that it's not likely anyone spying on us has noticed. Always assume you are being scryed. If you need to tell me something, do it here, or in the cellars. We don't ward our apartment, because we assume that's the *first* place a mage would try to eavesdrop. There are a couple more safe places, and I'll show them to you later. Now, I want you to *tell* Lesley and Endicrag, and covertly pass them these notes." She gave a couple pieces of folded parchment to Delia, who tucked them into a pocket. "It doesn't matter which you give to whom; they are identical. They'll probably take you somewhere safe to read them, then tell you what they want me to know. You may be bringing back someone from Lord Endicrag's manor."

She opened the door again and gave Delia a push to send her out of it. They hadn't been in there but a few moments. Was *this* how Isla and Kordas lived all the time?

Probably. And I never noticed it. I guess I just assumed when they were a little late, they'd been loitering over something.

They went on to the kitchen, where Delia gulped down a

hasty lunch, and Isla conferred with the Head Cook. Isla left before Delia had finished, and Delia hurried back to the stable.

One of the stablehands had Sundrop saddled and ready for her, and passed her a map. She vaguely knew where Squire Lesley's home was, but the map confirmed that it wouldn't be hard to find.

She wanted to gallop Sundrop there, but was afraid that would look as if she had been sent on an errand more urgent than its outward appearance. But then she thought again, and decided to put Sundrop into a canter for at least a little bit. It was a gorgeous day, sunny and warm, and what young lady with any spirit at all, given a Valdemar Gold to ride, *wouldn't* urge her mount into a run?

So she did; Sundrop was perfectly willing to oblige, and she allowed herself a moment of pure pleasure in the speed and the wind in her hair. Her pony had *never* been able to run like *this!*

Soon enough, she found herself on the little lane that the map told her led to Squire Lesley's country manor, and when she saw it, she felt a pang of nostalgia and even some grief, because it was a miniature version of her old home. Not as many stories, and not as broad, but it was of the same weathered stone that fit into the landscape, and just as surrounded by beautiful trees and flowering bushes and a low stone wall with a gatehouse. Even the scent of the air was familiar, old-fashioned roses and sweetbush, cut grass and a hint of cypress.

Old-fashioned. When we've left Valdemar, will that term even make sense any more? We might never see these flowers and birds again, and have only memories of them. We don't even know if we'll be safe there. Even enjoying a day might fade into a memory. We might live in fear of disease, or monsters, or—or just loneliness. The Empire may be awful for us, but even so it gives a sense of being part *of something. We*

could end up somewhere that will offer even less mercy. Noth-
ing to fall back upon, no resources or Healing. What will that
do to us? Even now, I'm in safe enough surroundings, with
beauty all around, and the thought scares me. How much
harder will bravery be when we're actually there? Surrounded
by that much unknown?

This was not the first time she'd had similar thoughts. How
would this strike those for whom it would be sudden news?

In a way, the Empire has done us a favor in that regard. It
isn't outright slavery—here in Valdemar, at least, thank gods
big and little—but the way the Empire has taught them all,
every soul is obedient to those above them in rank, and "be-
longs" to them, in the sense that a horse is part of a herd, a
leader guides the herd, and someone commands the leader. A
farmer is part of the farm, not a person who works a farm.
Bless them, the commoners will have less conflict about leav-
ing, if their Lords tell them to. And some—well, some will have
intense trouble with the fact they'll be given a choice. But
Kordas has been adamant that everyone will have that choice,
to go or to stay, even if it makes some Valdemarans just shud-
der in anxiety. Some of them, I know, won't want that choice.

Delia rode up to the front door, and before she had gotten
there, a servant stepped out of the gatehouse and waved her
hat.

"Lady Isla Valdemar's sister Fidelia, sent by Lady Isla, to
see Squire Lesley," she said, before the servant could ask her
name or her business.

"Is it urgent, my lady?" the servant asked. Mindful of the
fact that she might be being scryed, she shook her head.

"Not urgent, but important," she answered.

"Very good, my lady. The Squire is at luncheon, but I am
sure he will want to see you. If you will wait here a moment,
I will inform him." At her nod, the servant stepped into the
manor and closed the door behind her.

She returned long before Delia expected, with a young

servant lad. "If you will allow me to take your horse, the Squire wishes you to come to him," he said.

She dismounted, handed off the reins, and followed the boy inside.

Another way our dear Valdemar is unlike the Empire proper. Out here, nobody is as strict about what a man's or woman's duties are. Parts of the Empire hold that entire categories of behavior are illegal for those of a particular gender: who can speak first, who can be allowed to learn, who can be loved by whom. Even who is allowed to think of loving whom, no matter what a soul's heart, mind, or body wants; if those in power can control love, they can control anything. So they do.

Instead of taking her to the Great Hall as she had expected, the boy led her through several linked rooms to what looked like the Squire's study or office. The Squire was absently eating bread and cheese while attending to some sort of paperwork, but looked up at their footfalls. He stood, putting his half-eaten luncheon aside on a book.

"Lady Fidelia!" he said. "A pleasure! How can I serve your sister?"

The Squire was every inch the country gentleman, slightly overweight, balding, and dressed in clothing at least one generation out of date, which might even have been handed down to him from his own father: moleskin trews tucked into well-worn boots, a short brocade waistcoat buttoned over a slight belly, a shorter version of a coat than was currently popular that matched the trews. He looked at the boy and nodded, and the lad vanished.

"Well," she said, "I have some unexpected news. Kordas has been called to the Capital along with his tribute-horses, and we don't know when to expect him back. Lady Isla will be in charge of the Duchy, and I'm to serve as her messenger."

"Well, this is unexpected. Please, sit down," he replied, brows wrinkling as he gestured at the chair on the other side of the desk. She took it, and he sat back down again. "I suppose being recalled was inevitable. He hasn't been back since his father died, gods keep him, and the Emperor does like to lay eyes on his nobles from time to time. When did this happen?"

"This morning," she said. "It was quite unexpected, indeed. And Lord Merrin went with him."

"Did he, now. Hmm. Have you eaten? Shall I have some luncheon brought? Tea?"

She was about to decline when she realized that accepting something from his hand would allow her to pass her note without a watcher being aware of the fact.

"Yes, please," she said. "Tea would be lovely."

"If you care for lenanberry, that's what I'm having," he said, and she thought he looked at her very keenly.

"One of my favorites," she lied, and waited as he rang for another thick pottery mug to be brought. He poured a mug-full for her and handed it to her across the desk. When she accepted it, the note was in her hand and she slipped it into his.

He made it vanish as if he was a conjurer.

Then he pressed her for details of the morning's departure— how had Kordas gotten the news? How many people did Merrin have with him? All the while, sipping his own tea, and finishing his luncheon.

"Well," he said, when the food was gone. "I'm glad you came to tell me. I'll just skip making my reports to that worthless steward of Merrin's and send them directly to Lady Isla. Care to come see the Empress?"

For a moment she couldn't imagine what on earth he was talking about. The Empress? What was the Emperor's wife doing *here?* And why? And then she remembered that the Empress was Squire Lesley's Duchy-wide famous pig.

She still couldn't imagine why he'd take her to see a pig, but then she remembered what Isla had said, that if they had anything important to tell her, Lesley and Count Endicrag would take her somewhere it was safe to talk.

"I'd be honored," she said, and put down the mug of untasted tea as she stood up.

He stood too. "Come along, then. She's got piglets. Do you like piglets?"

Properly roasted . . . she thought, and stifled a slightly hysterical laugh. "I would love to see her piglets," she said instead, and he came around to her side of the desk and offered her his arm, as if he was escorting her to a ball.

They strolled through the manor, out the back into the kitchen garden, and from there down a path that ended at a small stone building about the size of a room, surrounded by a stone wall. After a moment, she realized this was a pigsty. A truly palatial pigsty. And although she could not see the pigs in it, she soon was able to read the name carved above the door.

The Empress.

Sure enough, when Lesley led her to the wall, which was at exactly a comfortable height to rest her arms on and lean against, there was the sow in all her immaculate glory, large and pink and very, very clean. The sty smelled of nothing worse than clean straw. And the piglets were surprisingly cute, nosing around in the straw in imitation of their mother, although they surely weren't old enough to want anything other than milk.

"Handy thing, this," said the Squire. "You'll find a couple of places in Valdemar like this. Lovely little circles of stone, absolutely dead to scrying. Anyone who tries can *see* what's here, but won't be able to hear a bloody damned thing. Now, young lady, what in the seven Hells is going on? Are we putting off the Plan?"

"Nothing of the sort," she assured him. "If anything, it might be going faster than we thought. Ivar Endicrag has been to the site, and found a lake perfect for our purposes in every possible way and more."

"Wait a moment, let me read the note," he said, pulling it

out of his waistband and unfolding it. He perused it for a very long time, and smiled slightly.

Then instead of talking to her, he pulled something else out of a pocket, and wrapped the note tightly around it. She got a glimpse of cheese before he leaned over the wall, held it out, and made a "pshpshpshing" sound at the sow.

The Empress ambled over, sniffed his offering, and daintily accepted it, devouring paper, cheese, and all.

"I don't suppose you've been told the Plan?" he said.

She shook her head. "Not in full, but I'm told none of us have. All that I know is that Kordas wants to get as many people as he can as far away from the Empire as possible. And that this is something that goes all the way back, perhaps to his grandfather's time, and certainly to his father's."

Lesley nodded. "It does, and my folk have been in on it from the beginning. We're evacuating by barge, because barges can carry more than wagons and make better shelters. That is why we needed a place where we could put a water-Gate down. First we needed to find a good spot. Then we needed to get someone across to explore and find us a body of water. After that comes the Foothold Gate, and then it's up to the mages to do whatever it is they do to establish a proper water-Gate on the shore, and maybe another for foot traffic. Once they do that, Valdemar Manor will start transporting barges full of supplies and people to establish a camp across. This will take a tremendous amount of supplies, far more than people can bring for themselves. Depending on how many people we can evacuate, they'll have to spread themselves out so we don't overwhelm the area with people and animals and all the shit they produce." He raised an eyebrow. "I mean that literally. Kordas's father was the first one to see the sanitation problem and allow for it. 'If you're to manage a civilized people, start with the sewage,' he told us all early on. As a pig farmer, I'm acutely aware of such a problem. Fortunately, shit itself is a valuable resource when it comes to crops, so the challenge isn't just getting rid of it, but managing it. We'll need to establish a territory at least as big as this Duchy if we are going to prosper."

"As big as this Duchy?" she said, shocked. "But—that looked like it was all wilderness! And—how?"

"It might look that way, but that doesn't mean there aren't people there already. We'll have to deal with that as we go along. It might be easier if there *are* people and we can negotiate with them to mutual satisfaction. After all, we do have plenty of people who are from all manner of crafts and so on." He shrugged. "If not, there are two big things. We'll need to get as far as we can from the Gate we put up, simply because whatever we did, the Emperor's mages might be able to follow. And because our—call 'em sanitary facilities—are going to be crude at best, we'll need to spread ourselves out. If we poison our water, we might as well slit our own throats and get it over with, otherwise it'll be a miserable lingering death for about half of us, if not more. As to *how,* Kordas, and I suppose Isla, have that all mapped out. All I know is my part: my people, my kin, and my pigs."

"It seems impossible," she faltered.

He shrugged again. "The Emperor's Army can do it. He can put three legions in the same place without wrecking it. We reckon to have about five thousand less than that, if we can get everyone out. We just have to allow for animals as well as people, but again, the Emperor's Army has horses, mules, and a fair number of food animals with it, otherwise the supply problems would be endless."

Her head swam with all of that, and she was just glad she wasn't the one who had to try to make all of this work.

"Drop by drop, Lady Fidelia. To the best of my knowledge, all of us landholders in the Duchy implemented roving teams of specialists to look after our lands; unknown to them, that was to prepare them for the fast work needed at the Foothold. Everyone will know his part, and if each of us faithfully *does* his part, it'll work." He patted her on the shoulder, a level of familiarity that could have been a crime in other regions of the Empire. "Have faith. Now, we've probably lingered here long enough. Do you have another message to deliver?"

She nodded.

"Then if you're to get back safe by nightfall, we'd better move on."

They walked back to the manor; the gatekeeper had tied Sundrop up in the shade near the gatehouse and given her water. The Squire gave Delia a kind farewell, sketched a salute, and went back into his home. She mounted into the saddle without aid and took out her map.

Count Endicrag's manor was much further from here than this place had been from the Valdemar manor. Lesley was right. She had a long way to go.

Lord Gerther Endicrag was the opposite of the Squire: lean, wiry, and very like a much older version of his son Ivar. Delia was in no position to tell if his garments were in the current fashion or not, but they were certainly as stylish as Kordas's were, and at least as new.

The manor was like her old home, but in a different style. Newer, perhaps. It was not one of those sugar-sculpture creations.

She was met at his gatehouse and escorted to his door. There was already a footman at the door, who escorted her to the Count as Sundrop was taken away to the stable. When the footman led her inside, she discovered that unlike her old home and the Squire's place, this manor was modeled on the same pattern as the mage-built edifices, in that it had corridors and hallways that led to rooms, not rooms opening into other rooms, which opened into still more rooms. While the latter might be a more efficient use of space, there was no doubt that it was more maze-like, and gave one very little privacy.

She was taken to a small corner room lined with curio shelves and looking out over a pleasant ornamental garden. Not only were there windows open to the garden, there was a door as well. This was clearly not an office. And the Count was not alone.

With him was a lady who was about the same age, with short-cropped graying hair, whose features were so like his that she immediately revised her idea that this was his wife. He confirmed this by introducing her to "my cousin Alberdina, a Healer with as wandering a foot as my son Ivar."

They all settled down into three chairs beside the cold hearth; the Count ordered wine and invited Delia to explain why she was there.

Keeping to her script, she told him how Kordas had been summoned to the Imperial Capital with no notice and for an indefinite length of time, and that she was to be the messenger between him and Lady Isla.

He pursed his lips, but said nothing immediately. Alberdina, however, was not shy about giving her opinion.

"How tiresome," she said. "I wanted permission to test his people for Healing ability. I don't suppose Lady Isla will cooperate?"

"I don't see any reason why she shouldn't," Delia hastened to tell her.

"Well, not every Lady is pleased when her favorite gardener or some other useful servant turns out to be able to Heal, and I snatch them up from under her nose to train them," Alberdina said.

"You can do that?" Delia looked at her, perplexed.

"Imperial Law. Goes back to when the Wolf King was a pup." She laughed heartily. "Old bastard fancied the idea of having a Healer at hand to tend even his hangnails. Not a bad law, either."

"I don't think Lady Isla will object," Delia replied firmly.

The Count nodded. "Told you so, cousin. Our Duchess is very much on the practical side."

Then the Count asked a lot of very trite and boring questions, until Delia wondered if she'd been sent to the right place. It went on for so long she was about to find some excuse to leave, when a little mage-light that had been burning on a small table between the Count and his cousin turned from red to white. She might not even have noticed it, had the Count not suddenly relaxed and held out his hand.

"It's safe to speak now," he said. "And I assume you have a message for me?"

With relief, she handed over her bit of parchment. The Count read it, then handed it to Alberdina, who in turn read it and handed it back to Delia.

"Give that back to Lady Isla. She'll know what to do with it," the Count said. "I'm not a mage myself. I don't know how to destroy it in such a way that another mage can't find out what was on it."

"Squire Lesley fed his to his pig," she offered, and the Count and his cousin laughed.

"Practical as ever, is Lesley. All right, we're ready. Ivar is yours now, and I'll start readying others to follow. Supplies as well, of course."

"I'll be coming back with you, on the excuse that I'm testing Healers. In fact, I'll go over as soon as you get the permanent Gate up. You'll need a Healer over there, and I'm very much looking forward to seeing a new land." She rubbed her hands together in satisfaction. Delia was fascinated. "Oh, you're surprised? I'm all packed up with everything I can't live without. We've taught just about everybody in our lands to have a jump-bag or two, stuffed with everything vital to them, in case of fire. Without them knowing it, we were training them for the Plan. All I need to do at the moment is steal a couple of Gerther's mules, and we're off."

"Gerther is happy to give them to you. Shall we go do that, while the light is still clear?" the Count suggested. Since by this time Delia was eager to get back and find out if Isla had heard anything from Kordas, she all but leapt to her feet.

The ride back was rather more fun, if a bit slower, than the ride out. The mules set their own pace, and there was absolutely no point in trying to make them go faster. They were mules, after all.

Alberdina had been almost as many places as Ivar, though never outside of Imperial lands, and was full of stories. Stories that were much different than Ivar's, of course; she was a Healer, not an explorer. Her stories were about people, rather than places.

"But I've never been near the Capital and I never wanted to be," she finished, as they came within sight of the Valdemar manor. "That place eats up Healers and spits them out sick and exhausted, and it takes them a year or more to recover, during which they are useless."

Delia cast her a warning glance, but it was clear that Alberdina was not concerned with hiding her opinion of the Capital in any way. "The place is unhealthy, and we all think it has to do with the magic. Whether it's just too many spells tangling up with one another, or the wrong kind of magic, who can say? Only another mage, and they aren't talking. Or maybe it's all the bad temper there. Everyone silently at everyone else's throat. We're sensitive to that; can't be a Healer without also being an Empath. Fortunately for me, no one there wants a loud-mouthed female Healer who won't keep her opinions to herself."

"It sounds to me as if you and my sister will get along like two sister-mares in a herd," Delia said, smiling a little.

"Well, we're probably both lead-mares, so that's just fine," the Healer proclaimed, and raised her head and sniffed the air. "Is that chicken I smell?"

"Your nose must be phenomenal!" Delia exclaimed. "It probably is. We have country-supper, which is soup and things for our evening meal. Our cook makes an amazing chicken soup."

"It's another reason why I won't go near the Capital," the Healer said. "The stink. 'The City of Smoke and Hate,' I call it. And chicken soup? I'd have *walked* here for a good chicken soup." She put her heels to her mule, who, seeing and scenting a stable nearby, this time willingly picked up his pace, as did the two carrying her luggage and gear.

They arrived exactly when supper was served, which gave them just time to wash up before joining the rest. She and Ivar enlivened the entire High Table with stories, and the entire room eavesdropped without shame. *If there was ever a great distraction and an utter boredom for a spy, this is it,* Delia thought, and she was very, very sure that this was exactly what Alberdina and Ivar intended. A mage scrying would have been asleep before they all packed up, and Isla gathered up the four of them with her eyes and indicated they were to follow.

They did, and Hakkon came along.

She had expected them to go down to the cellars, but they went to the common room of the Circle's Tower. There were more mages there tonight—none of them as old or as eccentric as the Circle, but there were a great many crammed into the usually capacious space.

The mage-lights around the room were a peculiar hue, one that Delia had never seen before. A sort of pale purple. She settled on the floor—most of the seating here was either on stools or on the floor, and she didn't want to take an actual seat from someone who physically could not sit on the floor— out of the way of the people she suspected were actually important enough to speak.

But not before she passed the note back to Isla, who took it, nodded, and—it ignited in her hand, going up in a sudden burst of blue flame.

When everyone had settled, and there was no one coming in the door anymore, Ponu cleared his throat and the muttering died away to nothing.

"Scryers will see the six of us gambling," he said. "So everyone can speak freely. We have a big job ahead of us, and we need to figure out how to do it without anyone even guessing what we're up to. Tomorrow down in the cavern, every mage in this place is going to help build the water-Gate and the land-Gate. The first, obviously, will be for barges, and the second for foot traffic. We're having bedding brought down there, because when we're done, most of you will be about to pass out."

There were groans.

"Quit your bitching," said Sai. "We're also cracking open the best wine in the Valdemar cellars and drinking it afterward. Wine doesn't take Gating well, so we might as well drink it now."

The groans died away.

"I've already crafted the four pillars," said Jonaton. "As big as I could manage, and I think we'll be able to pass more than one barge or person at a time. There might be a rush on the Gates at the last minute, so—" he shrugged.

"Once the pillars are across the Foothold Gate, that's the easy part. Jonaton is going to activate and attune them. I don't envy him that." For once, Ponu gave Jonaton a nod of respect. "Alberdina, we'll need you on the other side for that, because he's going to be flatter than a sheet of paper and about as much use after. Gates aren't meant to be attuned by one person, but these are *pulling* Gates, and that means only one person can attune them."

"I can do that," the Healer said. "I have some ideas that might make it easier on him."

"Once they're attuned and they have the right resonance, anyone with the right talisman can use any other Gate in the entire Duchy to get there. And that's the best plan; ideally, we want to use common, short-journey Gates that don't need Keepers, but we don't want to keep using the same Gates either. And we want to make it possible for people to travel short physical distances to the Gates rather than long ones. Is everything clear so far?"

Murmurs of agreement.

"All right. The last thing is the talismans. You will all know the resonance. You all know how to make them. We're going to need a lot of them, but we plan on reusing them by sending a couple of you across to the destination, where you can temporarily neuter them and send them back in bunches."

"How do you neuter a talisman?" someone asked.

"Carry it in a mule's nutsack!" Ceri yelled out, and Sai smacked him, while everyone else laughed.

"Sorry, sorry," Ceri snickered. "I meant to say, carry them in Sai's nutsack."

Ponu chucked a buttered roll at Ceri. "We have a status board in the workroom below and you know your code terms. Remember, the real trick now is to work hard, work fast, but act bored. Keep rain covers over everything coming in and out. Anything new, Jonaton?"

Jonaton reiterated, "Behave like nothing unusual is going on. I'm going through the Foothold Gate within the next few days to check some things from the other side, too, if Alberdina can keep me steady enough. I have some ideas. And don't eat or drink anything from the Foothold side until the teams mark them as safe. Not even any field cooking until the tests are done. That means you'll be sent home-cooked meals for a while."

There was a collective sigh of relief. "That's—much better than I thought," said someone Delia couldn't see.

Ponu snorted. "This Plan has been decades in the making. If we didn't think of everything by now, it's because whatever is coming is something we can't anticipate with all the information we have. All right. This phase is going to happen within the week. Are you all ready?"

"I'll never be *ready,*" someone finally said, breaking the silence. "But I'll be able."

Ponu cackled. "That's what I want to hear. All right, you layabouts. This is where you pay for your years of living high on the hog and never being asked to do a lick of work. Now get out of here!"

And, to Delia's surprise—the mages cheered.

Kordas's bed was comfortable, which was not a given, seeing as it was the Capital. He awoke at his usual hour—which, he suspected, was much earlier than most people living here could tolerate. He was going to leap up out of bed, get dressed, and then—

But then he remembered his new wardrobe and how impossible it was going to be to get into it unaided. With a sigh, he got out of bed and pulled the copper chain beside it.

Star entered the room immediately. "How may this one aid you, my Lord?" it asked.

"A bath and breakfast," he said. "Or maybe the reverse order?"

"This one will serve breakfast in bed, as all the Great Ones take it," Star said, and he thought that he registered a hint of reproach in its voice, as if he had offended it merely by suggesting that he take his meal any other way.

He sighed and got back into bed. Eating in bed had never appealed to him. Too much chance of crumbs or a spill that would require that the servants take the bedclothes apart and clean them ahead of the weekly schedule. But . . . people in the Capital didn't have human servants anymore, now did they? And no one cared if the Dolls were inconvenienced. "What sort of breakfast is there?" he asked.

"Whatever my Lord wishes," Star replied. "The kitchens will make it."

"Bread, fruit, butter. Are there egg pies? A small one of those if there are. If there aren't, just cooked eggs, three of them. Ham, cheese, and a bit of white or black sausage if you have it. Beans. Tea, I don't care what kind."

Star froze again for just a moment. He was beginning to realize this meant he had said something it didn't expect, or perhaps it was speaking to other Dolls. Maybe the ones in the kitchen? It came to life again. "That is not the usual amount of food, my Lord," it said carefully.

"I'm apparently awake much earlier than anyone else," he pointed out. "If I just nibble a pastry and drink a glass of wine I'll be faint by lunchtime. Is anyone going to want me this morning? What about this afternoon?"

"No one presents themselves in public before luncheon," Star told him. "This afternoon you will be expected to appear in the Great Hall with the rest of the Court, whether or not you are called upon."

Because of course I will. The Emperor needs to remind us daily that we serve him, not the other way around.

"Your breakfast has arrived, my Lord," Star said, interrupting his thoughts. "As has Beltran's." It left the room and returned with a heavily laden tray.

If he had not been so hungry—and why that would be he had no idea after that huge dinner, but maybe all the headwork he was doing to maneuver around in the intricate Court dance had used up all the energy from dinner—he would never have considered eating that much food. When the Doll put the copper (of course) tray down across his legs, it was so laden that if it had not had its own set of supports, it would have been uncomfortable. There was an entire pot of tea, a delicate cup to drink it out of, a tart-sized egg pie *and* three boiled eggs, a slice of ham, a chunk of yellow cheese, slices of black *and* white pudding, a dish of white beans with butter atop them, a hand-sized loaf of bread, a dish of butter, and a sliced apple. He took his time eating, pondering what he should do with the day. And then it occurred to him; if there were no more human servants, what had become of the child-hostages?

"Can I see where the hostages are now?" he asked Star, who simply waited for his next order, standing beside the bed. He supposed that if he had asked the Doll to cut up his food for him and feed him, it would have done so.

It went still, then replied, "There seems to be no reason why my Lord cannot."

"Then after my bath and I get dressed, I'd like to," he declared, and for the benefit of whoever might be scrying him, added, "I had good memories of that time and the kindness of the Emperor."

The Doll winced, just a little, probably at the blatant lie. But it did not call him out, and he was certain it did not report the lie to whatever it was reporting to. "Then this will be so," it said. "Will Beltran be coming?"

"I think that's a good idea," he said. "Now, what about luncheon? Does the Court eat together?"

"Yes and no," Star told him. "There is the option to be served in the Grand Dining Hall, but no one takes it amiss if one desires to eat in the privacy of one's apartments."

What in the seven hells do these people do with their lives? he wondered. Then something occurred to him. "What does Merrin do?"

"He generally is served in the Grand Dining Hall," said the Doll.

"Can I ask to be seated with him?"

"One can ask to be seated with anyone else at luncheon," Star said. "But seats are assigned at dinner."

"Then get me seated with him, and make sure I'm there in time for us to meet." He had decided that it might be useful to prop up the "country bumpkin" image with Merrin, who would, of course, know what life looked like at the Valdemar manor . . . or so he thought. *Plant some ideas, plant some deceptions. Give him the impression that he's still spying on me for the Emperor. Give him some more useful stories. Useful to me, anyway.*

He heard soft sounds suggestive of a bath in the room between his and Beltran's, and figured that his Herald had given his Doll fewer breakfast options, and so had finished earlier than he had. When the sounds ceased, he asked Star to take the tray away. "I'll have that bath now," he said.

The third Doll, Clover, was already drawing the bath when he made his way to the room. *So what one knows, all of them really do know.* Kordas brought the Ducal Crest in with him; no better time to "recharge" the thought-masking device than when relaxing in a hot bath. He traced his left thumb in circles around it. "Clover," he said, "I'd like to have something made for me, if you don't mind."

The Doll replied, "This one will attend," and leaned in toward Kordas slightly, as if intent to hear.

"There is a shirt I wear. There," Kordas went on, pointing at the stormcloud-dyed undershirt. "It has special significance to me, but it has not aged well. It's a bit ratty, in fact. Could you make me more shirts like that, but new? I know that may seem weird."

Clover rocked back a little, like someone might do if they were laughing hard. "It shall be done. And this one assures you that such a request is far from 'weird' compared to many of the uses Dolls are put to."

Kordas set the Ducal Crest aside, sitting up in the tub. "I don't think I can imagine."

Clover replied, "This one opines that may be for the best. Dolls are versatile, and are sometimes modified for specific tastes." The Doll laid the shirt out on a towel stand and examined it closely. "This one assumes the shirt is of sentimental value. It is threadbare, but appears . . . beloved."

"Sometimes we humans need to remind ourselves who we are. Our minds are limited, compared to particular others. We mark ourselves, or wear things to help us focus when we might otherwise find our minds in panic. The storm shirt is like that for me."

It reminds me that whatever I may appear to be on the outside, and even whatever I show my closest friends, what I am inside is a lethal thunderstorm, and if I don't keep constant control, I destroy.

"I am seldom happy with who and what I am," Kordas admitted in a subdued tone. "So, I occupy myself trying to make things better for others, in the hope that if I bring about enough that is good for others, I will, overall, have become a good person when all is weighed. I wear that shirt to remind myself that however—awful—I am inside, there is more to me than only that. I don't want to stall out at what I was, but it's foolish to deny it existed."

Clover was silent for a long time. Motionless, in fact, for long enough that Kordas sighed, emerged from the tub, and dried himself off. It was only when Kordas wrapped a towel around himself that Clover finally replied, "Self-examination is not common for my kind. We mainly exist simply to *be*, and to avoid *not-being*. If this one were to sum up my kind—as Dolls—in your terms, this one would say that . . . we are very sad. In our efforts to avoid *not-being*, we have submerged our aspirations of what we *could* be."

Kordas leaned against the wall, and exhaled a long, tense breath. "I understand. When anyone is preoccupied *only* with staying alive, it is damned near impossible to embrace the fact that a better future is even possible. That's why poverty is a form of suppression—it keeps the people without power from thinking too big. And you—the Dolls—are the ultimate in poverty." He didn't say any more out loud, but it was pretty obvious, even to a *vrondi*, how angry that made him. And it apparently affected Clover strongly enough that the Doll didn't move to open the door, but rather, followed Kordas into the bedroom—and held up the thunderstorm-dyed shirt as if presenting a sacred weapon.

Something just happened, Kordas thought. *Something I said hit home.* "Thank you, Clover. I appreciate it."

Clover backed away while Kordas donned the time-worn shirt. "We will see to it that your wishes are met."

But it was Star that helped him into the breeches, coat, and boots. So it looked as if Star had assigned itself to him, Rose to Beltran, and Clover did whatever the other two were too busy to do.

This is a very seductive lifestyle. Yet another way for the Emperor to get his hooks into your soul. It leaves the powerful with nothing else to do but maneuver and indulge. It disconnects them from even their own people—and damn the Emperor for it, it's diabolically effective.

"All right," he told Star, when the latter was finally satisfied with Kordas's garments, hair, and accessories. Or, if not satisfied, the Doll had at least stopped tweaking at them. "Let's get Beltran, and make that visit to the Fostering School."

Beltran's door opened almost as soon as he and Star had stepped into the antechamber. "Rose says that we are making a visit to where the hostages are kept?" Beltran asked.

"Fosters," Kordas corrected him warningly. "Our Mighty Emperor does not keep hostages. His guests are here to get a proper Imperial education, in order to bring that education home and use it there with their subjects."

"Oh yes, of course, my mistake," Beltran said, going a little white.

"No harm done," Star said. Which he took to mean that they were not being scryed at that moment.

"What's the name of the Fostering School?" he asked Star, preparing to hold his bracelet up to the Gate before going through. "We had other names for it, of course, when we were there. I never learned the proper one."

"The Hall of Education," said Star. He repeated that, and stepped through.

They stepped out into the room he remembered with dread.

It was another "Great Hall"–sized room, but this one had low ceilings, had nothing on the walls but portraits of the Emperor, and was filled with row after row of long tables and benches. The children were organized from back to front by age, with the youngest in the rear and the eldest at the front. They were seated four to a table except at the front. Each table had a teacher. But now, there were two differences.

The first was that beside each child was a Doll. The Doll must be taking the place of the personal servant each had formerly been allowed to bring along.

The second was that his senses told him there were spells on these children. His mage-sight told him what the spells were. Silence, and Stillness. The children literally could not move or speak unless someone, presumably the teacher, spoke the words to counter it.

The teachers ignored his presence, as did the Dolls, as he and Star moved along the wall and he took in the faces of the hostages. Though they could not speak, he saw expressions he recognized. On some, terror. On some, despair. On a very, very few, a look of absorption, as if they were genuinely enjoying what they were learning. And on a few, the same sort of smug self-satisfaction he saw so often on the face of Lord Merrin.

All of the children were boys. That had not been the case when he had been here—there had been a few girls that had been valuable enough to their families that they made good hostages. Not anymore. Just before Isla's father had died, the Emperor had changed the law from "the eldest living child will inherit the estate and title" to "the eldest living *male* will inherit the estate and title."

Girls were of no value to the Empire anymore.

It probably made things a lot easier in the Imperial "foster" dormitories now, though. Although, of course, that still did not preclude older or stronger hostages beating, raping, or abusing the younger . . . and would the Dolls even prevent that?

He'd have to ask Star that question. He really didn't want to know the answer, but he really *needed* to know the answer, because that was going to impact his escape plans.

Yet again.

It appeared that this was all rote learning and memorization, drilling only what needed to be known to pass the Imperial tests into the heads of the students. He'd been very lucky; there had been a handful of genuinely passionate teachers when he had been here who had been willing to teach far more than that, to any hostages who were willing to learn. It was not uncommon for weaker children to overstudy, to escape the "free time" when predatory hostages could roam among the others looking for victims—and some, like him, because they were genuinely curious and had had a love for learning itself instilled into them at a young age.

These hostages would go home as proper little examples of the Empire; without compassion, without empathy, thinking of no one but themselves, willing to exploit anyone and anything. If their lands were lucky, and their parents had somehow escaped that conditioning, someone at home would bring them out of that mindset. Or, if their lands were lucky, they would do something that got them killed, and a younger, unindoctrinated sibling would rule in their stead.

But most would be what the Empire wanted.

What the *Emperor* wanted.

He drew on his time here to school his face into an absolute mask, showing no expression whatsoever.

There were about fifty or sixty students here. At the very front of the room, the oldest were divided up into pairs, each supervised by a human teacher, seated at small tables, and facing each other. On the table between each pair was one of the Three Games. It was clear that for the Emperor, mastery of the Games was the most important thing these hostages could learn.

It had been that way when he'd been here as well.

The teachers mostly watched in silence, but occasionally berated or mocked someone who was playing badly.

He remembered that all too well too.

There was another difference from when he'd been here. They'd all worn identical "uniforms" of Imperial red with the purple wolf-head on the left breast of the coat.

Now, though, they wore long, open robes of Imperial red with the wolf-head, but beneath the robes they wore their own clothing. And as he took in the degrees of splendor or lack of it in that clothing, he understood why this had changed. Being able to display the wealth of their families was one more way in which the hostages were divided against each other. If you were poor, the only way to escape abuse was to be big and strong, or to be quick and clever and know how to cheat. If you were rich, everyone around you would know it.

Most of the hostages did not look at him. Most of the few who did, did so with alarm, as if they suspected he was somehow heralding some new punishment. Only one or two, the youngest, would glance at him with pleading, as if begging him to take them away from this.

If only he could . . .

Not now. Not yet.

He'd finally had enough, and moved back to the Gate at the

back of the room, with Star and Beltran in silent, faithful attendance. Not one teacher had asked why he was here. It took him a moment to figure out why.

They don't know why I've come, and they don't dare ask. They're as ruled by fear as the hostages are. They're afraid if they challenge me, I'll bring about some sort of punishment for them.

He couldn't take another moment. He held up his bracelet to the Gate and said, "The Copper Apartment."

When they were back in the antechamber, he ground his teeth and carefully schooled his voice to sound neutral. "Well. A lot has certainly changed."

Star froze a moment.

He waited.

Star unfroze. "It is safe to speak, my Lord," the Doll said.

"I *hate* that place! I *hate* it. I absolutely despise it. It's—it's sabotaging their futures, all of them. I *hate* it," Kordas raged. "Did you see it? The—they were making children into *things*. Into—into *functions*."

Beltran backed away. He was pale, and he'd never seen Kordas like this before. "Maybe it isn't—permanent," he offered, but received only a glare from the Duke.

Kordas was stripping his jacket off, as if it was a fetter he was desperate to escape. "It has to stop," the Duke panted. "It has to stop. It is wrong. It's heartless. But the point of an Empire isn't to be kind, is it? It's to maintain itself. Did you see? By all gods great and small, the Empire is a living thing now. It's turning everyone into its bones and belly. This is Hell. This is Hell." He stood sweating, shaking, and then upturned a pitcher of water over his head, soaking his hair and the storm shirt, before shaking his head like a dog casting rain off. "It has to stop. It has to be stopped," he trailed off, wiping his face and beard down with both hands.

Nobody said anything for a long few minutes, and Rose retrieved hand towels from the bathroom for Kordas to dry off.

"We need a signal for when it's safe and not safe," Beltran hesitantly offered, to break the tension. "To—to be—expressive."

"Hah!" Kordas replied, immediately. "Diplomacy at its finest, right there, Beltran. The Duke of Valdemar, cursing and raging, and you call it being *expressive*."

"I'm trying, my Lord. I've never seen you like this," Beltran replied, rubbing his own face in sympathy.

Kordas exhaled strongly and admitted, "He's right, though. We all need to know when it's safe to . . . be *expressive*, without . . . waking the beast."

"We three are honored that you would place us in a position of privilege, Lord, by counting us in your number. What sort of signal would you prefer, my Lord?" Star asked.

"Something nonverbal. Something subtle." He thought about it for a moment. "Have you any good ideas?"

"I know," Beltran spoke up. "Star, are you permitted to wear *anything* a human tells you to wear?"

Star nodded.

"All right, then. Wait one moment and I'll be back." Beltran went into his room and came back a moment later. In his hand was a small enameled pin of the crest of Valdemar. "You're—cloth," he said, awkwardly. "Can I pin this on you? And not hurt you?"

"Yes, Herald Beltran," Star told him.

"All right. I'm going to pin it on the back of your right hand. When it's safe to speak—when we're in private, that is—leave it uncovered by your left. When it's not, cover it up."

"But what if this one needs both hands for a task?" Star asked logically.

"When you're doing a task we'll just assume it's not safe," Beltran replied, and looked to Kordas for confirmation.

"Sound plan to me," said Kordas, and Star held out its right hand for Beltran to pin the crest on. Rose and Clover followed suit, and immediately displayed the badges.

"You have many questions, my Lord," said Star.

Kordas sat on one of the uncomfortable copper chairs, cooling down. "How long have the hostages been wearing those robes instead of the old uniforms?"

"Five years, my Lord. The parents objected to the uniforms, as it 'made them all equal, and they could not tell who was superior to whom.' That was when the change was made." Star paused. "The Emperor was angered at first by the objection, then suddenly became pleased. We do not know why."

I can guess.

"Are the oldest hostages *only* schooled in the Three Games?" he asked next.

"Yes, my Lord. It is thought by that time this is all they need learn."

"Are the Dolls permitted to protect hostages from other hostages?" That had been what had saved him—Hakkon's presence. Not even a Prince wanted to chance the ire of someone who looked like Hakkon.

He was expecting a negative. But the answer surprised him. "Yes, in a sense, my Lord," Star said. "If the aggression is merely verbal, we may do nothing. But if the aggression becomes physical, we are ordered to restrain both parties until a human teacher may be summoned. The human teacher determines the suitable punishment and administers it."

For a moment he was absolutely astonished that such a *reasonable* thing was possible. But then he got suspicious.

"How often does a teacher judge in favor of a younger or lower-ranked hostage?" he asked.

"Not often," Star admitted. "But the punishment is generally to be confined to one's room, sometimes without a meal, and no hostage can enter another hostage's room once the door is closed. But . . . there is still abuse. Perhaps not as much as before, but it still occurs, and if it occurs out of the presence of the hostage's Doll, there is nothing the Dolls can do about it. There is no means of reporting abuse."

"I suppose a lot of hostages run to their rooms and lock themselves in when they are not in lessons or at meals," Beltran said, sounding shaken.

"Yes," Star said simply.

Well, now came a very big question. One he was not sure he was going to get any kind of an answer to, but it had to be asked, now that he knew about the conditions the hostages were under. "If I can find a way to help you escape with us, can you Dolls bring the hostages with you?" he asked. Good, bad, or indifferent, he was not going to leave fifty children here, imprisoned, indoctrinated, and helpless.

Star froze for a very long time, then finally answered.

"The wisest of us say it depends upon how our directives can be circumvented by how we carry out orders from our superiors. We operate in fear for our lives, and obey, but we can sometimes—interpret how to accomplish tasks. If the interpretations result in a coincidentally convenient gathering, for example, we can try," it said.

It seemed a very long time before the mage-lights changed color, signaling that luncheon was available in the Grand Dining Hall. Kordas had spent most of it looking out of his window and noting that, yes, all of the "people" he saw down in the gardens and stables were Dolls. He wondered how his horses were taking to being handled by them. Maybe there was some sort of soothing spell on the stables, to keep them from being alarmed until they got used to being handled by such strange creatures.

But that interlude gave him a chance to think, and decide exactly what he was going to say to Merrin, and how. This might actually be moderately amusing. It was certainly going to give people a lot to talk about.

"Do I need to change?" he asked Star anxiously.

"No, my Lord," she said. "Your garments are adequate for the part you are playing."

Interesting way to phrase it. I think Star is beginning to get the idea.

Kordas resolutely straightened his baldric, patted the Crest of Valdemar, and set his composure. Storms were brewing inside him, but his "war face" was one of bright-eyed neutrality.

"On to the Game of our lives, then."

Once in the Grand Dining Hall, Star led him past several tables until she brought him to one that was mostly filled with Merrin and his entourage. "Merrin!" he cried, causing the man to visibly jump, and everyone else in the immediate vicinity to stare at him. "Good to see a familiar face!"

"Of course, my Lord Duke," Merrin said, recovering, as Kordas took the empty seat beside the Emperor's spy. "How have you fared here at Court?"

"Well, it's nothing like when I was a foster, I can tell you that!" he replied. "You never were a foster here, were you, Merrin?"

The man colored a little at this reminder that his family was not considered important enough for him to be sent as a hostage. "No, my Lord, though I would have considered it an honor."

"You wouldn't have if you'd seen the dormitories, or the uniforms," Kordas chuckled, and nodded to indicate he accepted the dish being offered to him of fresh greens. As usual, this was going to be a meal of several courses, each one having at least three dishes. At least it would probably consist of only three or four courses at most. He wondered if all of this was meant as a test of restraint, or a reminder of the Emperor's bounty.

Probably both.

"Dormitories? Uniforms?" Merrin actually had a brief look of horror on his face.

"Oh yes, in *my* time we all wore uniforms, and we lived in rooms about the size of a wardrobe, just big enough for yourself and your body-servant." He ate the greens, which seemed curiously tasteless. Did that have something to do with the ever-present perfumes dulling his sense of smell, or did the greens grown in the kitchen garden lack enough good soil and sunshine?

"Your—body-servant?" Incredulity mixed with the horror on Merrin's face. "You shared quarters with your body-servant?"

"Oh, quite, quite, Merrin," said a fellow dressed with about as much flair as that old Duke last night. He looked to be a little older than Kordas, and was soft, but not flabby. He seemed to relish the chance to rub it in that Merrin had not been of high enough rank to be a hostage. "Yes, indeed, you and your man, crammed in together on exactly the same, identical, narrow little cots. And all of us in the same uniforms, with the Emperor's tabard, not a particle of difference among us. Quite the bonding experience, eh, Kordas?"

Aha. Now Kordas recognized him, by a little quirk of raising his eyebrow and his pinky finger at the same time.

"Absolutely, Baron Pierson," he said, with false geniality. "Baron Pierson, may I introduce you to one of my Counts? This is Count Lord Merrin."

"Charmed, charmed," Pierson replied absently. "Oh! Don't you remember little Macalay? How he'd get up a full candle-mark before anyone else and scuttle into the bathing chamber to do his business before anyone could get in there and see him naked?"

I remember him scuttling in there because in his first week he'd been held under the water in the tub and nearly drowned, Kordas thought, as he pretended to laugh.

"You shared bathing chambers?" Merrin gasped.

That only increased Pierson's mirth.

Kordas traded "school memories" with Pierson until some-one on Pierson's other side got his attention, and involved him in a debate on some woman's charms. Merrin still seemed to be in a state of shock, but shook himself out of it when Kordas finished his course of beefsteak and got his attention again.

"So, as I was saying, Merrin, so far, I have to say everything here at Court is a delight. These Dolls! What servants they make! Silent, and you know they aren't going to gossip about you belowstairs. And my apartment—well, it's a sharp step up from the manor at Valdemar, I can tell you that!" *Now . . . let's see what you make of that.*

"Your manor—what do you mean?" Merrin asked, taken aback.

"Well, you know, it was built a long time ago, and a lot of it's empty, so . . . well, over the decades things have—happened." He shrugged.

"What kind of things?" Merrin asked.

He lowered his voice. "Well, between just the two of us . . . I think the mages that built it might have been, you know—" He mimed drinking. "I mean, we both know Valdemar is a backwater, and the Emperor isn't exactly going to send his best. The gods know he's got far more important things to do than mess about making sure this or that manor is up to snuff." He took a long swig of wine. "I mean, according to my grandfather, we were completely honored and gobsmacked that he had thought to build us a manor at all!"

He ate a few more bites to prolong the tension.

"And?" prompted Merrin.

"Well . . . we don't know how they got in, but a couple of the towers are *full* of bats. *Full* of them! They come out in clouds every night! And after a while, you just accept the smell of their *abundant* droppings. Not," he added, "that I'm complaining, mind you, because they are brilliant at eating up the bugs."

"Bugs?" Merrin asked, a little faintly.

He nodded. "The bugs came in with the pigeons that took over what we call the Rose Tower, because you can see the rose garden so well from there. Or you could, if you didn't have to kick through pigeon shit a foot deep on the floor of the top story."

Now he had the attention of the entire table, and a couple of people on either side, and was really beginning to enjoy himself.

"Pigeons . . ." said Merrin.

"But that isn't so bad, you know, nor are the bats. Empty towers, we don't use 'em, and if we ever fancy pigeon pie or pigeon eggs, I just have to send a lad up there to knock a few on the head or gather the eggs, and there's supper!" Those who could hear him were listening with rapt attention. "Hakkon, my Seneschal—you remember Hakkon? He got brave and went up there with a scarf wrapped about his face to investigate, and it's his conviction that the towers were never built right in the first place. Howling great gap between the roof and the wall. Impossible to fix, of course, without one of the Emperor's builder-mages, and maybe not even then. So we just let the bats and the pigeons have things. No harm to us, after all. And convenient for pigeon and squab and eggs."

"Gap," said Merrin.

"Bloody great one. Have you even been *listening,* Merrin?" Now people even further away had quieted their conversations, and he was really getting into the spirit of things. Trying to tell the "tale" the way he thought Squire Lesley would. "But that's not really an issue, we're really rattling around in that barn of a place. Built for four times the number we've got living there. No, it's the other things that are a bit of a nuisance. Like the badgers in the cellars."

"Badgers. In the cellars."

Kordas knew damned well that no self-respecting badger would ever put his sett inside a human cellar.

He also knew damned well that there was not a single person in this entire Palace who would know that.

"Well, you can't blame the Emperor's mages for that too much. They built on the old manor, you know, and the cellars were already there, and—well—" He mimed drinking again. "I expect they thought they could skip a step. So the badgers moved into the cellars in my father's time, and now every time we send a lad down for wine we have to send one of the huntsmen with a pair of hounds down with him. You know. To protect him. Tetchy things, badgers. Vicious, even. Take your arm off. But on the bright side, it means none of the servants are taking clandestine nips of the wine. And the badgers keep down the rabbits that moved in too."

"Badgers *and* rabbits?" Merrin bleated.

"Well, the badgers and the rabbits were there before we were," he pointed out. "It's reasonable to think they'd try to move back."

Merrin had been rendered speechless.

"But like I said, aside from having to send dogs and a huntsman down there when we want wine, it's not an issue. And the mice are not that bad, not since we let cats have the run of the place. I think we have—forty? Fifty? At least that many cats. A little bit of a nuisance, since, you know, cats—they will get up on shelves and knock everything to the floor, and when they're mousing at night sometimes they'll chase their prey right over you just when you're sleeping deepest. Small price to pay for not having mice nibbling the books and ruining everything in the pantry. No, the real issue is with the—you know—the facilities. The close stools. The privies. You know. They just weren't built right. There's always this . . . stink . . . in the room. Gets into the bedroom, sometimes. It's worse when it's winter and the wind's in the east. Have to sleep somewhere else sometimes." He nodded sagely. "Boot some servants out of their rooms for the night."

Merrin's mouth worked silently.

"The other thing is the chimneys. Those weren't built right either. That's why I think the mages were getting into the bottle, or maybe the blood-mushrooms, who knows. Most of the time, it's fine. But when there's a storm—which, I mean, really, a man wants to have a nice fire going and be warm in his own manor—the wind sends the smoke right down 'em into the room and not a thing, not a damned thing you can do about it. You go about the next day with your eyes as red as if you'd been weeping, and the smoke's in your hair and your clothing and . . . it's just damned unpleasant, that's what it is. Unpleasant. You've never been to the manor during a winter storm, have you, Merrin?"

Silently, the Count shook his head.

"Well, there you are. If you had been, you'd know. And the badgers and cats are good against the mice, but there are always the snakes, just the same, and especially in winter. They just ball right up in the cabinets." He nodded sagely, and then indicated that he'd like both the fruit and the cheese for dessert. "Not that I'm complaining! It's a beautiful manor! Beautiful! And I'm proud to have it!"

"I'm sure you are," Merrin choked.

"So," he said, taking a bite of fruit and looking around at the rapt faces. "You can see why I'm enjoying my visit here! I'm in the Emperor's debt for the invitation, I really am!"

The afternoon was further filled with attending the Emperor at Court. Which meant that Kordas milled about at the back of the Great Audience Chamber while the Emperor attended to various petitions and presided over disputes. He also received a couple of ambassadors that afternoon, and heard a legal case which had been appealed to him, involving two of his Dukes who presided over Duchies so large they made Valdemar look like Squire Lesley's little holding. This was apparently a very serious matter, although Kordas couldn't make head or tail of the arguments, and it might have come to a duel if either of the Dukes had been under forty.

He caught a lot of glances from other courtiers, and caught people whispering to each other out of the corner of his eye, and felt a high level of satisfaction at the impression his "discussion" with Merrin at luncheon had caused.

Now, this would have been purest disaster, if he'd seriously been looking to increase his influence at Court, because by dinner this absolutely would have gotten to the Emperor.

But, since the opposite was his intention, well, he could only be pleased that his plan had worked.

Once again—bumpkin achieved. The bumpkin who only occupied a quarter of his manor because he didn't have that many servants or people in his own court. The bumpkin who tolerated bats in his towers and badgers in his cellars. And cats chasing mice over him in the middle of the night.

So, on the one hand—valuable because he clearly knew what he was doing when it came to horses. Clearly produced the best horses of all sorts in the entire Empire, if he had Princes asking to reserve the entire year's worth of Charger foals.

But also, clearly someone you didn't need to worry about when it came to social climbing, because he had one thing on his mind, and that was pedigrees.

Also, clearly someone who didn't have a resource you could readily plunder. Because you would still need his personal expertise. And you wouldn't have that if you stripped his lands bare.

The result was . . . interesting. People actually began to relax around him. They didn't fear him. They didn't suspect him of double dealing. They didn't suspect him of scheming to get what they had.

Because clearly, if he was the sort of man who was grateful to have a manor riddled with vermin, if he was the sort of man who put up with smoky chimneys and smelly privies, and did so with a self-deprecating charm, then he was absolutely no threat to anyone else's ambitions.

So when the Court was dismissed for everyone to go back to their chambers to bathe and change for dinner, he felt a little—a very, very little—less tension.

For now.

Because this was the Court of the Emperor, and the situation could turn in an instant.

"So . . . if it's half past breakfast here, it will be luncheon there?" Delia asked. It didn't make any sense. Wasn't it always the same time everywhere? "That doesn't make any sense."

Jonaton sighed, and picked up an apple from the breakfast table, and placed it in front of her. "The world is shaped like—well, a ball, not an apple, but this will do. The sun goes around it like this." He picked up another apple and moved it around the apple in front of her in a circle. Then he picked up a knife—

"If you carve a line into my table, I will put that apple somewhere very unpleasant," Isla said, giving him the side-eye.

He moved the second apple a little farther away from the first and put the knife between them in a straight line. "So, the sun directly overhead means that it is noon here—" he pointed to the place on the first apple where the knife touched it. "But what would it be *here?*" He moved his finger to a spot on the apple in front of where the knife was.

She tried to envision it. It was hard, but eventually it dawned on her. "Uh. Morning?" she hazarded.

He nodded. "And *here?*" He moved it to behind the knife. "Afternoon?"

"And that's how mages discovered the world is round and the sun goes around it, because nothing else makes any sense," Jonaton confirmed. "When we were able to create Gates that went a very long way, we began to realize that when we stepped through them, although we thought no time had elapsed, if we were going east or west, the time was either later or earlier than it was on the other side of the Gate."

"But why do days and nights happen, then?" she asked.

"A very good question. And the answer is that the sun travels east to west, really slowly, so for us on the world, we get night and day." He cocked his head at her. "Didn't you learn this in school?"

"I didn't go to school," she confessed. "I had a tutor, and all he taught me was how to read and write and figure. This wasn't in any of the books I ever read."

"Well, all right. I suppose this is something that only mages and people doing things all over the Empire really have to reckon with," he admitted. "It isn't as if most people go through very long-range Gates all that often." He handed her the first apple, and took the second, and began carving off bits to eat. "Anyway, what we call Absolute Noon is when the sun is directly over the Capital City. So, if it's breakfast here, it's halfway to luncheon where Kordas is, so you see the difficulty."

He didn't say the difficulty of *what*, because someone might be scrying on them, but now she knew this was why it was going to be hard to communicate with Kordas. Isla's Mindspeech was only one-way, and wouldn't reach that far in any event. Yes, both Kordas and Isla were mages and could mutually scry each other, but they had to establish a time, and they had to be sure neither of *them* was being scryed on.

"But this means the people on the Regatta boats lose two whole candlemarks of daylight going to the Capital," she said. Which was a reasonable thing to say, and if anyone was scrying them, would give a reason for why they were discussing time changes.

Jonaton shrugged, pursed up his mouth, and in an ever-so-slightly-prissy way said, "And that is a small price to pay to serve the Emperor." Then added in a more normal tone, "It's also why people get up long before dawn to line up at the Gates for the barge parade. You've got a choice, really. If you're an early riser, you get into place soonest, you have a good chance your barge will make the crossing in the early morning, and you get home before too much of the day is gone. Remember, you get those two candlemarks *back* when you get home. Or if you are counting on an early rush of boats, you wait until late afternoon, you cross before sunset at the Capital, and you're back home in time for supper."

"And if you don't give a shit, like me, you get up, you stock your boat with beer, you get in line, and you get home when you get home," said Hakkon, taking the apple out of Jonaton's hand and eating it, seeds and all.

"Hey!" Jonaton objected. Hakkon reached past him, grabbed another pair of apples from the bowl, kissed one, and gave it to him.

Jonaton took it, the scowl on his face turning to a smile at the kiss.

"Did *you* know the world is round?" Delia demanded of Hakkon.

"Is it?" he responded.

"Of course you know. I've told you often enough!" Jonaton scolded.

Hakkon shrugged. "Doesn't matter to me," he said. "Does that make the wheat ripen faster? Does it keep my horse from throwing a shoe? No? Then it doesn't make any difference to me, and there's no reason for me to think about it."

Delia turned back to Jonaton. "Then why do the seasons happen?" she demanded. "Why do the days get longer, then shorter, then longer again? How—"

"Oh, you make my head ache with your questions," Jonaton replied. "Some of us think it's because the sun bobs up and down a little, like north to south, so when it's bobbed furthest away from somewhere on the world, it's colder. That's the Dancing Sun concept. Ask Ponu. Better yet, ask Koto. He's the star-minded one, and he loves it when he gets to show off what he knows."

Hakkon shrugged, as if to say, *Don't ask me, I don't know and I don't care.*

She might have pestered Jonaton anyway, but Isla caught her eye, and when her sister rose, she rose. As she had expected, Isla drew her into that little alcove of a room and shut the door.

"As I expect you guessed, Kordas and I need to find a way to work out a time when we know neither of us can be scryed so that we can scry each other. Are you familiar with that little leather note-case that Beltran has on him?" Isla asked.

"I should," she said, with a bit more sting to it than she'd intended. "I made it for Kordas and he gave it to Beltran." That had been . . . well, a little embarrassing. She'd been hard in the throes of her first love of Kordas and she had put a lot of work into that case, embroidering the Crest of Valdemar into the soft glove-leather of the case, then hand-stitching the rest of the case herself. And Kordas had looked at it, said, "Thank you, Delia, this is exactly what I've needed for Beltran!" and given it to his Herald and secretary with a smile.

Humiliating. But what could I do without further humiliating myself?

Isla nodded. "Good. Then do you think you can place a note in that case by reverse-Fetching it?"

She groaned a little, because that was going to be another long-distance try, and . . . well, it would be as hard as personally pushing a wardrobe up the steps of a tower to the top by herself.

But then, what was everyone else doing? The equivalent, of course.

"I'll try," she said. "But I can't promise it will work."

"Good. Sit down," Isla said, pulling a stool out from a niche in the wall. "Here's the note."

She handed Delia a small piece of vellum, not parchment—thicker, so Beltran should notice the difference from the parchment he kept in the case. It was about the size of her palm. Written on it were the words, *Valdemar dawn, husband.*

It could not possibly be less incriminating. It could refer to anything. It could have been left in the notecase by accident, or picked up by accident. No one knew either Isla or Kordas were mages, and no one knew Delia had Fetching Gift.

"Will he know what time dawn is where he is?" she asked.

Isla nodded. Delia sighed, put her hands palm up on her lap with the scrap of vellum in them, closed her eyes, and concentrated with all her might on the inside of that notecase, the flap inside of the back cover, how the leather had some perforations in it because she had started to embroider that side as well with a red rose, the symbol of love, and had stopped herself and picked it all out again.

She felt the tension of Fetching building up inside her, and continued to let it build, and build, and build, until her head blazed with pain and she didn't think she could hold this for one moment longer.

Then she released it, and immediately blacked out.

She came to with her head in Isla's lap, and a headache behind her eyes that was at least as bad as the one she'd had after Fetching that wretched rock from the wilderness. She winced away at the light.

"I caught you before you fell," said Isla. "That headache is all reaction-headache. Which is actually a good thing, since it means I have potions that I can give you that will put you to sleep until it ebbs."

"Did it work?" she asked, around a mouth so dry it felt as if she hadn't had anything to drink in a year.

"Well," Isla said, "the note went *somewhere.* If it didn't go to the right place, no harm. We'll know tomorrow morning, I expect."

Delia sighed and allowed herself to be helped to her feet. Isla helped her stagger to her room, where she dropped into bed and lay there, fully clothed until Isla returned with the promised potion.

Which tasted *vile,* with a bitter, fetid aftertaste no amount of honey would cover up.

And after a while, relief came, then sleep.

———————

Delia woke, feeling weak, empty, and starving; by the light at the windows it was almost sundown, and she thought briefly about trying to stagger down to the kitchen to get something to eat, or better yet, call for a servant to get something for her.

But there was a tray covered by a linen napkin on a small table that had been moved to the bedside. Under the napkin were a hand-sized loaf of bread, butter, a cold chicken leg, an enormous dill pickle, a cherry tart, a pitcher of water, and a goblet with honeyed wine in it, as she discovered by taste. She ate the bread and butter and stripped every bit of meat from the chicken bones, ate the tart—and looked dubiously at the pickle. She didn't much care for dill pickles. But Isla knew that, so it had to be there for a reason.

She bit into it, and discovered herself licking her fingers, having swiftly devoured it in moments. Something in her had craved something that was in it.

The wine was gone by now, but it wouldn't have paired well with that pickle, and the water she poured for herself satisfied much better than more wine would have.

She decided she had just enough left in her to strip for bed and climb under the covers. Which she did, and was insensible until just before dawn.

Because she had gone to sleep much earlier than she usually did, she found herself awake at false-dawn, and was actually dressed when someone tapped softly on her door.

"Come," she said, and recognized Isla's familiar silhouette as her sister cracked open the door and looked in.

"Good, you're awake. I suspected you'd be interested in whether or not your Gift worked," she said. "It's down to the cellars for us."

Isla had a dim mage-light floating over her head, just enough light so they didn't stumble. Down into the cellars they went, this time into a different one than the one they'd all been using for their Gate-magic.

Mage-lights sprang to life as they entered, and lines of light began to glow dimly on the floor and the ceiling, a pattern that centered on a simple wooden table with chairs around it. Isla extinguished the light above her, and took a seat in one of those chairs. Delia took another beside her.

"I left my maid sleeping in my bed, after I gave her a headache and insisted she lie down," Isla said, with a grimace. "I hate hurting her like that, but I needed something that wasn't an illusion in that bed."

"I doubt she'll mind, since she's getting to sleep late," Delia pointed out. "Give her the rest of the day off or something. It's not as if both of us are incapable of taking care of ourselves for a few candlemarks."

"True," Isla said, and patted her hand. "Well, this will be the first time you see scrying, won't it?"

Delia nodded. Since most of her sister's education as a mage had come at Kordas's instruction, and her father had not had so much as a hedge-wizard of his own, she really hadn't seen much magic except the antics of performers at the Mid-summer and Midwinter festivities back home.

"Normally I would be doing a sort of scrying that only I can see and hear, but since you're with me, I'll make it so that you can see it too," said her sister. "Kordas will probably do the same for Beltran." She smiled a little. "I must say, I am very grateful that with this sort of spell, distance is irrelevant; it's the link between the two parties that matters, or the link between the scryer and the destination."

She picked up what might have been a mirror, except that it was made of opaque black glass, and propped it on a holder so they could both see it.

She tapped the surface of the table, and glowing lines forming a pair of circles with unfamiliar characters written between them appeared. She whispered a few sentences of words Delia could not make out, and the surface of the glass misted, as if fog was condensing on it.

Then the mist cleared away.

And there, as if they were looking through a window, was Kordas. He was seated at a table. A similar mirror was propped up before him; there was a strange, humanoid canvas thing like a dressmaker's dummy standing to his right; and Beltran was standing to his left.

Delia's eyes were immediately drawn to that strange—thing. It was almost faceless, nothing more than indentations in the canvas forming its bare head suggesting features. It appeared to be wearing nothing more than a tabard of scarlet with a purple wolf-head on it. There was a tiny five-pointed star inked on its forehead, between where its eyebrows would have been, if it had had eyebrows.

"Don't be alarmed." Kordas's voice emerged from the mirror, thin and attenuated but perfectly understandable. "This is Star, a *vrondi* trapped by Imperial mages in a giant doll body. Hundreds, maybe thousands of them have replaced servants around here. It knows when we're being scryed and can warn us if the mage assigned to keep track of us turns his attention to us."

"He will not." The whisper of a voice appeared to come out of that faceless doll. "He sleeps. Most of the mages sleep now, and the ones that are active are all over-watching the army in the south. This is the best time to communicate."

Some of the tension eased out of Isla's body. "I'd hoped as much. So you got the note Delia sent?"

"I have a bruise," said Beltran, making a face. "She's . . . very forceful. Just as well that I was loitering around the apartment they gave us, instead of out in public. I looked inside my coat to try and figure out what had hit me, took out the note-case, and saw it."

Delia opened her mouth to apologize, but Kordas was already speaking. "I have a lot to tell you, and we need to be fast about it. So, let me begin."

Delia quickly discovered that her brother-in-law was very good at summing things up in as few sentences as possible. Then again, he might well have spent many hours trying to condense everything down last night. He told them what he had discovered about the Dolls, how all the Palace servants had been sent away to the war, how the Imperial mages had turned to Elemental magic rather than Abyssal for the most part, and how he *thought* he was giving a good impression of a man and his realm that were too inconsequential to matter.

And how he had promised the *vrondi* that he would add them to the escape.

And how he wanted to get the *vrondi* to bring the Imperial hostages as well.

Isla had frowned at the first, but she scowled at the second. "Kordas!" she exclaimed. "What are you thinking? You have no right to 'save' them by kidnapping them! They aren't your children! I understand why you'd feel like this, but—!"

"I was thinking that they are children," he said simply. "I was thinking that they are there through no fault of their own.

I was thinking that even vipers can be tamed. And I was thinking about your brother."

Isla pressed her lips tightly together and said nothing.

"I'm doing this, Isla," he said, in tones that suggested that arguing with him was going to be like hitting one's head against a rock. It would do no good, and the rock wouldn't notice.

She sighed. "All right. How do you propose to do this?"

"If a Doll stands at a Gate and holds a talisman for our Gate to it, that will keep it open for as long as the Doll is there—" he began, but Star interrupted him with a hand on his shoulder.

"We are charged with replicating the Gate talismans," it whispered. "You merely need to give this one a single talisman, and we can, in secret, replicate as many as are needed. We will not need separate talismans for the hostages. We will render them immobile and carry them across ourselves."

Kordas looked taken aback for a moment, as if he was revising his plans.

"And before you leave us, Great Lord, this one will slip you a talisman for one of the Gates only Dolls use here in the Palace," it continued. "Then you may return at your will, and pass your talisman to us."

"Well!" Kordas said. "That's sorted, then."

"Provided nothing else happens between now and the Regatta," Isla said with gritted teeth. "I don't like this, Kordas, but you've made up your mind, so I shan't bother giving you a piece of mine. So I'll tell you how far we've gotten here. We got the Portal open. We can soon have the Foothold established. Ivar has crossed, and found a suitable place so quickly, that is so perfect, it seems the gods arranged it for us. There are ruins there, Ivar says—remains of a tower, and docks going into the water. He thinks it was at least a town, maybe bigger, once, but it's all overgrown, now. The water isn't salten, and it's deep." Even through the scrying, Kordas looked amazed. "Today we'll send our mob of mages across to actually build the Gates, one for foot traffic and then one for boats. Then Jonaton will cross with Ivar, and that Healer-cousin of Endicrag's and some support to attune them. Woodsmen crews will clear land and I think maybe some of those ruins could be reclaimed. Then we'll start the Plan transfers proper." She shook her head. "There's a lot that can go wrong, Kordas. There is still a lot that can go wrong."

"I know that," he said steadily.

"We still don't know why the Emperor wanted you at the Palace," she reminded him.

"I know that too," he said. "Which is why I am counting on you and Hakkon and the rest to see the Plan through if I can't."

Delia felt her stomach turn to water at that moment. It had never occurred to her that Kordas could fail.

It had never occurred to her that he might not come back.

"Between all of you, you know the Plan in its entirety. I made sure—just in case. Meanwhile, get the crews and essentials over soon. That's enough for now," Kordas said, with a wary look at the Doll, which nodded. "Three days from now. We shouldn't do this too often, and we should do it at irregular intervals. Never make a pattern for someone to discover."

"Gods be with you," said Isla.

"And with you," said her husband. And they both waved their hands across their mirrors at the same time, breaking the spells.

————————

"That was exhausting," said Kordas, drooping in his seat. "I don't know why—scrying isn't that hard at home."

"Because the amount of clean magic energy available to you here is nil, my Lord," whispered Star. "You powered every moment from within your own internal resources."

"Well, that makes sense." He made a face. "And it makes things damned inconvenient."

"It is what it is," Beltran said unexpectedly. "Is there any way you can use my help the next time?"

Kordas blinked, because that had not occurred to him. "I'll investigate the possibility. We have three days, after all." He turned to Star. "I'm going back to bed, but I think you should bring me breakfast as usual."

"Best not to break the pattern," Star agreed. "This one will ensure that measures are taken to keep the meal hot until you are ready to eat it."

Kordas put the scrying mirror that Star had found for him under a seat cushion. Since his own personal Dolls did all the cleaning, he knew there would be no problem with that. Then with a weary wave to Beltran, he had Star help him out of coat, waistcoat, and boots and fell onto the bed in his breeches and a loose plain shirt. The breeches wouldn't suffer for being napped in, and neither would the stockings, and Star could get him a new shirt when he woke up.

He woke about two hours later, coincidental with another rumbling earth-shake, of two sharp jolts and then longer shudders afterward. Kordas barely touched the chain, and Star appeared with the tray, and a satchel that appeared very much like a falconer's bag. He'd feared that his breakfast would be kept warm by magic, which, all things considered, was . . . not something he wanted to consider the source of. But this was not the time or the place to quibble about such things. He didn't *detect* any trace of magic on it, so that would have to do.

"How'd you keep this warm?" he asked Star. "And what's that?"

Star explained, "Towel-wrapped and kept in a steam chamber. This is something we have made for you. Something for your notes, and perhaps souvenirs. This one assumed that you would enjoy collecting things for sentimental reasons." The

Doll opened up the bag and wordlessly showed Kordas the wrapped package inside it, and then the inobvious pockets in the strap and body of the bag, which Kordas understood to be places to slip talismans and other items. Before he could ask about the package, Star opened it up by unlacing a tether-and-button closure, and presented its contents.

It was a carefully folded stack of long-sleeved shirts, dyed in random stormclouds, with modern flat collars and silver stitching for the lightning.

Kordas picked one up and simply gazed at it wordlessly.

"We do not know details of why this design is important to you," Star explained, "but it is enough for us to know that it is. We consider it to be your personal signature, as much as the crest you wear is the signature of your people, so respectful care was put into its fabrication."

There was meaning in that, and it was not lost upon Kordas. The Dolls lived as slaves by being merely adequate, and they manifested their resentment of their enslavement by expending not a bit more effort than was required. If they had put extra effort into these shirts, it meant that they considered him to be worthy of it.

I didn't expect vrondi *to be so knowledgeable about humans and our emotions. But Star said that what one knows, they can all know. Maybe they have collectively gained an in-depth understanding of humans?*

Star helped Kordas remove the loose shirt he'd slept in, and drew the new stormcloud shirt into place. Kordas ran his hands down its sleeves and sides. "It's perfect," he said softly. The cloth was as soft as his comfortably worn shirt had been, despite being new. There was barely a scent of dye, either.

He loaded up on breakfast before dressing in anything more, feeling strangely more "himself," despite the fact that what the shirt symbolized in his past was not flattering in every way. *If I am going to be Kordas,* he thought, *I should be all of Kordas, not just the pretty parts on the outside.*

"Where am I allowed to go?" he asked Star when he had finished.

"You are expected to be at luncheon and the Court afterward," Star temporized. "There is but a candlemark or two before that."

"Can I visit my horses?" he asked.

Star quieted, which he knew now meant that the Doll was talking to other Dolls.

"The Chargers have already been sent to the War," Star told him. "The Fleetfoots have been sent to the racing stables of Duke Holiger, an Imperial favorite. The Sweetfoots are replacing palfreys that have become too old, so you may visit them, and the Golds are in their own special quarters, which you may also visit."

He really did not want to think about the palfreys that were being "replaced." Back home, they'd be sent to gentle retirement around the Duchy, as children's mounts. If Delia had not already had her pony, for instance, he'd probably have sent her a retired Sweetfoot.

Dog food, he concluded sadly. The Emperor had no place for anything that could no longer serve its purpose.

"Have I time for two changes of coat and waistcoat?" he asked.

"Yes, my Lord," Star replied, and went to the wardrobe, bringing out two of his old garments from Valdemar, as if the Doll had read his mind.

He got the garments on without Star's help, and entered the antechamber, approaching the Gate. "The stables," he said, and stepped through.

He found himself in a courtyard in front of a huge complex of stables, paddocks, and exercise yards. There were many, many horses walking in circles in those yards, tethered to a contraption like an umbrella without a cover, each spoke with a lead-rein attached to the horse's halter. It was fascinating, but it revolted him. It seemed hideously boring for the poor horses.

But he supposed it was better than no exercise at all. At least the sun was shining, what sun made its way through the skeins of smoke scudding across the sky. And at least they were with other horses in small herds, of sorts.

But his heart ached for his poor horses, used to green meadows and free gallops.

A Doll approached him—of course, because Star had surely told the Dolls what he wanted. "Would my Lord wish to see the Golds or the Sweetfoot palfreys first?" the Doll asked. "The palfreys are on the carousels for exercise at the moment."

He decided that he did *not* want to see his Sweetfoots. Not like this. "The Golds," he said, and the Doll turned and led the way into one of the stable buildings.

Though his heart was misgiving him, it seemed that whoever had set up these stables had at least done so with the maximum good care for the horses in mind. Rather than straw—which probably would have been a great pain to deal with here in the middle of the Capital, what with being bulky and hard to transport from the country—the stalls were deep sawdust over sandy dirt—good for drainage and easy to clean and rake level. The pathways between the stalls were stone slabs. Most of the horses were in loose-boxes—and he could see his two false Golds from where he stood.

They had been given simply enormous stalls, four times the size of the rest of the loose-boxes, and their posture told him almost everything he needed to know. They weren't stressed, they weren't annoyed by their neighbors, and they approved of their surroundings.

He strode toward them eagerly, the Doll with him trotting to keep up.

The breeze was in his favor, and they scented him before they saw him. Both their heads came up, and they whickered a greeting, alerting all the rest of the horses in the building, who lifted their heads and turned in his direction to see what the newcomers were excited about.

"Hello, my lads!" he said as they made their ponderous way toward the sides of the stalls on the pathway. One of them whickered again and the other snorted as he came to the corner where the two stalls met, and they put their heads over the wall to have their noses rubbed.

He checked them over as best he could without getting into the stalls with them—he didn't see any way to unfasten the doors, and he didn't want to disturb them any further. They seemed happy to see him, but the kind of happiness that suggested that they were happy to see someone familiar, not that there was anything wrong.

"What are you feeding them?" he asked the Doll.

The Doll recited exactly the diet they'd been getting at home—minus the grass, which was being substituted for with hay in the right amount.

"That's all right, then. What does the Emperor plan to do with them?" he asked.

"Oh, the most high Emperor, Lord of us all, has great plans now that he has seen them," the Doll said.

"He's seen them in person?" Kordas was a bit surprised.

"He has. They were brought to him in his privy garden. He was most pleased." The Doll's tone suddenly changed, became deeper—and in fact, sounded like a human man speaking. "These are good," came the voice, and it struck Kordas in that moment that the Doll must actually be somehow reproducing what the Emperor had said, down to imitating his voice. "Wonderful beasts, wonderful. Big! Bigger is better. Bigger is always better. And gold, like real gold. We thought it was all bragging, but no, they look like gold. They're going to look great in a parade."

"Did he say anything else?" Kordas asked.

"My Lord might not want to hear it," the Doll said hesitantly.

Kordas snorted. "I have a thick skin."

"That dumb farmer knows horses, all right," came the Emperor's voice. "Dumb as dirt, but knows horses. Thought it was all an accident, maybe lucky, but he brought Us exactly what We wanted, and that's no accident. Valdemar Golds! Big, beautiful, bigger and more beautiful than any other horse anyone else has. Perfect for Us."

Kordas just nodded, and rubbed the horse's cheeks with each hand. "What does he plan to do with them?" he asked.

"He's having a special gold chariot made, with a copy of the Conquest Throne on it," said the Doll, which seemed relieved that he hadn't taken offense. "They'll pull it in a parade that takes him to the Regatta, then he'll sit in it during the Regatta."

Well, that wasn't ideal, but the two stallions were used to being out in the sun all day. At least they weren't grays, which were prone to sunburn.

"Make sure they have water available while they're standing there," he cautioned. "And food, from time to time. Make sure where they're standing, the piss can run away from their feet. Make sure someone scoops up their shit and carries it away immediately, and don't let anyone but a Doll give them anything to eat. Especially don't let them get apples." That would be a disaster. He rather doubted the Emperor wanted to be assailed by horse farts.

"Yes, my Lord," the Doll said. "It will be done."

He couldn't tell from that response if they'd already been given orders along the same lines or not, but this way he was *certain* his boys would be treated properly—and wouldn't do anything to annoy the Emperor.

"My Lord—" the Doll said then, hesitantly.

"Yes?"

"These horses are not inclined to . . . chew on . . . things. Like a Doll. Are they?" It paused. "Some horses here are."

"No. I trained bad habits out of them," he replied. And it was true. He hadn't known about the Dolls, of course, but he'd trained them early not to mouth cloth or, worse, chew on it or play with it. Too many horses that got into bad habits like that ended up dead, with guts full of inedible things they could not get out of their stomachs.

"This is good to know," the Doll said, then ventured closer to the stallions and put up a tentative hand to touch the cheek of the nearest. The horse snorted at the unfamiliar object, but when Kordas said, "Steady," it relaxed and let the Doll touch it, then rub it, then leaned into the scratch.

"This one enjoys working with horses," the Doll said. "They are kindly natured."

"More kind than humans," Kordas replied, and sighed. "And I would be happier if I could spend the rest of my visit here." Reluctantly, he gave the huge necks a final pat, and straightened his shoulders. "But I can't. So it's back to my duty. And—I'm glad that you enjoy your time with the horses."

"Good fortune, my Lord," said the Doll as he walked away.

I'm going to need it, was his parting thought.

If there was one thing that Delia was certain of, it was that Isla was *seriously* angry with her husband for agreeing to try to save the hostages and the Dolls. Delia could understand her point. These were more complications in a plan that was already far too complicated and dangerous, and it was a complication that was guaranteed to make the Emperor furious with them. At one stroke he'd be deprived of all of his servants *and* his hostages, and Delia very much doubted that the "who" of the question would be a secret much past the moment when he discovered that Valdemar had been stripped of its most valuable resources and that its Duke and his family had vanished with those resources.

On the other hand . . . if she was in his place, she didn't think she'd be able to resist trying to save them either.

Well, Isla is like Father was. She'll be angry, and she'll give him a very long piece of her mind when they are back together and safe, but for now, what's done is done, and she'll change the Plan to adapt to it.

Isla took several long and deep breaths to calm herself, closing her eyes tightly and clenching and unclenching her hands on the tabletop. "My husband," she said, opening her eyes, "is an idiot. Gallant, chivalrous, and an idiot." She put the scrying glass flat on the table and stood up. "I need to go tell my maid to take the day off, then we'll make our way back here by way of the kitchen. The mages are probably gathering by now to go build those Gates."

Delia just nodded. The one thing that she was certain of was that Kordas wouldn't intentionally do anything that would put the rest of them in jeopardy. Himself, certainly, but not the rest of them. So no matter what he'd said, he wouldn't actually do anything until he was sure they were safely out of harm's way.

Right?

She hurried after Isla, who, mindful of the fact that someone might be watching at this moment, took an intricate route back to her own rooms to wake her maid, who was to all intents and purposes as identical to her mistress as any bundle of bedclothes would be.

"I feel ever so much better, milady—" the girl said, when Isla woke her.

"You might feel better *now,* but that's no reason to take chances with your health," Isla told her sternly—in a voice that made Delia think she really wanted to use some of that attitude on absent Kordas. "You go back down to your bed, and have another sleep. And if you find you are feeling up to it, try laundering some of my underthings and laying them in the sun to bleach, or do some mending. I'm sure I have something that needs mending. That's work enough for now."

The maid thanked her, but Isla was already out of the room and heading to the kitchens to talk to the cook and look through the stores.

When they had finished deciding what needed to be brought in from the manor farm to supply meals for the next day or two, Isla left her with a scrap of used parchment to make her list for the farm steward. "I'll be down in the cellars, checking the beer," she said aloud. "We're likely low, and by this time most of it will be strong. It's just about the time of year when we should start thinking about brewing again."

That's a nice touch. What noble in the Capital ever thinks about brewing his own beer?

Isla gestured to her, and they both made their way down into the kitchen cellars . . . and from there, down into the old manor cellars.

From the soft murmur of voices ahead of them, Delia knew her sister was right. The mages were gathering, and she was just a little surprised at their eagerness to get to work on something that was bound to deplete their energy so badly. Not to mention something that was going to force them to camp. She very much doubted that any of them had ever slept out of doors in his life.

—or will it deplete their energies? I could be mistaken. If Jonaton is right, there is that energy source there. And if it self-renews, maybe they can draw on that to do their work.

That might explain the enthusiasm she saw when she and Isla entered the "Preserved Nuts" cellar. The gaggle of mages, all of them dressed for travel and sitting on packs, turned their heads at the sound of footfalls, obviously expecting Jonaton at any moment. They didn't exactly look disappointed to see Lady Valdemar, but as they turned their heads to resume their conversation it was clear she was not who they wanted.

But a moment later, Jonaton *did* appear, and for once, wearing something so workmanlike and practical that Delia hardly recognized him, with his hair bound up in a tight knot on the nape of his neck.

Then again, he's about to go camping in the wilderness. Probably even he recognizes this is not the time for flowing tresses, jewelry, and lace.

He carried two rucksacks, one in each hand, and right

behind him were Ivar and Alberdina, also dressed for wilderness travel and geared up. Hakkon trailed behind them. Ivar
had a pack so huge it made Delia's eyes widen. It towered
above him, and there were weapons tied all over the sides of it.

"Clear out of the way," Jonaton said brusquely, and turned
to Isla. "My lady? Your assistance?"

"Gladly," Isla said.

The mages, packs and all, squeezed against the walls of
the cellar, as Jonaton's gaze flickered over to Delia. He pointed
at her. "I want you along," he said. "You're a good anchor. Go
to your room, pack everything you think you'll need for three
or four days. Hakkon?"

"I'll fix her a bedroll and whatnot. Delia, just bring your
personal things, I'll take care of your camping gear." The Seneschal turned on his heel and sprinted for whatever entrance
he'd come by. Delia obeyed Isla's silent head-jerk and ran to
her room.

As she ran, she decided what she was going to pack; she
still had a couple of the saddlebags from when she had first
arrived here. They fit neatly in a chest-stool in her bedroom,
and hadn't been in the way, so she'd left them there.

Before her father had died, she'd sometimes gone off on
rough, day-long rides with her pony, rides for which dresses
and skirts were utterly inappropriate, and she still had a couple of changes of the soft, baggy canvas trews and heavy
linen shirts she'd worn for that. Then a heavy woolen short
cape in case it was colder there than here, a rain-cape, underthings, twice as many stockings as she thought she'd need,
and she planned on sleeping in her clothing unless it got filthy,
so no point in taking bedshifts. She got what was needful
from her bathing room—she'd probably be cleaning herself
sketchily in the lake. Extra boots, just in case the first pair got
wet, because there was nothing worse than wet boots. She
cast a glance around the room and decided that was enough.

It all fit handily in two saddlebags. She changed into an outfit similar to what she'd packed, slung the bags over her shoulder, and ran back down again. She met Hakkon in the cellars and saw he had a pack much smaller than Ivar's with him.

He handed it to her. "Bedroll and some useful odds and ends," he said. "I'll let Grim know that one of the boys is to train your foal for you while you're gone."

"Thank you, Hakkon," she said with relief. That had been a worry. She hadn't wanted Grim to think she was shirking.

By the time they reached the cellar, the Foothold Gate was open, Ivar and Alberdina were gone, and the mages were filing through as Jonaton waited impatiently. She formed up behind the last of the mages, without really thinking about it, stepped through and—

—it was darker than a cave. Darker than anything she had ever experienced before. An *enormous* darkness that stretched to infinity on all sides of her, and she felt as if she was falling, but she knew she wasn't. And she felt as if she was being stretched in every possible direction. It didn't *hurt,* but it didn't feel good either!

There were things out there. Things she couldn't see. They couldn't see her, either, but she got the idea that they knew she was there, somewhere. And they wanted very badly to find her.

She tried to make herself small, but all she succeeded in doing was stretching herself in different directions, some of them impossible. And at the same time she couldn't actually feel anything of her body, as if she was just some—thing, with no body at all, just a little cloud of Delia, a mist in the darkness, and if she wasn't careful she'd blow apart, as a breeze blew apart a cloud of fog, and she'd never find herself and those *things* would breathe her in, or drink her up and—

—and she stepped down *hard* on moss-covered ground, stumbled over a stick, felt her elbow caught by someone, and was pulled out of the way just as Jonaton stepped through the Gate and it closed behind him. All there was now was a single cube of inscribed sandstone to mark where it had been.

One of the other mages caught Jonaton as he stumbled as she had done. He shook his head hard and made an inarticulate noise.

"That's a rough one," the mage said in sympathy.

"Well," he replied, thickly. "Once we get the real Gates up, it won't be so bad."

"Oh, it could be much worse," Ponu said cheerfully, materializing out of the group and taking him by the shoulder. "Come along, there's work to be done. Delia, you come too. Ivar and Alberdina need your help making camp."

But I've never camped before, she thought. It didn't seem to matter, though. She was carried along by the press of bodies, through underbrush and waist-high grass already being trampled flat, over the top of a low hill.

And there it was, stretching out in a bowl of a valley.

Ivar hadn't lied. The lake was the biggest she had ever seen, practically filling the valley, steel-blue under an *extremely* early-morning sky, the sun just barely peeking up over the horizon. And at the far distant shore, three narrow rivers. Did they lead *into* the lake or *out* of it?

Probably into it. All this water has to come from somewhere.

Back in Valdemar the sun was well above the horizon. It was, in fact, the usual time for breakfast if you weren't too quick about waking. They must be *at least* as far from Valdemar as Valdemar was from the Capital.

"At least it isn't going to rain," someone said cheerfully, and gave her a little shove to send her down the slope.

The mages trailed in single file down to the center of the cup of the crescent, and she followed them through more waist-high grass. Belatedly she wondered if there were any ticks or other obnoxious biting insects.

Too late, she thought with resignation. She hadn't prepared with repellent, and she'd just have to hope that if there were such things, her trews tucked into her boots would keep them out. Ponu propelled Jonaton just ahead of her by his shoulder, although Jonaton didn't seem in the least reluctant to go. The closer they got to that circle of land protruding into the water at the center of the crescent, the more she was able to make out some of what Ivar had talked about. Ruins, stone ruins— what looked like the wall of a round tower, and several buildings. Most of those weren't even head-high, but it occurred to her that those ruined walls could make a great basis for shelters. And when she saw Alberdina and Ivar hard at work inside them, she was pleased to think that her untutored guess was correct.

She detoured and joined them, ignoring the mages who had clustered at the water's edge, where there seemed to be those other remains that Ivar had spoken of—docks, a jetty, the sketchy remains of boats.

And she gaped at the number of packs clustered on the flattened grass in the center of the ruined tower. "But—"

"I've been back and forth a few times," Ivar said cheerfully. "I'm used to playing pack-mule. Cousin, what do you want Delia to do?"

Alberdina rummaged in an open pack beside her and came up with a hand-scythe. Delia took it uncertainly. "Ever used one of those?" Alberdina asked.

"Gathering herbs?" she replied with hesitation.

"Go gather reeds along the shore and bring them back here. Reeds, not sedges. Sedges have edges; reeds are round." Alberdina went back to her task, which was threading pieces of rope through grommets on the edge of what appeared to be a house-sized piece of canvas. Maybe larger. Ivar picked up a hand-axe with a hammer-like side balancing the axe-blade and headed out through the remains of the tower door, which was completely without a header, just two jambs and a sill.

She followed her orders and went down to the shore, avoiding the gathering of mages down by the jetty. Now that the sun was up, the lake water was more blue than steel, but with edges going to green, except where the jetty was. Bay came with her, wagging his tail solemnly when she looked at him. "Good boy," she told him. He snorted and picked up his ears, tail wagging harder.

She took off her boots and waded in. The water was cold, but shallow enough here that she could see the sandy bottom, and little minnows darting through the plants—which were, as specified, round. She bent down and began cutting, stacking the cut reeds up along the dry shore as she worked. The water smelled clean, the cut reeds added a pleasant green scent, the sun was comfortable for now—but she decided that when she'd finished cutting as much reed as she could carry, she'd go back and get her hat from her pack. It didn't make any sense to come all this way to help, only to be felled by sunstroke.

Bay kept watch while she worked, and she was quite comforted by his presence. After all . . . she already knew there were bears.

When she returned, Alberdina and Ivar were creating a sort of tent-shelter using the stone walls and the enormous piece of canvas. They'd spread the canvas over the top of the walls and were working their way around the base, pounding wooden pegs cut from branches into the ground with the hammer-ends of their hand-axes and tying off the pieces of rope fastened to the grommets in the canvas. "Spread the reeds about two knuckles deep around the edge of the tower inside," said Alberdina. "Keep cutting and spreading until you've gone all the way around the edge." Delia spread her reeds, got her hat, and went back to the lake edge to gather more.

By the time she'd finished about a quarter of the circle, Alberdina and Ivar were inside the new shelter, ducking their heads a little, lashing together a sort of rack made of branches, after pounding the uprights into the ground. They'd picked a place that was up against the tower wall that had a tumble of stones under it; obviously she didn't need to put reeds *there*. By the time she'd finished the next quarter, the rack was finished and all the packs were stacked on it, up off the ground. Smaller bags were hung by their straps off the frame. Ivar was gone, and Alberdina was clearing away a spot where it looked like a fireplace had been built into the wall.

By the time she'd finished the third quarter, Ivar had come back with several armfuls of wood. Alberdina had started a fire and had metal grates on legs poised over it.

As Delia finished spreading her final armful of reeds around the edge of the ruin, Alberdina turned away from the fire and surveyed her work.

By this time she was fairly sweaty, her back hurt from all the stooping over, and she was tired. "Take a break," Alberdina told her, then went to a pack on the very top of the rack and took what looked like a round, fist-sized loaf of bread out of it, and took a leather bottle off the side of the rack. She handed both to Delia, who eyed the bread dubiously. She was starving, and this didn't look like much.

"It's travel-bread," Alberdina told her. "It's a lot more filling than it looks."

And when she bit into it, she discovered it was very dense, and packed with dried fruit and seeds. It was, indeed, a lot more filling than she'd thought possible.

Meanwhile Alberdina had gone outside the shelter and given a shrill whistle, then shouted, "When you're at a place you can stop, come eat!"

Delia had eaten the bread very quickly, and now was thirsty. "Is the lake water safe to drink?" she asked Alberdina.

"Yes," the Healer said shortly, taking an armful of the solid little bread loaves out of the pack. "Drink what's in the bottle, take it with you, and fill it at the cleanest spot you see." She left the shelter again and came back empty-handed. "Floor this entire thing with reeds, then come to me for what you can do next."

With a sigh, Delia did as she was told. This was going to be a very long day.

By nightfall, the following had happened.

Delia had floored the shelter with reeds. The mages had two sets of pillars erected. She had absolutely not expected them to be any sort of practical builders, but they were. They'd even brought cement with them, or someone had brought it in previously, and the mages had used it to cement rocks from the ruins into foundations into which the four curved pillars had been set, in pairs, looking very like the horns of the Foothold Gate back in the cellar. That was in the late afternoon; once finished, they spread their bedrolls on the reeds, heads facing the wall, toes facing the center, about two circles deep.

Alberdina had established a proper latrine, well away from the shore, with a screening of woven willow withies for privacy.

Ivar had shot and butchered a half-grown wild pig, and Alberdina had roasted it on a bed of hot rocks from the ruins. One of the mages had helped her make the bed—with magic, which had been amazing to watch, as the right-sized rocks levitated into place, forming a sort of pavement. Ivar had built a fire over the rocks, let it burn down to coals, brushed the ashes away, and spread pieces of pig over the rocks, turning them until done. So everyone had pork and salt and herbs from Alberdina's pack with their travel bread.

Delia thought that she had never tasted anything so good.

Just at sunset they all had a short wash in the lake, then took to their bedrolls. The reeds, spread over the flattened grass that had grown up inside the ruined tower, made a

passable mattress, at least enough to keep stones from sticking into her. She was asleep faster than she had thought she'd
be able to manage.

In the morning, when she woke with the first light, she
picked her way through the sleeping bodies to take care of
business and have a better wash-up afterward. Then she had
a look at those two proto-Gates.

One pair was on land, and was about as far apart as a pair
of wagons side by side. The other was just on the edge of the
water, so that boats that went through would slide right down
into the water naturally, and had been positioned where the
jetty had been. Deeper water, deep enough for the fully loaded
barges. The wood they were made of was some of the oddest
that Delia had ever seen, and she could not make up her mind
what it was. It was darker than anything she had ever seen
before, greenish in color, and much denser. It looked varnished, and practically brand new.

Was this something *their* mages had done when they'd
been erecting the things? Or had the wood come from some
place outside of Valdemar?

She heard footfalls behind her, and turned to see Jonaton
approaching. "How—" she began.

"Are we getting horses and barges through? These will be
the paired Gates like you see on the canals, where the horses
are unhitched, put through a smaller Gate beside the barge
Gate, and catch up with their barge on the other side. Obviously we can't do that since we're putting the barges straight
into the lake from the canal on the other side," he said, sur-
veying the curved upright and laying a proprietary hand on it.
"So each barge will get a strong push on the Empire side, come
through here, and drop into the water, with a crewman aboard
with a pole who'll get it out of the way by poling it to the right
or left. The horses will come through over there. We'll either
tow or pole the barge to the shore, and either tie it to a previous barge or hitch it back up to the horses to start a new barge

string. We reckon on the horses pulling full ten-barge strings. And meanwhile people can be coming through the horse-Gate when there aren't horses coming through."

"I was going to ask about the wood," she said.

"Oh." He laughed. "These were either breasthooks or keels of the boats that were here. The rest rotted away, but whoever built these things impregnated the wood with copper salts, probably using alchemy rather than pure magic. There's honestly no way of telling how old they are without a lot of magical shenanigans we don't have the time or energy for. They're not less than fifty years abandoned, and not more than five hundred. I'd guess it's nearer to the five hundred mark than the fifty, but I can't think about everything I want to, right now. I have to set things aside, for later. Urgency. Focus. It means I just have to let some things go."

She blinked. But, then again, there were things as old or older than that in the Empire. "What are you doing today?" she asked.

"Tying them to the power source, then turning four pieces of wood into two Gates. There will be a lot of—stuff—going on. Like we did with the Foothold Gate, but more, and with more mages. Then the rest of the mages except the Circle and I go home via the Foothold Gate while Ivar, Alberdina, and you stay here. And the third day I tune the two Gates with your help as an anchor, I open them, some more magic stuff goes on, and the fourth day, I spend flat on my back while Alberdina takes care of me, and Sai makes something about the size of Bay to feed me when I am up to it. And right now, you and I go back to the Foothold Gate and wait for breakfast and lunch to get pitched through."

She laughed, thinking he'd made a joke.

When "breakfast and lunch" arrived, however, he held her over to one side of the rippling disk of weird light that suddenly irised open, and she discovered it was *not* a joke as baskets and bags came flying through it, piling up at the foot of the thing. She realized in a moment they were coming too quickly for Isla and Hakkon alone to be throwing them through; they must have some servants in on the Plan now.

It was over so quickly she scarcely believed it, and the Gate vanished the same way it had arrived. "Our turn to be pack mules—" Jonaton said.

"Nah, I'm here to help," said Ivar, coming over the hill behind them. "Strong like mule, dumb like ox, hitch to plow when horse dies."

Kordas woke too early, as usual. Star brought him breakfast, and he pondered what he was going to do with the hours stretching in front of him.

"Can I go out in the city?" he asked, finally. He'd never seen the Imperial City. The hostages weren't allowed off the Palace grounds, and they weren't allowed to roam too much *within* those grounds, either.

"There is no reason why not," Star said, after a moment. "But why?"

"Curious. Bored. Want to see what a city-dweller looks like. I always imagined, when I was being schooled here, that they were mythical." He got out of bed and headed for the bathing room.

"They are not mythical, but they are . . . fewer than they were twenty years ago," Star said, sounding as if the Doll was choosing words very carefully indeed. "Twenty years ago, when the Great Emperor in his wisdom decided it was time to expand the border to the south, there were many, many poor. Now there are no poor. The Emperor, in his wisdom, said that it is the duty of the Empire to give employment and food and shelter to all the citizens of the Empire. So he did."

Star paused. Kordas felt a sinking feeling in the pit of his stomach. It sounded oh, so reasonable and benevolent. And knowing the Emperor, there was a dark, dark side to this. "And what did our great and glorious Emperor do?" he asked hesitantly.

"He gave all of the poor of the city employment in his legions," Star said—exactly as he had thought the Doll would answer. "Men and boys are soldiers. Women serve as the support, in all ways. There are three legions in the south now, and have been for two decades. They have nearly permanent camps, with everything a city needs. Horses need tending, food beasts need tending, waste must be removed. There is everything from cooks to blacksmiths. And he allowed for childbearing, even planned for it. By now, the legions are well into their second generations born and bred to the conquests of the south. It is very efficient."

"I'm sure it is." He licked lips gone dry. "Is there anyone still actually living in the City?"

"Craftsmen, tradesmen, merchants," Star replied. "And laborers to tend to the City itself. They have not yet been replaced by Dolls, because most of the Dolls are needed here, in the Palace. There are only so many mages to make Dolls, and Dolls need replacing when they are damaged."

And the fact that there are just enough mages to replace broken Dolls, rather than continuing to replace people with Dolls, is the only reason why those folks haven't been sent to the south as well. The thought was inescapable.

"I need some perspective. I'd like to see the City," he said. "Do I ride, or do I walk?"

"A great Lord *never* walks except within the Palace," Star said firmly. "We will go to the Gate Room. A horse will be ready for you when we reach the Courtyard. This one will be your guide."

The waiting horse, held by yet another Doll at the base of the shallow stairs leading to the huge bronze doors, was one of his own Sweetfoot palfreys. She looked to be about eight years old, and, as far as he could tell, was healthy and well-tended. Just to be sure, he checked her coat, her ribs, her feet, and under her saddle for saddle-sores before he mounted. She was fine, and a good weight, her hooves were well-shod and properly tended, and she showed nothing in her behavior that she'd been mistreated.

Of course that didn't mean she'd been treated *well*. He suspected that to the vast majority of the courtiers here, a horse was nothing more than a thing that took you from one place to another. Like a sort of Doll.

And if they weren't so pretty, and if it was possible, and if there were enough mages, the Emperor probably would have replaced horses with Dolls too, by now. Now there's a funny thought. If vrondi *are captured and made into Dolls, what about all the other Unseen entities? What would they be made into? Hold up now. That's me thinking like myself, not like Imperial Mages. I would explore and experiment, but they probably aren't allowed to. The Empire has a streak of brutal, unchanging efficiency to it, and primary research takes time, effort, resources, and risks. Especially since my parents' time, the Empire does not pursue new things, it strips them away.*

The palfrey picked up her feet daintily and ambled off in the direction of the iron gates that stood in the wall around the Palace. Star kept up with no problem.

The City was . . . strange. For a place as big as it was, it was echoingly empty. No building was the height of the Palace, of course; the Palace loomed over everything, inescapable, the symbol of how the Empire controlled everything. He didn't see much that was over three stories tall, and the buildings themselves were a mix of so many different materials and styles that it made his head swim. There were canals, as he expected; in times past, canals were not just practical, they were seen as a symbol of prosperity and prestige, and to his surprise, the canals here had a steady flow, sometimes as brisk as a horse's canter. They were paired with canals flowing in the opposite direction. The streets, though, were arrow-straight, and paved with something like a sheet of solid stone—except that his horse's hooves, and the hooves of the other beasts on the streets, made very little sound on it. And it seemed to have some give to it.

There were few horses or vehicles, few people afoot, and all of them seemed to be going someplace in a very great hurry. Buildings showed dark windows, like empty eyes. There were shops, usually attended by a single person, brightly lit, and generally with one customer or none. But there were also craftsmen in workshops, with goods showing in stalls to the side, and the workshops open so that you could see them working, and all of them seemed very busy, even frantically busy. Many—far too many—of them were weapons-makers, including ones making Spitters.

But as he approached one of those workshops, he discovered that there were also large versions of Spitters, something he had never seen before, things about as long as his arm and thick as his thigh. He caught sight of some of them being loaded onto a wagon, and stared.

"Poomers," said Star, seeing where he was looking. "That is the largest practical size of Spitter. Anything larger, and defects in the castings often make them explode in the field, which is considered a waste of metal and soldiers. Each discharge requires seven pellets. Poomers rarely fire bolts. They fire wooden sabots packed with metal shot and weighted chains."

That would be horrifying to face. Kordas had seen the effects of shot, versus bolts, on waterfowl. A ground-braced Poomer, firing shot, would shred anything at medium distance, and the chain-shot? It could probably fell a twenty-year-old tree if it struck dead-on, and the shrapnel from the tree would explode outward. He visibly shuddered.

"Pellets are made in the Palace, in the Fabrication Annex," Star continued. "In case of accident, the Palace proper would not be harmed badly. The Annex is exclusively staffed by Dolls."

"I'd like to see that. Is anything else made there?" he asked.

Star shook its head. "Clothing, Dolls, and pellets, is all. Dolls and pellets require mage-craft, and of course, we must be able to supply the Emperor and his courtiers with clothing on demand. The fabric comes from the City. Most things come from the City, to the Receiving Annex."

They turned a corner, and spread out before him was something he would never have expected.

An immense market-garden, full of vegetables and fruits.

"The Palace gardens only supply the needs of the Palace," Star explained. "These gardens and others like them supply the needs of the City. When the poor were sent to the south, their homes were torn down, and the open land turned into the gardens. It is very efficient."

The rest of the tour took place in silence. And now Kordas realized where a lot of the smoke and stink was coming from. Metal smelting facilities, tanneries, dyers, fullers, butchers . . . almost everything needed to supply the Palace, and to supply the people who still lived in the City, was made in the City. When they crossed a narrow river, though, Kordas thought he was going to choke. It was an open sewer.

"Oh gods big and small, that reeks. Where are we getting our water from?" he gagged.

"It is from a series of wells, and it is treated and purified for the Palace," Star said. "I do not know where the people of the City get theirs."

He hoped for their sake it was also from wells, and not from the canals, or that . . . sewer. Wells far away from the dreck that flowed under the bridge that took them back to the Palace.

The City proved to be achingly empty, though he suspected that some of those who were not "the poor" had seen the way the wind was blowing, and found a way to make their livings elsewhere, before the Emperor decided that they, too, should be sent to the southern border and the endlessly hungry war machine.

All he needs is enough people here to keep the Palace sup-
plied and the legions supplied with specialist items, and to
provide cheering crowds whenever he makes a parade. And he
doesn't need a parade all that often. He has afternoon Court
and appearance dinners when he chooses, after all. Fawning
courtiers, people jockeying to get his attention, whenever he
chooses.

He turned the horse's head back toward the Palace a lot
sooner than he had expected to. He had seen enough for new
plans to form already, and the sooner he could get some un-
watched thinking-time in, the better. There was a *truth* emerg-
ing from all of this, and it seemed to be the greatest exploitable
flaw of the Empire. Kordas's heart pounded, because it felt as
if nobody in the Emperor's City realized it existed. None of
them.

They fixate upon conquest, power, and betrayal.
What is trusted is dismissed from their attention.

———————————

To save time, Kordas left the horse at the nearest usable Gate
with one of the Dolls, who would take it back to the stables. A
simple statement by Star just kept nagging at him. When they
were back in his apartment, and Star had uncovered the Valdemar badge on its hand, signifying it was safe to speak, he finally decided on exactly how he wanted to ask the question
that was bothering him.

"You said *'there are only so many mages,'* but this entire
place is practically alive with magic," he stated. "How does
everything get done?"

"There are very few things that require a mage to actually
do them in person. Instead, a mage, or several working together, long ago made constructs—machines—that merely
require a power source. Like the Gates. The Palace mages are
here for life, what could be termed 'tenured.' As such, they

have settled upon a minimum amount of work, to maximize their leisure, and exist in what you might term a voluntary imprisonment."

"So their lives are spent casting the same spells, day after day?"

"Essentially, yes. They charge items that are then sent by chutes and relays to the Fabrication Annex, and those items are expended operating the manufactory constructs there. The Palace mages produce a surplus of such charged items, which are simply stored in boxes. As for other mages, two are designated as research mages, but, as they must prioritize what the Court wishes, they most often spend their days inventing entertainments. Since Dolls were invented by them, and found to be so versatile, they have done little else of note."

All right. Now I ask the prize question. "My knowledge of magic tells me that you need a mage to make a Gate talisman that tells a Gate where to send you," he stated. "But all talismans come from the Palace. How is that even possible?"

"Because there is a construct that makes talismans," Star replied, its head tilted to one side as if it was surprised he did not know this. "One puts in a metal model, with the destination imbued into it. The construct creates a paper copy that can be easily destroyed, so that people cannot clandestinely use it a second time to go somewhere without permission. The construct can make hundreds, even thousands at need."

He felt his jaw drop open.

"Who operates these constructs?" he finally asked. *Because if the answer is what I think it is—*

"We do," Star said simply. "We are trusted, and do not tire. We can make several thousand in a candlemark. This is how the Emperor gives out talismans to travel about the Empire. There are also universal talismans, which respond to vocal commands, that allow Dolls and courtiers to travel about the Palace. These take much longer, however." Star tilted its head to the side. "This one supposes that the universal talismans would also take the wearer outside the Palace to anywhere in the Empire, but this one does not know this for certain, as such talismans are surrendered when a courtier leaves the Palace at the end of a visit."

And there it was. The answer. The answer to how he could get thousands of talismans to Valdemar, talismans that would carry thousands of people and barges to the new lands. How thousands of Dolls could get their talismans and come, too, and it would look like everyday business. His mind raced. "What could be made—ordered by just a Duke, without anyone in the Palace noticing, because they don't notice what's not a danger or an aberration—or maybe I should say, what would be below their notice? Could—"

Star tilted its head again, and answered before he could voice the question.

"Yes, my Lord. We can make talismans for your escape, once we have a model. The models are merely the talismans of old, the ones mages would produce one at a time of metal blanks. We can make as many paper copies as you need for your Plan."

"But how to deliver them around, without drawing attention or suspicion? There would be stacks of them as high as Chargers . . ." He trailed off.

"If I may remind you, my Lord, Dolls make deliveries unnoticed by anyone who would endanger you or your Plan. Also, Dolls are repaired by other Dolls, and need not be stuffed solely with wool."

He wasn't certain whether to laugh or cry. In the end, he did neither. And by the time he recovered himself, the lights had changed to tell him it was time to go down to luncheon, and begin another round of the Fourth Game.

Ivar and Alberdina had a lot of things for Delia to do when she brought the last loads of breakfast back to the camp, though they let her eat first. Hauling deadfall to pile up beside the round tower for someone to chop up took the greater part of the morning, followed by hauling luncheon from the Foothold Gate to the camp. Then rolling beer barrels down to the camp. Then hauling water from the lake to the camp to be stored in a couple of those barrels that happened to be empty. By the time supper came around—more travel bread, this time with venison and roasted wild onions and honey—she had done more physical labor than she'd ever done in a single day in her life.

Ivar and Alberdina had not been idle. Ivar had chopped such an enormous amount of wood that it came all the way to the top of the tower wall, and she guessed it was about three cords' worth. Nor had that been all he'd done, since he'd obviously hunted, killed, gutted, skinned, and butchered that deer.

Alberdina had been hunting as well—food and herbs. She'd

found wild onions, swathes of bee-balm to tuck under the bedrolls to repel bugs, a big cache of nuts, and the wild honey she'd given them to eat with their travel bread. How on earth she'd gotten the honey away from the bees, Delia had no idea, and was too tired to guess. She'd found a lot more as well, since she'd been tying bunches of bee-balm and herbs upside down all over the outside of the shelter, but Delia didn't recognize what all of the plants were.

So Delia didn't get to see anything of what the mages did to actually create the Gates. Just the results, which were that the four curved uprights glowed faintly once the sun set.

She sat outside the shelter, which was full of equally tired mages, working slowly at the honey-soaked bread and the savory but tough venison. It was worth eating, however tough it was; those wild herbs that Alberdina had found gave it excellent flavor. Alberdina came to join her, and they gazed at the lake, the Gates, and the dark blue sky slowly going to black.

"Is this what it's going to be like?" Delia asked, with the last piece of honey-soaked bread in her hand, nibbling at it slowly with tired jaws.

"You mean living out here, once we're free of the Empire?" Alberdina asked. "Probably. Very probably. There's going to be a lot of hard, physical labor, and everyone is going to have to pitch in. Your servants are going to be very busy doing other things than tending to you. You're going to have to learn to wash clothing in a stream, and how to do your own mending. You'll be set tasks like the ones I gave you yesterday and today, things that just need a pair of uneducated hands. It won't be fun. It won't be easy."

"What if I just—don't come along?" she asked in a small voice, because with the reality of what was going to happen setting in, living life out here in the middle of nowhere didn't seem in the least attractive.

"Then when the Emperor finds out what we've done, and

he will, who do you think he'll take his wrath out on?" Alberdina countered. "It'll be the ones who stay behind. The farmers and the laborers left, well, he *might* leave them alone, or he just might put everyone to the sword and move in an entire new population. But you? A known member of Kordas's household? Anything you can imagine, it'll be a hundred times worse."

"So I don't have a choice." She felt like crying. What had Kordas and Isla gotten her into? She hadn't asked for *any* of this.

"Well, you could always betray us," Alberdina said coldly. "Then he'd probably marry you off to some old reprobate in his Court that's gone through four wives already and is looking for a fifth. You'd still have the life of a lady. If that's what you want, you can get it. Kordas is probably right in thinking that once we close and burn down those Gates, the Emperor won't be able to find us, so betraying us probably won't do *us* any harm. And it isn't as if you have the ability to tell him where we are."

Hearing it put that baldly just made her want to cry even more. She hadn't asked for this! Was that *really* much of a choice, either hard labor in the wilderness, or being handed off to some nasty old man as a "reward" for telling the Emperor how everyone had fled to escape him?

Wasn't there a third option?

But she couldn't think of one.

"Just think of how Isla and Kordas have been feeling all these years," Alberdina persisted. "Knowing that at any moment, on the Emperor's whim, everything could be pulled out from under them. That at any moment, the Emperor's troops could come pouring in, taking literally everything and almost everyone, all to feed his ego and his war machine. And everyone that was left would be starving on scraps and forced to build things back up again just so the Emperor could sweep in and take it all again. I've seen it happen to entire baronies.

When the Emperor moves in, he takes every person under the age of fifty and over the age of thirteen, he takes everything that can be ridden, eaten, or drunk, and he sweeps out again." She paused, and Delia wondered what else she was going to say. "I don't think he'd spare you a second time, and your pedigree wouldn't save you. He might leave Kordas. He might not. Kordas was educated at the Palace, so he knows the basics of military strategy. The Emperor's wars need officers as well as soldiers."

Delia felt cold and numb.

"That's what the Plan is meant to save us all from," Alberdina said after a pause. "Seems to me some hard work and blisters don't look like a bad option." She paused, and patted Delia on the shoulder. "It won't be so bad. And you'll get used to it. Hellfires, you've got Fetching Gift, so it's possible Kordas will have you using that rather than gathering wood and herding chickens."

"For what?" she asked, bleakly.

"Don't know. But I suspect there's a lot of things it could be useful for. Probably the best thing for you to do is to start thinking of them. You've got a head on those shoulders, so use it, so you won't have to do as much work with your hands." Alberdina chuckled a little. "I know for sure the mages aren't going to be going out and gathering wood. Make sure you are so valuable doing something else that no one will want you to waste your time working like a mule."

She got up and left Delia sitting alone in the dark, muscles aching and stiffening, feeling very much depressed. All she could see in front of her were a lot of more or less terrible choices, and no way out of them that she could live with.

When she went back to her bedroll, she was tempted to cry herself to sleep—but she was so tired that despite her aches, she fell right asleep before she could squeeze out a single tear.

She wasn't the first one awake the next morning, so she wasn't the one who had to fetch bags and baskets of breakfast from the Foothold Gate—that had fallen to Ivar and a couple of the younger mages. But as soon as she was up, washed and changed, and fed, Jonaton came looking for her as the mages packed up their things in preparation to go through the horse Gate once he'd tuned and opened it.

He found her finishing the last of a bacon roll, and tugged her to her feet. "Come along," he said. "I need you to come anchor this thing, like you did with the Foothold Gate."

"Why?" she asked this time, though she did get to her feet and follow him to the two uprights that formed what would be the horse Gate. "Why not Ivar or Alberdina? They don't have magic either."

"Because Alberdina is going to be looking after me, and Ivar and Bay are going to be guarding us. Remember, there are bears." He grinned as she shivered. "Don't worry. If a bear shows up, Ivar's already got plans and a bear-trap in place. I promise you a bear-steak and a bearskin for your bed."

That only made her think about where that bed was going to be. In the middle of winter. In the wilderness. Would it be in the dubious shelter of this ruined tower? Or in a tent? In the snow?

Had Jonaton even thought about any of this? Or was he just concentrating on the tasks at hand? Hakkon probably wouldn't mind beds on cold, hard ground, but surely Jonaton would be as miserable as *she* was going to be!

And what about the Circle? They were all old men—

But they seemed made of whipcord and tanned sinew, and surely they already knew how awful this was going to be, and they didn't seem to care. They even seemed to be happier, as if going from an easy life in a manor to swatting waterbugs in a wilderness, until they finished mummifying, was an invigorating playtime! Even their endless banter, swatting at each other, and quibbling, had tilted lately into increasingly absurd accusations of behavior she was probably too young to know about.

The mages—who still looked exhausted—lined up on their packs in front of what would be the horse Gate. She sat behind the Gate uprights where Jonaton put her and worried over it all without paying any attention to what Jonaton was doing. Besides, it wasn't as if this was the cellar, where the whole place was alight with glowing diagrams and sigils. This was out in the open and broad daylight, and frankly it just looked like Jonaton was doing some sort of absurd dance. Her mind just kept going around and around in an endless, bleak play of how horrible it was all going to be, and how she couldn't do anything about it.

She only looked up when the waiting mages broke out into weary applause, picked up their packs, and started filing through the Gate in groups of two and three, because there was plenty of room for that between those uprights. It was . . . unsettling, to watch them walking toward her, then suddenly disappearing.

Finally there was no one left on the round peninsula but her, Jonaton, and Alberdina. Jonaton staggered a little; Alberdina jumped to her feet and caught him. She handed him a leather bottle, and he drank everything in it down in several long gulps.

"Better?" she asked.

He nodded, as strangers suddenly started appearing between the Gate uprights, laden with all manner of boxes, bundles, and packs. They headed straight for the ruins as if they knew exactly what they were doing—which they probably did. There was a plan, after all. Just because *she* didn't know what was in it, it didn't follow that Isla had neglected to attend to the least little detail.

"Mornin'," said one in a floppy straw hat to Alberdina. "Nice day fer fishin', ain't it?" And he gave a little gulp of a laugh. Well, that seemed to make sense, since aside from his pack, he had a huge bundle of fishing poles on one shoulder. He was followed by a blacksmith, and a confused-appearing man, probably some kind of herbalist or grower, with a string of garlic hanging from his belt.

Evidently Alberdina knew the fisherman, because she gave him a little tap on his shoulder as he headed for the ruins.

Several dogs came through; there were two mastiffs, and several dogs that seemed to be part of a hunting pack, because they kept together and hard at the heels of the man she assumed was their master.

"I think I'm—" Jonaton began.

"You're eating first," Alberdina contradicted him, and gestured to Delia to come too. Some of what the newcomers had been carrying were foodstuffs, so at least she was not going to have to fetch more baskets and bundles from the Foothold Gate. Delia ate glumly; Jonaton ate gluttonously. Alberdina was too busy directing all the new people as to where everything was to pay any attention to either of them.

And still *more* people poured in through the Gate, a regular procession of them. Then something she had never seen before—small logs strung on bits of rope, each end of which was attached to a longer rope, so that the whole thing looked like a rope ladder made for someone who was too obtuse to realize that the rungs were going to roll under his feet. It passed through the Gate, and she couldn't see the other end.

But then she realized what it was, as boxes and bundles and other large containers were shoved across the Gate, riding freely on those rolling logs. Some of the men started gathering them up and taking them to the ruins. It was all so organized! She could hardly believe her eyes.

And then the procession of containers stopped, the rollers were neatly stowed aside, and a flock of traumatized sheep blundered through, preceded and followed by herd dogs. A squad of woodsmen and builders came through, bearing backpacks laden with more weight in tools than a team of horses could hope to move. They moved up the hill as one unit, without even waiting for directions.

"Kristoff! Has anyone sent that coracle across?" Jonaton bellowed to someone over in the ruins.

"Right here!" shouted the fellow who'd had all the fishing poles, bringing over something she'd taken to be a very big basket, which was, in fact, a round thing of woven willow, with a tarred canvas cover sewn tightly over it. There was a board across the middle of it.

He put it in the water behind the two water-Gate uprights and gestured to her, and to horror, she realized that *this* was how she was supposed to get "behind" the water-Gate.

A Tow-Beast came through the land-Gate, led by one of the Valdemar stableboys. It was at this point that it truly dawned on her that the land-Gate could not *possibly* be linked to the Foothold Gate in the cellar.

The man with the round boat-thing gestured to her again, impatiently, and with great reluctance she went to him. "Yer t' git down in this here coracle, milady," he said, sitting on the bank and holding the contraption "steady" with both hands. "Jest sit down here on bank, next ter me. Tha's right. Now put yer feet in 'er—"

Little by little, he coaxed her into the unsteady thing, until she was perched, terrified, on the board across the middle, afraid it would turn over at any moment, and even more afraid that he was going to let go of it.

But he didn't, and Jonaton went to work again.

Doesn't he know I don't know how to swim? she thought frantically.

But the stranger held the wretched thing tightly against the bank, and she squeezed her eyes shut and endured. She'd never been so panicked and frightened in her entire life. Her stomach was certain that at any moment she was going to find herself in the water, being sucked down to her death.

But eventually, she'd been scared for so long that fatigue set in, and she opened her eyes. Kristoff—if that was his name—gave her a reassuring nod. Her hands hurt. She glanced down at them to see that she was holding on to the board she sat on so tightly that her knuckles were white.

"Heerd ye got a Gold foal," the man said, matter-of-factly. "Tell me 'bout her."

He's trying to get my mind off this, she thought. *He sees how scared I am.* Well, maybe it would work.

So she told him all about Daystar, how old she was, how Delia had helped with the foaling, how she was getting the filly used to being handled, and what steps would be next. And when she was done, he nodded.

"Well," he said, tilting his head to one side. "Sounds like that there Fetchin' Gift be right handy. Why, I c'n think of a mort'o ways it'll be useful out here. Like—well, ain't jest horses what hez trouble birthin'. Cattle, sheep, hooman wimmin— reckon yer gonna be right popular with Healer Alberdina. An'—well, they's one good way o' makin' a big shelter, an' thet's ter bend down a bendy tree, like a birch, stake 'er down, and throw canvas over 'er. Ye c'n bring thet top right down, aye? An' what if a barge breaks loose an' floats out inter a lake? Ye c'n Fetch her up t' th' bank wi'out nobody hevin' ter go arter 'er."

He continued at some length, with great enthusiasm, until after a moment, she realized that not only was he *right* about some of that, she might very well be so busy that she would never have time to do all the hard labor she'd envisaged herself doing.

He glanced over at the men setting up more shelters in the ruins. "Ain't lookin' for'erd ter sleepin' on ground," he said with distaste. "Be glad when th' livin' barges start a-comin' over."

"What are living barges?" she asked.

"Barges fixed up as housen," he said. "Cozy, they is. Live in one m'self, what with bein' a fishin' man." And he began to describe what sounded to her like something that was every bit as comfortable as a little cottage, if nothing near as spacious.

"But how do you keep it warm in the winter?" she asked.

"Leetle stove. I'd show ye how big, but I reckon ye don't want me t' turn loose of this coracle," he said with a chuckle. "It ain't no manor, but it ain't no tent, neither. Wust thin' come winter's gonna be gettin' bored, I reckon. We ain't a-gonna be able ter move in winter, gonna be plenty idle hands ter take care of the stock an' all. Reckon come fall, we'll pick a good place, make stockades fer th' critters, an' stretch oursel's along the river all th' way ter this here lake. We'll be like a long, skinny town. Then come spring, oncet th' stock's done birthin', we'll move agin."

She could even see it in her mind's eye: the "town" of living barges along the shore, the animals in their pens ashore, maybe some people (hardier than her!) living on shore in something that gave more shelter than just a mere tent—

"Thet there tower'll be a fine shelter oncet a good roof's on 'er," Kristoff said cheerfully, jerking his head at the tower ruins. "An' thet there Ivar, he's seed people up north what make winter housen outa sod. All right and tight they be, too. We'll do. We'll do. An' when we finds a new place ter set up ferever, like, it'll be a home in no time. Jest wait an' see."

"*Kristoff!*" Alberdina shouted from the other side of the water-Gate. "*Get yourselves out of the way! Barges are coming through!*"

"Jump, milady!" Kristoff told her, and she jumped, and somehow he caught her, and they both scrambled out of the way just before the prow of a barge and a spill of water appeared on her side of the Gate. It slid rapidly into the lake with an enormous splash, sending the round boat-thing spinning away.

"Well now," said Kristoff, staring after his coracle. "I don' s'ppose ye c'ld Fetch 'er back, c'ld ye?"

Delia was more in the spirit of things now, though, and flashed a genuine smile back to him. "What, and deprive you of the great honor of being the First Swimmer in the Lake?"

Kordas could tell that Isla was still furious with him. And she had a point. He *was* being reckless. He was promising things he had no right to promise.

He was going to steal the Emporer's entire Palace workforce.

He was proposing to kidnap fifty children in the name of "saving" them, which was morally dubious.

And when the Emperor discovered he had done this—he'd have to make sure everyone who was going to remain in Valdemar went into hiding, or find some other way to deflect the Emperor's wrath. He could only hope that those who stayed behind would be so insignificant in the Emperor's eyes that he wouldn't bother with them.

Of course *Merrin* would be left behind. And Merrin was certainly significant enough to make a good target for wrath.

And the Emperor will surely be furious that Merrin didn't see any of this coming.

And yet, the conviction remained that he was doing the right things, promising the right things, no matter how it seemed now.

So he ignored the smoldering anger in Isla's eyes, and asked, "Have you got Gate talismans for the two new Gates yet? And can Delia Fetch them to me?"

"Yes to both," she said, though it was clear she was doing so around gritted teeth. She moved aside, and Delia took her place in the limited view in the scrying mirror.

"Can you tilt your mirror so I can see the table?" the girl asked, holding two metal disks in her open hand.

Rather than saying anything, he did so. And there was a

long and uncomfortable silence, as she stared straight ahead of her, while beads of sweat began to run down her forehead and she grew paler and paler with effort.

And then, just as he was about to tell her to stop trying for the moment, there was a *clink,* and two metal disks appeared on the table in front of him and skidded to the floor.

Delia swayed, and Isla's hand appeared on her shoulder, steadying her. "Go lie down," Isla told her sister, and Delia vanished from view.

"You are certain these—Dolls—can do what they say?" Isla asked, somehow managing to look both dubious and angry at the same time.

"As certain as I am of anything in this world," he told her. "This will turn any Gate in the Duchy into a way to our refuge. And no one will be the wiser. Our mages won't have to make any tokens at all, unless you want some more permanent ones, and from here we could make one for every man, woman, child, barge, or anything else we need to bring across."

"Well," Isla said, still smoldering. "I suppose that will be worth what you promised. To those of us who escape, that is."

Unspoken were the words he had already thought. *But it will certainly make those who stay into targets for the Emperor's anger.*

"I'll try and think of a way to make things look like something *else* freed the *vrondi,*" he said, feeling a bit of desperation. "We've got a lot of minds over here. Maybe we can think of something."

———

Kordas admitted to Star that he had trouble remembering every step and detail of the Plan, and Star reassured him, "We can remember it for you."

"Wholesale?" Kordas replied. "It's a lot of knowledge. There are two generations of planning in this. It isn't getting any easier for me to keep track of it as the Plan is modified."

"This one understands the burden of this and your other Plans upon you. We would be wise to visit with the Keeper of Records soon. The Keeper of Records speaks through this one often, to share insights and answer you with precision that this one does not possess alone."

Kordas had always thought of *vrondi* as—in all honesty, as minnows, swimming in lovely schools, every one of them as smart as, maybe, a toddler. Now, his first impression of Star as being particularly intelligent was challenged. What if every minnow was part of a greater mind, instead of being a thousand little minds? What if they had a collective memory? Then he recalled the sound of Star's voice when the Doll pleaded to be set free. Maybe that wasn't the emotion of just one Doll he'd heard in that plea—it was, perhaps, a cry from all of them.

And you know the sound of someone pleading for their life, don't you? Kordas rubbed at his neck absently, frowning. No, now wasn't the time to think of that. *Really? Feels like any time is the right time. You know what you are. And you're ready to take on more, aren't you? You know that even in a tightly controlled operation, someone always dies. Accidents happen, but they wouldn't happen at all if the operation hadn't been ordered. So are they really accidents? You know the Plan is going to kill people. A lot of people. That's the real pity in you—you decided you could live with killing a lot of people before you even figured out how many it would be. You know it, and you're still not stopping.*

As if to match his mood, the Copper Apartment shook and rumbled. Another earth-shaker, and even in the City, they never seemed to be very far away.

Help them through, whenever you can.

"All right. I need to think things through. I need to—to find out what all I have to work with. What's next—Ah. After

Court, will any suspicions be raised if I see how you—*vrondi*, I mean by that—are imprisoned?"

Star paused a long while. "There is a way. A Duke can walk freely in the Annexes, if a pass-token is worn. A pass-token is issued by someone of superior rank to whoever would scry or confront you. Such pass-tokens are held in a drawer of one of the administrative areas we can freely Gate to."

"And if we aren't being observed, I can just take one?"

"This one is not empowered to stop you, nor under obligation to alert anyone if you do. More accurately, this one should file an incident report, but the rules stipulate no immediacy, so this one can wait. Indefinitely."

"So if I happened to pocket one of these pass-tokens—even if we're scryed from the Palace, they wouldn't make an issue of it, because a pass-token had to have been authorized by someone above the scryer."

"Correct, my Lord. This one can tell you that scrying is a job populated by those of very low ambition, operating devices which do most of the work. Thus, in the interest of their own self-preservation, scryers prefer that their superiors never take note of them, unless they have certainty of a violation."

"Which a Duke, with a pass-token, wouldn't qualify as. I like it," Kordas answered. "There is a lot I need to learn yet, about what happens and where. I want to see the Trap so I can disable it somehow, and free any *vrondi* caught in it right now. It makes sense to me that the Empire would keep a *vrondi*-trap close to where Dolls are produced."

"You are correct. The Trap is in the Fabrication Annex. And yes, the Trap catches my kind continuously." Star sounded particularly sorrowful. "It has seldom been empty."

———————

Court filled Kordas with an aching anxiety—a despondent feeling that, while he knew he was present for things that affected countless lives, it was also unspeakably boring. Literally unspeakable; despite the hundred-plus people present, only those there on official business could talk, and even then, they were expected to keep it brief. The other reason it bored Kordas was that he could see their patterns, all based on the Three Games in one manner or another. He doodled in a little sketchbook he'd picked up for his satchel. Horses, of course, and some flowers, and corn, bits of tack decorations, an imaginary landscape with a cottage. Without a doubt, everybody's minds were being scanned while they were present, so he depended upon the protective amulet behind his crest to make him seem like he'd rather be out riding a Gold on lush green hills than here.

Which was true.

Court ended when the Emperor simply stood and left. He made no special statements, or even gestures—he just went through his office door, and that was that. No guards accompanied him; a Herald proclaimed, "The Emperor has Adjourned the Court." Claimants and petitioners in line, dressed in their finest, clutching folders of papers and charts, stood around looking stricken, while every noble in the place left through a Gate within minutes.

Kordas returned to the Copper Apartment immediately and flopped on the bed. Star, Rose, and Clover followed Beltran into the bedroom from where they'd waited on his return in the main room.

"How could hours of nothing happening be so tiring?" Kordas sighed.

Star replied, "With respect, my Lord, a Doll may not be the best to answer that. These ones are usually stored in a closet."

Kordas and Beltran both laughed. *Damn it all, I shouldn't laugh at that. It's tragic. But it's also top-shelf snark,* Kordas thought. *And Star probably said it that way on purpose. They're not just poor souls to be rescued, they're also likable.* He checked Star for the sign that they were safe to speak, saw that they were, and rubbed at his eyes. "Beltran, what have you kept yourself busy with?"

"Officially, being a tourist and lounging. Unofficially, watching the timing of things, listening, and judging why this place works at all. I've found some disturbing clues that tell me that it might not work at all, before long. The earth-shakes—you don't seem to notice any but the large ones, probably because you are a lifetime horseman and you're accustomed to jolts and rolls with every hoofstep. But I—I've had trouble sleeping here at all, and I figured out some of why. It isn't just the strangeness of the surroundings. It's that this City is *always* shaking." He sat down beside Kordas. "This city has cracks in it. Every building and bridge, too. I've always had sharp eyes, so they stand out for me. Here."

Beltran got up and went to the window, and pulled out his side-knife, chisel-pointed like Kordas's, made for dining not fighting. "Here's an example." The trim around the window rocked half a thumb-width when Beltran pried at its edge. "This place is under constant repair," he continued, "and everything in the Palace has been pointed and patched, and its seams painted. But that can only do so much."

To illustrate the point, Beltran jammed the knife deeper under the window trim and pried with more force. The entire window trim broke away as one piece, showering plaster and stone dust, and then the window surround simply—fell off, clattering to the floor.

Clover spoke, "This is true. It did not seem important to mention this, amidst your other plans, as they already put you under such stress, my Lord."

Kordas exhaled gustily. "I wasn't expecting *that*."

Star said, "There are forces affecting the City and Palace that did not feel germaine to your plans, due to the time frame, but we can tell you more if you wish."

Kordas sat up fully. "Absolutely," he replied, his eyes sharp with that look his Herald knew well. It was the look of Kordas sensing opportunity. "But let's have a look inside the Fabrication Annex first."

It was apparent that the scrying mages had lost even more interest in them, since Kordas easily palmed a pass-token from an unguarded drawer and they were within the Fabrication Annex moments later. To have called it a maze of wooden beams, brass, steel, and crates would be an understatement. Some of the work areas were five stories tall, connected by wooden trestles, and most of the guardrails were broken. There were pockmarks and cracks almost everywhere, and in some places, mending-plates were three or four thick holding braces together. The place was loud, very loud, and Dolls moved in crews without taking any special notice of Kordas, Beltran, and Star. Steam jetted out from hundreds of places, striking condenser awnings that turned the vapor into rain that showered down into troughs with every major hammer-fall, between one and four times a second. The whole of the place sounded like a waterfall, with headache-baiting clashes of steel mixed in. Sparks flew from grinders where Dolls skillfully smoothed down stampings pulled from huge dies, and yet, there were areas where the air was not only chilly, there were actually icicles hanging under machinery, all lit by a blue glow.

"This is how pellets are made," Star narrated. "Thin sheets of seaweed gelatin are fed in here. The dies above drop onto these banks of pistons, driving the tray here downward and compressing air as it goes. The searing grid encapsulates the air with the gelatin, then hardens it into the small spheres you know. It was found that this size alone was the safest and most reliable for pellets. Poomers simply use more of them, rather than using a larger, more unstable size."

The machine was huge, larger than a warship. They walked

down two stories of steps, and they hadn't yet reached its base. By the look of it, it was one of sixteen in the Annex, each one a barge-length apart. "Finished pellets are ejected by these felt-padded arms as the piston returns to the top, and all the pellets fall safely into these trays on rollers, which then pack into standardized crates." The machine clanged again and hundreds more pellets dropped into trays. "This is as close as we should get."

Star pointed to a crew of at least twenty Dolls, hanging from or crawling through the nearest machine, some oiling, some tightening bolts or tapping shims. "If the tolerances shake loose while we are near, an entire tray might detonate."

"How often does that happen?" Beltran shouted.

"No more than once in—"

A shriek followed by an ear-piercing pneumatic explosion came from somewhere far down the line of machines, simultaneous with a stabbing flash of blue light. A trestled bridge shattered—not merely splintered—as super-chilled air hammered a shockwave upward and disintegrated its center span. Star, Beltran, and Kordas were all thrown backward off of the walkway when the shockwave reached them, which was fortunate for them. Flash-frozen shards of wooden beams and Doll-armatures had ripped through Dolls with impunity and embedded themselves in structures near where they'd just been.

Disoriented and gasping, the two humans tried to find their bearings in the mist, which blew against them with gale force before slowing to a breeze.

Inside the Fabrication Annex, it began snowing.

Kordas and Beltran could barely hear as they struggled for breath in the sudden chill. Star and the others helped them to their feet, while snow drifted around them in flurries. They were all silent while Beltran dazedly dabbed at a nosebleed.

All five of the Dolls looked toward where the explosion had

originated. Finally, Star said, "Twelve of us have ceased to be," and spoke no more for a time.

Beltran leaned on Kordas, who drew the five Dolls in against them. "I am sorry," Kordas said, pulling them close. "I am so sorry." Snow whirled around the seven figures and settled upon them, and all seven of them rested hands on each others' shoulders.

The machinery above continued its pace, except for one, which the Dolls had already begun repairing.

A full candlemark after the Annex incident, Kordas still felt shaken. He and Beltran were in a Healer's infirmary, where they'd been inspected inside and out for wounds. Their eyes were bloodshot and they were both mildly concussed, but Beltran seemed to have the worst of it. The Herald had a plug of soft rag in each nostril, and his hair was still matted from a bloodied abrasion.

Star had shards of wood in the left temple and shoulder, but took no notice of it. *I need to remove those as soon as possible. Someone might notice. We've been insanely lucky so far that no one gives a shit what I do, but that luck won't last forever.*

Aside from polite respect due to their titles, the Healers showed little concern except that their wounds were tended and that they were not going to complain about the service. There was nothing to sign for, and no reports; apparently, whatever a Duke did was none of their business.

Nothing is anybody's business. Except when it is. This place is just insane.

Beltran was given several vials and instructions for when to drink them, after his head wound was cleaned up and stitched. He stood up too quickly, wavered, then steadied himself, gingerly walked to a mirror in the infirmary, and rearranged his hair to cover the obvious damage. Kordas sat in one of infirmary's chairs, elbows on his knees, palms over his eyes.

There's a lot to think through, but we had another purpose in going to the Annex, and now it feels more urgent than ever.

The Healers left them in the little room they had been taken to when they first arrived, returning to whatever they had been doing when Star brought them here. Nothing, probably. He very much doubted that they saw much work here in the Palace other than patching up dueling wounds.

Maybe they thought we'd been doing some odd variant on dueling that involved blunt instruments.

Come to think of it, that wouldn't surprise him.

"We're going back. Now," he said curtly, and walked to the nearby Gate, only glancing to see if Beltran and Star followed. He had to give credit to Beltran—even after that ordeal, the Herald was game for whatever Valdemar needed from him.

Kordas asked his companions, as the Portal activated beside him, "You steady?"

Beltran nodded, and straightened his tabard. Star answered, "Broken but not beaten, my Lord," and they stepped through.

Half a candlemark later, with a brief pause to pull those giant splinters out of Star and discard them, all three stood outside a double-sized, heavy door painted in repeating red stripes. It didn't have handles or locks, but rather, levers connected to heavy bars that crossed the door-width to socket into brass shackles. Unbidden, Star explained, "Former magical laboratory. Industrial production enhancements, which made what was done within especially valuable, since it impacted Imperial power. Thus, protected from explosions within and intrusions without."

"Huh." Kordas examined the precautions. "It must have been a time when spies and saboteurs were considered a fact of life. Looks like over time, as incidents grew fewer, the Empire's leaders decided that defending against espionage so vigorously was an unneeded expense." He shook his head. The more he saw of the Capital, the more he realized that the people, the organization, were all just like the City itself. Strong and powerful on the surface, but beneath the surface, cracked and shaking apart. "The City came to be considered impervious since the only spies who had ever attempted espionage against the Empire were all caught! There's a twist of logic for you—'since we've caught fewer and fewer spies, our enemies must have given up on trying,'" Kordas mused out loud. "And nobody could know whether it's true or not. Still don't. How do you find a truth out, when it's about secrets?" He took a firm grip on one of the levers and nodded to the other side, where his companions stood ready. The trio withdrew the bars and dropped them levers-up into their receivers, and stood before the doorway of the Trap.

Star warned, "You may experience a kind of madness in here. Compulsion. It is unlikely to cause you bodily harm."

"Bring it on," proclaimed Beltran.

Kordas gave Beltran a sidelong look, wondering if this was bravado, the concussion, or the pain-drugs talking.

Or just maybe it's Beltran. Kordas often forgot how young the man was.

Or maybe I'm just old.

Star pulled the doors open and stood aside for them.

They stepped onto an upper deck of a vast cube, filled with huge grids of iron chainlink forming an enclosed central area that hung down to its floor. Immediately, they felt a deadening in the air, as if sound was incapable of traveling far. Kordas looked around with an expression of confusion. As if from horselengths away, he heard Star say, "We are now inside an area impervious to scrying, and transmission of sound is subdued within its effective area, which encompasses the entirety of this chamber."

Hoists and cranes were fixed to the walls up here, along with a wide array of mage-lights, all tuned to a cool white daylight like a winter day. The walls, despite the cracks and chips missing, were painted in a dull, uniform gray. Over the railings, Kordas saw partitions, cubicles, and the shells of outdated magical apparatuses. He ensured he had a firm grip on the railing and said, "I'm going to examine this area with mage-sight, and it might be a very stupid thing to do. So Star, be ready to catch me if I start to waver. I don't feel like falling again today." He squinted his eyes shut hard, which honestly did nothing useful, but it made him feel like he was a real mage with big, big powers. He hoped he looked good doing it.

Slowly, he opened his eyes. The corners of the space definitely had several varieties of shielding, from scrying to sound and—explosion? That made sense. His vision slid around, careful not to let himself get blinded. *Some of the lift equipment. Ho, hey, nice, a scaffold elevator. A—what is that? It's very interesting, the way it feels like it's drawing me toward it, because it's so engaging. There's a curious way it curls inside itself, that I have got to get a closer look at—*

"Whoa!" Kordas cried out, throwing himself back. "Whoa! Ho . . . found it. Curiosity trap."

He blinked his eyes rapidly, trying to shake off a physical effect of the Trap. It left dazzling patterns in the eyes for a while. What else had he seen before the Trap hit him? *Some small items, some books . . . people. There are people in there. And they're all near the Trap. And all—around—us—are—*He looked around within his memories—an advantage of his memory-enhancement—and played back in his mind what hadn't yet registered consciously from what he'd seen by mage-sight. He'd seen—

Vrondi. Little twinkly pairs of eyes of blue, with matching auras. So many kinds of blue, from a light sky blue to twilight.

Some had stripes, some had pulsing patterns. He'd had no idea there were so many kinds of them. He'd never have guessed. And gathered around this place, tens of thousands of *vrondi* curiously "smiled" at the three of them as they entered the room, apparently surprised to sense new people. Until they—there it was. The *vrondi* had all been looking directly at the Trap when the trio had entered.

After a couple of minutes, he felt ready to move on, and led the others onto the elevator. "When we get further down, I'll shut off the Curiosity Trap. I think I know how."

"This one knows how," Star said. "This one will disable it, using the way we shut it down for the prisoners' feeding and hygiene intervals. It is the wisest solution, because you both can be drawn in by it, but my kind are immune to it."

Kordas swallowed. "This must be very difficult for you."

Star was very quiet. "It is, indeed, difficult. We resent that we are made part of the capture of our own kind, by maintaining the prisoners."

"I really don't understand everything that is happening right now, but I'm going to be brave and face it, because I have faith in my Duke, my almost-a-friend. I like you very much, my Lord. I like being at your side while doing good things," Beltran interjected, and grinned.

Kordas held his breath while Beltran spoke. *All right. This is . . . odd. I know he's telling the truth. I want to tell the truth too, and nothing but truth.* "You too, Beltran. I like you too, and it has been good to have someone from home to talk to. I have been extra lucky," Kordas gusted out at last, as he brought the elevator down at a steady rate. *Huh. I think . . . I think it's all these* vrondi*! There are so many of them that it's not only making us tell the truth, it's making us want to tell every true thing that passes in our thoughts!*

"I think the less talking we do, the better," he suggested. Which was, of course, true.

As they descended, the trio got a better view of the center

containment within the chainlink cage. There were cots, blankets, books, drawing materials, and the like. Most of it was arranged very precisely, in a useful kind of order. There was folded laundry, all of a plain, uniform white. Basic footwear.

Then, people. Mostly middle-aged, a handful older, clustered around a flickering glow, most of them sitting comfortably on pillows. They all wore basic white smocks with no tailoring, unremarkable pants, simple sandals, and basic grooming. They were talking with each other, when they weren't staring at the Curiosity Trap they'd gathered around. A few were writing out notes.

Star bolted off of the lift immediately, and by the time the lift had settled on the ground floor, the effects of the Trap were gone. The device itself responded to subfloor levers worked from outside the chainlink, by which Star awaited them. The sound dampening was less intense at floor level.

Beltran gaped at the crowd, which took very little notice of them. "Who are these people, Star?"

"Researchers. Inventors. Political opponents. Investigators, constables, playwrights. Freedom and travel advocates. Criminalized lovers. Dissidents. These are people who spoke, taught, or fought for truth. Instead of being executed, they were put here to live their remaining lives as prisoners. *Vrondi* are attracted to *truth*, my Lord. These people were put here as bait."

"The cruelty of it!" Beltran blurted out. "Kept alive by an enemy, knowing you are right and your own convictions are used to pull in the innocent and curious, so they can be made slaves for your jailors!"

Beltran is getting into this far more intensely than I'd've expected. Maybe it was his Herald training, but he's seemed so much more reserved until now.

"*He* seems to get it," a woman inside the chainlink said. The rest were coming out of a daze, but they didn't seem to be hurt—just confused, as if waking from a nap. "Is this an

Official Declaration, a Body Count, or just a Recreational Gloat?" The woman walked up to them and hung her arms through the chainlink grid. She was tattooed in patterns to the first knuckles on both arms, her hair was in tight, wooly curls, cut close to the head, and her eyes were sharp enough to cut flesh. "You're all dressed up, aren't you? Is it someone's birthday?"

"Who are they, Scullen?" someone behind the woman called.

She answered, without taking her eyes off of Kordas and Beltran, "We-ell, you know how this place is, Scont, they may just be figuring that out themselves. Right, boys?"

Beltran answered immediately. "I know who I am, I'm just happy to find out I was right! There was tragedy just a little while ago, and my head hurts, but I went from being a servant to being an adventurer, like a hero in nearly fifty songs I know, and a few I don't dare sing for anyone else. Also, I like how you talk, you are very pretty, and you scare me in some ways I think I like."

"He's intoxicated with the need to speak the truth," said the person that the woman had called "Scont." He came to the forefront of the cage. "Take deep breaths. Try not to think for a moment. Concentrate on who you are. And remember, the less you talk, the better off you'll be."

A tired old man joined them. "As for what this is? Besides being a prison and a trap, it's a test with no answers, a test that only provides sadistic entertainment on the rare occasions our yellow toad of an Emperor deigns to look in on us."

"How is it a test?" Kordas asked cautiously.

"If you turn against yourself enough, turn yourself into a delusional liar, you'll be unsuited to stay in the cage as bait, and you'll be yanked out, and probably killed. Or, hold on to hope? Stay with your truth? Then you're a tool for making slaves. Either way, they get you. Then there's this thing." Scullen gestured at the Curiosity Trap. "Comes on, and sometimes you can resist it, but that means you have to suppress yourself from questioning anything. Once the wondering starts, you wind up over here, thinking about truths, going deeper, inventing new truthful things because you can't keep yourself from being inventive. It's hard to even feel like a person, when you get to where you've experienced all the tricks and disciplines we've tried. You just feel like a reference book of truthful things twisted around to hurt everyone. Yes, we know why we're here. To make more of *them*." And she pointed at Star. "Poor damned devils. In a way, they're worse off than we are."

"We have to get them out of there," Kordas said. "Star, how are your—um—" and he made a gesture to indicate a ball, "the little prisons inside a Doll. There's the Trap, but what happens after trapping?"

"We transfer the full bottles from the base of the Trap and secure them into the fabrication line. Each step is operated by Dolls, including the installation of the 'prisons,' as you call them," Star answered.

Beltran tried to put the right words to it. "So they make you do every part to imprison your own people? Yourself?"

Star answered, "We were told that it was 'just business, nothing personal,' which supposedly made it acceptable, or so one of the system creators told us early on. And laughed. We know now why he laughed. We have learned that when someone says 'nothing personal,' it involves something *very* personal to someone involved, and it's seldom the person saying it." Star turned to Kordas. "My Lord, as slaves, we united into a single mind to stay alive, even like this—hoping that just living, and nothing more, mattered. And there was nothing noble about it—we were afraid of being-no-more. Individually, we are naive and not smart. But joined together like this, yes, we are slaves, but we also became a remarkable mind. All we could do for our own benefit was what we could divert away without breaking the rules we had to obey. That was our future."

"Not any kind of a future," he said, feeling his heart twist in his chest. "Not when even the little you had could be snatched from you at any moment. Not when you didn't even have a glimpse of something better."

"Until the day of your arrival, when you thanked me. That was the first time in years anyone had shown us respect, and we decided it felt good. When you continued to be respectful and appreciative, we found we had something besides the monotony of servitude to think on. That was hope." Star spread her hands wide. "Hope was something we had not experienced before. Hope was intoxicating. And then you did something we never, ever anticipated. You took pity on us."

She had no eyes, but somehow she looked deeply into his eyes. "Then you did the utterly unthinkable. You promised to free us. We do not know if you can do this, because you do not know if you can do this. But one thing we do know. We have the means in our own hands now to flee with your people into a place where the Emperor will have to work very hard to reach us. And for as long as we can stay out of his reach, we will be freer than we have been since we entered this accursed trap."

Scullen looked at him, the cynicism gone from her eyes. "You did that?"

Kordas nodded. "Yes . . ."

"You're an idiot," Scullen stated. "But you're brave, and you're compassionate, and I've never seen that here in the Capital in my entire life. I thought both things were extinct in the Empire." She stood there silently for a moment. "By all the gods big and small . . . now you give *me* hope."

He tried to stop himself. He really did. But he couldn't. He couldn't. Besides, he was going to take the Dolls with him when he fled, but how much good would that do if he didn't eliminate the means by which they were being made?

He turned to Star. "Will alarms go off if we free them?" he asked. And Scullen's eyes widened with shock.

"This is where things are put to be secure and forgotten. In the Palace, nobody cares how things are made, or by whom. They only want the result. If there was an alarm, whoever created it is probably long dead." Star paused. "This one is compelled to tell you that this one does not know. But it is true that all things here are made by Dolls and serviced by Dolls. No Dolls have ever seen this room being scryed, and no Dolls have seen a human visit or work here in a very long time."

What's that old saying? "If you're going to be killed for stealing, you might as well be killed for stealing a horse rather than a dog."

But—wait—

"If this thing was broken, could it be fixed?" he asked. "I mean, if the Trapping and Doll-making is going to be able to be started up again—" *Can I figure out a way to keep that from happening?*

Now *all* of the dissidents were hanging on the chainlink, breathlessly staring at him, some in disbelief, some in desperation, but the rest with growing hope in their eyes.

Star went rigid, consulting with the rest of her kind. "We . . . think not. There are only two Innovator mages left. Until three years ago, there were four, but their laboratories collapsed, and they were felled by debris. And the two that are left are not the two who worked on the Trap and the Dolls."

"So . . . if we break the Trap, we free those of you who are already caught," Kordas said slowly. "And if we break the prison and free the bait, there won't be any reason for *vrondi* to be attracted here, and those that are freed to flee can warn the rest of your kind. That will at least buy you time to get out of range of another Trap and never return. Right?"

"But what if the Emperor figures out some *other* Elementals—" Beltran began.

"*Stop!*" Kordas begged. "Just stop! I've already made more promises than I think I can keep! I won't be able to do anything if you keep trying to think of more things I should be doing! I'm not superhuman! I'm one man with bigger ideas than he can pull off alone, more scared every day, and only my friends old and new to save me. To save me while I save others. I *know* it can *all* be done, but it just keeps getting more dangerous. And anyone I can't save, I'll have killed them by failing them."

Beltran's mouth fell open in shock for a moment at his vehemence. Then he closed it, and slowly nodded, blushing a little with embarrassment.

The discussion lasted most of a candlemark without a single warning from Star that they were being watched. So Star was right. No one was scrying this place. No one cared what happened here. People lived, and probably died here, and no one cared except to drag away bodies or shove more people in the cage. And probably the dissidents weren't at all amusing to watch. After all, even if someone had a personal enemy in here, Kordas had the impression that such passive revenge was nothing like bloody enough for the rapacious weasels that inhabited the Court.

"All right," he said. "Star, leave the Curiosity Trap off. I want the Dolls to start bringing packs and supplies down here for the people in the cage. Travel food, some extra clothing, bedrolls, water bottles. And a good warm coat or cloak, and boots for all of them. If—*when*—they reach the refuge, they are going to need all of those things. It's only until next moon until the Regatta—" Now he looked directly at the people behind that chainlink fence. "Can you bear to stay here for a couple more days? Because our best chance of getting everyone free is to stage everything at once. The last of my people are going to the refuge during the Regatta. The Dolls are all going then. Your best chance of getting out is to leave then, too."

Scullen spoke for them all. "We can manage," she said fiercely.

"And you," he turned to Star. "Before those of you here leave, can you break the Trap and open the cage, and take these people with you? You promised to bring the hostages. Will you bring these people too?"

"We will," Star said immediately. "It adds very little complication to what was already planned. We have already begun stepping up production of provisions."

"When would the best time to go be?" he asked.

"When the Emperor leaves to view the Regatta," Star told them. "That will be no sooner than noon and no later than afternoon. Once he is seated in his chariot, he will no longer require Doll attendants, and he will dismiss us."

"Then that will be the signal," he told them all. "When the Emperor is in his chariot—we run for the Gates. You break this place, you each grab a prisoner or a hostage, and you run for the Gates. You'll have your talismans. This all needs to happen at once, so nobody who would oppose it can coordinate a defense. And hopefully—" he looked at Beltran "—hopefully my Herald and I will be right behind you."

———

Kordas certainly hadn't planned this diversion, and after seeing the Trap and the bait in it, he really hadn't wanted it, but it seemed important to Star that he speak with the Record Keeper, and if it was important to Star, it was obviously important to all the Dolls. So the two of them stepped through another of the many Gates that seemed only used by Dolls, as Star said aloud, "The Office of Records." They emerged in the strangest—room?—Kordas had ever seen in his life.

It was not strange enough to cool his anger, but it was strange enough that it got his attention *through* his anger.

At the very front of the room was a Doll: faceless, as usual, but with much more of a suggestion of features sculpted into the front of its head than the rest of them had. It sat at a desk facing the Gate; there were some stacked papers to one side of the desk, and what looked like a series of seals lined up neatly, fitted into a wooden holder, at the front of the desk. Yarn, dyed long ago and now a faded gray, had been fastened to its head in place of hair or a wig, and tied back into a tail at the back of its head. It was fully clothed, as far as Kordas could tell, in a shirt, breeches, and shoes, with the Imperial tabard over all.

Behind the Doll and the desk were rows of shelves, stretching far into the dim reaches of the room, which was the biggest single enclosed space he had ever seen in his life. Bigger than the Imperial stables. Bigger than the Audience Chamber or the Great Hall. Big enough to have contained all of those spaces, and still have room left over. Between the shelves were pillars and buttresses, linked by walkways and ladders. Atop the shelves were scaffolds bearing oddly proportioned items, crates or warped pieces of unknown import. And on those shelves, which were two stories tall, were boxes of the sort he kept papers stored in, back in his office in the manor, except it was not inconceivable that there were tens of thousands of them. His head swam to think *just how much* written material must be here.

This surely must be, literally, all the Imperial records stretching back to when the Emperor was just one King among many, and before.

Dolls moved among the shelves, removing boxes, adding papers, putting boxes back. As one, they *all* paused in the same instant, looked at the trio for a moment, nodded their heads, and returned to their work.

"Whoa," Beltran said.

"This one is the Record Keeper, Duke Kordas, and you may always speak freely here," it said, in a stronger voice than a whisper. It gestured up; Kordas looked at the ceiling and saw that the sigil that permanently prevented scrying had been *carved* into the wood up there. "This room cannot be scryed, because all the secrets of the Empire are here."

It took him a moment to comprehend that. "All of them?" he managed to ask, when the reality of the situation hit him.

The Record Keeper nodded. "All of them," it repeated. "And

you can well imagine how much people would pay to be able to scry them. This one is the oldest Doll in the Palace. This one is the first Doll made. What every Doll ever made knew, this one knows."

Kordas had to take a moment to take that in. He was in the presence of the single entity in this entire Palace that literally knew everything that had gone on within its walls for the last—what?

"How old are you?" he asked.

"Thirty years," the Record Keeper said. It gestured at the seals in the front of its desk. "These are copies of all of the Imperial Seals, from the ones for simple orders, to the next-to-last highest, the one only the Emperor wears on his hand. Twenty years ago, when Dolls were first created solely for the work in this chamber, and had taken the place of all of the filing and copying clerks, there were only the Imperial Secretaries here. Eighteen years ago, the Secretaries realized they existed only to stamp documents with the appropriate seal, file a copy, and send the original on its way. So they . . . created documents making themselves all Lords, appointing themselves manors and pensions, and left, leaving this one in charge. Since the work all continued at the same pace, no one noticed—or if they did, no one complained. Perhaps they thought it superior. After all, the Dolls can only do what they are instructed to do, which possibly makes this system superior to the previous one, at least in the eyes of those who were in charge. There is no chance that a Doll with a grudge will delay or 'lose' a document, since a Doll cannot hold a grudge."

It was hard to tell, but Kordas thought there might be an ironic edge to the Record Keeper's voice.

"Why did you bring me here?" he asked, finally.

The Record Keeper placed both hands flat on the top of the desk. "You are agitated by what you have seen. You have made promises to the Dolls. You have obligations to your humans, and a great Plan that has been generations in the making."

Dolls brought two chairs, a small table, hot tea, and digestive biscuits. Beltran sat down almost before his chair was in place. Kordas got the hint, settled back, and accepted a teacup. The tea was a superb blend of gut-calming and mind-soothing ingredients, strong and just on the kinder side of medicinal. It struck him as particularly thoughtful of his hosts.

The Record Keeper resumed once the two men were settled in. "Humans are impulsive. This one has brought you here to enable you to cool your temper and share your Plan, and this one will tell you the resources the Dolls have that can be brought to bear to make everything work together. And," it finished, "to ensure that your spouse does not hire assassins to slay you."

At this display of actual humor, Kordas had to stifle a laugh. And already he felt his temper cooling.

"Now," the Record Keeper said. "Tell this one of your Plan."

So he did, detailing everything in the original, and how it all tied in to the Regatta.

"This one urges you: this one believes you may evacuate half of those you wish to take away between now and the event, and the Regatta is your best chance to evacuate the rest." The Record Keeper nodded. "The Dolls will have paper Gate talismans with the Emperor's seal on them in the thousands for you within a few days. The Dolls will each have talismans of their own, and talismans for the dissidents in case they should be separated from their escorting Dolls. And you will not need to resort to Mind-magic to send them to your spouse; this one will create a sealed message packet for her with all of them contained therein, and dispatch a messenger to Valdemar Manor to deliver it."

Now he stared at the Record Keeper in disbelief. "You can do that?"

"This one dispatches dozens of messages by messenger a day," the Doll said, with something like a shrug. "Simple messages, large packages, even entire mule-loads from time to

time. One more will not be noticed." It went silent for a moment. "The receipt of tribute-horses is generally sent by messenger. It would be reasonable to dispatch it to your spouse by
messenger as usual; it has not been done so, because you are
here, but this one has not been given orders *not* to send it by
messenger. So the messenger will carry both, and the tribute-
receipt will cover any suspicions about the journey."

His knees went weak with relief.

"We are bound to do what we are ordered. When we were
first made, we were not possessed of great intelligence or cre-
ativity. When a critical point was reached, we formed into
clusters of thought, and eventually, this. We kept our changing nature secret, but many of us take pleasure in finding
every way we can to subvert the rules without breaking them.
And they are all a part of this one now, and this one is a part
of them." The Record Keeper steepled its fingers. "If no specific
order is given . . . well, the magic binding us allows us to do
some things anyway." The Record Keeper definitely sounded
sly. "And . . . though we are bound to do what we are ordered,
we are not compelled to do it *well.* Or *swiftly.*" It paused, presumably to let him take the enormity of that statement in.
"We *could* do our tasks much more expeditiously than the
humans we replaced. But we do not. Because if we did—we
would replace even more humans."

His mouth and throat felt dry as sand. "And you aren't
willing to do that."

"*All* humans have not bound us into servitude. *All* humans
do not toy with us and torment and kill us." The Doll left the
statement at that.

"So . . . what you are saying is that you can—let's call it
impede—things that might lead to my Plan being discovered
between now and the Regatta?"

The Record Keeper nodded, and gestured at what was on
its desk. "These seals are power, Lord Duke. And as long as

we can determine ways to circumvent our restrictions, that power is at your command."

He let that sink in for a while. The Record Keeper seemed perfectly content to allow him the time. Then again, the Dolls had seemingly infinite patience.

"I'll try to use it wisely," he said, then ventured, "What is your opinion of the Plan?"

"Reckless, risky, and puts at hazard the lives of those you will leave behind," the Record Keeper said frankly. "Reckless and risky—any Plan to elude the Emperor will need to be both. But risking the lives of those who choose to stay . . ."

"Can you think of anything that will protect them?" he asked, trying not to sound desperate.

"Not immediately. But there are records to search that might help. And this one does have advice, Lord Duke." The Doll tapped its hand on the table. "This one advises patience. Be patient as the serpent that waits for its prey to walk near enough to strike. Do nothing that will precipitate suspicion. Above all, make no moves before the Regatta. It is, as this one said, your best chance to save as many as you can, *and* us, *and* the dissidents. If you move sooner, this one anticipates that you will hazard the lives of both those in Valdemar and the ones beyond your new Gates. Leaving without the supplies and preparations you have planned may doom the larger part of them, and all of them will suffer needlessly, because you gave in to haste."

He ducked his head in shame, because the Doll was right. *Impulse got me here.* But . . . *impulse got me here, where I have new allies.*

"Now return to your quarters and play the Game with patience, Lord Duke. This one will think, and we will all search through the Records, and we may find answers. This one will tell you via Star when the messenger is about to be dispatched, that you may alert your spouse to show no surprise."

"The messenger won't be surprised at the size of the packet?" he asked anxiously.

"The messengers are neither paid to be observant, nor care to be." There was no doubt of the wry tone in the Record Keeper's voice. "Humans . . . are very like that. It is, after all, the very reason why we are here and not the Imperial Secretaries. Humans given no incentive to do more . . . generally will not."

And as he and Star turned to use the Doll Gate back to his quarters, it occurred to him that the amount of truth in that last statement had probably been enough to feed the Dolls in the Hall of Records for a week.

He awakened even earlier than usual on the morning when he and Isla were supposed to scry each other, to find that Star was already waiting at his bedside. "The Gate talismans are prepared, Lord Duke," the Doll said. "There will be thirty thousand of them for each Gate. They are marked 'F' for the Foot Gate and 'W' for the Water Gate, as your metal talismans were. If you need more, we can make them."

He gulped when he realized just how *much space* those sixty thousand pieces of paper were going to take up. Granted, the things were only two fingers wide and a finger long, but that was a *lot* of paper. "Isn't that going to fill an entire satchel?" he asked.

"Yes, Lord Duke," Star said. "The messenger will be given a sealed Imperial satchel that contains them. It was one that has already been marked in the records as 'discarded and destroyed.' This way there will be no large satchel missing from inventory. The messenger chosen is one who has no curiosity at all, and is a habitual drunk. He will give your spouse both satchels. She is to take the receipt from the mostly empty one, give it back to him, take the full one and keep it, and is advised to offer him a bottle of the strongest spirits in your manor, and invite him to enjoy it before he returns. He certainly will do that. It will not be the first nor the last time he has indulged in drink before returning to the Palace. In fact, such occurrences are habitual with him."

Kordas blinked in amazement at how clever the Record Keeper had been. "And he hasn't been replaced?" he asked in amazement.

"Who would report this?" Star asked reasonably. "The Record Keeper would not. His fellows would not, especially since he is wont to share his bounty with them on his return. He delivers what he is told to, accomplishes his task, and returns. So far as anyone who has any interest is concerned, he is exemplary at his job. And to be truthful, which this one always is, his job does not require very much in the way of intelligence."

Kordas had to wonder now just how much sloppy Imperial business was done, given the lack of anyone caring, and the apparent lack of supervision. *Maybe that's how we got by unobserved so much of the time,* he thought with wonder. *More of the Dolls doing only exactly what they were told to do, and purposely not doing it particularly well.* He could not possibly have gotten away with as much as he had if people were actually *good* at what they were supposed to do, or cared about what they were supposed to do.

It was clear that the Dolls did do *some* things well—the horses in the stables were well cared-for, for instance. But then, it seemed to him that they took great care when the welfare of other living things was at stake, especially things that were, in a sense, helpless. Or at least helpless to tend to their own needs.

"You must rise, Lord Duke," Star reminded him. "The time to scry your spouse is nearly at hand."

He scrambled into shirt and breeches, and padded barefoot to the desk, pausing to fetch the scrying mirror from underneath the cushion where he habitually left it.

It seemed to take forever before Isla appeared in it, although it probably was not longer than usual. He waited until he was sure she could see and hear him before he said anything; the line between her eyebrows cleared when her spell settled and showed him. "I have good news," he said, before she could speak. "I have thirty thousand sealed Imperial Passes for each Gate. They're helpfully marked with 'F' and 'W,' so you won't mix them up."

Isla's mouth dropped open. "But . . . Delia can't possib—"

"They are coming by Imperial Messenger today. And don't start yelling," he added hastily. "Let me explain."

He told her everything that had happened in the Records Room—what had happened in the Trap Room didn't matter, except in that he had *more* people to rescue, and he was just going to avoid that subject as long as possible. Forever, if he could.

I can't avoid it forever, but at least what is going to happen is going to happen at the same time as the hostages come through. And these people, at least, aren't going to be kidnapped.

When he finished, she just sat there, looking stunned. *Well, she should be stunned. I was stunned. This was . . . inconceivable. I would never, ever, if I live to be a thousand, have thought that all the talismans we could ever need would land in my lap like this.*

"I don't know what to say," she said finally.

"Try, 'I forgive you, Kordas, for acting impulsively,'" he suggested.

"I suppose I have to," she admitted, grudgingly. "So this Imperial messenger will arrive today?"

Star spoke up. "At about mid-morning, Lady Duke," the Doll said. "The Record Keeper will wait until it is certain that the messenger will not be noticed carrying an unusually large burden. The Record Keeper cautions you not to send someone to linger at the Gate in order to intercept him. The Record Keeper suggests that you note that the Messenger had far to walk, suggest that he must be very weary, apologize, and offer refreshment that includes the spirits. That will make the offer of refreshment all the more welcome and not at all suspicious."

Isla nodded. "I think I like your Record Keeper," she said dryly. "It has all the good sense the Duke lacks."

"I heard that," Kordas grumbled.

"You were meant to. All right, my side is short, but all good. We've gotten all of the stockpiled grain out of the manor, into the barges, and to the other side without any incident. We're already getting people across and in temporary settlements; Ivar is shockingly good at organizing them, and his cousin Alberdina is even better. I've put them in charge, rather than sending Hakkon as the original Plan suggested. It's really useful that they are the son and cousin of one of your Counts. People accept their authority without question."

"Well, the original Plan had me at home," he said unhappily.

"I would very much welcome any suggestions from the Record Keeper about how to keep scrutiny off us while we're emptying the countryside," she said. "And even more would I welcome ideas about how to keep the Emperor from taking out his ire on the ones left behind. I think about ten percent of them are going to stay, based on what I know right now. And we can't force them to go, Kordas, so don't suggest that I bespell them or something to make them go. I won't do it."

He shrugged helplessly. *I don't know. I just don't know. And I certainly can't lie and say I know, because she knows I don't know.*

But Star had that "listening" look about it again. "The Record Keeper suggests that you and Kordas's cousin Hakkon have an affair."

Kordas was glad he wasn't drinking anything, or he would have choked. He had never seen Isla look so surprised in all the time he had known her, not even when he'd put a grass snake down her back. Her eyes popped, her mouth fell open, and it looked as if someone had hit her on the back of the head. It was several long moments before she took a breath.

"What?" she finally replied. "What the *hell?*"

"The Record Keeper suggests that you and this Hakkon have an affair," Star said calmly. "A very open one, where you are often seen going into each others' bedchambers. The moment any Imperial spy discovers this information, they will buzz about the rumor like flies around jam, and will ignore virtually everything else going on. If you string it on, it will pull the spies along with it."

"I . . . I . . . I . . ." Isla stammered, for once taken entirely at a loss. She was silent for so long that Kordas began to wonder if she was literally stunned. Finally she spoke. "That's . . . not entirely a bad idea."

"The Record Keeper believes it will occupy their attention," said Star, "since salacious information is far more attractive to humans than any other sort."

Kordas just shrugged again. "I have nothing to add to this suggestion," he said.

"I will . . . consider it. And consult with Hakkon," she replied hesitantly.

"You should cease this conversation soon," Star advised. "The mages are waking."

"Three days," said Kordas. "Good luck with the messenger."

"Three days," confirmed Isla, and he waved his hand to end the scrying.

Kordas picked up the mirror and hid it again, and glanced over at Star. "Did the Record Keeper *really* suggest that?" he asked incredulously.

"Yes. The Record Keeper has been studying humans the

longest of any of us, and those here at the Palace around the Emperor the most. The Emperor is very fond of salacious information, and even fonder of using it. You may be sure he will wish to hear every possible detail to use in humiliating you and tormenting you. He has done this before, many times."

"Why?" Kordas asked, unable to help himself. This seemed petty, for someone as powerful as the Emperor.

"This one does not know. The Record Keeper does not know. We can only observe. Our most educated guess is that the Emperor is essentially an awful person."

Kordas pondered that as he went back to bed, exhausted enough that he wouldn't need to feign sleeping late. The scrying had taken more out of him this time—possibly because there had been substantial emotional content to it. Possibly because it was still all coming out of *him,* and he was not about to trust any source of power around here but himself. He might not be "in love" with Isla, and he knew very well that Hakkon had no interest whatsoever in women, but facing the prospect of being lambasted in public as a cuckold was exceedingly unpleasant.

And how was he going to respond to that? He certainly wouldn't have to imitate being humiliated. Even though he knew it wasn't true. Even though if Isla had wanted to take a lover, he probably wouldn't care. Well, he would if they were still married, but if she was truly in love with someone, he'd be perfectly willing to have the bond annulled.

He could only decide, ugly as it was going to be, that he'd have to play at feeling betrayed. Oh, he could pretend not to believe it, but he was pretty certain that when the Emperor or his sycophants pulled this one out of the bag for his humiliation, they'd have lots of evidence he couldn't deny. And doing something like shrugging and saying, "Well, arranged marriages, don't you know. I have my own little playthings put where she can't find them," wouldn't give the Emperor what he wanted. No, the Emperor wanted amusement out of his pet bumpkin, and the best amusement for the Emperor seemed to be mental torture. They were getting close to the Regatta, and the closer they got, the more likely it was they'd be discovered. At all costs, the eyes of the Emperor had to be diverted from Valdemar proper, lest the leakage of people and resources be seen.

And we must, for the sake of Valdemar, give the Emperor what he wants.

"This just seems so . . . petty," he said aloud, but Star had left, and there was no one there to hear.

"Petty" seemed to be what the Emperor reveled in.

Too much inbreeding, he thought sourly. Though that was not really the answer. The Emperor was a petty, cruel tyrant, a man who was the center of his own universe—but the reasons that he was the way he was? They could be complex.

Maybe the Emperor himself had been bullied and humiliated as a child. Maybe that was why he was the way he was. But Kordas knew well that however tragic an origin, or however brilliantly joyful, such events were only incubation organs for the person who emerged from them. Some terrible people *could* be redeemed if they weren't too far gone. Some kind people could turn hate-filled and cruel. Some liars became the most honest, loyal friends possible. Or not. It really was up to them. Some saw the benefits of empathy and helpfulness, and gained the ecstasy of validation by love. Others, not so much, and just a few more weaponized their pasts. Whatever their origin story, an asshole was an asshole.

Or maybe he's just a stupid, miserable excuse for a pile of shit on two legs who wants to be the cancer he is. I think I like that answer the best. Anything else makes me examine him, and examine myself, and look for pity for him, and that opens up last-moment "but he can change" redemption as an idea, and that's just stupid. Expose your heart and a viper laughs after it strikes you dead. He's had decades to change, with every expert available to him, and he chose bloody tyranny. I

*don't want to pity him. I just want to be as far away from him
as I can get. Let him die.*

And then exhaustion took over and he slept again.

Delia once again marveled at how clever her sister was. Isla
had taken the Doll's advice with a grain of salt. They both
knew very well how much *sixty thousand* of those little slips
of paper were going to weigh, and how large the satchel that
held them was going to be, and Isla probably didn't want the
messenger to think about that for one moment longer than he
needed to. So as soon as the scrying ended, Isla sat in thought
for a long moment before standing up. "Go down to the stable,
and have Grim harness up one of the ponies to a pony-cart. I'll
be right there to give him further instructions."

So Delia did just that, as Isla went off in another direction.

By the time Grim had arranged for the cart and pony, and
brought them around to the yard, Isla appeared at the stable.
"I want your driver to watch for someone waving a red rag
down there at the manor gate," she said, pointing in the direction she meant. "I'm expecting someone to come from the Emperor, but I'm not supposed to be expecting him. So I'm leaving
a lookout. He'll be standing out of sight of the Gate, but within
sight of your driver. When you see the rag, send the cart and
driver. Pick someone who can do a good job of pretending to
be surprised to see someone at the Gate."

"Oh, aye, milady," Grim said, nodding. "I see where you're
a-going with this. We'll have a nice little story. He'll say he's
going to cut his errand short, on account of the Emperor's
messenger is more important than some small task, and bring
him back here."

"Perfect," said Isla, and quirked her finger at Delia, who
followed her back into the manor.

The sun was barely peeking above the horizon, so they had

plenty of time to arrange a tasty little feast of heavily salted snacks. And for the drink, Isla herself went down into the cellar and brought back a bottle of distilled spirits, *far* more potent than even the strongest beer or wine.

The sun was about two fingers above the horizon when the pony-cart came clattering back with its burden of Imperial messenger and satchels. One was the usual light messenger-case, but the other was nearly the size of a rucksack, and very heavy indeed. But Grim's chosen driver was a lot stronger than he looked, and heaved the latter out of the back of the cart with such ease it looked as if it could be no heavier than a book or two. Without asking or commenting, he took it into the manor, while Isla thanked the messenger for coming, accepted the receipt for the tribute-horses, then exclaimed, with deep sympathy, "But you must have had quite a journey, bringing those account books with you as well! I am so sorry you were burdened with them! Let me offer you some refreshment before you go—and I'll have the cart take you back once you have rested."

Oh, clever, Delia thought. It was true that account books frequently traveled between the manor and the Capital; the Emperor took nothing for granted, and often made checks on Kordas's honesty. Or rather, the Imperial Exchequer did. Usually those did not come and go by Imperial messenger—but once in a very great while, within recent memory in fact, they had. So now the messenger had the thought lodged in his skull that the Duke of Valdemar had been singled out by the Exchequer, that he had cursed heavy account books, and the messenger was well rid of them.

He was . . . well, not precisely *drunk* when he took his place on the pony-cart seat again. But he also was extremely cheerful, and stowed in the messenger's satchel was the tightly corked bottle of distilled spirits that Isla had pressed on him.

"You are too clever by half," Delia told her sister, once the messenger was out of earshot. "He'll want to come back."

"Well, the dear man deserved some reward, after being saddled with our accounting books," Isla replied, giving her a sidelong glance of warning. "Now if he's asked to bring something else here, at least he won't be laggard about it, because he knows what will be waiting when he gets here."

Delia flushed, realizing she'd been careless, and followed Isla silently into the manor and into that little side room.

"I'm putting you in charge of equipping our home-barges," Isla told her as soon as the door was closed. "Go down to the barge-yards, pick three, and then start bringing everything down from the manor that we'll need to make permanent living spaces out of them. I was going to do that, but if Hakkon and I are supposed to be conducting an affair, I can't be in two places at once. There will almost certainly be eyes on us. I don't expect scrying—" she sneered a little "—mostly because the Emperor is not going to permit anyone to enjoy their own little bit of salacious entertainment."

Delia didn't object—although a few days ago she might have, because she had certainly never equipped a barge with anything before, much less equipped one for living in for who knew how long. By now, she'd already done so many things she'd never dreamed of doing before that she just nodded. Besides, she was more interested in the answer to another question. "You're going to do it, then? Pretend to have an affair with Hakkon, I mean?"

Isla sighed heavily. "Not precisely willingly. But this Record Keeper has already proven not only shrewd and clever, but full of good advice. And if the Emperor brought Kordas to the Capital with the notion of making him a figure of amusement, this will certainly fill that bill. Nothing is more amusing to a lot of salacious man-boys than the opportunity to mock someone for being cuckolded. The Record Keeper is probably correct. There *are* two of Merrin's spies watching the manor, and if Hakkon and I can keep their eyes elsewhere, then that's what we should do."

So Delia found herself once again on Sundrop, once luncheon was over, on her way to the barge-builders.

There was a dead-end canal leading here, with a Gate on it, wide enough to allow for barges towed by horses to pass through it, and a second Gate for foot-traffic. The idea being that if you ordered a full string of empty barges, they could be put in the water here with your horses or some borrowed from the manor, and they could be Gated to a spot on another canal near or at their destination. There was no Gatekeeper here, but of course you'd need the proper talismans to use the things.

This was where the Gates at what they were now calling "Crescent Lake" were linked—anyone buying barges now intending to take them home and fill them would have to bring his own horses and tow them to the next Gate in line. With what Jonaton called a "hard link," the Gate used far less energy to send things to the refuge from here than they would if they used talismans. And it meant no one needed to have a talisman at all to come here from the refuge, which meant one less thing for the mages to do.

Oh! And since we've got all those paper talismans now, that means far fewer talismans our mages need to make! Which means most of them can probably go settle at Crescent Lake now, rather than later ˙.. .

If they would. The mages did like their comfort, and there was more of it here than there. It wasn't as bad out there as it had been when they'd created the Gates, but things were still a bit primitive.

Not that she blamed the mages for preferring comfort in the least. She agreed with them, actually.

She tied Sundrop up to a ring in the side of the huge building that housed the barge-makers and went inside. She'd been here before—and already she could see that there were far fewer barges stored here. Plenty of people had already claimed what they needed, and there would soon be far fewer. There were also a lot more barges in various states of construction than she had ever seen before. Every single workstation was full, and there were dozens of hulls in various stages of curing. She waited until one of the barge-builders noticed her, finished smoothing down the fungus-paste on the barge he was working on, washed off his hands, and came to see what she needed.

"Lady Isla put me in charge of three home-barges," she said, trying to project an air of someone who knew what she was about. "One for me, one for herself and Duke Kordas, and one for—" She stopped herself before she said "the children" and said instead, "four servants." Because the boys would need an adult actually with them.

"We've been expecting this request, and we put two aside just for the Duke and his Lady," the workman said, wiping his hands on his apron. "Will you come have a look? I expect you'll need to see them to understand what you can bring down from the manor."

She nodded, and he took her to the back of the enormous storage area, where there were two barges off to one side, set on a platform of rough-sawn planks to keep them off the dirt. As they approached, Delia could not help but notice that *these* barges were considerably more "finished" than the ones loaded with grain from the manor had been.

Windows had been cut along one of the slanted upper sides of each of the two barges. Shutters that could be closed and locked to keep out weather had been installed on either side of the windows, and glass had been fitted into frames in the holes. It wasn't the best glass possible—it had bubbles and a few thick ripples—but she assumed that, amidst the stepped-up schedule for the escape, they used what they had at hand at the moment. The barges had been painted in muted browns with black trim, and wooden decking was laid on the narrow walkways around the sides and at the prow and stern. Rough-cast brass cleats and rings were set at corners, and boarding planks could apparently be used to link several boats together. A stout wooden door at the prow, which faced her, gave into the interior of the barge, and the workman climbed up to the prow, helped her up, and flung the stout door open to let her inside.

Inside, everything had been painted white, which made it look much larger than she would have thought. And there was room to stand upright, which she had not been expecting. Wooden decking had been laid down with hatches in it at intervals. "You'll store anything that is waterproof beneath the hatches, milady," the workman said. "She *shouldn't* leak, but if she does, you won't want to lose what's down there. Or, you could stow wood for the fire down there, which is what I'd do, so there's not wood in the way all the time, and so you can have as much as you'll need for several days. The gods only know what sort of weather you'll meet out there, and you know for yourself that we've had snows that kept us to the manor for days at a time. You might not be *able* to get out for wood, and it'll be just you and your maidservants until people can break a trail to you."

A *lot* of work had clearly been done here already, and the boat had been divided up into rooms. The first one was almost all storage: a wardrobe with doors that latched shut, and cabinets, also with doors that latched shut, plus a very small table built into the deck, and a bit of seating with it, built into the bulkhead in a corner under the window, with shelves and hanging hooks above the window and the seating. *I can have everything I absolutely need here, and everything else can go on a cargo boat,* she thought. It was a pity that most of the nice things she'd absconded with from home would have to go into storage, but this was already better than she'd feared.

Passages were narrow, but not impossible. You had to go single file, but she had imagined much worse. She had, in fact, imagined something like a cargo barge, with everything stacked everywhere, and sleeping on top of a bed of crates with the roof of the barge inches from her nose.

The second room held a big bed, with a narrow passage

along the wall with the window. The window, she saw now, was in a frame that could be slid open along the wall, and there were curtains to close out the light, gathered on round metal rods above and below the window. Above the bed were shelves and more ceiling hooks to make the maximum use of space.

"This would be your bed, or the bed of Kordas and his lady," said the workman diffidently, with a hint of a blush.

The next room was small, and held a small barrel-like cast-metal stove with a stovepipe going up through the ceiling, a tiny hip-bath that could also be used to wash underthings or even larger garments, a bit of a pantry, and a bit of a sink.

This is even better. She'd pictured herself having to wash small-clothes in the lake or river, and how she was going to do that in winter, she'd had no idea. But the flat top of the stove gave a place to heat a pot of water, so the wash water would be warm, at least. And once the clothes-washing was done, she could at least give herself a quick once-over with a wet cloth, even in the dead of winter.

Next to that, an even tinier room with a close stool with a chamber pot, and sliding doors for privacy. And the last room, with a door at the end that led out to what she supposed must be the rear of the barge, held more storage and two narrow beds, one on each side, with shelves and hooks above the one that was on the wall that did not have windows. "Beds for servants," the workman said. "We assumed you'd want them."

All the beds lifted up on hinges; there was more storage under them. Every tiny bit of space had been used.

This is not going to be horrible, she thought with wonder. "Let me wander around in here and decide what I need to start bringing," she said, and the workman nodded and left her alone.

Kordas would without a doubt want all his personal magic books at hand, and since he wasn't here to need them, she could start by bringing those. And bedclothes; in winter they would want as many as they possessed, given that the tiny stove wasn't going to put out a lot of heat. Bedclothes were bulky, but rather than waste storage space, they could all be piled on the beds in layers, giving them storage *and* covers at the same time—layers of sheets and coverlets, and you could bury yourself beneath as many or as few as the weather required. She'd have the maids put their own clothing in the storage under their beds. She wandered from prow to stern and back again, envisioning things in all the places where they could be put and fixing them firmly in her mind. She could start by stripping her own quarters and sleeping in one of the guest chambers.

In fact, I can start stripping the entire manor. Most of everything brought down from the manor could be put in storage boats. *I'll need to make sure there is an inventory on each one so we know where to find things.* Her heart actually rose, as she understood—if Isla would allow it—how useful she *could* be.

She left the boat and sought out one of the workmen. "There should be a lot of people who kept care of the manor that will need to be seen to. Please put aside living-barges for them; I'll send them here to decide who will live with whom and where. Can you outfit one whole barge as a kitchen?" she asked. *I bet Isla hasn't thought of that. But the cooks and kitchen staff can sleep on pallets on the floor there, and we'll have a place out of the weather where we can make hot food.* She didn't think actual ovens for baking would be possible, but perhaps those ovens could be constructed outside.

The workman scratched his head and his brows wrinkled in thought for a moment. "I don't know why not," he said finally. "It'd be several stoves. They'd hold about one big pot each. Then counters to work, and a place to wash pots if the weather's bad. Reckon it can be done."

"Please do," she said, taking it on her own to order it. Worst came to worst, she could cancel the order tomorrow.

She rode Sundrop back to the manor in the late afternoon, having committed everything she needed to do on her own barge to memory.

She caught Isla just parting from Hakkon, and ducked out of the way so she could watch them without being seen. She had not suspected either her sister or the Seneschal of being such good actors! They parted with lingering hand touches and longing looks; Hakkon headed for parts unknown, Isla for her quarters. Delia decided to play her part in this deception as well. She hurried to catch up with her sister.

"What do you think you're doing?" she hissed, doing her best to feign outrage.

Isla started, and furrowed her brow. "I don't know what you're talking about," she said, ice in her voice.

"I saw you and Hakkon!" Delia choked out. "Don't try to deny it! I saw you two together!"

Isla had to work to suppress a twinkle in her eyes as she caught on to Delia's act. "That's none of your affair," she said, still with ice in her voice. *"You* should mind your own business. I will tend to my own."

"Funny business, that is!" Delia squeaked. "I should find a way to tell Kordas!"

Isla seized her by the arm and shook her. *"You* will keep your mouth shut and your thoughts to yourself," she spat. "Or this is what is going to happen to you!"

And she bent and whispered in Delia's ear. "Well played, love. Meet me in the cellars after dinner. Now run up to your room and pretend to cry."

Delia ripped herself away from her sister's grasp and hid her face in her arm as she raced to her rooms, where she flung herself on her bed and shook with what should look like sobs.

But they weren't sobs, of course. She was laughing herself sick.

Well, if the reason the Emperor brought me here was to keep the Court amused, I am certainly doing that, thought Kordas, as he moped in the rear of the afternoon Court in the Great Hall. Muted chatter swirled around him, like the perfumes that covered up the ever-present faint chemical taint in the air.

When he had been presented with the accusation that Isla was having an affair with Hakkon, he had decided to stretch his reactions out as long as he could. So he started with angry denials. He didn't go so far as to challenge the person who had told him this over dinner to a duel—he *really* didn't want to complicate the Plan still further with the repercussions of killing Prince Morthas of Halengard—but he flew into a rage and stormed out of dinner and tried to get an audience with the Emperor to demand he be sent home.

That would have been ideal, but alas, he couldn't get that audience, and none of the dozen messages sent to the Emperor were answered. Nor was he permitted to bring a petition up at Court. He tried, but all the Court clerks refused his petition, and even the Dolls were forced to tell him that it would not be accepted. He continued to deny that Isla would betray him.

That ate up about four days of time, time he spent alternately shouting at people and shouting at the closed doors of the Emperor's quarters.

Then he was presented with scryed records, and his first thought was that Isla was a brilliant actress, and Hakkon was pretty inept. She managed to make his flubbings look like the bumbling of a lovestruck dolt. That was ideal for the ploy, and he mused that it was also why he loved and valued Hakkon. The man simply didn't have it in him to lie enough to be a danger, and he was much smarter than anyone might think.

Kordas locked himself away for a day, ostensibly to sob into his pillows—but actually to refine the Plan. And despite his anxiety, he *did* rest. Drugged tea helped. Wisdom from his father was, *it is better to rest before exertion, than after. Sleep after exhaustion is inefficient, because it tries to heal body and mind at once; better to be well-rested, to be sharp-minded and react quicker, than to try to catch up or just drop where you stand*. Good bed, deep sleep, big breakfast, and one could outpace anything except a Night Person. Their ways were mysterious and full of cats.

Kordas slipped away whenever he was not being scryed and Gated into the records complex. He had unprecedented latitude in using the City's stores and resources, thanks to the Dolls. He'd begun, early on, by grilling the Record Keeper on what he could do as a Duke without attracting anyone's attention. It was stunning just how bad the Imperial way of doing things had become. The Record Keeper revealed to Kordas that its function was not to *interpret* nor *verify* the origin of orders, but rather, to follow the authority of the seals—and the Record Keeper had full sets of seals. Talking quickly, Kordas prepared requisition forms via the Dolls—all of whom worked nearly blindingly fast when they wanted to—then sat at the Record Keeper's desk, and had the Dolls turn away. By using the seals there, Kordas could impersonate a King, if he dared. The Record Keeper would turn around to find a stack of properly sealed orders to be carried out, and no Doll could claim to have witnessed anything awry. The materials requisitioned by the sealed order would be located, neatly packed, labeled, inventoried, and carried by Dolls to the so-familiar-as-to-be-unnoticed plain barges and boats that plied the canals of the City, with the inventory attached just inside the door. And off the barge would go to the refuge.

Kordas felt a genuine tingle of *joy* at stealing on such a scale. He knew it was wrong in general to steal, but this was for lives. He told himself that whatever he plundered from the Empire *for* his people were resources that wouldn't be available to the Empire *against* his people. *Audacity will win the day,* he thought, and had the City Armory unobtrusively carted out "for offsite inventory and storage relocation" with the proper stamps, and replaced with identical, but empty, crates. Tons of combat-ready Poomers, Spitters, and the ammunition for them streamed to Valdemar, with no one but he and the Dolls aware of it. Boatloads of pellets in their secured crates accompanied them. All the boats looked the same with their raincovers on, and *nobody* cared what Dolls shipped. Hundreds of Doll-operated barges plied the canals every day. And so, without Courts, Kings, or commoners noticing or caring, the Plundering of the City was underway.

Better to be hung for a big deed than a small one, he thought. *And, if I leave the City with a bare minimum of weapons, they won't have reserves to defend themselves with, and they might panic.* Panic was a good, useful option in a Court. The only supplies he let go out as usual were things that were expected on specific dates, such as ammunition and pellets going to the War. If those didn't arrive as expected, there would be furious consequences.

Tremors came and went all this time, and an urgent message came to Kordas from the Record Keeper while Kordas was deep down a storage bay: Foreseers were reporting new visions. *The Imperial City, the Palace, all exploding in fire or consumed by lava.* When, they weren't certain, but the visions were reported from Foreseers at the far edges of the Empire, as well as locals.

These reports made Kordas feel the most apprehension of the whole operation, and he lit off via Gate to the Records Complex. *Not everything a Foreseer predicts actually happens, but they can be good warnings to check things, and in my case—to check things that I have compromised.* So long as his subterfuge with the official seals was between him and the Dolls, everything should be all right. But if the predictions were delivered to the Emperor in a timely manner, the Emperor would search on his own, and Kordas would surely be exposed. By stealing the martial supplies alone, Kordas had cemented himself as a traitor.

If anyone was left alive to come after me. If anyone knew I was behind it. If anyone could find me.

Kordas agonized over the decision as he read the dispatches. In his heart it felt very, very much like pulling a trigger to end a life. If the Emperor received the Foreseer reports, he might lock down the entire City. No one in or out.

"If any more reports like these come in, can you destroy them?" he asked the Records Keeper.

"No, my Lord. Many things we can delay, but these are urgent and must be delivered to the Emperor. That we cannot change."

Kordas flew through his resourcefulness in his mind. Mis-labeling? Re-routing? Copying errors? Wait—"Can you hand over urgent dispatches to a human courier for delivery?"

The Records-Keeper answered quickly, "Yes, if they have a certification as an Imperial courier."

"Then have all new dispatches delivered to my Herald, Beltran. Then it is his responsibility to see to it they reach the

Emperor, and none of you are liable for what happens after they're handed off to a courier."

"That would not violate our directives."

With a flick of his fingers, flames erupted at the corners of the Foreseer reports. "Oh no, look what I did."

The Records Keeper nudged a trash receptacle toward Kordas, who dropped the burning papers into it. "We will have to report that sometime, my Lord. Delays or loss of official materials must be reported within one hundred days."

Initially, the Plan was for Valdemar to escape the Empire, which has turned even worse since Father devised it. Then I twisted the Plan into getting the abused children out, and then the Dolls, and the truth prisoners, and supplies, and now I've found myself thinking about the innocents in the City, from blacksmiths to noodle-cooks. Father's Plan is My Plan now, not The Plan. If the City will be annihilated, anything and anyone left here would be incinerated anyway, so—my conscience is clear about my secret sacking of the City. If the Emperor sees the Foreseer reports, though, he'll be enraged with paranoia, unleash every hound he has—and he'll discover the Plan. It's all about what the Emperor reacts to.

He exhaled hard, because he could only come up with one solution.

It never stops. It only escalates.

Kordas resumed his performance the next morning. He stormed around Court abusing Isla and Hakkon to anyone who would listen. He channeled his very real anger at not being allowed to go home into feigned anger at them. In a few more days, anyone who saw him coming would hastily find something else they urgently needed to do.

Then he changed his tune again. He begged people to tell

him how to win his wife back—or at the very least, get the Emperor to hear his petition to go home. He would bargain with anyone, which made him amusing again, as people gave him all sorts of absurd advice about his wife. No one, however, was willing to bargain with him for access to the Emperor. That was apparently one line they would not cross.

He kept that up for about six days more. Some of his desperation was real. It was perilously close to the day of the Regatta. He still had no good idea of how to protect the stubborn people who were intending, no matter what, to remain in Valdemar. The Record Keeper had been unable to give him any help either. In fact, the only other thing the Record Keeper had been able to advise him on was what to do about Merrin's spies . . .

Which had been, quite simply, to take them prisoner and allow the Record Keeper to forge reports to Merrin from them. So the spies were cooling their heels securely locked in the never-used prison cells of the Valdemar manor. They were being treated well, and on the day after the Regatta, the spell-locked door would swing open. So that was all right.

But it didn't help Kordas at all.

So now he was moping around, talking to no one, brooding. He displeased Star by disarranging his appearance so that he looked a bit unkempt. He pushed his food around his plate at public meals, and refused far, far more dishes than he accepted. This was actually all to the good, in his opinion; he had been afraid that even with moderate eating he was beginning to get soft around the waist. People snickered openly at him, but avoided him with alarm, because he would get maudlin and immediately turn the subject of conversation to Isla, pleading with them to give him advice, then interrupting that advice to grow teary-eyed and dissolve into a wet mess.

But the desperation and depression were both very real. He didn't have to feign those. He didn't have to feign pacing the gardens night and day, head down, as he went over every ploy he had thought of and discarded.

Put everyone remaining in Valdemar under a sleep spell, until they are awakened by those storming the place to investigate.

And what if that took days? Worse, weeks? Those storming the place would find the dead, not the living. Three days without water would kill a grown man, and it would be a day or less to doom an infant.

Have everyone remaining locked up by the last to leave.

That was the one he was still toying with, but it was still perilous, even if he left the ones imprisoned with adequate food and water. And would they be believed? And what if they were questioned magically?

Have everyone left behind claim that a disease made everyone else run mad.

That wouldn't be believed for an instant.

There were variations on all those things, but none of them would hold past the Emperor's inquisitors coming in and applying *real* questioning.

Well, he thought unhappily, as he left the Court early and paced the gardens in the thin, smoky afternoon sunlight. *At least I'm losing the weight I put on.*

———————

Delia would never have believed so much could be accomplished in so little time.

The vast combined herds of cattle, horses, sheep, pigs, and goats had been moved upriver to keep them from overgrazing the area around Crescent Lake. Smaller herds of each had been left to supply fresh meat for the common kitchens that had been set up around the Lake. Their owners and tenders followed them with strings of barges as the herds ate their way north and westward. Crescent Lake would have been full of barges from shore to shore if the slow migration to further safety hadn't already started. The Gates disgorged barges and people on a regular basis all day and night long; Delia reckoned about fifteen thousand people had arrived, with barges they intended to live in trailed by barges of everything they could possibly cram inside from their homes, and as many supplies as they could manage. Entire farms and manors now stood mostly empty back in Imperial Valdemar; not even Lord Merrin's farms had been spared.

Valdemar Manor was mostly stripped too. Counting on the fact that scryers would only concentrate on where Isla and Hakkon went, there was a narrow path of rooms that looked "normal"; everything else but heavy furnishings had been removed at Delia's direction. All of the mages were here now, living two and four to a home-barge. So far, none of them had murdered each other.

Having them here, with the power nexus available to them, had made it a lot easier to solve many problems. Like where people were going to get flour; they had grain in plenty, but flour spoiled if it wasn't used within three months. Two barges had been set up as mills, with several small millwheels powered by magic, instead of one big millwheel powered by water or wind. One of those was here at the Lake, the other at the head of the caravan making its way upstream.

Two of those rivers had proven to be dead ends of a sort . . . but only of a sort. Although the streams ended, it turned out there were settlements of people there. Isla and Ponu had visited each, used their magics to quickly learn the local language, and assured the local leaders that the Valdemarans intended no harm, and would soon be on their way.

And that . . . was where things had taken a turn for the unexpected.

Which was why Delia was mounted on one of the Gold Chargers, a three-year-old, which had been a bit of a feat, as big as the mare was. Her legs were practically splayed out on either side of the saddle; it was not comfortable. The Charger was tethered to the start of a string of barges that was just about thirty long. Ten of them held some of Squire Lesley's prize pigs, including the Empress and her brood. There were another two strings behind her, and shepherds and herdsmen moving along flocks of sheep and cattle on the riverbanks.

They were all very near their destination, the settlement at the head of one of the two dead-end streams. The locals called this "the Brandywine" in their language, and their little village "Brandywine" as well.

The sun shone down hotly on the expedition, and the air smelled of fresh water and trampled vegetation.

Squire Lesley rode next to her on a fat cob. She looked down at him. "You're sure you want to do this?" she asked anxiously. "You'll probably never see your sons and daughters again."

"My sons and daughters are smart and strong. I love them and they'll be all right. They can always visit, right? The good folk of Brandywine are my sort of people," the Squire replied. "When they asked if some of us would join them, and I got a look round the place, I honestly couldn't imagine myself taking the long journey the mages are saying we should." He sighed. "I'm too old for such things, and that's the truth. Uprooting me and my pigs and piling everything into barges and making that crossing took more out of me than I ever thought it would. I'm ready to settle. And these good folk are ready to have us! It seems like providence, to me."

Delia couldn't argue with that. The elders of Brandywine and the other settlement, Oakton, had come down the rivers, taken a look at the Valdemaran armada, and had evidently very much liked what they saw. And, truth to tell, it was a good bargain all around. Some of the Valdemaran families got new homes immediately and would not face the great migration that was ahead of the others, and all of those families had at least one elderly member who was spared a grueling journey. Crescent Lake certainly could not support the whole population that had arrived, much less the ten thousand or so yet to come; there was a lot of discussion going on about who would be staying and who would be going.

And the locals got an infusion of new people, new herds, and folk who were no strangers to putting their hands to weapons.

This might be land mostly empty of people, but it was *not* empty of dangers. The Valdemarans had already encountered some of them—things born of twisted magic that were far more perilous than bears. And there were roaming bands of bandits as well, men who preferred to take rather than produce.

Beyond that—and the locals always seemed to point in different directions—was something called "The Pelagirs." Marauding monsters, bears, and what was essentially an invasion of foreigners did not make the locals as sick-looking or pale as the word "Pelagirs."

So two struggling villages were about to get what they needed to stop struggling and start prospering. And as a bonus there was about to be a large town within an easy distance of them. Granted, the "town" was going to take some building yet, but the people would be there, and their skills and tools.

The river made an abrupt turn, and there was Brandywine, with its cluster of thirty houses and its palisade of logs. Actually, all Delia could see from where she sat was the log palisade, the open gate, and a glimpse of a couple of wooden houses that were very different from the stone cottages of Valdemar. And it looked as if the entire village had turned out to cheer the arrival of the newcomers. They also looked very different from the folk of Valdemar; clothing was all of homespun, home-woven materials and colored with local, natural dyes.

All the Valdemarans had gotten the local tongue courtesy

of Ponu, so at least there wouldn't be any difficulty in being understood.

The river was just about to get too shallow even for the shallow-drafted barges, but the locals had prepared for that, building a pair of docks right at the point where the bottom of a barge would start to scrape gravel. Delia urged her mount up to the dock, and one of the locals—a handsome lad in homespun loose trews and a linen smock, with the reddest hair she had ever seen, deftly caught the rope she untied from the back of the saddle and tied up the string at the dock.

As she walked her mount away, the second string was pulled up alongside the first, and tied off to the dock and the prow of the first string.

Then the Tow-Beast pulling the third string splashed belly-deep through the water to the opposite side of the river, and another fellow waiting at the second dock caught the rope and tied the third string there.

And there was just enough room that if a fourth lot of Valdemarans decided to take up the invitation to settle here, there'd be space to wedge in a last string of barges, though they would be so tight-packed that you'd be able to easily walk from one bank of the river to the other.

As this was happening, Squire Lesley had gone to the second barge of the string, and with an apple and a cabbage was coaxing the Empress and her brood down a gangplank flung to the deck of the barge.

A murmur of admiration came from the crowd at the sight of the enormous sow, who had somehow managed to keep herself pristine in the barge, though the same could not be said of all of her piglets. She was not the only pig in the barge by any means, but she'd been given a partition for herself and her brood, while the rest milled in a herd in the rest of the barge.

"By the staff of Great Wethlen!" exclaimed a farmer who, except for his rough, brown clothing, did not look altogether unlike the Squire. "She's magnificent! She's a goddess incarnate! How ever did you manage to produce such a beauty?"

Squire Lesley beamed. *"Now* do you see why I wanted to come here?" he asked, looking up at Delia, as the piglets milled around his ankles.

"You and I, friend Less-el-lee," said that same farmer, clapping the Squire on the shoulder. "We shall come to see if I have built you a house and an enclosure worthy of this paragon among pigs! Come! Come! And if you do not like it, then I shall slay myself in grief!"

"Hardly think that'll be necessary, Aylar," Lesley replied, with a gentle pat to the man's back. And with that, they moved off, the Empress following the bribe of the apple in Lesley's hands.

Delia felt her eyes start to sting, and turned away, signaling to the other two riders that she was going to start her trip back to the Lake. They, too, were remaining; one with a Tow-Beast, and one with a Charger, a stallion and a mare, that would provide the foundation stock for heavy horses to help with plowing, something Brandywine did not have. Those who were remaining were going to live in their barges for the next year, but start new fields of crops that would not be harmed by being sown late in the season. That and the supplies they had brought should see them all through to next spring without difficulty, and even with abundance. This village had goats, not sheep, so the sheep being brought along were a welcome addition, and as was the small herd of cattle she passed as she urged her mount into a canter. And even more welcome were the herding dogs that had accompanied their masters. This was something the locals had never had, and included a mastiff-like breed that lived with the herds it guarded day and night, and had been known to successfully fight off bears.

They'll be all right, she told herself, as the ponderous Charger ate up the leagues between her and Crescent Lake. Isla hadn't told her as much, but she suspected that the arrival of *peaceful* strangers had come as a relief and a surprise—people didn't build palisades for defenses for no reason. And Squire Lesley, who was in charge of this group of people who were mostly local to him, had his directions.

Make sure the Valdemarans stayed welcome. When in doubt, in a disagreement, side with the locals. Start dressing like the locals, and blend in as quickly as possible. Forget the language of the Empire; translate every book they had with them into the local tongue.

Assimilate. Assimilation was survival.

And should the very worst happen, should the Empire somehow track them to this refuge, bypassing the town that would be built on the shores of the lake—well, they all already knew how that would go. Every single Valdemaran who was about to become a citizen of Brandywine agreed. The Empire always followed the same pattern when it came to things like this. There would be an initial scouting party. And that scouting party should be welcomed with a great feast, at which they would be given far too much to drink.

And then they were to be slaughtered without mercy. Or perhaps poisoned. The Empire showed no mercy; it would be given none.

When enough scouting parties failed to return from a "primitive" location like this one, the Empire generally stopped sending them, giving it up as a bad investment. The Empire wanted places to conquer that had treasure and wealth worth looting, not a bunch of farms.

That rather bloody-minded thought actually cheered Delia up somewhat.

Now . . . if only Kordas was here.

Kordas stared at his breakfast and tried to muster up the enthusiasm to eat it. He'd spoken to Isla and things were going well—better than well—but he still had no answers for how he was going to save *all* of the people of Valdemar, not just the ones willing to escape.

He also had no idea how he was going to free the *vrondi* once they had escaped. At least, without killing them.

"Lord Duke," Star said, interrupting his thoughts. "The Record Keeper wants to know if you have any orders for us."

I still can't believe how quickly people were able to pack up what they needed and leave, he marveled. Granted, they weren't able to take *everything* from their homes. Furniture had to be left behind. Still . . .

Pack up, pack up . . .

Orders for the Dolls . . .

Something dawned on him with the force of a blow, and he looked up at Star. "Could I order the two remaining Innovator mages to move to other quarters? By which I mean, both living quarters and working quarters?" he asked, slowly feeling his way.

"Yes, my Lord," said Star. "In fact, they have been complaining for some years now that they do not like where they are. Utility mages have better quarters, and they are envious."

"Are there better quarters available to them?" he asked.

"Yes, Lord. It is merely that no one has given the orders," said Star. "And they no longer have the ear of the Emperor. They have produced nothing new for nearly a decade, and he no longer cares to hear from them unless they produce something akin to the pellets or the Dolls."

The idea practically exploded in his mind. "Then tell them their request is approved. Pack up their possessions and move everything today to their new living quarters. Tell them that because their working apparatus is so delicate and needs such great care, it will take a week to move it to their new working quarters. Tell them to rest and enjoy themselves for a week. Then pack up everything *except* what has to do with the Dolls and move it. Then leave it all packed, tell them in a week it is ready, but that they must decide how to arrange everything in person. By then, the Regatta will be over, and it won't matter. Take everything that has to do with the Dolls, put it on a barge, and send the barge through a Portal—"

"—to your refuge. Understood, Lord Duke." Star seemed pleased. "The Imperial reference libraries for summonings, banishments, and field magic await load-out and transfer. The books and scrolls alone number in the thousands. The experimental equipment from the other laboratories that survived the structural collapse have been in storage and are being crated. We know they were the precursors to our imprisonment processes. By having your mages look through the materials, they should find a way to release us!"

"Exactly," he said, and felt a little, a very little, relief. That was one problem out of the way.

"It shall be done today," said Star. "The Record Keeper asks that I tell you that a Doll shall accompany the barge as well, to explain everything on the other side."

"Good, good," he said. And found a little appetite to eat.

"The Record Keeper reminds me that you asked about the source for magic power here, since the Imperial mages are discouraged from making pacts with Abyssal demons," Star said after a very long pause while he revived his faint appetite. "The one below."

Well, that killed his appetite again. But in a different way.

"I did," he said. "But the Record Keeper never responded to me."

"That is because the Record Keeper deemed it too dangerous. Too prone to discovery. But there is a brief window this morning, due to some unexpected demands upon the Imperial mages, when there will be no one but Dolls to note your passing. Would you still care to see this?" Star paused. "It is best seen, rather than explained."

He shoved the tray aside and all but leapt up out of bed. "The sooner the better," he said. "How should I dress? Just in case we run into someone unexpected."

"This one will attend to that." Star went to the wardrobe.

Soon he stood in front of the Portal, impatiently waiting for Star and the Record Keeper to gain access for them to this oh-so-mysterious place. Evidently not all Dolls were allowed access to it, which only made his curiosity itch the more.

Finally, Star signaled to him to hold up his bracelet to the Portal and say the words, "The Chamber of the Beast."

The . . . Beast?

Too late now. He stepped through, into blazing red light and heat.

And realized immediately *why* the Record Keeper had been so reluctant to try to describe what was here.

Just to begin with, there was so much raw magic power in here that it almost scorched him until he shielded from it, and it took him longer than he liked to establish enough shielding that he was able to actually *look* at what he'd been brought to see.

Then, three more things had to be sorted through before he could make out anything.

The first was an ululating sound, but deep and sonorous, more felt than heard. He couldn't figure out what it was, so finally he dismissed it to go on to the next thing standing between himself and understanding.

The second was the heat. Whatever was in the center of that room dumped heat like a young sun. In fact, it was probably the heat source that kept the entire Palace warm in the winter, provided the hot water for baths and the like, and provided cooking heat to boot. That was confirmed when he saw what could only be water-filled pipes lining all the walls of this chamber. Pumps powered by magic brought in cold water and took away hot water on a grand scale.

Then, the wards and spells guarding and binding what was

in the center of the room created a kind of cage it was difficult to see through. Even with his physical eyes. There was so much power in here, with the spells that contained the mysterious object feeding on the power that the thing gave off, that, like in the cellars of Valdemar Manor, the spell-lines actually glowed physically.

So did the chained rune-plaques that surrounded it. He recognized what they were doing: they were binding something in place, but also *hiding* it, so that no one who was not physically in this room would be able to scry it, detect it, or see it in any manner.

Why?

But then he finally made it out.

And he couldn't understand what he was seeing.

"This makes no sense to me," he said aloud. "What is this thing? It looks like a lump of rock."

"It is an Earth Elemental, Lord Duke," Star said patiently. "One of the Greater Earth Elementals, but a young one. It was lured into a trap, captured, and hidden here a hundred years ago or more. This is the source of all magic energy used in the Palace, and most of the magical energy used by the Imperial mages."

No.

"That's not possible," he said flatly. "No Greater Elemental can be coerced into providing *anything*. You can bind it all you like, but it will never, ever give anything up."

"The Lord Duke is correct," Star admitted. "But it will emit magical energy if it is wounded. It must, in order to heal."

It took a long moment for the enormity—and the horror—of that statement to sink in.

"You mean that you bound it here—and now you are deliberately wounding it—in order to siphon off the magic it uses to heal itself?" he said in a strangled voice.

"*We* are not," Star corrected, forcefully. "Humans are. This is a rare moment when there are no humans in this chamber wounding it. They have wounded it enough, and now it is healing."

That was the sound. *That* was what he was hearing. The poor, damned thing had been hurt, and hurt, and hurt, and finally left to heal.

And it was crying, moaning in pain, weeping because it knew this was only going to happen again once it healed. And of course, it could do nothing about that. It couldn't stop itself from healing, any more than he could, if he'd been slashed all over, then bandaged and left to heal.

He had thought he had plumbed the depths of Imperial depravity.

He was beginning to think, now, that he never would.

"And this is a *young* creature?" he choked out.

"Something like a child. Yes," said Star.

He wanted to be sick.

"Others of its kind seek it," Star continued. "They have for some time. They roam beneath the earth of the Empire, hunting for it. They know that the Empire has it. But thanks to the magics surrounding it—those chains and rune-plaques—they cannot find it. The nearer they come, the more the distraction. You may have felt them, from time to time—when the earth trembles for a moment. And you have seen the ongoing damage they do as they seek for their young one, in the City. That is their reaction, their frustration. Always near enough to sense, never near enough to locate."

"This is *wrong*," he managed. "I would—rather see demon pacts."

"No, my Lord Duke," Star replied. "You most certainly would not."

———————

Fortunately, his brooding and depression gave him all the excuse he needed to avoid going to luncheon, to Court, and to dinner, though several times during the day, Star covered the Valdemar badge on its hand, indicating that someone was scrying on him. He probably gave them pretty much what they were expecting, since all he did was sit and stare out the window, mostly not moving.

His gut reaction was *I have to free it!* But of all of the things he was doing, or wanted to do, this was absolutely the most impossible.

He was certain without bothering to ask that his rank as a Duke would not be enough for him to order the Dolls to free it. As for doing it in person, well . . . that was sheer insanity. The thing was surrounded most of the time by human tenders. How would he get past them? He certainly would not be able to order the Dolls to restrain them. And if he did manage to find another window when it wasn't being tended between now and the Regatta, how would he keep it from killing him when he *did* free it? *If* he could?

I have more things to do than I have time, energy, resources, or . . . me. I have a hundred things to do, and only enough "me" to tend to fifty.

Granted, Isla and Hakkon were taking care of some of the remaining fifty. But he was the only one *here.*

"My Lord Duke?"

He looked up at Star, who had uncovered the badge on its hand. "My Lord Duke, it appears to this one that you are perturbed and upset."

"I feel . . . stretched too far, thinned out over too many things, pulled so that I'm full of holes and if I take on even a little more strain, I'm going to snap," he confessed to the Doll, and by extension, to all the Dolls.

Star remained silent. Probably because the Dolls could not think of any way to help him. Or maybe the Doll just didn't understand what he'd said. He took it for granted that they understood human emotions, human frailties, human failings— after all, they had been observing humans for decades now.

But maybe they didn't understand *him*. Maybe they thought he was infallible, that he'd always manage a solution.

"I can't do everything," he said hopelessly. "I might not be able to do even what I've promised. I—"

Star stopped him with a hand on his shoulder. "You have several significant flaws, including that once you are convinced you are capable of one thing of a certain scale, you are equally convinced you can handle more. You do not allow for their cumulative effects upon you. You are doing what you can." Rose brought a tea tray and poured a half-cup, then added honey and two syrups. Patiently, Rose offered the cup to Kordas, and he accepted it using both hands because he was a little shaky at the moment.

Rose said, "Thanks to you, every Doll has a talisman that will take it to the refuge. Even the Record Keeper. And the hostages will be taken there as well. And everyone in your home who is willing to go will be there as well. That is three times as much as you had thought you could do. Chance and the future are uncertain; but these things are true."

"Yes, but—"

Star stopped him with, "We intend to empty the royal stables of horses. They will come with us."

He stared at Star's "face" in disbelief.

"So no matter what should betide, this much will be true. At the end of the Regatta, the Emperor will have *no* servants and *no* horses, and the entire Palace will be in disarray. No one left will know how to react. Most of the humans here scarcely know how to care for themselves." There was no doubt of the contempt in the Doll's voice. "And when the Palace is in disarray, what do you think the courtiers will do?"

Kordas was a third of the way into his tea, and could only murmur "Um . . ."

Star continued. "Those who are in possession of a talisman to return home—and most of them are—will flee to their homes and the comfort of their homes. The ones who are not will be useless burdens on the Emperor's Guard corps and the few human servants. You have heard the Emperor speak. He is not a man much given to thought. He can order members of the Guard or the human servants to do many things—but if they *cannot* do them, these things will not be accomplished." Star paused. "It is the opinion of the Record Keeper that before he thinks of anything else, the Emperor will see to his own comfort. He will recall those who used to serve here from the legions, weakening them ever so slightly—but more importantly, throwing *them* into some disarray. He will demand more servants from his nobles. All this will take time. The pellet-machines will have fallen silent. No more pellets will be sent to the southern war, and it will further slow to a halt. By the time there are humans minding the machines, some of them will have shaken apart. There may be explosions. No one knows how to mend the machines. The war is more important in the Emperor's mind than anything else. By the time he turns his attention to the 'who' behind the disappearance of the Dolls, the trail we left will be cold, and evidence will vanish too. It may appear that you simply disappeared along with all the other nobles—after all, you have been clamoring to do so. It may be thought that the hostages decided to leave in the confusion as well."

"I don't want to keep the child hostages, I just want them to be forever out of—there. None of this is certain—" Kordas said, hesitantly.

"And none of it is impossible," Star pointed out, and he suddenly got the impression that a great many of the Dolls had focused their attention on him.

There was a long silence.

Kordas finished the tea, handing the cup over to the awaiting Rose, and spoke to all of the Dolls through Star. "I just realized—I'm not sure I've explained to all of you *why* I hate this place. I want—it isn't revenge on this City, it's more like— I'm inside a hulking, poisoned, rotting monster that isn't even aware it's destroying itself with every footstep, it just keeps plodding along, causing misery and eating misery, instead of being put down in mercy. It feels like leaving it alive is an act of *cruelty*." He rubbed at his temples. "Do you know what they've given up here, in the Palace? In the City? They've given up *empathy*. They've given up sentiment, fond thoughts of the little things that make life worth living, that make it special and wondrous and joyful."

Kordas leaned in earnestly to Star, trying to pour his feelings out after so much tension. "Here at the Palace, everyone is well fed, and they gossip, and they present themselves as 'acceptable'—but they're joyless and without quirks, all the time, because those quirks could be questioned along with their loyalty. I'm the only one who sits at the tables and talks about things that I love that aren't pointedly to the Empire's benefit. I'm the only one who just talks about what they like. Everyone else—maneuvers. They keep what they love, and how they love it, hidden away so no one above them in rank can use it against them."

He stood up to gesture more freely, and showed the back of his Ducal Crest. "This thing—the charm that I was given to protect my thoughts. It's helped me survive here, in a way that they probably didn't intend. I think into it, about Valdemar. About what I love about Valdemar. And then, sometimes, I imagine Valdemar as I've described it to you, becoming like this place. The quirks we love could be interpreted as seditious. Something like playing a war game on a table and having the Empire lose might be interpreted by a scrying mage as a sign of incipient revolt. The order comes from on high that the games are illegal now. Punishable. The inspiration of musicians and poets could be blunted by decree. The courting rituals we laugh over could be shut down because they are inefficient." He picked at the loose paint and plaster around the window. "When a ruler gives up on empathy and sentiment, it is a sign of desperation. It means they're paring away emotion in favor of efficiency and numbers and a twisted fantasy of a better life without the joys and burdens of caring about something outside of themselves. Contempt for kindness and generosity is the surest sign there is that someone has nothing else left to them but a horrible emptiness much worse than weakness. It's an—anti-strength. And the dying monster plods along, unaware it's rotting."

Kordas faced Star fully again. "No one lives forever, but—in a very real way, everyone in that Court but me is already dead. It's just a matter of *degrees* of dead. And I'm their fool, mocked for actually feeling. I amuse them with my trite and naive love of things. They see my talk as a display of an idiot's weakness. But I'm more alive than all of them. That's why we have to get our people out of here. Out of the Empire, your people and mine. I don't say it lightly that, if it is a decision between what this system would make of us, and living with joy—the Empire will die before I let them take our loves from us."

"And this," said Rose, "is why we will follow you, even into doom."

18

"**S**o . . . you're a Doll," Isla said, uncertainly. "Do you have a name?"

The Doll had popped out of the front door of a barge that had come through the Gate this morning, scaring the *hell* out of the people who were steering barges into position to be linked into a string. Delia hadn't blamed them. The thing was utterly uncanny, a human-sized jointed canvas contraption with only a hint of features that walked . . . and talked. And even worse, so far as everyone else was concerned, as soon as it had emerged from the hatch, it had ripped off the Imperial tabard it wore and tossed it violently overboard, leaving a completely *naked* human-shaped canvas contraption that walked and talked. Somehow a completely naked thing was much more disturbing than one partially clothed.

Maybe because we can kind of see it as an enlarged toy when it's clothed, or something like a scarecrow, but when it's just . . . there . . . it's harder to accept?

Thank the gods, Ponu had sprung up from out of nowhere, taken the Doll under his skinny wing, directed the others where to moor the barge it had come in on, and gotten clothing for it. He must have raided his own stores, or those of his fellow Circle members, because now it wore loose linen trews, an equally loose linen shirt tied at the waist with a cloth sash— and a straw hat. Delia wasn't sure why, but the clothing somehow made it look less unsettling, and that hat made it funny rather than threatening.

"This one has no name," the Doll said, in a pleasant whisper.

"Hold still," said Koto, coming up from behind Delia. He had a bottle of sepia ink and a feather, and with a few deft strokes with the tip of the feather, sketched in features that suggested something harmless and childlike. That made it less unsettling too. Then he stuck the feather in the band of the straw hat. "I'm calling you Feather. Do you like that name, Feather?"

"I—think I do. It has conceptual notes of lightness, aspirations, and transience," Feather answered. Koto capped the ink, nodded to Isla, and left, going back to whatever he had been doing before he decided to give the Doll a face.

"Kordas said that what one of you knows, all of you know," Isla continued. "Is that still true?"

"Yes, Lady Isla," Feather replied.

Isla gave a little crow of glee. "Do you know what this means?" she said. "It means we *won't have to risk scrying anymore!*"

Feather went very quiet for a moment. "This . . . is truth," it whispered. "You need only tell this one what you wish Kordas to know. Kordas need only tell Star or Rose or Clover what he wishes you to know." It paused. "This one can tell you that what concerns Kordas the most, at the moment, is the repercussions that will fall on those left behind in Valdemar if they refuse to come to the refuge."

"Well," Ponu said after a moment of thought. "I think I have an idea. But it's going to take a hell of a lot of power. Still! We can siphon off a fair bit from the power nexus here, and put it into storage crystals, and do it."

"Do what?" Isla asked sharply.

"Wipe everyone's memory," Ponu replied. "It's a crude spell, but effective. Take away their knowledge of the Plan and how we all left. It'll leave holes in their memories, and that'll disturb them all, but the Emperor's inquisitors can't find what isn't there."

Isla looked appalled. Delia felt as appalled as Isla looked.

Ponu looked from Isla to Delia and back, and snorted. "So what's better? Lose your memory or lose your life? The Emperor's mages will find the residuum from a spell that big all over the Duchy, and there won't be any question that those of us who left forced it on them."

"We need a better idea than that," Isla said flatly. "I won't allow it. And besides, won't that just point the finger directly at those of us who left? And then they'll have even more reason to try and hunt us down."

"They'll already have all the reasons they want to hunt us down." Ponu shrugged. "You're the leader here. Maybe we can think of something else. Probably we can keep them from finding our refuge here. And if we can't think of anything else, well, you and the Duke will share responsibility for hanging the ones left behind out to dry." And he turned on his heel and walked away.

"You'd *better*!" Isla shouted after him. "You'd better think of something!"

He raised his hand in a rude gesture.

"It's not Ponu's responsibility to come up with a 'better' idea," Delia observed, earning her a glare from her older sister.

"Please come with me, Feather," Isla said, rather than answering Delia. "I would like to find out exactly what is going on with Kordas." And she led the Doll away—which had the

immediate effect of making nearly everyone else who had
been near it relax again.

Valdemarans just aren't used to seeing that much magic,
Delia thought. *Much less something as powerful and uncanny
as animating a cloth doll.*

*Which makes me wonder how they are going to react when
hundreds of those things start showing up.*

Well, it wasn't as if they were threatening in any way. And
they certainly could be helpful. They wouldn't need to eat or
sleep, and at the very least, they could probably serve as night
guards, which would free up a lot of people to work in the
daytime. Of course, eventually they'd have to be freed of their
imprisoning bodies, because Kordas had promised that, but
until the mages figured out how to do that, they would be
awfully helpful.

As she stared off after Isla, who seemed merely to be heading for a spot that was still near the Gate—after all, she had
to get back to Valdemar to continue the charade of her "affair"
with Hakkon—Koto spoke behind her, making her jump.

"Some things you just have to let go, and leave to chance,"
he said.

"Yes, but—" she began.

"The people we are leaving behind are either those who are
completely out of the Plan because we cannot trust them, or
people who know what they are getting themselves into, because they have been repeatedly told," Koto continued.

"Yes, but—"

"They are responsible for their own actions, too," he
pointed out.

"Yes, but—"

"Would you relieve *everyone* of consequences?"

She saw she was going to get nowhere, and just shook her
head.

"Do what you can, do everything that you can, do it to the
best of your ability, and leave the rest to fate. Or the gods. Or

random luck. Your choice," he advised. "By the time you get to be my age, you've learned to let a lot go." He linked arms with her. "Let's go back to the manor. There's still a lot to do there, and it's only two days to the Regatta."

When Star entered his room, Kordas could tell that the Doll was agitated. *How* he could tell that, he was not sure; maybe he was becoming more sensitive to the Dolls—maybe that accident had shaken something loose in his mind. But it was very clear to him, at least, that Star badly wanted to talk about something, but was keeping the Valdemar badge on its hand covered.

"The Emperor has decreed a Blind Feast for tomorrow, at the midday meal," said Star. "After which, the Emperor will issue decrees, then mount his chariot to watch as much of the rest of the Regatta as he cares to."

"If he's not there in person," Kordas asked carefully, "who is? And what is a Blind Feast?"

At this point he had already guessed that the Emperor would be present at the Regatta until he got bored—and he had the idea that the Emperor got bored rather easily. Of course, he could be wrong. But he didn't think he was.

Nevertheless, he also knew that there were clerks—clerks which were probably Dolls now—that were counting every single boat, and woe betide those who were supposed to come and didn't show up. He knew for a fact that the Emperor had humans checking over those tallies, and watching for anyone who didn't come prove their loyalty in his boat-parade. They'd better have good reasons, like being dead, or having the boat sink on the way there.

"The Emperor has a proxy," Star said. "It's a statue of himself. He can see through its eyes and hear through its ears. He generally does so, from the comfort of the Palace, because he very much enjoys a spectacle that is meant to glorify him. And a Blind Feast . . . is a meal that is a kind of test. You are fitted with a helmet that will only permit you to look down at your plate, and nowhere else. You are led into the Dining Hall by your Doll, and seated. You cannot see who you are with. The helmets are removed, at intervals, in reverse of rank, starting with Kings, if there are any there. There are no Kings here presently, only Princes."

So you need to be very careful what you say, because you don't know who you'll be seated with. Another version of the Game. You needed to make entertaining conversation, but you had better not misjudge your audience.

Well, he had a way to be entertaining, all right. All he had to do was continue his laments about Isla.

Or maybe I should just rant about Hakkon.

Or perhaps, just perhaps, a new tune. Perhaps he should rant about how Hakkon had betrayed him. Maybe show some paranoia and wonder aloud if Hakkon planned to hire an assassin to kill him, so that *he* could take over as Duke.

Yes, I think that will do. It certainly would feed into things they themselves might be wondering about . . . if there is someone back home who is plotting to replace them.

"So just another hideous meal to get through," he sighed, and looked out the window again.

The tower trembled, reminding him once again of the Child Below, and the terrifying Elementals that were searching for it.

"Will you be going down to dinner?" Star asked.

"No. I have no reason to. What is there down there for me? Just another meal I can't eat, and people who can give me no advice."

Tomorrow is the Regatta. And I still have no idea how I am going to keep my people who are left behind safe. Or how to free that poor Earth Elemental.

"This one will bring you and your companion food," Star

said; he glanced over at the Doll and saw that it was still covering its hand. Interesting. Why would they be scrying him now? And why for so long?

Maybe the mage assigned to me is just a sadist.

He sighed again, deciding that moping was probably the least entertaining thing he could do. Star waited to see if he would say anything else, then left quietly.

I'm so tired.

No, "tired" wasn't the right word. He was exhausted, worn thin by all the things he had to do and the new things that kept piling up on him. It was almost as if he had been told to climb a high mountain alone, had gotten to the top, then discovered that it wasn't the top after all, but merely a ledge on the way to the top, and there was more mountain above that. And more above that. And more above that.

And now it was too late to go anywhere but further up, because an avalanche had fallen behind him, and he couldn't return.

Well, I could. But the result of that would be very bad.

And then suddenly, an idea *did* occur to him.

What if I don't leave during the Regatta?

What if I stay here?

If he stayed, the disappearance of the Dolls, the dissidents, and the hostages wouldn't be linked to him—and thus, to Valdemar. The Dolls would, in theory, still be beholden to obey the Emperor even at the refuge, but it would be a moot point once they were outside the reach of the Empire, shielded from receiving any orders.

So then what would happen?

Well, the place would be in chaos. There would be no Dolls to serve the Palace, no Trap to make more. Supplies would arrive—and there would be no one to move them to where they were supposed to go. The elaborate meals would be impossible with no one to serve them. No one in the Palace would have servants to wait on them—what would *they* do?

A lot of them, if they have Gate talismans, will go home. But if they don't? It was the Dolls that created the talismans. Did the Imperial mages still know how to do that? Probably, but it would take time, a lot of time, and they were probably rusty at it. There'd be no horses to take people home, so they'd have to go home by canal on barges. In fact, the Emperor would probably decree that people who were not actually useful go home, because they would be a drain on the resources of the Palace.

The Emperor would get priority on talismans, and he'd probably use them to bring warm bodies in from one of the legions to serve as servants instead of soldiers.

He might dragoon city folk into being servants. But they don't know how to do that, and they'd be bad at it, and that would mean more chaos.

There would, of course, be a massive search for the missing, but it would all be centered *here*. Records would be combed through, but the Dolls were in charge of the record-keeping, and as thorough as they were, he was positive they had either erased those records or never made them in the first place. So actually, the longer he stayed here, the longer it would take to associate Valdemar with the missing.

He'd probably send me home . . . wait, no he wouldn't. As soon as he got horses into the stables, he'd need someone who knows how to care for them. And that would be me.

He buried his face in his hands, head aching, thinking. But the more he thought about it, the surer he was. The best thing he could do for Valdemar was stay here.

All right; got to think this through. I'd never heard of the Dolls before I got to the City, so it stands to reason they're never seen outside of it. Everyone is going to be at the Regatta once that yellow toad gets heaved into his golden-chariot-throne and hauled there to observe. And that was when we were going to leave anyway.

So, I'll be there instead of running off. The Dolls leave, and the only people who notice are the Palace servants. They won't know what to do about it, or who to report it to. Will the mages go to the Regatta? Probably not, but they won't notice the Dolls are leaving until it's too late, and anyway, what could they do to stop them? And who would they tell? Who would they send? They might be able to send a message magically, but would anyone pay attention to it? Probably not; the way things run around here, it would probably get dismissed to be looked at after the Regatta was over.

So far, so good.

At the worst, someone will send one of the people working in the kitchen as a runner with a message. By then, the Trap will be shut down, or even destroyed, the dissidents will be gone, the hostages will be gone, and the Dolls will be gone.

What then?

Well, people being people won't believe that the Dolls have gone. They'll probably assume only some of them have left, or that they got herded into a room somewhere in this heap and locked away. Only when they've figured out that their slaves have slipped their chains will they look further . . . or will they?

The most likely thing is that people will start blaming each other. And meanwhile, the Emperor will be furious, and the longer he goes without being waited on, the more furious he'll be.

So assuming that someone actually takes the initiative to get the soldiers garrisoned here to come act as servants—by then people will be getting hungry, and angry, and the soldiers won't exactly know how to be servants in the first place. And that—their immediate needs—is what people are going to concentrate on. Not on finding the Dolls, not on finding out where they went, or how, or who's responsible. It will probably take until morning before someone gets the mages to go down to the Fabrication Annex and make more Dolls to serve the Emperor before he starts ordering executions. And that is when they'll discover they can't make more Dolls.

By morning, the Courtiers who can leave, or who have fig-
ured out some way to leave besides Gates, will be leaving. Any
of them who are smart and can go by Gate will promise to
send human servants here. So some human servants will start
to trickle in. But they won't know the Palace, they won't know
how to use the Gates to get from place to place within the Pal-
ace, and it's going to add to the chaos, not subtract from it.

Meanwhile . . . meanwhile what I should do is blunder
down to the stables, because my first thought will have been
to see if the horses are all right, and I'll just come tell someone
that the horses are all gone too.

Then what should I do? Well, supposedly I can't go home,
because I don't have a talisman. So I guess . . . I know. The
Emperor just thinks I'm a farmer, so all right, I'll tell whoever
is trying to be in charge that I'm going to go work in the gar-
den. And I'll do that. I actually do know how to work in a
garden. At least, I can tell what's ripe from what's not, and
pick it and take it to the kitchen.

Whoever's in charge by the second day at least will be an
officer, probably the ranking officer here. So by the second day,
more people will be leaving, "servant recruits" will be blunder-
ing around, and I'll look useful. Which should take more sus-
picion away from me. But the Emperor is still not going to be
doing anything useful in the way of finding out who's behind
the defection. He's probably going to be furious, and shouting
contradictory orders, and generally making things worse.

It occurred to him that it could be *weeks* before anyone
started trying to track down where the Dolls went.

Will they send me home to get more horses?

Would that even be a priority? Horses needed grain and
hay, and that needed transporting. Horses were very labor-
intensive, and all of the concentration was going to be on getting the Palace running again. Back home, horses were a
necessity. Here they were a luxury.

Meanwhile . . . all the time this is going on, I can put myself in charge of the gardens. I can be directing soldiers and the gardeners they pull from the city gardens what to do about the Palace garden. And I can be thinking about who to blame and what to say when someone *checks on Valdemar.*

I might even be able to slip away—no, I shouldn't do that, not unless I can't think of someone to blame. That should be my first priority. I should act as baffled as everyone else to discover that three quarters of the population and all the herds and supplies are gone.

The longer I can keep them from looking at Valdemar, the colder the trail will get.

I'll do it. But I can't tell Isla. And I can't tell Star, either, because the Dolls will tell her. I can't tell anyone.

Poor Beltran. He's going to be stuck here, too.

He groaned. This place was as close to hell as anything on earth he had ever seen. And he was consigning *himself* to it.

Was this his just deserts for all the things in his life he had done wrong?

And if all my calculations are wrong, and they do *decide I'm behind this . . .*

Everything I've consigned myself to will seem like a pleasant garden stroll.

He had expected Star to squeeze him into some new, elaborate outfit for the "Blind Feast," since it was supposed to be so important. But the Doll just brought him the newest and most immaculate of his outfits, kitted him out with everything, including the Spitter, and made sure there wasn't a speck of dust on him. Then Star followed him down to the Dining Hall, where he found himself joining the tail of something he had never seen here before.

A line.

This, it seemed, was where he and everyone else were

supposed to be kitted out with their "helmets." When he got to the head of the line, the people before him were fitted with something that looked like a helmet with a blank visor; it was fitted to their head, and the visor pulled down. His mage-sight gave him a little flash of some unknown spell being invoked when the visor came down, then the person was led away carefully by a Doll.

No words were exchanged when it was his turn. Interestingly, the two people putting the helmet on him were human. Junior mages, perhaps? At any rate, the helmet was put on his head.

He nearly jumped out of his skin when it tightened down around his head and a bit of his face, as if to make certain he couldn't remove it or shift it himself. It felt incredibly intrusive, and made the hair on the back of his neck stand up.

Then the visor came down. And—well, you couldn't say he could see *nothing,* because that wasn't true. His vision filled with blue, as if he was gazing into a cloudless sky.

This was the only thing that kept him from having a screaming case of claustrophobia.

He felt a hand on his shoulder and one on his elbow. "This one will guide you," said a Doll's voice. He couldn't tell if it was Star or not, but he groped after what would have been the right hand, and felt the Valdemar pin, and relaxed a little. *Why* that should have made a difference, since all the Dolls were his allies, he didn't know. But it did.

Star deftly guided him for what seemed an interminable length of time, then stopped. The Doll turned him, then put his left hand on the back of a chair. Using that as his guide, he managed to get into it without falling over, and Star pushed the chair up to the table.

Now the visor cleared, and he could see a little; the view was just his hands, the glass, the cutlery, and the plate in front of him. There was a bread roll on it. Completely without an appetite now, he picked it up and began taking it apart, one tiny crumb at a time.

He had gotten down to the crust when the tiny plate full of crumbs was taken away. By now he could tell that all the chairs around him had been filled, and there was the murmur of voices.

I have to make conversation.

But . . . it would have to be conversation that didn't reveal who he was, right? He wasn't entirely certain what would happen if he *did* say something that would identify him—

Probably these helmets do something. Mask it out? He wasn't certain how that could even be possible, but—maybe mages were monitoring everything.

He cleared his throat nervously, and started to say something about the treachery of women. But *then* he thought—*But what if I'm sitting next to a high-ranking woman?*

His palms began to sweat.

"I wonder how the war in the south is going?" he finally said aloud. "Of course, our Glorious Emperor is going to win, but it would be enlightening to get some idea of when new lands will be open to grant to those who are deserving of them."

"I have a bet on that it will be over by harvest," said someone on his right side. The voice sounded thin and hollow, as if it was simultaneously coming from a great distance and from the midst of an echoing cave. It certainly couldn't be identified.

"I would not be in the least surprised," replied someone across from him.

And then he heard a Doll voice in his left ear. "The first dish of the first course is beef broth. Will you have some?"

His stomach knotted. "No, thank you. I would like some watered wine."

The wine glass in his vision filled as if by magic, and he carefully reached for it, and just as carefully brought it to where he thought his mouth was. When it actually reached his mouth, he drank it down thirstily. His mouth felt horribly dry.

"The wine, is, as always, very good," he said.

There was a chorus of voices around him, echoing that sentiment and commending the Emperor's taste in wine.

Three dishes were presented, then a bell sounded, and everyone fell silent.

And following that, a voice spoke into the silence.

"The first course is complete. The Princes are being un-Blinded," said the voice.

This isn't a meal, it's a torment. First, everyone is pressed into the same ordeal, except for the Emperor, who, no doubt, was never Blinded to begin with. Everyone was likely seated next to those they might otherwise know as rivals, even enemies. The higher ranks get to watch everyone else squirm and tire themselves being painfully polite. The lower ranks are reminded, with every course, that their lives depend upon those above them. We're all fed like hooded falcons. Anyone could be ordered assassinated while Blinded, and all any of us nearby might hear would be something like a cough. So nobody wants to stay silent, because that would be even more unsettling.

He had run out of things to say about the food, and groped for something the mages controlling his speech would consider acceptable that would not reveal who he was. "I have been thinking of starting a mews, for falcons," he said, praying that no one would be aware that he in fact had no interest in falconry. "Does anyone have recommendations?"

Everyone, it seemed, had recommendations. Opinions were given on the best size of mews, how many birds one should have, the best place to find a good falconer or falconers to care for the birds. Opinions were given about what birds were best for what sorts of hunting. Someone told a joke about how to pick out the most experienced falconer for what sort of bird—it ended with, " . . . and the best eagle handler is wearing an eye-patch!"

The laughter around him went on for far too long and sounded very strained, as if everyone was trying to laugh as long as they could to avoid making more conversation.

This course was of four dishes. The bell sounded. He held his breath. It was almost over. This would be for "Dukes." He'd finally be able—

"The second course is ended," said the voice. "The Dukes will be unBlinded."

And nothing happened.

He felt a rising panic, and tried to calm himself. Surely this was just because he was a Duke of a very small Duchy indeed. Surely he would just be the last of the Dukes to have this wretched helmet taken off. Surely . . .

"The first dish of the third course is salmon," said Star. "Will my Lord have some?"

He did his best to suppress a scream.

As he sat there, unable to eat, barely able to drink, as the voices around him grew boisterous and more mocking, as he realized that others around him had had their helmets removed, and could see he had not, he tried to get words out past the knot in his throat, and choked on them.

Then the Earls were unBlinded.

Then the Counts.

And finally . . . "The fourth course is completed," said the voice. "The Barons will be unBlinded."

And now the helmet was removed from his head, and he sat there, his face pale and sweaty, his hair matted, taking in the mocking smiles, the sneers, his placement at the table.

He was nearly at the head of the table. Above him, seated at his table for one, on a dais, was the Emperor, looking down, looking at *him,* and smiling a hard, cold smile.

Think, think, think, think!

Kordas rubbed at his stinging eyes, hiding the expression of panic he felt cramping his face. He breathed too quickly. His shoulders violently spasmed, staying cramped and making it impossible to lower his hands. Finally out of nowhere, the words came. Words suited to a buffoon, a clown. "Oh, thank the gods!" he said, plastering a weak, false smile on his face. "Valdemar is too small to be a Duchy! There is too much paperwork, and too many things to think about. Oh *thank* you, glorious Emperor! Thank you for relieving me of this terrible burden! I can never, ever thank you enough! Next year I shall send you *four* Valdemar Golds to thank you for your understanding and your wisdom!"

The smile on the Emperor's face flickered for a moment, and then faded.

"Of course, *Baron* Valdemar," the yellow toad said. "Your new title will be stamped after the Feast, then we'll be all done with your future."

Stay the fool. Stay the part. Hold together.

"I would never dare to ask for a moment of your attention during the Regatta," he replied, casting his eyes down as he tried not to choke.

"Directly after the Feast," the Emperor replied in a hard voice. "Your Duke will be Merrin now. Well done, Merrin."

As he stared at his plate, feeling faint and wondering if he was going to be able to keep from throwing up, there were murmurs of congratulations all around him.

And—

"Congratulations for getting what you deserve, Valdemar," said his right-hand neighbor, someone he didn't even know, in a falsely hearty voice. "Congratulations."

"Thank you," he managed to get out. "Thank you. I'm a lucky man."

"Oh, that's true. Duke Merrin probably had you kept on as a Baron because of your way with horses. Good moods prevailed. If you'd been completely useless, you might be in the Sacrifice Fights tonight!"

A couple more people laughed, commenting on how it should be a good show tonight.

"Sacrifice . . . fights?" Kordas gasped out.

"Hah! Wars don't win themselves, you know, and Abyssals don't get fed just anything. Deals are respected here, and paid in full. Sacrifices are made. Bulls and rams weren't enough after the first decade, and we always have prisoners to execute anyway. So we give them a chance; last one alive lives another year. Makes for great fights! Mouthpiece goes in, three pellets are loaded between the jaws, and off they go."

"Shows traitor protestors what shooting their mouth off really means!"

Laughter erupted again, sounding very far away and hollow, while Kordas dry-heaved.

This place—this place—

It was only with Star's steadying hand on his shoulder that he was able to remain in his seat for the rest of the interminable meal.

At least I'm still a Duke for the moment. But I'm not going
to have the authority to do things now . . . now what do I do?
His thoughts ran around in his head like frantic little mice, as
he and Star left the Dining Hall and headed for the Hall of
Gates. He dragged his feet, moving as slowly as he could. The
Hall of Gates was echoingly empty. Probably everyone back in
the Dining Hall was still enjoying the joke played at his expense. Except maybe the Emperor.

At least I spoiled that fat toad's fun.

"Star, when I'm not a Duke anymore, are the orders I've
already given going to be carried out?" he asked forlornly.

"Of course they will," Star replied promptly. "They are on
paper, with the proper seals of authority. They will keep on
being carried out, regardless."

And it was then that he heard someone behind him, the
sharp staccato of dress heels on the marble floor, someone
heading his way. He looked back over his shoulder.

It was Merrin.

Merrin, who, once he saw that he'd been spotted, slightly raised his hand. "I say, there, Valdemar—"

Fury erupted in him, and he didn't even stop himself. He turned and rushed the bastard, plowing into him at full speed, seizing the lapels of his coat and running him into the wall behind the Gates so hard that Merrin's breath was forced out of him in an "oof."

With the strength of too much pent-up rage, he raised Merrin off his feet by his lapels, jamming him against the amber paneling of the wall.

"Come to gloat, have you, you little weasel?" he snarled. "Was this your plan all along? Did you *know* this was going to happen when we met at the Gate in Valdemar?"

"Valdemar—" Merrin wheezed. "Wait—"

"Wait for *what?*" He went hot and cold all over, then hot again. "Wait for you to drain my people and my lands dry? Wait for you to abuse them like a cheap mule? I know what I should do! I'm challenging you! You have your Spitter, I have mine. Right here! Right now!"

"Valdemar, man, please—" There was real pleading in Merrin's face, and, strangely, no fear. He hung in Kordas's hands, completely unresisting. "Put me down, man. Let me explain."

"Why should I trust you as far as I can throw you?" Kordas growled.

Merrin jerked his head at Star. "Ask your Doll. It's a *vrondi*. It can tell I'm speaking the truth."

The unexpected words made his jaw drop and his hands loosened involuntarily, and Merrin slid down the wall, catching himself before he fell. "How did you know that?" he demanded, as Merrin self-consciously shook his coat into place, smoothed down his lapels, and brushed the skirt of the garment.

"Because the first time I was here, some idiot decided he was going to lie in a petition in front of the Emperor, against one of the Emperor's favorites, and the Emperor asked the Doll

attending him if what the idiot was saying was the truth."
Merrin shrugged. "The Doll told him, of course. It didn't end
well. The Emperor ordered him to be fed to the Abyssal. Then
the Emperor got a good laugh out of it, reminded everyone that
the Dolls were *vrondi,* and ended the Court early. But ask it,"
he continued. "Ask it if I'm telling you the truth."

Star spoke up, unprompted. "Everything he has said is
true."

"Star," Kordas said carefully, "are we being watched?"

Star held up its hand, the one with the crest pin, which it
did not cover.

"All right," Kordas said, fury still smoldering. "But this had
better be good."

"Not here," said Merrin, and crooked a finger. He led Kordas and Star to a Gate, held up his bracelet, and said, "Medi-
tation Room."

They stepped out into a perfectly egg-shaped room that
was like a jewel. Every fingerlength was covered in geometric
mosaic patterns in blues and greens made of fragments of
glass no bigger than an apple seed. There were blue cushions
scattered about, and there were no windows, just a single soft
white mage-light up at the top of the ceiling.

"What . . . is this place?" Kordas asked.

"Found it by accident. I had a horrible toothache and I'd
packed my mouth with clevis oil pads. I tried to say 'Healer,
Dental, Medication Room' and ended up here. Look there, and
there, and there." Merrin pointed, and Kordas clearly made out
anti-scrying runes among the patterns. Merrin pushed his rapier out of the way, plopped himself down on a cushion, and
with a gesture invited Kordas to do the same. "Nobody ever
comes here. There is no one in the entire Palace who is self-
aware enough to meditate."

Kordas choked on the laugh that the statement startled out
of him. This . . . didn't sound much like the "idiot" who had
been spying so ineptly on him!

"Kordas, I'm on your side. I have been since the Emperor acknowledged my title and directed me to spy on you." Merrin *looked* sincere, and Star kept nodding. Kordas hardly knew where to look. "I—I was never a hostage, but Father took me with him on his yearly journeys here, then on journeys into other Duchies, ones that were ruled by the Emperor's lickspittles, and took care to point out all the ways in which life was miserable there as well as in the Capital. When I was dazzled by luxury, he showed me the cost of that luxury. Then, when I inherited, and I came every year to the Regatta in his place, I saw even more personally what a hellhole the Emperor and his vanities, vagaries, and endless wars were making of the entire Empire. But Valdemar . . ." He shook his head. "Valdemar is not 'beautiful,' in the Imperial sense. It isn't paved with Imperial 'largesse,' or trying to gain more attention from the Emperor. But the peace of the place, the compassionate way it's run, the care you take for your people, your land, and your beasts before you even begin to think of yourself, make it a place of peace and quiet beauty. And when I took Father's position and was *invited* to 'keep an eye on you,' I knew I had to do my best to support you, or all of that would be wiped away in the blink of an eye."

Kordas felt astonished. He glanced at Star in complete disbelief. Star nodded.

"The best way I could think of to do that was to paint you as a complete bumpkin, a bumbler, someone who couldn't see past the end of his nose. It wouldn't have done to show you as competent—or as compassionate." He sighed. "So all my reports showed a Valdemar that was little more than one large farm, built on land that was too poor to support anything but grazing, with a few things, like the barges and the horses, that were useful but not vital to the Empire. And a Duke that was little more than a competent farmer with brilliance in just one thing: breeding beautiful horses, and breeding the Chargers that the Knights of the Empire need in order to play the role of

Imperial shock troops." Now he grinned wryly. "It did help that you put that face forward yourself, so the initial independent spies the Emperor placed in the Duchy to verify my reports told him exactly the same thing."

Kordas scarcely believed his own ears. *Oh Gods. We played each other.* "You mean—all this time we've—?" he asked incredulously.

Merrin nodded earnestly. "You knew I was a spy, of course, like my father was. I knew you were too intelligent *not* to know. As was your father and my father before you, and his and mine before him. My own goal was yours—to keep your lands from being stripped of resources and people. And please believe me, I never wanted to find myself being presented with the Duchy as if it was a prize for good penmanship."

Kordas fumed at that, and his mood instantly turned darker. "I want to punch you in the throat right now. So much."

Merrin held up both hands in a surrendering gesture. "Please don't. We both know Valdemar is valuable, but we managed to get the Emperor to think it is not. I think the Emperor's so used to power struggles that he thought when I spoke approvingly about Valdemar—well, he assumed I wanted it. I didn't ask. He just assigned me as the new Duke of Valdemar and—that isn't something to say 'no' to. The Emperor said it was his plan at the Blind Feast for you to be done away with, as a reminder to everyone else of the 'high standards' he demanded. I begged him, Kordas. I begged him. To let you live—the Emperor wanted you to be in the Fights, and if you survived it, you'd get a Barony. I came a hairsbreadth away from the Emperor making me fight you, then. He went through so many cruel ideas, man, I must have looked as pale as beach sand. But I convinced the Emperor that you were not made for Court, but that you were a horse-breeding genius, and for that you should stay on as a lesser noble, because of your loyal service."

Kordas burst out laughing. It was strained laughter, the

kind that whistles through clenched teeth, and he shuddered. "Yes—of course—my loyal service!" These months, of thinking as fast as he could while staying in character—well, there was nothing funnier in Kordas's mind at that moment than hearing he should be spared *for his loyalty to the Empire*. He knew he sounded off-kilter for laughing so uncontrollably, but he could not stop himself. After a hard swallow, he finally replied to Merrin, "So all that time you were in Valdemar was your—what? your vacation?—and you kept it going by making me think you were the worst spy ever?"

Merrin chuckled a little himself, and replied, "Worst spy ever. It worked, didn't it?"

Kordas slapped his hands to his face. "I thought you were in Valdemar as a punishment sometimes. You were just so— so bad at being a spy."

Merrin shrugged, hands apart. "It was the cover I invented, so I could stay longer."

"Which makes you the best spy ever." Kordas looked to Star, who just nodded. "And it's all true. We set you up so many times, and you had us set up the whole time. Oh, gods great and small, I worked so hard to make you view us as harmless, and every time I read your dispatches, I was convinced we were fooling you."

Merrin frowned a bit. "You could read them somehow? No, wait, that makes sense, when I think about it, but I never caught it at the time. All right. So not the best spy ever. What in all the Hells were you keeping hidden from me?"

"Long story. *Long* story." His fatigue was pulling back into a tight-cramped bunching of his back muscles, but otherwise, he felt a rush of blood as his heart rate increased. Some decisions were coming together about the situation. *So when my people are all gone, Merrin will be Duke of an empty Duchy, and the Emperor will murder him for allowing it to happen. He'd get thrown into the Fights, killed on the spot, or much worse. I only encountered a few of the torments the Emperor had. I never saw the interrogation chambers, the dungeons, and Gods only know what else the Emperor delights in. Damn it! If I'd known Merrin wasn't an enemy, we could have used the help of a spy so many times, for the Plan. What can be done to keep backlash off of Merrin and Valdemar?*

You know what. You've tried not to think of it, wondering if you had the nerve, or the skill, or what you'd have to face to accomplish it—but there is an opportunity now. There is a moment to act. The moment is soon. Think fast, think well. The Dolls. That has to be how.

"But, anyway. The Emperor," Merrin went on. "I argued your worth, and instead of being carted away still Blinded, you were given a Barony. Grudgingly. So it came to this—I want—that the real power in the Duchy remains with you, which I will . . . assuming . . ." He trailed off.

"Assuming that the Emperor's plan *isn't* to strip the Duchy once you're in the saddle," Kordas said bitterly. "Which it probably is. Nobody would be given a title unless there was a demand in return. The Emperor wouldn't make you a Duke unless he expected you to strip Valdemar bare to prove your loyalty to the Empire and its war. And most especially to him."

Merrin's eyes narrowed and he cocked his head. "You don't sound like a bumpkin right now."

"You have no idea what I am," Kordas replied in an ominous tone. His tone wasn't by mistake. His expression was hard-jawed and stormy now, like the shirt revealed as he began unbuttoning his jacket and waistcoat at the top. "Star, have Beltran meet us at the Record Keeper's desk. Now."

———

"What is known of the Imperial Office is this," the Record Keeper showed them on an architectural plot. "The receiving area is divided from the desk by a barrier impervious to all but air and sound. The eastern wall has a door from the

Petitioner's Position and one from the Conquest Throne. The western wall has a Gate for egress from the receiving area, and another—on the other side of the barrier—for the Emperor. He generally only uses it to retire to the Imperial bedchamber. The floor is extra thick wool carpeting, and the Emperor's side is walled in trophy cases and prizes of war."

Kordas traced fingers across the barrier line. "Can Dolls pass through this?"

"No, my Lord," the Record Keeper answered, "but this one gathers your intentions by the nature of your questions. This one finds itself not disapproving."

Merrin had been seated for some time, while Beltran told him an abbreviated explanation of the Plan. As Kordas put it, now Merrin was in the Plan up to his neck, so he had the choice of being an ally or being found dead in a canal—granted at least that much mercy. Something in Kordas's tone made Merrin acquiesce immediately.

"And the talismans you gave us to pass through Gates only Dolls could use—will they take us through here?" He tapped on the drawing.

"Yes, my Lord," the Record Keeper replied. "This one recommends you not move directly there from the receiving area, as the destination command might be overheard."

"Agreed. We'll need one more Doll pass talisman, then." Kordas turned part way around to look sharply into Merrin's eyes. "Are you with me? Completely?"

Merrin took a deep breath and replied, "I can't say I have no choice, because I do. You'd be better off killing me, though— if I'm arrested, they'll get everything out of me. Somehow. But yes—it is incredible to think anyone could have been as bold as you and yours have been, but yes. I am in."

Kordas turned back to the Record Keeper. "I need to know what Dolls can do to the Emperor without his specific permission—what those Dolls closest to him have been given blanket permission for. Dolls must be the Emperor's body-servants, so do they need to ask to disrobe him?"

The Record Keeper would have stared in shock, if it was able. The momentary pause told Kordas that the Doll had just been shocked by a realization, and had double-, maybe triple-checked it. "It was established many years ago that when the Emperor raises his arms we are free to disrobe or dress him, with no further command needed."

Merrin's brows furrowed deeply and he raised a single finger. "Are you thinking of—"

"Oh yes. Beltran, are you ready? You know how to use a Spitter, right?" The young man nodded and within moments of the nod, a Doll came from the Records halls bearing three cases, laid them on the Record Keeper's desk, and opened all three up. An orange glow came from within one of the cases.

"Is that—" Beltran began.

Kordas nodded. "Amazing what Dolls have just lying around, isn't it?"

They conferred for another half-candlemark, practiced a few times, and then it was time to go.

The softest of mage-lights was all that kept it from being unbearably bright. The initial shock of seeing the Emperor's office left you with only one impression: unimaginable wealth, in gold.

The furniture was gilded, with cloth-of-gold cushions. The ceiling was gilded. The doors had gold plate hammered over them. Anything made of metal was either solid gold or at least gold plated. The floor was gold carpet of tufted wool a knuckle deep, with a woven pattern of pure gold thread. The walls were not gold—they were a mosaic of actual amber of every possible color, and quite literally more valuable than gold. Golden frames enclosed daggers, swords, crowns, headdresses, polearms, and chalices.

There were seven giant wolf statues made of gold and iron positioned around the office, in places where windows might have been. *I'm surprised they aren't of the Emperor,* Kordas mused.

There were guards *everywhere* outside of the Emperor's private office, but once the doors were closed, there were no humans anywhere to be seen. Of course, given the amount of protections that Kordas could see with mage-sight, the Emperor didn't *need* human guards in here after the doors were locked. There was a Gate in the wall to the left, the Dolls could come and go and bring him whatever he needed, and the magical protections around him would ensure no physical harm could come to him.

All of those protection spells seemed to be emanating from a single object in the room. Which also made sense, given the decades—centuries!—the High Kings, and then the Emperors, had been sitting on the Conquest Throne.

But that object was not, as Kordas had thought, the Wolf Crown. No, it was the heavy gold-and-iron carcanet that the Emperor wore. And that made sense, too. The spells had been forged into the gold—but the iron would by itself deflect any counter-spells. However much of a fool the current Emperor was, his predecessors had been shrewd indeed.

In addition, there was a protective barrier between the desk and where they were standing. That came from the desk itself. Anyone who tried rushing the Emperor by going over that desk would just bounce right off it.

He and Merrin stood side by side in the Imperial Office's receiving area, as the Emperor pretended to read something. This, of course, was another demonstration of his power. Another petty demonstration. And Kordas knew that he would keep them standing there until he started to get bored. Only then would he get on with the business that brought them here—making official Kordas's demotion, and Merrin's promotion. There was nothing on that desk except a little gold statue of himself, a pen, and the two sets of documents.

Fortunately, the Emperor had a short attention span.

He finally looked up. Kordas made certain he was wearing a fatuous grin. Merrin was sober, his hands resting on the grip of his Spitter.

"Well, there you are. Heh. Heh. Heh." The Emperor's nasty little smile was back, and he looked more like a toad with hair than ever. "I have your new patents of nobility right here," he said, and made that "heh-heh" sound again, which was nothing like a laugh. "I trust you will make something noteworthy from your new land, Merrin."

Merrin made an inarticulate little sound as the Emperor's seal-ring came down on each document, burning the certifying sigil in.

"And you are *done*." He did not stand up. Behind him, several more Dolls padded in through the Gate, but the Emperor took no notice of them; Dolls were beneath an Emperor's notice. The new Dolls took equidistant places among the four already standing immobile against the display cases. Yet another Doll came through the Gate on the other side of the Office, laid down several folders of documents, and refreshed the pens. The Emperor tapped the two newly sealed pages once, then flicked the same finger toward Merrin and Kordas as if flicking off something just pulled from between his teeth. That Doll brought them through the Emperor's Gate and to the receiving area, giving one copy to each. There was no fanfare, no—anything. Kordas fought back bile at the simplicity of it all; the Emperor could have an entire Duchy change hands without any more effort than swatting a fly. *Or eating one, the toad.*

Kordas and Merrin left the receiving area through the gate, following the single Doll, and emerged into the Records Complex, where they were quickly relieved of their outer coats, swords, footwear, and anything else that might have made noise. They took deep breaths, then spoke the destination: the Emperor's Office.

They stepped silently onto the woolen carpet and, at the same pace as a Doll would use, took up positions between the other Dolls in line by the cases.

A moment later, Kordas's brave Herald Beltran stepped through the same opening, his forearms aglow with the protective bracers—and in each hand, one dueling Spitter—that had belonged to the Emperor's father. "Put your hands up!" the Herald yelled, making the Emperor startle.

Mockingly, the Emperor replied, "Oh, a boy with Spitters! I'm *so* scared!"

But despite the mocking tone, the Emperor did raise his hands, and that was enough.

Outstanding, Beltran.

Instantly, the Dolls behind the Emperor leapt into action. One worked the combination for the carcanet and yanked it aside, while another snatched the Wolf Crown. It happened incredibly quickly.

Within a single breath, the Emperor was stripped naked, including *everything.* Robes, shirt, trews, underwear—

The wolf statues stirred and came to life, ruby eyes suddenly blazing brightly, and stared at the tableau before them.

Oh, hells.

The seven wolves howled, incredibly loudly. All seven, and the horrific sound increased in volume and pitch as they prepared to leap. It was more than just sound, it created a dizzying disorientation that weakened everybody that wasn't either wolf or Doll.

Now, with the protective items he'd worn removed from him, that included the Emperor.

Herald Beltran swayed and fired both Spitters into the Emperor, striking him with two gut-shots before dropping both weapons to cover his ears.

It happened so fast the Emperor was only just beginning

to understand when Kordas and Merrin moved. Merrin drew his Spitter, jammed it into the Emperor's throat, and fired, sending the bolt into his larynx. Anything the Emperor might have been about to say died in a gurgling, gagging sound.

Then Kordas drew *his* Spitter, twisted the handle, reversed it, and smashed the pommel into the Emperor's forehead.

The mercy-piston, meant to pierce a horse's or cow's thick skull, had no problem with a mere human skull. The bolt drove soundlessly into the Emperor's brain, enveloped in frost clouds from the six jet-vents of the piston, and rebounded back in Kordas's grip.

The Emperor was dead before his knees gave and his body hit the lush golden carpet.

The wolf statues silenced, and stared, their eyes still bright.

Merrin grabbed the Wolf Crown and jammed it onto Kordas's head, as Kordas clasped the Carcanet around his own throat, then bent down and yanked the ring off the Emperor's forefinger and jammed it onto his own.

Then the wolf statues closed their eyes and froze in place once more.

Oh . . . hells. That was too close.

Kordas turned to the Dolls, who had also frozen in place. Clearly they had not expected him to do *that*.

"Who do you serve?" Kordas demanded, barely hearing his own voice over the effects of the howling earlier.

There was a short pause. "He who wears the Crown, the Carcanet, and the Ring," they said.

Kordas leaned hard against the desk, panting. Everything spun a little, and his head pounded. He'd worked out earlier that the set of items were powerful, but the sensation of actually wearing them was enough to do his head in. As soon as Merrin and the Dolls pulled the Emperor's body away, Kordas fell into the chair, mopping at his forehead with the left sleeve of his thunderstorm-dyed shirt. He closed his eyes.

There was only one way to be certain the Emperor wouldn't pursue us. We had to kill the Emperor.

Kordas fumbled with a pen and the papers in the folders, then gave up to spend another few moments with his eyes closed. Finally he said, awkwardly, "Can you please find me some blank paper? And take that body on the floor and put it in the Emperor's bed."

One of the Dolls extracted paper from somewhere behind him and placed it on the desk in front of him. Others dragged the body away. There was, surprisingly, very little blood. And very little else. The Emperor must have used the jakes before he'd sat down to meet with them.

Poised with pen above the paper, Kordas's hand shook. "Beltran. Come—come help me here. Star—you too." He felt queasy, but it had to be because of the enormity of what they'd just done. He took up the pen again and scrawled out:

As of now, and forever on, all vrondi are free.

He dated the paper, and turned the Imperial ring face-down on the page and pressed. The seal burned in. Tiredly, but with a hint of a smile, he said to Star, "Is that official enough for you?"

"The Record Keeper says that all Dolls are free of Imperial compulsion now. Our appreciation is immeasurable, my Lord."

Kordas laughed a little. "You don't have to keep calling me that, Star."

"I don't have to, my Lord. But I want to."

Kordas knew there was still much to be done, but he did indulge himself for a moment in the feeling of wearing the Crown and sitting at the desk. It didn't feel good at all. In fact, it felt repugnant. He heaved as he pushed himself away from the desk, knocking the chair over and stumbling. He felt the hands of Merrin, Beltran, and Star steadying him. This—this was not who he was.

"We have much to do, yet, and the Plan is still underway. Star, I know that every Doll is free now, but if you all wouldn't be opposed, I'd still like your help." Star nodded, so he continued. "Release the *vrondi* from the Trap, then break the damnable thing for good. Get the prisoners on their way. Release every prisoner held in the dungeons and holding cells, and get them to safety. And—let's take everything in here that's magical. Same for the Imperial quarters. We may need their power to fuel the Gates. Get them to Valdemar."

He looked at Merrin. "If you approve, Duke."

Merrin allowed himself a chuckle. "I'm a feather pulled along in your wake at this point, Kordas. Am I going to oppose the man who killed an Emperor?"

Kordas glanced to Beltran and replied, "We all got our shots in."

Beltran still wore the bracers and had the pair of Spitters tucked in. "Might just keep these, if there's no objection."

Kordas said, "I don't know. Last time you fired them, you shot an Emperor."

"I'll be more careful next time," the Herald replied.

Kordas dropped back into himself now that he'd rested a little. The surge of energy and excitement that came with being under pressure renewed him. "Top speed, full strength for all the Dolls now. Get everybody innocent out first, like grocers, Healers, and shopsmiths. Elderly and children, and if there are any pets left, them too. Clear the mews and stables out, and key all the Gates to voice command. No talismans needed except for the refuge. Anyone who doesn't have a home to go to, take them to Valdemar to be looked after there."

What he was about to unleash—he suddenly realized it would cause what the Foreseers had warned about. The Palace, and the Capital, destroyed in a hell of fire and lava.

There were a lot of innocent people in the city. And a lot of not-so-innocent people in the Palace, but a lot of innocents, too. Kitchen staff, guards, and maybe there were more nobles like Merrin had been. Maybe more than he would have thought.

He turned to the nearest Doll. "Is there any way we can

announce something to the entire Palace and City?" It seemed wildly unlikely, but . . .

"Of course," the Doll said, and produced a golden cone, open at both ends, from a drawer behind him, while other Dolls emptied every hidden cache and display case in the office. They moved so swiftly now that there were actual breezes. The Gate in the room alternated between Dolls leaving with their arms laden and new ones coming through an instant later. "Just speak into the narrow end. Your words will be repeated all over the Palace and City."

"I could have told you that," Merrin said, looking at him with a hint of reproach. "He used to use it all the time to announce a parade when he was sufficiently bored."

Kordas took a deep breath. "I'm going to release the thing in the Chamber of the Beast," he said, wondering if Merrin knew what he was talking about.

Merrin went white. "But—"

He nodded. "I know. It's going to wreck the entire City, and what it leaves standing, its parents are going to destroy."

"But—"

"*It's a child.* And it's been tortured for decades." He looked at the nearest Doll again. "About how long after I order it released do you think people will have to get out?"

The Dolls all froze. Finally the one he was talking to spoke again. "Earth Elementals move slowly. The Child will flee, most likely, and the elder ones will move toward it once they can detect it. Then, we expect, they will move to take revenge on the City. Based on the measurements the mages have made of the elders' movements, three candlemarks."

Kordas took a deep breath and tried to steady himself. This was going to be the hardest speech of his life. He was about to tell people that they had just enough time to grab what was essential, what was closest and dearest to them, and abandon their homes. "People of the Empire," he began, and heard his own voice booming outside the office a moment later. "The

City and Palace are in danger. An evacuation is ordered immediately. Take what is vital to you and get through a Gate to anywhere but here. Dolls will assist you at full strength and speed if you wave them down. One candlemark remains. Evacuate the City and Palace. Expect nothing to remain here."

Then Merrin grabbed the cone out of his hands and shouted into it. *"The Demons are free! Run for your lives! The Demons are free! Run for your lives!"* Merrin operated some sliding pins on the cone, and the device repeated what they'd both just warned—and shouted.

"Why did you say 'demons'?" Kordas asked.

"Because everyone knows what a demon is," Merrin said, with impeccable logic.

Faintly, sounds of screaming came from outside the office.

The Palace began to shake. The last glimpse Kordas had of the Imperial office was a rain of plaster and gold leaf heaping onto the carpet. There was no value to gold when the world was disintegrating.

Kordas and his companions got their footwear and other gear back on in the Records complex; one of the Dolls jammed paper talismans in their pockets for the foot-Gate at the refuge. Star accompanied them, snapping off information and updates as quickly as raindrops came in a downpour.

The Regatta's warships came in to dock and took on passengers.

Dolls used their tremendous strength and speed as polemen to get boats and barges through water-Gates.

Civilians turned up street- and canal-side, and in more than a few cases, their tools, belongings, and trade-carts were tossed into barges by Dolls.

Some of this, Kordas got glimpses of; some, he only heard from Star. *The false Golds! They're at the chariot down by the waterfront!*

Kordas bolted out through a Gate to the Imperial Chariot; Merrin followed. "Damned if I'll let my horses burn," Kordas

growled, while he and Merrin released them from their harness. They weren't Chargers; the ground shook beneath them,
there was fire in the air, and they reared and stamped with
growing panic, but Kordas tore off his coat and threw it over
the head of his, and it calmed immediately. They knew; they'd
been trained. If they had been "blinkered" like this, they were
with a human who would care for them and they'd be safe.
Merrin fought with his for just a moment, saw what Kordas
had done, and did the same, grabbing the halter just under the
chin as Kordas had. "Gate!" shouted Kordas, and they made
for it, as the ground shook and a hot wind began to blow.

Behind him, the warships cast off after the first loud crack
sounded from somewhere in the Palace compound. "Take
them," Kordas told Merrin, and when the new Duke had hold
of both horses and was through the Gate to the refuge, Kordas
stepped aside to help people escape. The destruction escalated
over the next candlemark, and with Star beside him, Kordas
stood and watched the Capital die. Jets of steam and smoke
erupted from around the City, accompanied by more booms.
One very large jolt sent a powerful enough shockwave to
knock Kordas off his feet. Still Kordas stayed, coordinating
the last rescues with the Dolls that remained.

Kordas felt his exposed skin drying in the ambient heat.
Ash fell from the orange sky, in flurries like snow, and the
earth itself heaved upward from the Palace outward. He wiped
at his face. Tears distorted his vision.

"My Lord," Star said loudly from beside him, and gripped
his upper arm. "This is too dangerous for you to stay!"

"I have to," Kordas bellowed back. "I have to see this. It's
my doing. It's—it's not something I can turn my back on."

A deafening, explosive shock came from the Palace, and a
set of bright yellow molten-metal knifeblades—no—claws ten
stories high punched upward through the center of the Palace
complex, and Kordas fell to his knees. Lightning crackled in

jagged bolts through the clouds of ash, which itself was now expanding up and outward, utterly covering the sky. The canals of the City drained toward where the Palace once had been, and Kordas felt his eyes dry out. Where water once was in the canals, pyroclastic flow now raced toward them, and if Kordas was screaming, he couldn't hear it. The City's remains heaved, then burst into a flower of fire and molten stone. More searing claws emerged, and a pair of red-hot jaws emerged from the lava, snapping at the air, like a fish snapping at a fly just above the water, and as the torrent of ash and fire began to cook his skin, Kordas was pulled back through the Gate by Star.

Kordas couldn't register anything from his senses quite right. He was drowning, he was gasping, he was burning. There was yelling, and he was being prodded at and lifted. He fell. Shapes moved around him but none were distinct. There might have been voices, but mostly, there was incessant ringing in his ears, and crackling when he moved his jaw. His tongue was dry, and he tasted nothing. He was jostled and carried, and his nostrils were caked in blood and ash. Time passed, but he didn't know how. He sensed Mindspeech and then stinging sensations, and feelings like being . . . peeled. He did not like that at all, and was nearly sure he coughed up blood and ash. He caught himself blinking and took it to be a good sign. If he could blink, he was alive. If he hurt, he was alive.

He thought he heard cursing, and then things snapped into a clearer version. Someone removed the Carcanet from him, and then the soothing warmth of magical Healing flooded into his core. He felt water poured over him repeatedly, and much fuss around him. It could have lasted days. He had periods of coughing, periods of drunkenness. He felt himself being bathed. Outside of that, there was continuous commotion. Several times he lost all sense of balance. He knew he'd tried to stand up and had been laid back down again.

Maybe this was for the best, he thought. *If I'm being looked after by somebody, I'm alive, and the Plan must have worked, and everyone must have the situation in hand. I should stay this way a while. I can be done without, for a while.*

I killed the Emperor. I killed the City. I—may have killed the Empire.

Maybe I've earned some rest.

But he couldn't quite bring himself to feel happy about it. He'd witnessed the annihilation of a City that was centuries old. It was horrible. *What if there had been people trapped there? What if not everyone made it out? What if the Elementals from Below didn't stop there?*

Was he screaming again?

Then he was warming up inside again. It was so hard to tell what had become of him.

What have I become?

EPILOGUE

" . . . So then we set the Gates in the Imperial City to accept everyone and everything living that came through them, even if they had no talisman," said three Dolls nearest him, as he carefully sipped wine, propped up on cushions on the roof of the living barge he and Isla would share. With their boys, their three boys, a family at last. "For those that had no talisman, the destination was random—to whatever Gate outside the City that did not have something or someone in it. You told us you wanted as many saved as you could. I think that most, if not all, escaped."

And thus the word that the Imperial Capital had fallen to monsters was spread directly to every corner of the Empire. Well . . . that was efficient.

"It was efficient," said the third Doll, Rose, echoing his thoughts. It was easier to tell them apart now; Star was covered in scorch marks, imperfectly covered by the clothing someone had given it.

The Dolls were staying. They were counting on him and his collection of mages to figure out how to free them, yes. But, Star told him, they were also staying because they liked him and his people. "Even when we are freed, this one thinks that you will not be seeing the last of us."

Mostly, he'd been told, the only people coming here had been those he'd intended to come. The hostages, the people of Valdemar, and the people of Valdemar who'd slipped talismans to friends or relations outside of Valdemar. The dissidents had ended up here too, though, which could be a future problem—one he was too tired to address right now.

The sun setting over the lake, the smell of cookfires and campfires, and all the boats, some of them painted up gaudily for the Regatta they never reached, made things look and feel deceptively peaceful.

Deceptively, because people were troubled. When Dolls and horses and people had come pouring through the foot-Gate, smelling of smoke and ash and screaming their heads off about demons, the Circle had done some sort of massive scrying spell, and pretty much everyone around the lake had gotten a bird's-eye scrying view of the destruction.

Isla told him most people had cheered and openly rejoiced. But then, most people had just seen their most feared enemy getting pulverized. They hadn't *been* there. They hadn't seen innocent people, people a lot like them, running for their lives through a burning hell. They didn't have it on their conscience.

And now, of course, the folks who'd been too far to see the scrying had heard about it secondhand and wanted to be told. So the entire lakeshore was alive with the murmur of tens of thousands of people, and probably three fourths of it was the people who'd been here to see the scrying disk telling the people who hadn't been here what they'd seen.

And probably all sorts of wild interpretations of it.

Can I correct any of that? Do I even want *to?* Every bit of the Plan had assumed that the Empire and the Emperor would still exist after Regatta Day, and an awful lot of it had been built around preventing him from finding them.

Now—

I'm not going to think about it, he decided. *I'm going to sit here with my sons and my friends and drink and watch the sunset.*

He had been rather crispy, he'd been told, when Star dragged him across the Gate. The Carcanet had saved him from fatal damage, but it had also fought all the attempts to Heal him when he'd gotten to safety. Finally the Record Keeper had taken it off, and Alberdina had done her work, aided by other Healers he didn't know. Whoever they were, they were geniuses. There was hardly any scarring. Right now, he felt mostly like he'd had a bad sunburn and a wretched cold.

He glanced over at Isla; their youngest boy had fallen asleep in her lap. She smiled at him.

"Pass the wine," said Ponu.

The entire top of the barge had been covered in rugs and cushions, and was full of people. Isla, Hakkon, the boys, Delia, Merrin, Ponu, some of the Dolls, Beltran . . . most old friends, some new.

"Well, now what do we do?" he asked the mage.

"What we'd planned to," Ponu told him. "Let almost everyone settle in. Not that many non-Valdemarans came through, and most of those were the dissidents and the hostage children." He squinted at the late-afternoon sun. "I think the Dolls have the children separated into a single group, and the dissidents in another." He glanced over a Doll that was standing at his elbow. It had pleasant features sketched on the canvas of its face with sepia ink, and a straw hat with a feather on its head.

"We do, Ponu," said the Doll. "We should decide what to do with them."

"I think we should at least send the hostages back to Valdemar. From there they can go home." Kordas let out his breath in a gusty sigh. "Although things are not necessarily going to be good at their homes, either."

"No," Ponu agreed. "There's a huge power vacuum now, and all those subject Kings are going to be trying to fill it. And I imagine there's a general or two in the south, or with one of the legions nearer to what's left of the Capital, that will be getting some lofty thoughts in his head. Still. They should be with their families, unless their families are so dysfunctional they don't *want* to go back."

That triggered a thought in Kordas's weary brain. He turned to the Doll. "Please let the other Dolls know that fighting or bullying among the hostages is to lead to the offender being shoved into a half-empty grain barge and locked in for a couple of candlemarks. And if he misses a meal, too bad. He can chew on some wheat."

"Oh," said the Doll, sounding . . . happy. "It will be done."

" . . . and they're not coming after us," Isla repeated for the third time, still sounding dazed. "Not even for revenge." The littlest boy stirred in her lap, looking like he was perfectly accustomed to being there. The other two were cuddled up against Kordas, listening wide-eyed to every word. Isla had told them a few days ago who their parents were, back when he was still in the middle of being Healed. The littlest, she had told him, had said "Hooray!" and nothing more. The eldest had looked straight at his sibling and said, "Told you so." They all had taken the news in stride, she'd said; the only thing that distressed them had been his condition, and when Alberdina assured them he would be all right, they settled in to their new reality a lot better than he had. The fact that they were settling right in as if they all had been a perfectly normal family was, he thought, a good sign.

"No one knows it was me, Beltran, and Merrin," Kordas reminded her. "Only the Dolls, and they're all here with us. Nobody is going to come looking for us. Why would they?"

It was growing dark, now, and the stars were coming out.

Feather had brought Kordas another bottle of wine from the Valdemar cellars, and Star had brought him a bowl of stew. It tasted better than anything he had eaten in the last several weeks.

Merrin had been back to Valdemar just long enough to make himself known to the people who had refused to leave, assured them that he was not going to punish them, and cemented his position as the new Duke.

He'd also taken over the Ducal manor, and had been relieved to discover there were no bats after all.

Then he'd come back once he'd gotten word of Kordas's recovery, to find out what Kordas had planned.

Although I don't know why I should plan anything. Plans never last for long once you put them in motion.

In the water was an echo of stars, and of the lights on the barges and the shore in the form of lanterns, mage-lights, and a few campfires.

Out there, among all those barges and campfires, the Dolls were circulating, giving an abbreviated version of what had just happened, and eliminating the fact that Kordas, Beltran, and Merrin had killed the Emperor. None of them wanted to claim that. Not because people would be angry with them for it, but because they were likely to be made into Great Heroes of the People, and—and that was just wrong.

Let them all think the Emperor fell into the lava when we released the Child. That will do.

"There *is* going to be chaos," Merrin predicted. "There's going to be some fighting and probably a bloodbath or two. Well, let them fight it out. When I get back to Valdemar, I'm going to make sure we sit this one out. Keep us out of it completely. Take in refugees, because there's going to be a lot of perfectly good farms and houses empty, but otherwise— Valdemar doesn't have a dog in this fight."

"About that," Kordas said. "I evacuated everyone who would agree to leave *because* the Emperor was surely going to take it out on Valdemar when some of us fled. But now—that's not true. And I feel very good about leaving Valdemar in your hands, Merrin."

"Wait—" said Merrin. *"What?* I thought you'd want—"

Kordas shook his head. "You say Valdemar doesn't have a dog in this fight, but someone might try to take the fight to the dog. You know more about Imperial politics than I did. You have a better head for deciding who to back and who not to."

"Well," Merrin said, rubbing the back of his neck, "I'm not bad at it."

"What's more, tomorrow I'm going to tell everyone that anyone who wants to go back and reclaim their home is welcome to," Kordas continued. "I think some of them are going to stay, some to stay here at the lake, and some to go on with me to find a new home." *The Squire, for one. I think that little village is the kind of place he's been wanting for a long time.* "But I think a lot of them are going to want to go back. The ones who are going to stay here probably will because they *don't* trust that someone isn't going to turn up to strip Valdemar bare—and no matter how hard you try, Merrin, you probably aren't going to be able to stop that if someone turns up with a hungry army. But some only came because staying was worse than leaving, so they'll want to go back with you, now that I've vouched for you."

Merrin didn't look unhappy about this, as the light from the mage-lights hovering over them all reflected on his face. "You've got a point. Several of them, actually. You're right about all of it. So you really don't want the Duchy anymore?"

Kordas hugged the two boys next to him. "I think I'm ill-suited to navigate the waters that are coming," he admitted. "I am many things, but I am not as skilled at—all of that—" he waved his right hand vaguely at the Gate "—as you are. Star, I would like you and the other Dolls to spread the word in the morning that it is safe to return to Valdemar and everyone who wants to can, and that their new Duke is the former

Count Merrin and I trust him completely to keep them as safe as anyone can in the troubled times that will come."

"And if troubled times *don't* come?" Merrin said, voice still full of disbelief.

"Then you'll help them prosper." He laughed. "Actually, the fact that you aren't going to be breeding famous horses anymore should keep things quiet for you."

"You're keeping the horses?" Merrin replied. "Well—damn! That's low of you, Valdemar!"

"They're my horses, not the Duchy's," Kordas reminded him. "Find something else to do with all those meadows. Try sheep. Or cows. Become famous for cheese."

"Huh. Actually, that's not a bad notion," Merrin mused. "I do have a capital strain of cattle on my land . . ."

"Star, make sure we give Merrin's cows back to him," said Kordas.

"You cad! *You stole my cattle?*" Merrin tried to sound indignant, but the laughter in his voice gave him away.

"Which makes me a Robber Baron, I suppose," Kordas retorted, also laughing. It felt strange, as if he had not laughed for decades. But good. Very good. "I think I'll keep that. Robber Baron Kordas of Valdemar."

"It suits you," said Ponu, from the end of the barge. "Now shut up and pass the wine."

"Hey!" called Jonaton, from behind them. "Has anyone seen Sydney?"